Hoops and Seeds
A Pause in the Harvest

by

Roger Johnson

The characters in this novel are fictional except for the political figures.

All rights reserved.

ISBN   978-8-9872510-1-0

Email: rogerj47@gmail.com
Website: Roger_Johnson.com

To my first baseball and basketball coaches, my older brothers Jay and Rick, who impacted my formative years. I don't hold them responsible for how I turned out as an adult, but I thank them for their guidance over a half century ago.

Acknowledgements

Four college/university women's coaches provided critical insights into their journeys through The Pause. Each coach faced unique challenges in how they approached The Pause. Their political views may differ from mine, but their love for their players shone through consistently.

Charli Turner Thorne, Arizona State University in Tempe (retired). Coach Turner Thorne opened her soul about her journey. ("Ask me anything.") She also read the manuscript and offered support and suggestions about its shortcomings. Her experience working with the Diné of northern Arizona provided me with valuable insights.

Todd Holthaus, Pima Community College in Tucson. He and his staff have provided access to his practices and players for several years. His ladies play without athletic scholarships or on-campus housing which made for a unique situation during the pandemic.

Mike McLaughlin, University of Pennsylvania in Philadelphia. UPenn lost an entire season as the Ivy League cancelled the 2020-2021 season too. None of his ladies transferred out when their seasons were canceled, and that speaks volumes about the relationships he develops with them.

Yvonne Sanchez, Assistant Coach, University of Michigan (during The Pause and The Restart seasons). Former Head Coach, University of New Mexico in Albuquerque. Coach Sanchez provided insights on the critical value of assistant coaches during the pandemic.

Joe DesGeorges. Joe is my patient and precise formatter. This is the seventh novel we have worked on together. Joe is also integral to the cover design of each book.

Wendy Constantine and **Wally Towne**, editing assistance.

Books in Print by Roger Johnson

Laments for the Dead
Layers of Darkness
America's Soul

The Cheetah Basketball Series
On Point
Gifts: The Return
Coach Izzy
Hoops and Seeds: A Pause in the Harvest

Other manuscripts in the queue include

Lines (Due out in early 2024)
Jegos
The Hill, '67: A Love Affair

Hoops and Seeds: A Pause in the Harvest

Roger Johnson

IngramSpark

2023

Hoops and Seeds

"They cry, they yell, they tell us how unfair it is, they withdraw, and they cry some more. They're hurt and confused. We've broken protocol more than once to hold our girls."

Coach Nancy

"It's like I've been dragged by a horse and all my skin has been scraped off."

Dyani Dehiya

"The Pause was maybe my best year of coaching."

Coach Charli

MARCH 2020

Things are and then they are not

Agriculture and Basketball. Blog, by Ken Davidson

Harvests take place year-round in the San Joaquin Valley; each crop ripens on its own time. "To everything, there is a season," as my minister so often reminds me, "a time to plant and a time to pluck." It appears there is a natural rhythm to life mostly ending in positive results in America, the bountiful harvest. And yet. The farmer deals with a fickle Mother Nature, often a harsh Mother. She can yield both good and bad, and the farmer learns to expect both. "Know your crop" is sound advice. "Nurture your soil." Sometimes the most valuable life lessons are disguised by Mother Nature. The Valley, America's most productive agricultural region, represents the dichotomy of farming and that natural rhythm. For the farm laborer, low wages, substandard housing, and poor-quality health care are exacerbated by bad air and tainted water. Mother often displays inequalities on the same farm.

So it is for a basketball coach and her team. Basketball's season appears to plant in the fall with the first practices and reap in the spring with the tournaments, but there is growth year-round. As with the farmer, a solid planting does not always result in a bountiful harvest. An injury to a key player can be as devastating as a summer hailstorm but healthy soils improve the seeds' chances.

Members of the California State University San Joaquin Valley Sequoias women's basketball team usually come from poor neighborhoods, not exclusively, but often. Most were overlooked by major programs, as if invisible. Coach Molly Rascon recruits these kids, offers them a chance, challenges them, and then fans their fires. She calls them her tribe. Dyani gave her permission. It is an ongoing narrative. When Coach Rascon interviewed for the position five years ago, she promised the committee that her squad would reflect the student demographics of SJV and represent the university with passion, dignity, and humility, and in short order compete for championships. In any given year, the SJV roster blends Hispanics, Blacks, Asians, and Whites. This season, however, it includes two Native Americans, a Guatemalan, and a sort of Mexican (a Dreamer). Coach promised to mold everyday student-athletes into extraordinary women. She has kept her promise.

Her tenure has shown steady improvement. In Coach Rascon's first year, inheriting a squad that won just five games the previous year, the team finished two games under five hundred and won their first game in the conference tournament, albeit a weak conference. Year two saw a third-place finish in the conference, and year three they were runners up, but won the conference tournament earning the automatic NCAA bid, but as a sixteenth seed. Last season, her fourth, the Sequoias earned their second automatic bid into the NCAA tournament, a fourteenth seed, but were humbled by a three seed in the first round. One and done again, but necessary steps, as she would say. This season, the Sequoias finished undefeated in the Ring of Fire Conference and 26-2 overall. Non-conference wins over two high-major schools, Arizona and Southern Cal, should provide them with a higher seed, giving them a realistic chance to advance past the first round of the NCAA tournament, assuming they can win the conference tournament again and receive that automatic bid. Otherwise, they might get an at-large bid, but that would almost certainly mean an opening game against a number one seed and another early trip home.

It's tournament time in America, the first step along the path that is universally known as March Madness, the Big Dance. It's all those cliches that are used to describe the excitement that accompanies a championship team with high expectations. SJV is such a team, a conference champion, a squad knit together by journeys not related to basketball but forged by that basketball experience. Officially, the Sequoias. Unofficially, the Tribe, the Trees, the Warriors, the Cheetahs, Our People. Whatever, this is a team with a chance to advance beyond the limits of its past. One and done won't suffice this season. It is the team coaches Molly Rascon and Ryanne Powell have built from the ground up, and one that does not want excuses for coming up short. Quick, athletic, skilled, and well-coached, Cal State San Joaquin Valley from central California. Its time is now— "the time to pluck"—a time that may not come again soon.

It's March 5, 2020, the last conference game, which SJV won tonight in a romp, is in the books. The focus now is on the upcoming conference tournament which begins a week from tonight, March 12, in Santa Barbara. Let the journey begin, the best month in sports— the bountiful harvest!

A university bus arrives at the Best Western Inn in Goleta, California, just after 2:00 in the afternoon, Wednesday, March 11. It carries the Cal State San Joaquin Valley women's basketball team. The last half hour of the trip has been on the 101 along the coast, and what the ladies notice is the clean air. Tulare and the central San Joaquin Valley suffer from poor air quality. "America's Salad Bowl" is situated in a geographical depression which holds the pollutants close to the ground. A temperature inversion. Farming, oil production, dry soils, interstate traffic, and offshore winds that blow the urban contaminants far inland contribute to the dangerous haze. It is especially hazardous to those laborers who work in the fields for extended hours. Childhood asthma is a serious problem in The Valley. On this day, however, crystal clear skies greet the team as the players exit the bus and enter the motel's courtyard. The motel's host advises the team to enjoy the moment, because tomorrow's forecast is for clouds and rough days ahead.

Chapter 1

Coach Rascon's ringtone for her players is "We Are the Champions" by Queen. Freddie Mercury wakes Molly just after 5:30 on Friday morning. It's Kaori Park, the Sequoias' small forward.

"Morning, Kay-kay. What's up?"

"I'm sorry to call so early, Coach, but my grandmother is in the hospital."

"Oh, no! What's wrong?" When Kaori was recruited by Coach Rascon two years earlier, it was Kaori's grandmother who told Molly that her granddaughter was going to attend either Stanford or Berkeley, that sports was not the family's main emphasis. Neither university offered Kaori an athletic scholarship, so she took her exceptional academic record to SJV, much to her grandmother's chagrin. Kaori is the team's single exception to the economic background of the players' families.

"They think it's pneumonia. My father didn't tell me until last night after the game, because he didn't want to have me worry about it before the game, but it's serious. She's really having a hard time breathing."

"What can I do? Do you want to come over and talk about it?"

"No. I called to ask if I can miss practice this afternoon to go see her."

"Of course, you can, Kay-kay. I can talk to your professors."

"No, Coach. I can drive home if it's okay that I miss practice. It's only about three hours. I can go to my morning classes, and then drive back tonight after I've seen my Nai-nai."

"Don't worry about practice. I was going to have you work a little with Coach Powell, but mostly it's a walk-through to get our soreness out. Just keep me informed about your grandmother." Molly thought she heard Kaori sniffle. "How about this, Kay-kay. I'll meet you at the student center before your first class and have a coffee."

∽

When Molly arrives at her office, her top two remaining assistants from the scaled-down staff are already watching film on Cal State Indio, the last place team in the conference and SJV's first-round opponent in the tournament. Ryanne Powell is Molly's age, 41, from Chicago, and has been Molly's assistant at two colleges. "Severely Black," she describes herself with a hint of humor. Nicole Aikins played for SJV before Molly arrived and asked Molly if she could be a graduate assistant that first year. Nicole is a statistics geek, and her analytical analyses taught Molly that basketball is more than a game of skill, heart, and sisterhood. At least that's how Molly introduces Nicole to other coaches. Nicole desires to become a high school head coach and calculus teacher one day. Out of health precautions, several assistants and team personnel have been told to stay away until further notice. The staff now looks more like a high school staff than a D1 cadre.

Molly fist-bumps both ladies as she walks past them to hang up her jacket and get a soda from the refrigerator. "Did you get my message about Kaori?" Both assistants nod and Ryanne asks what else Molly learned at her coffee meeting with Kaori. "She'll be back for tomorrow morning's practice. I guess her grandmother is pretty sick. She's old but has been mostly healthy. Rapid decline. Evidently, the doctors aren't sure it's just pneumonia, so Kaori may not be able to visit in person. Fear of being contagious."

"Oh, that's just what we need, for the whole team to get the flu before the tournament. We finally recover from sprained ankles, jammed fingers, and wrenched backs." Ryanne shakes her head and pulls out a chair for the head coach. "Did you tell Kay-kay to be careful?"

"I did, but she already said she would." Molly sits and slides a legal pad across the table. "What do you have?"

Coach Nicole hands Molly a computer readout. "With the new guidelines, since we'll be practicing with just the scholarship players, and our six practice players won't be allowed in the gym, these analytics are condensed. It'll seem strange, but we can direct full attention to the ladies who will be playing. What you're holding is a breakdown of time each of us can spend with each player along with the statistics from the last four games."

Ryanne holds the printouts and shakes her head at the younger assistant. "Whatever happened to the old school axiom, 'Just roll the ball out and get after it'?"

"So says the coach who teaches cross-court passes, doesn't like fifteen-foot jump shots, and rails against men who say women don't deserve even the meager money allotted to them. Your favorite phrase to the girls is 'That's a low-percentage shot!' Analytics is just statistics on steroids. Your olden days are gone." Nicole smirks as she hands Ryanne another handout. "Do I need to interpret these for you too?"

Ryanne raises her hand in a mock attack against her younger colleague.

For the next half-hour, the three coaches analyze Indio, a team SJV dominated in their two previous games. They conclude that unless the great California earthquake happens, SJV will advance. Freddie Mercury ends this part of their meeting. It's Kaori again. Her father has told her to stay in Tulare, that grandmother is too sick for visitors, so Kaori will be at practice. The coaches take up their phones to reply to the dozens of text messages from just this morning. And as always, Coach Rascon has donors to contact.

Practice is relaxed, to say the least. It begins, as it often does, to warmup dancing at 100 decibels to "Come and Get Your Love," by Redbone, a Native American rock band from Los Angeles. Then, stretching, passing and cutting drills, partner shooting, reviews of last night's game mistakes, late game specials. The Sequoias will begin the playoffs in good health, the healthiest they've been all season. They will have no excuses. Dyani Dehiya, the vocal leader and senior point guard, tells her teammates that it's "Rez Time!" which means 40 minutes of hell to their opponents. Dyani is Navajo. Diné. A gift. She came to SJV via a Tucson community college that allowed her to play as she did on the reservation. Her coach there told her that Coach Rascon's teams play fast. Dyani upped the tempo a notch. She hates it when Molly subs her out for a breath. She can rest after graduation when she returns to the reservation.

Emerson Loki's motivation stems from one season at UC Santa Barbara where she sat on the bench throughout her freshman year after being selected to the All-Southern California all-star team her senior season from Santa Monica high school. Twenty-plus points per game and defensive player of the year and several D1 scholarship offers! This year's conference tournament will be held in the UCSB gym, a neutral site. Emerson intends to score more points in that first game against Indio than she did in an entire year playing for the Gauchos. Emerson is the team's leading scorer. Dyani calls her running mate "Lope," short for Antelope, because of her gracefulness. Coach Moses Robinson, formerly a junior high coach in Oxnard and once an NBA forward—back in the previous century—came with Emerson. Sort of a package deal. He says he'll retire again when she graduates, but Coach Rascon doubts that. Robinson is the Gentle Giant, the coach who never yells. Grampa Robinson. Molly fought the staff reductions due to the health precautions to keep him and won.

Dyani tags all her teammates with a nickname. Her Uncle Hector taught her that these names give people extra strength, power they never knew they had. Few of the nicknames stick, however, except in Dyani's mind.

Coach Rascon blows her whistle ending practice and gathers her squad on the bleachers. She hands her laptop computer to Danelle Weston, the team's senior center. No player on this year's team has grown more than Danelle. Molly took a chance on her, trusted a former teammate who coached Danelle in high school and saw her anger erupt on so many occasions that she had to be benched or suspended. A community college experience helped Danelle grow, but no four-year college extended an offer to Danelle to continue her play. That's when Molly's high school teammate reached out, told her that

Danelle had been a ferocious rebounder and defender in high school. Molly offered a partial scholarship that first year.

Molly opens the computer and directs Danelle to begin reading.

For the NCAA selection committee, seeding a low-major team is usually a formality. Fifteen or sixteen, or in a rare case, fourteen. A warmup game for UConn or Stanford or South Carolina or Baylor. 'Thanks for playing, but now the tournament can get serious about its games.' The Power Five conferences can begin playing each other in contests that matter. Maybe a couple of mid-majors can sneak in. In men's hoops, mid-major conference champions often advance into the Sweet Sixteen, but not in women's hoops. The divide between the top and bottom is too great. That's why the first weekend, the Round of 64, is played at regional campus sites. Friday, March 20 and Monday, March 23. On Tuesday the tournament can get serious with the sweet sixteen. Sweet for a reason.

San Joaquin Valley? Is that in Texas down by the Alamo? Near San Antonio? Oh, Cal State San Joaquin Valley is in Tulare, California, the champions of the Ring of Fire Conference. When was that conference created? Just five years ago, huh. Low Major. Nice record. 26-2. Didn't they qualify last year and get drilled by Oregon? You say this San Joaquin squad beat Arizona? But the game was played at a high school gym on the Navajo Reservation back in early December as part of a four-team cultural celebration. Sounds like an exhibition game to the committee. And Southern Cal? Okay. If they win their conference tourney, we'll think about a number twelve seed. Send them down to College Station to play A & M or maybe up to Palo Alto to play a Pac-12 school. Only if they win their conference tournament though. At least they'll get a plane trip and a few days away from classes.

Coach Rascon steps to Danelle and pushes close the computer ending Danelle's soliloquy. "I'm not sure our favorite retired journalist can be more sarcastic, but I think you get his gist. We won't get any respect from the selection committee." Molly pauses, taking the computer from Danelle and motioning for her to take a seat with her teammates. Molly stretches out her message, allowing her team to lean forward just a bit. After handing the computer to Coach Aikins and whispering something to Coach Robinson, Molly smiles and turns back to her ladies. "My high school coach seldom swore or raised his voice, much like Coach Robinson. If he was really angry, he might use the cuss word . . . *ass,* but he had to be really angry." She pauses again, looking back at Coach Robinson and nodding her head. "Well, I don't give a rats' *ass* where the selection committee seeds us or who we get in the first round or how far away they send us. As far as I care, they can come kiss my tight *ass.*" A few of the team giggle. Molly takes two steps to Ryanne and puts her hand on her shoulder. "We're going over to Santa Barbara and win our little tournament, and then we'll come back to Tulare and prepare like we always do." She pauses again but doesn't take her eyes off her team. "Honestly, I don't know if we can beat a number one or number two seed, but I do know that you can compete with all those threes, fours, and fives." Her eyes have not released her team to respond just yet. "*March Madness*," she says in a whisper. "We win our tournament, and then," Molly pauses again. "And then, for us, for you, March Madness becomes, as Dyani and Char always say, *War!*" She says that defiantly, and her team stands and whoops and claps. "GET US OUT OF HERE, DYANI!"

Dyani Dehiya begins chanting in her native tongue, "Warriors, Warriors, Warriors." Her teammates pick up the rhythm, dancing around their captain and emotional leader. They are not Sequoias at these moments. They are The Tribe.

The coaches watch the ladies leave for the locker room, arms around one another's shoulders, laughing. Coach Robinson watches and says, "Coaching without yelling is a fantasy world. Only an old man who's seen it all could get away with that."

Molly's husband has dinner on the table when she returns home from the gym. Frankie, Jr. has already started eating. He's eight, in the third grade, quick, and athletic. And perceptive beyond his age. Molly kisses her husband and son on the tops of their heads before sitting down.

"Your AD called a little bit ago," says Frank. "He wants you to call him this evening at home. No hurry, he said. How did your day go? Are your young ladies excited?" Frank Martinez is a pediatrician with his office in Visalia about fifteen minutes from Tulare and the university. They met in Los Angeles when he was in residence there and Molly was the assistant coach at UC Irvine. Thirteen years ago. She became the head coach at Division III California Coastal College in Thousand Oaks in 2009, and he proposed to her after her first year. She told Frank that she was always going to be a coach and hoped to get a D1 job at some point. He told her that pediatricians were in demand everywhere and would go where she went.

"We had a good practice; only our top twelve since we released our six practice players last Thursday. Not hard or anything, just great vibes. We'll get after it tomorrow morning." Molly looks at Frankie. "You're welcome to come." Turning back to her husband, "How was your day?"

"Normal, sort of. We're keeping an ear to the ground for new news about this coronavirus thing. Since Trump declared a public health emergency and the CDC is warning about a pandemic, we've been on alert, but you know all of that already. Some new cases have been reported in the San Francisco area, Santa Clara County. Older people. If the country is vigilant and well-led, maybe it will be minor."

Molly hesitates to put the forkful of enchiladas in her mouth. "Well led? Yeah, right."

"Not Trump, but the public health people around him. He just needs to level with the country about how serious this virus could be and then allow the medical community to do its thing."

Molly shakes her head. "That would require that he cares about the people of America."

"No politics at the dinner table," says Frankie, Jr. His parents nod. His world is nearly perfect, and they'd like to keep it that way.

After dinner Molly calls Dr. Calhoun, the university's athletic director. He tells her that the NCAA is monitoring the virus, advising caution, but taking no other action. The AD gives her a tentative schedule for the upcoming conference tournament in Santa Barbara, asks about any team injuries, and tells her that the men's team lost the coin flip for the seven-eight seed and will have to play Atascadero in the first round. "Bad matchup. Coach Galvan isn't optimistic." When she hangs up, she prepares a practice plan for the morning and makes six copies, one for each assistant and one for her notebook. Paper copies as well as in the computer. Then she calls her high school team-mate Izzy Soto to wish her luck in her next game at the Colorado State High School tournament and thank her again for Danelle Weston. Molly then changes hats from her coaching one to her CEO one and emails four donors to her program. These are not large money donors but crucial anyway. Her husband comes in to remind her that Frankie is ready for his story. Afterwards, she will continue with the administrative portion of her sixteen-hour day.

Chapter 2

Ken Davidson's March 5th blog congratulated the team on its undefeated league season and highlighted the play of Coach Rascon's substitutes who, because of the lopsided score, received extended playing time. Davidson once wrote for the *LA Times,* an award-winning sports journalist whose beat mostly focused on professional teams and athletes. In retirement he returned home to his beloved San Joaquin Valley to "scribble notes about the hard-scrabble families and their children in America's food basket." *Agriculture and Basketball* is the title of his blog, but the focus has become the athletics part, because when basketball enters a person's body, it "courses through one's veins forever." He understands that blogging is passe, old-fashioned, but he's not searching for a wide audience. He has always been a print journalist, and blogging allows him to maintain a connection to his previous profession. Davidson's connection to Coach Rascon's team came through Moses Robinson. Davidson was having a cup of coffee at Apple Annie's in Tulare when Mose entered. Davidson had written a piece on Robinson for the *Times* back in the late Seventies just after Mose retired from the NBA and returned to his hometown, Oxnard, California, to become a junior high teacher and coach. The journalist thought that path unique and column worthy. Davidson is a sentimental old man with a fondness for honest conversation, underdogs, public education, harvest times, and dilemmas. In Tulare he is back home, and the women's basketball team at SJV is his new favorite beat, even if it doesn't pay anything or get national coverage. He often travels with the team—the bus trips but not the plane rides—and listens to the conversations of a remarkable group of young women, both players and coaches.

On this Saturday morning, Davidson sits in the bleachers with his notebook watching Coach Rascon's ladies battle one another for one more rebound. When either Sylvia Castro or Danelle Weston is on the court, it's difficult for any other player to get the ball, although the Dreamer, Esther Santiago, is a fearless freshman, and Greta Espinoza is growing. Rebounding drills are one of Coach Rascon's "everydays." These drills begin on Day One in the fall and continue throughout the season and are full contact. As Coach Rascon says, "A coach needs to have a few pet peeves, and when a player messes up on these, I need to go ballistic, just to remind them that there are little things in life that are important." Block outs are one of hers, and unlike Coach Robinson or her high school coach, Molly yells.

Davidson is searching for an angle. He's written thousands of words about Dyani and Char, the team's two Navajos from northern Arizona. He's praised the selfless work that Danelle and Sylvia have done all season in the trenches. They are the number one and number three rebounders in the conference. Back in the fall, he wrote about their religious views, one a devout Catholic, the other an Evangelical Baptist, who both carry their beliefs on their shoulders. Because of the nasty debate about whether Dreamers should be allowed to stay in America, and because Esther is so delightful and erudite, Davidson wrote a blog about her life that was picked up by the *Times* after Christmas. Kenti Solorzano, the team's third point guard, is from Guatemala. She's 26 years old, missing two fingers on her right hand, and in the States working on a PhD in agronomy. She was on Guatemala's national soccer team, but she loves basketball too. This is her first year as a member of the team.

SJV under Coach Rascon has always played an up-tempo style, lots of fastbreaks and quick threes. Always that aggressive full-court press. When Dyani came on board two years ago, Coach Rascon envisioned a new level of speed. She recruited Emerson Loki and Kaori Park to complement Dyani's skills. Emerson and Kaori are 5'11" svelte athletes who look like they should be running the 400-meter hurdles at the Olympics, but with sweet shots and no fear to attack the basket in transition.

Kaori and Emerson. Davidson ponders. What is it about these two players that brought them to this place? Both had outstanding academic records in addition to their athletic prowess, but here they are in central California at a university that isn't known as a flagship in either. Solid, yes, but not Ivy League academically or Pac-12 athletically. SJV caters to minorities and students from lower income brackets. They had choices, and yet, here they are.

He takes his eyes from Kaori and Emerson and finds Coach Rascon. Physically, she is the least imposing figure in any arena. 5'5" maybe only 5'4". Shorter than any of her players and assistants. Over a foot shorter than Coach Robinson who stands nearby. But in this gym, one always knows where she is and who is in charge. Davidson believes it's her eyes. He did his research; Molly Rascon has been a winner at every basketball level despite her stature. He wishes he could have interviewed her high school coach to get a glimpse of her home, of her soil. He remembers something Ryanne Powell said to him at the beginning of the season, at the planting. "Molly honors her roots every day." Ryanne said it in response to his question about why Ryanne has been Molly's assistant for over a decade instead of seeking a head job herself. Non-sequitur. Ryanne continued, "I'm coaching young women with my best friend. Why would I want to be anywhere else?"

Coach Rascon blows her whistle. Every player stops instantly and holds her ball. "Ladies, we have five days to get a little better." She pauses, as she usually does, but every player knows it's not an act. They know she was an All-American twenty years ago, that she knows what it takes. Her girls know she is fuming inside, because someone was casual, but she's trying to control herself. Davidson pulls his feet off the bleacher in front of his butt and leans forward to hear Coach Rascon's words. "You're paired up for a reason beyond having someone rebound your lazy-ass shots. What I see is a group of girls going through the motions, over-confident. What I want to see is twelve ladies trying to get ONE SHOT BETTER!" Standing at center court, Molly turns slowly to see each girl at the six different baskets. "Maybe not against Indio or even Palm Valley next week, but against that number four seed in two weeks, ONE SHOT will make the difference." She pauses again. "Quit being so nice to your partner. When she's lazy with her footwork or her passes are soft and off target, say something!" Coach Rascon is about to explode.

The Gentle Giant, who has been working with Danelle Weston, Greta Espinoza, Sylvia Castro, and Joyce Hensley—the Bigs—clears his throat, not that the team can hear, but that Molly can hear. He speaks only loud enough to hear because the gym is absolutely quiet. "Big games are always about one extra possession, one extra stop, being one possession better than your opponent. That one play can be earned on a Saturday morning after the conference has been settled, when no one is in the stands cheering, when you're tired because your boyfriend kept you out last night." He looks directly at Keilani Russell and gives her a tight-lipped grin. "Players four through twelve think they know that that last shot will be taken by Emerson or Kaori, but it's not always the star who takes that shot. Guess what? Coach VanDerveer up at Stanford didn't win a thousand games without doing her homework. She knows who Coach Rascon will designate to shoot that shot and has a plan to deny them. So, who steps up when Dyani can't get the ball to Kaori or Emerson, when Sylvia has fouled out? Which one of you has the courage to prepare yourself to take the shot that might never happen . . . but could. It's that courage to imagine what *could be* that makes you a champion. This morning, this drill, could be that moment." Coach Robinson pauses, nods to the head coach, and steps back. His voice has been calm.

Molly Rascon doesn't pause, and her voice is focused. "Let's make this morning the *Could Be* morning." She blows her whistle, and the sneakers begin to squeak with new energy.

In the stands, Ken Davidson jots a note on his legal pad. *While Assistant Coach Robinson makes the point, his words are an extension of the head coach's purpose. "Dog gone it, ladies. If you sign up for something in life, put all your energy into it and get it right!"*

Morning practice ends at 9:30. The last 45 minutes are productive, one of Coach Rascon's favorite words. "I don't want good players; I need *productive* players." Maintenance lifting follows immediately after, and then each player meets with one of the assistant coaches for an evaluation/concerns meeting. Then lunch.

After that the team piles into a university bus for a short trip to the Tulare County Fairgrounds. They are never told the destination of these trips beforehand. At least once each month, the team visits a Tulare site to learn a bit of local history or culture. Coach Rascon believes that the team owes back, as she calls it, to the people who share their town with the ladies for a few years. "You will not be allowed to be placed on a pedestal. You will be like all other SJV students." She wants her team to be humble, to understand that the money spent on university athletics comes from somewhere, that it doesn't just appear magically. It's someone's tax dollars that pays the bills. These trips are an extension of the team's community service activities.

The team is met by an old man who farms a few miles west of Tulare closer to Corcoran. As the ladies stand in front of the bus, he begins his lesson.

"Seventy-eight years ago, Americans of Japanese ancestry stepped off buses and trains near here and then were marched under armed guard through the main street of Tulare to this location. The majority were women and children from southern and central California. Mostly Nisei, first generation American citizens. They were housed in hastily constructed barracks here at the fairgrounds for four months in the heat of the summer while more permanent camps were being built in other locations. 1942. Most of those incarcerated here eventually were transferred to a concentration camp at Gila River, Arizona." The man pauses and looks kindly at the twelve young women. Then he steps forward and shakes each one's hand, introducing himself and asking their names. The team wears their brown and gold team traveling sweats, and every girl holds a plastic water bottle. The SJV coaching staff stands in the background. The man raises his right hand slightly and waves the team to follow him to a horse barn nearby.

"The prisoners were housed in barracks similar to this one, about 20 feet wide and 100 feet long. The barracks were crudely divided into multiple family units in order for families to stay together. A family of four had about 330 square feet of living space." The man sees a raised hand and acknowledges Greta Espinoza.

"That seems tiny. Did each family have its own bathroom?"

"Oh, no. Group toilets, showers, and sinks were located at various locations around the fairgrounds. Conditions were quite primitive. The family units were equipped with a minimum of furniture, mostly just wooden cots with thin mattresses. The inmates set out constructing basic furniture on their own out of crates and other wood. They also planted gardens and generally tried to make the grounds more amenable while they were here." He acknowledges another hand.

Joyce Hensley clears her throat. "We read about the Japanese internment in high school, that it was done out of a concern for safety along the coast. My teacher said that the government later released them and said they had made a mistake. That seems to me like it minimizes this event."

"Often, when we make mistakes, we don't want to talk about them, or we want to minimize them and move on. The country won the war and a wave of euphoria passed over us. The nation experienced very few acts of sabotage during the war, and so the prisoners were set free. Let me emphasize a few details first. About 120,000 people were imprisoned in all, the majority being citizens. Nearly 5,000 of that total were imprisoned here at Tulare. These people were rounded up simply because of their appearance because they looked like the people who attacked Pearl Harbor. While President Roosevelt issued an executive order to make it appear legal, it was a suspension of their basic rights and liberties. And property. They lost their homes and most of their possessions and generally were not welcomed back into their communities after their release." He again waves his hand for the team to follow him. He leads them into a cafeteria where he has them sit.

"As I understand it, your coach involves you in projects that make you get to know Tulare better." The old man pauses to get the ladies' assent. "Coach Rascon contacted our local county museum. The director put her in touch with me because I'm a big basketball fan, and because my family spent the summer of 1942 here in Tulare before being sent to Arizona for the next three years." He allows that fact to settle over the team.

Kaori raises her hand, and the man points to her. "Were you born in the camp?"

The man laughs slightly. "No. Do I look that old?" The team giggles. "I was born years later, after my parents finally settled near Fresno.

When I was about ten, we moved here to begin farming. I learned in school that Americans believed the incarceration of Japanese Americans was an injustice, that it was a black mark in our history. If that's all it was, I don't think your coach would have brought you here to listen to an old man tell his family story. Along our southern border today, migrants are being held under conditions that rival what my family suffered under during World War II. Children are being separated from their parents and forced to live under terrible conditions." Again, the man pauses. "Words matter. Tulare wasn't called a *temporary jail;* it was an *assembly center.* I'll bet you learned in school that the camps were *relocation centers, temporary relocation centers,* and not *concentration camps.*" He allows that term to hang in the air over the team. "Fortunately, few people died in America's camps, but imagine what might have happened if the war turned out differently. Why weren't Germans rounded up and sent to camps on the east coast?" He stops there to collect his emotions. "I love this country, but right now I see a rise in intolerance, and looking at you young ladies, I see a diverse group of Americans. And, as I spoke with your coach, I began to see what she wants for you."

For the next fifteen minutes, the old man answers questions about his past, but always deflects them to relate to current conditions. He shifts their questions to episodes in their own short lives. "That was then, this is now. How can you better the lives around you?" The session ends only when Molly walks to the front of the room and tells her team that they have practice soon and will have to get back on the bus. She instructs her ladies to thank Mr. Fuchigami. The team stands and applauds, and Mr. Fuchigami bows slightly. One by one, the women approach him and hug briefly. Kenti Solorzano is the last to thank Mr. Fuchigami.

"Could I meet with you sometime . . . after the season is over?" she asks. "I study soils, what to grow in particular soils. I'm from Guatemala, a small city called Nebaj."

"Of course, but why wait? I'll be attending all your tournament games in Santa Barbara. We can talk there."

❧

The late afternoon practice is all shooting. Game shots at game speed, position oriented. Threes, free throws, one-dribble jumpers, driving lay-ups, powers. More threes. As always, the coaching staff emphasizes the pass that precedes the shot. The Sequoias won't practice on Sunday. Heading into the playoffs, the most important thing is the team's health. Give the subs the bulk of any scrimmage time on Monday and Tuesday. The Sequoias are ready.

Monday, March 9, 2020, four days before the conference tournament begins at the UC Santa Barbara gym. Practice is crisp, and the coaching staff is pleased. Emerson Loki has been especially focused, which removes some of Coach Robinson's anxiety. He knows she wants to show well in that arena, and he was the one who steered her to SJV. She played middle school ball in Ventura, just up the 101 from Mose's middle school in Oxnard. He had watched her and gotten to know her when the schools had boys-girls doubleheaders on Saturdays. After her eighth-grade year, Emerson transferred to Santa Monica, a school known for its hoops. They reconnected when she enrolled at UCSB, and after Mose had retired from teaching. Mose is a 71-year-old grampa, but he still loves basketball. That feeling never goes away. He was just as frustrated with her lack of game time as Emerson was. Mose and his wife Sally had watched SJV beat UCSB that year with Emerson sitting the bench the whole game, and he loved Coach Rascon's pace.

At 6:00 that evening, the athletic director meets with both Molly and the men's coach in his office. "It's been decided, out of an abundance of caution, that our tournaments will be played without crowds. It's a conference call, not mine. The games are still on, but they'll simply be played in empty gyms. As far as I know, most conferences have decided to do the same. Empty arenas, but the tournaments will go on as scheduled. The Big Dance will do the same. It's a billion-dollar event that gets most of that money from TV. This damn coronavirus has everyone running scared, maybe too scared, but nobody wants one of theirs to catch it. Lawsuits, you know." He stops.

"So, the rumors are true," says Molly. The AD nods. "My girls will be extremely disappointed if this decision holds. I assume the conference won't change its mind tomorrow or the next day." Again, the AD nods. "I need to get to my team tonight before the word gets out, and rumors start flying again." She stands and places her hand on the men's coach's shoulder as she leaves.

"She'll have her team ready regardless of the circumstances," says the men's coach. "I'm not sure my guys will be up for this."

In the hall Molly sends a group text instructing her team to gather in the team room immediately. They are all aware of the rumors.

THE TOURNAMENT IS STILL ON

This is the sentence that greets The Tribe as they enter the team room. Coach Rascon, Ryanne Powell, Nicole Aikins, and Jackie Jakino are at the door greeting each player as she enters. Coach Robinson didn't answer the text and hasn't arrived. Most of the team are dressed casually or in study pajamas, as Coach Powell calls them, since the girls have been instructed to get ahead with their class assignments, as they will be out of school beginning on Wednesday. This is an irregular meeting, so they know that something important will be revealed.

As the coaches walk to the front of the room, Emerson blurts a question. "Is Coach Robinson okay. He hasn't been hurt or something, has he?"

"No. No. He'll be here as soon as he checks his text. You know how he is about texts," answers Molly. "This isn't about that. It's about the rumors circling about the coronavirus." There is a noticeable relaxation in the room. Emerson's question hadn't occurred to the others, but when she posed it, they tensed. Molly clears her voice. "It's been decided to hold the tournament without spectators because of the threat of the coronavirus. I guess the number of cases is increasing rapidly around the country, but especially along both coasts. California has seen hundreds of new cases just over the weekend. The conference doesn't want to put fans in any danger. I think this is the decision that is being made in every conference everywhere." Molly's cell begins playing "We Are the Champions." She looks at it briefly, then hands it to Coach Powell who walks to the back of the room. "It's Coach Robinson. He just got the text." The team laughs.

Coach Rascon continues. "Okay, this is what I know. This doesn't affect the games; they're still on. We have the 6:00 o'clock game on Thursday, the primetime game. Indio is the sacrificial lamb, as you already know. We'll have to bring our own energy. Bench! You especially will have to provide an atmosphere. Be loud! Practice tomorrow at 4:00 as scheduled. We'll take the bus to Santa Barbara on Wednesday morning, so pack for four nights. We are the two-time defending tournament champions." She stops and looks back to her staff. They shake their heads. Nothing to add. "Questions then?"

"Will our families be able to watch?"

"No, probably not. You'll need to call them and explain. Maybe the ban on fans will be lifted for the NCAAs, but I doubt it. I know they'll be disappointed."

"Trump said the virus was under control."

Molly masks her political feelings. "Maybe he's trying to reassure us. It's definitely not under control yet."

Assistant Coach Jakino puts her head down so the team doesn't hear her response. "It's just going to magically disappear."

"Is there any danger to us, that we could get it?"

"According to the best medical advice, you're safe. Seems as though the virus is hitting the very old, especially in nursing homes.

Molly and her staff answer several more questions, and when she ends the meeting, the team seems secure about their own health, but they are disappointed that fans won't be in the stands. As they file out, Dyani mutters, "I've never played in an empty gym before. On the rez, it's the event of the week. Full houses, and our high school arena holds more than SJV's."

When the team is gone, Molly sits on the front table with her staff sitting in front of her. "Disappointing to the max," says Ryanne.

Nicole Aikins has been mostly silent all evening. "It's not fair! Only a few old people have died. We haven't heard of any cases in Tulare or on campus. What's to say it's not just like the flu."

The other coaches remain silent. The door at the back of the room opens, and Coach Robinson enters carrying a small cooler. "Thought tonight we might all need a cold beer."

∾

When she gets home, Molly sends a personalized text to each of her girls. Her husband sits next to her on the couch reading to Frankie, Jr., who senses something is amiss. When she finishes, she catches up on several emails from her former teammates, both from college and high school.

"Want to talk?" asks her husband.

Molly closes her laptop and lays it on the end table by the couch. She shifts and puts her legs over Frankie's lap so that her feet are in Frank's lap, a not-so-subtle act that will let him rub them. "This decision to close the games to spectators is disheartening. I tried to focus on the fact that the tournament games are still going to be played, to minimize the loss of fans, but it will change the nature of the event. I hope my girls didn't sense my disappointment. We have all the momentum in the world going for us right now. I don't want this virus to steal it." She goes quiet, and her husband and son wait. "I don't feel much like their mama tonight . . . or their coach. More like an administrator handing out edicts." Frankie fiddles with his mother's kneecap, and she smiles at him. "When the girls left the room, I was still standing at the front. They just filed out like zombies. There should have been an air of excitement. We're the league champs, and we're closing in on a positive seed. Imagine that, maybe a twelve seed from our podunk conference. Five years in and a twelve seed, maybe even an eleven. One strong weekend, and we're into the Sweet Sixteen. For these girls, it's possible. And nobody there to see it unfold."

Frankie suddenly throws up his arms. "And the crowd goes wild!" His parents laugh.

∾

Tuesday's afternoon practice will be the last one in the SJV gym before the Sequoias board a university bus in the morning for a three-and-a-half-hour drive to Santa Barbara, 210 miles. Just down the road to the coast. Check into the motel and then hold a shoot-around at

The Thunderdome in Isla Vista. Opening round versus Indio. Very little thunder.

Coach Rascon uses "the last everything" to motivate her charges. "If we're not sharp, this could be the last whatever." Fill in the blank. Kenti Solorzano cracks up her teammates and the coaching staff when she says, in her peculiar English vocabulary, that while the thunder might be missing in the Thunderdome, SJV will bring the lightning. "We scorch and burn Indio!"

Loose but precise. The coaches like what they see. Lots of chatter, but no horseplay. The journey has not lost its mission. Coach Rascon extends the rez ball drill because of its intensity. Danelle feigns disdain because she gets no shots in this drill, only throwing long outlet passes. Emerson pretends to dunk on Dyani and falls hard to the floor. No harm done, but Molly ends the drill and sends six players to opposite ends to run through set plays and inbounds plays. Dummy drills. Now the coaches demand execution, and Molly reminds her girls that "Every drill is a passing drill!" Coach Ryanne is the footwork queen. "If you can't pivot, you can't play. Do it again!" She supervises the starting five plus one, while Coach Nicole and Coach Jackie have the subs. Coach Robinson works with the centers on both ends, while Molly stands at mid-court and commands both groups. Eyes in the back of her head.

From sets, the ladies move to free throws. These will end practice after they run their misses. Then they will towel off while Coach Rascon critiques the practice. All positive comments this afternoon. On normal practices, there would be corrections, but not today. It's all good. The Tribe is ready, and there is no mention of the crowdless games. The team stacks hands, and Dyani yells, "Warriors." Ken Davidson, who is observing this last regular season practice from high in the stands, shakes his head at the number of nicknames this team assigns itself. "The mascot of the day," he once blogged. On that day after an especially high scoring game against Riverside, one of SJV's main rivals, Molly called her team the Cheetahs. She wouldn't tell him why.

∾

Molly and Ryanne relax after dinner with a glass of wine. A one-hour break. Her husband chides them; a poor Chicana and a poor Black from the Chicago projects drinking wine. They are never far from next season, even during this season's playoffs. Frank teases his wife frequently that she can never retire, because she wouldn't have anything to talk about. Frank and Frankie do the dishes. When they complete this chore, they move to his study to work on Frankie's homework. Frank canceled their motel reservations in Santa Barbara when the NCAA called for the banning of spectators at the tournament. Molly and Ryanne move to the kitchen table and pull out their legal pads.

"How do we replace Dyani next year?" asks Molly. It's the first question one of them asks each time they plan recruiting trips. They've seen a dozen California point guards, all highly rated, but only one meeting their needs who might slip into their grasp. None possess the potential to replace Dyani.

"Right now, it's Char. Not bad, but she needs at least another year to fill those big shoes. Not so much about her skills as her leadership ability." Ryanne flips a page on her legal pad and scans the list of out of state point guards on Molly's radar.

"I've been thinking." Molly puts her pen aside, interlocks her fingers, and puts her hands under her chin. "Keilani. I don't want to lose her via transfer, and we both know she's frustrated playing behind Emerson and Kay-kay."

Ryanne nods her head slowly, pondering. "We obviously aren't going to get another Dyani." She tilts her head into her left hand and reaches for her wine. She holds the glass without taking a sip. "It would give Char that extra year."

"Dyani has allowed us to play two small forwards for the past two seasons. If Keilani was our point, we could subtly transform Kaori into an off-guard. Work on her ball-handling skills over the summer. Not so much different than how she plays now. She'd still run the left lane. Having those three out front would certainly nullify opponents' pick-and-roll on top. We'd switch everything."

Frank comes to the kitchen to get ice for his tea. "That would leave just the center position. Who replaces Danelle?"

Both coaches give him a look that asks, "Why were you ease-dropping and who do you recommend?"

Frank closes the refrigerator. As he passes behind his wife, without looking at either coach, he says, "Sylvia. Think outside the box. Move her and let Greta and Esther battle it out for the four spot."

Both coaches smile. Ryanne nods again. "He has a point."

Molly's cell rings; it's the SJV athletic director. "Just a heads up, Coach. The Ivy League is cancelling both its men's and women's basketball tournaments. It's confusing as to whether or not they will allow the league champions to participate in the NCAA tournament. I'll know more tomorrow. Your schedule hasn't changed. The bus leaves at 10:00 and should get you to your motel around 1:00. Good luck."

Molly relates the call to Ryanne. "The Ivy League. I wonder what their coaches are saying." Her words mask her concern. When the Ring of Fire Conference was created five years ago, the year Molly was hired at SJV, the presidents and chancellors at the eight universities expressed a desire to become "the Ivy League of the West." Obviously, that was not going to happen, what with Stanford and other great universities in California, but the goal was to focus on academics and not just be diploma mills for minority students.

"Don't you know a couple of the coaches in the Ivy?" asks Ryanne.

"Yeah. They have to be devastated."

Although eight teams arrive in Santa Barbara on March 11 for the Ring of Fire Conference tournament, only one has a destiny. Five of the eight teams could win the tournament if the proverbial ball bounced their way, but only one has a realistic chance to win a game in the NCAA tournament. For seven teams, this weekend is the culmination of six months of sweat, the reward, but for one squad, the weekend is but another step along a path. For seven coaches, the goal is to win a game and advance. For one coaching staff, the goal is to get a little better, to tweak a weakness or polish a strength. Part of the process. For seven teams, Santa Barbara represents earth on the horizon. For one team, Santa Barbara represents the sky, an opportunity to soar above that looming horizon. For seven teams, the conference tournament is the ceiling; for San Joaquin Valley, it is the launching pad to greater possibilities.

Crystal clear skies and clean air greet the Sequoias as they exit the bus and enter the motel's courtyard. A giant banner welcomes the team. "The Best Western South Coast Inn Welcomes the Ring of Fire Conference Champions: Best of Luck to the San Joaquin Valley Sequoias." Three young men wearing white jackets pass out red roses to each team member. Playing at UCSB is a treat for the ladies. The men's tournament will be played in Fresno, a city not far removed from Tulare so not considered as a special destination. The SJV men are not expected to advance past the first round and will not be staying on site. The ladies are booked through Sunday.

While the team waits in the courtyard for their luggage, Coach Rascon tells them to unpack their bags and put their clothes in the chests and hang up their uniforms. "Don't live out of your suitcases!" After a light lunch, the team has a shoot-around in the Thunderdome at 6:00, exactly 24 hours prior to tip-off. Dinner will be served around 8:15, and Coach Rascon demands that the ladies be showered and dressed appropriately since they represent their university. Thoughts of playing in an empty arena don't enter the players' heads. The Tribe is giddy! It is all about the game. Reality can come tomorrow.

It's the eve of the second step of the journey. It's about earning a positive seed rather than simply filling a slot. It is the chance to be a factor. To become visible.

2019-2020 SAN JOAQUIN VALLEY SEQUOIAS

1	Dyani Dehiya	5'7"	Sr.	Chinle, AZ	Sociology
3	Kenti Solorzano	5'7"	Gr.	Nebaj, Guatemala	Agronomy
5	Char Betany	5'6"	Fr.	Window Creek, AZ	Undeclared
11	Keilani Russell	5'9"	Fr.	Inglewood, CA	Communications
13	Emerson Loki	5'11"	So.	Santa Monica, CA	Theatre Arts/Dance
15	Kaori Park	5'11"	So.	Sunnyvale, CA	Math/Env Science
21	Joyce Hensley	6'1"	Jr.	Fresno, CA	Nursing
23	Maria Sanchez	6'2"	Fr.	El Paso, TX	Early Child Educ
25	Sylvia Castro	6'2"	Jr.	El Paso, TX	Family Studies
31	Esther Santiago	6'2"	Fr.	San Diego, CA	Art
33	Greta Espinoza	6'3"	Fr.	Oxnard, CA	Agribusiness
41	Danelle Weston	6'4"	Sr.	Brighton, CO	Criminal Justice

HEAD COACH: Molly Rascon, Oro Hills, CO, 5th Season

ASSOCIATE HEAD COACH: Ryanne Powell, Chicago. IL

ASSISTANTS: Moses Robinson, Nicole Aikins, Jackie Jakino

Chapter 3

The tournament program includes the team's record and the fact that SJV is the league champion, the undefeated league champion. Molly, Ryanne, and Mose are having breakfast before the team and young assistants arrive. As the motel manager promised, yesterday's sunshine has been replaced by clouds, and the Channel Islands are obscured. The first game of the Ring of Fire tournament pits third seed Santa Clarita against sixth seed Chula Vista. Game two, the winner of which will be San Joaquin Valley's second round opponent, pits the four and five seeds, Salinas and Atascadero. The second-best team in the conference and the only team to challenge SJV all year, Palm Valley, plays number seven Long Beach in the late game. Unless SJV loses, it will be the only team from the conference to get into the NCAA tournament. If SJV loses either its first or second game, they won't get in either. Maybe if they lose in the finals. Maybe. Women's basketball facts of life in 2020.

Ken Davidson joins the three coaches. The four oldest people who rode the bus down from Tulare discuss the impact of the coronavirus on sports in America. "In all my years of journalism, this will be the weirdest season of them all. No fans." He shakes his head. "The NBA went on hold last night."

"Sort of like middle school games on Saturday mornings," says Coach Robinson. "Pure basketball with no antics." He pauses. "Except for a few overprotective parents."

Molly smiles. "Or high school basketball in Oro Hills for my sophomore season. Maybe a dozen family members. Did you ever coach girls, Mose?" He shakes his head. Molly goes into her past.

"I write for the fans," says Ken. "I'll be curious to see their reaction to my blog and other sportswriters' columns." He looks to Ryanne. "I see you react to plays on the floor but not the fans. You and Mose are the calmest people in the gym during games."

"Mose is just napping. I hear them, but I've learned to tune them out. Molly can tell you that wasn't always the case. My job is to suggest things to Molly that she might miss. My job isn't to wave my arms to rile up the crowd. Still, I do enjoy all that emotion."

Molly scoffs. "Let one of our girls take a charge, and you're the first one off the bench."

"That's because you're already standing. If the refs would allow it, you'd run onto the court to pick her up." Ryanne looks directly at the old journalist. "Molly thinks that taking a charge is the next best thing to an orgasm." The table cracks up at Ryanne's banter.

Ken reads a text and relays the message. "The MEAC quarterfinals have started; second game is in progress. Morgan State versus Delaware State. The conference is historically black universities. They play some pretty good hoops."

Ryanne raises her eyebrows. "That's a good sign."

Six SJV players led by Danelle Weston enter the elaborate dining area. A Best Western motel in Santa Barbara, California, is not the same as a Best Western in Brighton, Colorado. When Coach Rascon informed her team about accommodations, Danelle groaned. Now, she's amazed at the breakfast spread and her ability to order off the menu. Shortly, the remaining six players arrive in pairs. Ken Davidson begins taking notes in his spiral pad. Molly Rascon continues taking notes in her head.

At 10:12, Dyani Dehiya receives a text from her uncle, Hector Dehiya, wishing her good luck and asking if the games are still on. Dyani's eyes well up.

Coach Rascon receives a text from the Cal State Bakersfield head coach, a good friend of hers, that the WAC has cancelled its tournament.

Ken Davidson's phone rings at the same time his text alert buzzes. All five power conferences are cancelling their basketball tournaments immediately. A quarterfinal game between St. John's and Creighton has been halted at halftime and the players pulled off the court. At other venues in other cities, teams are warming up for their first contest.

Duke University announces it is suspending all athletic activities until further notice.

Coach Rascon's cell buzzes. She sees who is calling, and her stomach knots. She uses the f-word under her breath.

"Coach, this is Dr. Calhoun." He makes a slight noise. "Your tournament has been cancelled. I'm sorry. Bring your ladies home." Calhoun says more, but Molly will only remember his first words. *Your tournament has been canceled. Bring your ladies home.* She swallows hard and widens her eyes to fight back tears. Her jaw tenses. On either side, Ryanne and Mose each put a hand on Molly's forearms. They wait. She takes a few deep breaths and then quietly says, "Yeah.," and then stands, and with a spoon, taps her water glass to get her team's attention.

Ken Davidson will blog later about her handling of this moment when the season crashed, when SJV's season abruptly ended, when their championship run vanished.

"Ladies, your phones will start buzzing like crazy soon, people telling you the tournament is off. I just heard from our AD that the tournament is on hold, and we'll know more shortly, so ignore the rumors for now. What I want you to do is eat a good breakfast and review your keys that we went over last night. I'll keep gathering information, and we'll meet at 11:00 in the conference room. Remember what Coach Robinson always tells you. 'It goes by too fast, so savor every moment,' and he doesn't just mean the games. Moments like game day breakfasts."

Ryanne takes her eyes off her best friend and looks out to the team. "Go easy on the sausages. All that grease doesn't sit well during the game." She catches Sylvia Castro's eyes. "Especially you, Sylvia. Remember what happened at Atascadero in that first game. I don't want to have to clean you up again." The team laughs.

Molly sits and whispers to her table to stay for a while after she leaves. "They'll know soon enough." She stands, looks over her team at this moment, smiles at them while nodding to herself, and exits.

Back in her room, she calls her husband. He can tell that she's devastated.

∾

The coaching staff is waiting for the team as the ladies enter the conference room, each player wearing her warmup jacket. Sequoias now. Coach Aikins and Coach Jakino hand each player a tournament program. Emblazoned on the front cover is a photo of Dyani shooting a layup over a Palm Valley player. When they are all seated, Coach Rascon begins.

"First, I need to apologize for not being completely honest at breakfast. I knew, but I wanted you to have that breakfast." She stops herself to wipe a tear. She has a funny remembrance of a former teammate from high school who wore heavy eye makeup and avoided crying so as not to smudge it. Molly returns to the moment. "The tournament has been canceled." Coach Rascon has long ago learned to hold her girls not just with her arms but with her eyes, and twelve pairs of eyes look to their coach for protection. "There will be time later for anger, for that 'It's not fair' moment, but not now." Molly looks at Danelle and gives her center a stern, directive look. Danelle nods. "We will have to be satisfied with being the undefeated conference champions, the only team in the league's short history, either women's or men's, to accomplish that feat. In my heart, I know that we would have marched through this tournament to claim another trophy, which would have given us that NCAA berth. In the days ahead, we can imagine where we would have been seeded, where we would have gone to play, who our opponent would have been. Ryanne and I will not sell you short; we will most likely pit you against South Carolina in the Final Four and then get UConn in the championship game." Molly smiles weakly . . . and pauses.

"Seriously, this is extremely disappointing, but we will go on. For now, you need to go back to your rooms and pack up. We'll board the bus at 1:00 and go home. Contact your families; let them know. We should know more about school tonight, so after we get back to Tulare, we'll meet again for pizza and go over the news. Things are changing hour-by-hour."

Dyani raises her hand. "Is this how my senior season ends? Mine and Danelle's?"

Molly curls her lips inward. She looks back to Coach Robinson, who moves toward Danelle. Molly goes to Dyani and hugs her, while Mose hugs Danelle. Coach Powell claps first, and then the team stands and applauds its two seniors. When it quiets, Coach Rascon, still holding Dyani, says, "I just saw a tweet from a coach who suggests that seniors be given an additional year of eligibility, but that's just a straw to hold onto. We can't rely on that. If this is how your season ends, you go out as champions . . . and dearly loved by all of us."

∾

***Blog notes, March 12.** Kids aren't talking much, not like usual bus trips. Worried. Faces buried in their cell phones. Lots of sniffling. Emerson stares out the window. The coaching staff is busy with texts, no doubt trying to find more information. Molly and Ryanne share in whispers. Mose sits next to me texting his wife who evidently is with two of their grandkids. Kids. I'm surrounded by kids on one level, but really, they are all young adults. All nineteen or older. I wonder if Coach will demand they attend classes tomorrow since their tourney was canceled. She's a stickler about that. Tulare in about an hour. Still lots of laborers in the fields. Bad air, as usual. I love The Valley. Coach Jakino does too. She'd make a wonderful high school coach because of her ties and understanding of this valley, and her Yokuts ancestry. Molly's staff is tight. Mose and Coach Jakino came on two years ago. Not sure how long Mose will do this. He keeps saying "year-to-year." He maintains his house in Oxnard, but he rents an apartment near the college during the season. Sally (wife) stays with him parts of every week. Lovely couple. Old but still affectionate. Interracial. Oxnard all the way. Greta is Oxnard too. They're comfortable together, almost like uncle and niece. Greta and Emerson are why Mose is here. He has street cred with the team. Been there, done that.*

Maria is resting her head on Sylvia's shoulder. They don't often sit together on bus and plane rides. Half-sisters from Texas. Similar physical attributes but Coach is trying to get Maria to play as tough as Sylvia. It's not in her. I think Maria would rather play like one of the three small forwards. Kaori, Emerson, Keilani. Poetry. Mose told me Emerson was named after the Transcendentalist writer. That's worth exploring. What type of mother names her daughter after a dead male writer from long ago?

No subplots on today's blog. It will be all about the tournament's cancellation and the abrupt end to a wonderful and successful season. But incomplete.

❧

The SJV athletic bus pulls up to the dorm where all the players live except Kenti Solorzano who is not on scholarship. Five years older than the next oldest player on the team, a grad student, an international student on a visa program that ends this semester, Kenti plays purely for the love of the game. She is offensively the least skilled player, but she is "so darned athletic" that she makes a wonderful practice player when defending the guards. Kenti asked Coach Rascon for a tryout, telling Molly she simply wanted to play against good players, and practice time would be enough. Not once during the season did Coach have to encourage Kenti to play harder or focus, and the Guatemalan relished guarding Dyani—to the point of frustration to the all-conference point guard.

Coach Rascon stands at the front of the bus. "The pizza will be delivered at 7:00. Put your stuff in your rooms and meet in the lounge then. There's more information coming about classes too. I'll talk with the AD so that I can give you as accurate of info as I can. I know, it's been a hard day." She turns slightly, but then turns back. "Oh, and no practice in the morning; I'll let you sleep in."

The ladies laugh lightly, but they're tired. They exit the bus like a team that has lost a game they weren't supposed to. Quiet, subdued.

Four student managers remain on the bus. The bus will return to the back entrance of the performance arena, aka the gym, where the equipment will be unloaded. Normally, uniforms would be laundered immediately, but not tonight since they weren't worn. A subtle deviation that indicates that things are not as they should be.

Molly, Ryanne, Nicole, Mose, and Jackie make their way to the conference room in the dorm to prepare for the meeting. Ken

Davidson excuses himself to go home to his wife. "Keep me informed; let me know if there's anything I can do." A journalist, a compiler, a confidante. He senses a larger story, but his antennae indicate Coach Rascon wants this next meeting to be "team only."

Kenti is sitting at the back of the room with her bags. "No sense two trips to my dorm." Normally, the bus drops the team off at the gym, and one of the coaches walks her to her dorm which is closer to the gym. She doesn't drive. Coach Aikins tells Kenti she'll take her home after the meeting. Logistics.

"Kenti," asks Coach Rascon, "remind me of the stops you make when you fly home."

"Here to Los Angeles. To Houston. Then sometimes to Mexico City. Then to Guatemala City. My family will pick me up to take me home. I have only made this journey twice. Too expensive to go for the weekend." She smiles at her little joke. "Also, your president might not let me back in. Kenti is not joking about her last statement. She fears America's latest anti-immigrant policies will influence foreign students' ability to travel across borders.

Molly nods as she makes another call. Coach Jakino stands to answer the door, knowing it's the pizza delivery. It's a full-on dinner. Pizza, wings, breadsticks, sodas, and two pasta dishes, one for Mose and one for Ryanne. Ryanne isn't a pizza fan, and Mose just eats so much that he needs that second main dish. Molly kids him that it's the least she can do since his salary is the lowest on the staff—as per his demands—which he donates to the Tulare school district athletic budget. Coaching for the love of the game at his age. "Financially secure in retirement!" The staff sets the food out on the tables while Coach Rascon jots notes on her legal pad as she listens to the voice on her cell.

Ten minutes before 7:00 the team enters. Tardies are not acceptable, one of Molly's pet peeves, so the squad operates on "Lombardi time." Also, they're hungry. Kenti has already gotten her pizza slices and wings. When everyone is fully engaged with the food, Emerson stands and asks for their attention.

"In that alternative world that existed earlier today, we would be at halftime of our game and ahead by twenty points." Her teammates clap and whoop. "And Coach would be shaking her head and telling us we're not playing with intensity." Subdued laughter. Coach Powell lightly shoves Coach Rascon's shoulder. Emerson looks to her left to find her point guard. "And Dyani will be all over Danelle and Sylvia about their outlet passes. 'Gotta be quicker, Bigs! Gotta get us out and running! You know where to find me!'" Dyani tries to explain, but the team won't allow that. Emerson continues. "So, tonight we celebrate our victory over Indio, and tomorrow we'll see who we go up against, and I'll tell you all how that one turns out. One game at a time, right Coach?"

Joyce Hensley, who is at the food line refilling her plate, turns to the team. "In that alternative universe, if you starters have done your job, I'm about to enter the game and get a half-dozen minutes. In an empty gym, if I score, you guys will go nuts, like I never scored a basket in a game." Her best friend on the team, Sylvia Castro, reminds her that she scored six in the last Indio game. "All putbacks; cleaning up our misses." Joyce walked on her freshman year, the same year Sylvia arrived as Coach Rascon's prized recruit, a two-star prospect from south Texas. Three years later, Sylvia has lived up to her potential, while Joyce remains mostly a practice player, but a valuable one.

"Who do we get tomorrow, Coach?" yells out Kaori Park.

"Let's say Atascadero upsets Salinas. A close one, but the Earthquakes rumble past the Steinbecks for the right to play us. Game is at 7:00 tomorrow."

"Do we meet here again after dinner?' asks Kaori.

"Sounds like a plan."

The imaginary world continues until the pizza is consumed, and then Coach Rascon brings her team back to reality. "I have to ask, are any of you feeling sick right now?" Nobody is. "Good. Governor Newsom has asked that the public schools shut down for the next few weeks as a precaution, and I guess most schools are. Tulare and the rest of the Valley haven't announced that they will yet, but we'll see how this week goes. I spoke with our AD when I got off the bus, and he says that we here at SJV will continue to hold face-to-face classes, but that professors can opt to go to alternative modalities if they want, so you'll need to check with your professors to determine. So far, no cases of the virus have been reported here."

Molly is interrupted by Char Betony. "If there are no cases, then why did they cancel our tournament so fast? It sucks!"

Molly curls her lips inward before responding. "Char, and all of you, I think that because the Big Boys did, and by Big Boys I mean the NBA and the power conferences, I think our conference felt they had no other choice. I'm so disappointed for you, for us. You've worked so hard to get to this point, and to have it taken away is so heartbreaking." She takes a deep breath. "We're undefeated conference champs, and yet, it feels . . . at this moment . . . hollow, but it won't in years to come." Molly puts her hand on Ryanne's shoulder and squeezes. "Coach Powell and I have been together for over a decade, and this is the best season we've ever experienced with the best to come. You gals are the team I've always dreamed of coaching. Piece by piece. You make each other better." Again, Molly pauses.

It's Dyani who breaks the tension. "Is this the part where you tell us you love us again?"

Coach Rascon smiles and nods. "Yeah, Dyani, this is that time."

When the meeting ends, eleven players return to their rooms. Usually, these rooms are comfortable and predictable and secure, but not tonight. The coaching staff walks Kenti to her dorm, and then they go to their cars in a nearby lot. It has been a difficult day, unlike, however, the loss to Salinas in the finals of the 2017 tournament finals which kept the Sequoias out of the NCAA that season. That team had only itself to blame.

∽

"You want a beer?" When Ken Davidson answers in the affirmative, Coach Robinson tells him he'll be over in ten minutes. After the team meeting, Mose drove to his apartment to see his wife and update her on the events. But Mose has a story in his head, and Sally isn't a journalist. She suggested he call Ken.

Modelo for Ken. Coors for Mose, a holdover from Boulder 50 years earlier.

"Do you have any idea how many colleges had their games canceled?" It's a rhetorical question Mose is asking.

"And a hundred times that many high schools. And there's all those other sports."

"A minimum of twelve players per team."

"Millions." The two old men are on the same page.

"You showed Molly a lot of consideration by not attending tonight's meeting. You understood how personal it might be, and you respected her privacy." Mose takes a slow sip of his beer as if he's respecting its brewing process. "It did get pretty intimate. In my two years being around her, I've learned that she . . . is easy to get to talk about her kids, but not about herself."

Davidson nods. "She's a matador when I try to get her to reveal herself. Effusive in her praise of her girls. They receive all the credit for wins; she takes all the blame for losses. She won her hundredth game this season here at SJV, and I couldn't get her to comment. In just her fifth year." His throat makes a low bass sound. "I'm pretty sure no one in administration thought that was on the horizon when they hired her. From what I gathered when I started this gig, the suits thought they were getting a firebrand who would represent the university well, but a winning record wasn't part of the equation so much. The three men who drove that hiring committee are friends of mine. Good people, but they admit they got more than they ever imagined. A helluva lot more." The journalist is always writing another story in his head, even when all those stories don't get published. Blogging, though, allows for more random thoughts than a weekly column in the *Times* ever did.

Mose's turn. "You might want to let those three good men know that she'll be a hot commodity; that other universities will be lining up to hire her. And pay her a lot more."

"That queue will be shorter now that the tournament has been canceled. If this post-season had played out like I anticipated it might, a conference title and a win or two in the NCAAs, then the line would be long and financially enticing. But that's on the backburner now. She's going to miss a big payday."

Mose nods in agreement. "She and Frank are financially well-off, and neither of them grew up that way. Not sure that money matters much to her." The two men sip beers in silence for a few minutes. Mose repositions his long legs and looks at his empty bottle. "Need another one?" he asks his host.

Ken nods. "Yeah. Might help me sleep."

Mose gets up, goes to Ken's kitchen, and returns with two more beers. When he settles, he says, "You can't write about every team in America, but you need to write about this one and tell every team's story."

Davidson's head nods like a bobblehead doll in slow motion. "You're not talking about a basketball story, are you?"

"Not exactly. Bigger. Might not be a feel-good account."

Chapter 4

Agriculture and Basketball. Blog, The Day After, by Ken Davidson

The sun came up this morning, but yes, as is typical for The Valley, the brown cloud cast its pall over the fields. Apropos. The workers were out before I walked the dog. Naomi had my coffee on the table when I returned—as she always has. As you might expect, every sports column, podcast, and blog is about the loss of the tournament or NBA—as if the sports world is the center of the universe. I imagine the Sequoias slept in; I know Coach Rascon did not. She was most likely up before the field workers—if she slept at all.

I'm numb, almost directionless. In this eerie scenario, I hope I don't lose sight of the field workers. The missus and I will take a drive around the county this afternoon.

On Friday the last day of classes before Spring Break, SJV's president announces a Covid-19 Transition Plan for limiting face-to-face teaching, but not closing the university entirely. The voluntary conversion to virtual learning will be put in place beginning Monday, March 23, when the student body returns from their breaks. Ten days of official confusion. The basketball team's plans were to play in the first round of the NCAA tournament at one of sixteen sites determined by seeding. None of the ladies were heading to Cancun or Hawaii or Cabo . . . or even home. Nor did they want to. They would have packed uniforms for their trip, not bathing suits. Molly had promised the team at the Thursday night meeting that she would have some kind of plan for the week. She would get them home or provide support for those who would be unable to leave campus.

Ryanne brings Molly a latte, and the coaches sit down in the basketball office to "make lists," Molly's forte. "We can get the California kids home this weekend," says Ryanne. "It's the other six that will be difficult."

"Mose said he can monitor Greta, Emerson, and Keilani easily. They all drive and can make it home, but at least he can meet with them a couple of times if they need anything, if that's allowed. Kaori and Joyce will be fine too. Esther, though, will require something. Her mother is across the border, so maybe she can live with her aunt in San Diego." Molly makes quick notes for those six players. "The other six might all be staying here in the dorms." She squints her nose. "Will the cafeterias be open?"

"How come we never recruit rich kids?" teases Ryanne.

"I wouldn't know how to react around their parents." Molly laughs, the first real laugh instead of the ironic laugh of the past few days. "We get the ones we're supposed to."

Ryanne calls student services and finds that the cafeterias will be open over the break. She reaches across the table to check off one of Molly's bullet points. "Well, they all have a place to sleep and food. What's next?"

As if on cue, Molly's cell starts playing, "We Are the Champions." It's Kaori. "My father says not to come home. He thinks my Nai-nai has Covid."

∾

All five coaches sit in the team room along with Ken Davidson. The dam seems to have burst, if canceling the tournaments wasn't drowning enough. Duke University has suspended all athletics and won't play in March Madness even if it is rescheduled for later in the spring. The NCAA suspends all recruiting. "Shut it down!" is the official proclamation. On Friday, March 13, Coach Rascon is proceeding as if practices are not allowed but that team meetings are still a go, since academic classes can still meet face-to-face in small groups.

"What time are the ladies coming in?" asks Davidson.

"Three. Same as our practice would be held," answers Ryanne.

"Can you still have your ladies go to the training room for their rehab work?"

"Until we hear differently, we'll do that. Fortunately, we don't have any serious injuries to speak of. Danelle's back spasms up occasionally; Greta complained of a stiff neck on the bus back yesterday. Don't know where that came from." Ryanne looks over the roster. "Dyani always needs to have her floor burns rinsed out. Can't keep her from diving on the floor even during practice." Davidson is continually taking notes the old fashion way, a pocket notebook and pen. Ryanne teases him about his abundance of notes, but he tells her that an old White man who thinks he can write about a women's basketball team in the 21st century needs to do lots of research—research to unlearn his previous biases.

Coach Rascon, who has been standing with her back to her assistants, turns. "Let's be proactive as hell. Any bitching about having our season ended unfairly stays in this room. If anyone asks or goads you for a damaging statement, ignore them. Our official line is that public health supersedes games. The health of our players, their families, the student body, and the Tulare community are our paramount concerns. Our ladies may want to complain, but we, as a staff, are not going to buy into that. We can't because it will do no good." Molly looks to each assistant for confirmation. She gets to Davidson. "You'll have a hard job, Ken. You have this reputation for honesty and frank reporting, and I'll expect you to continue with that. Still, remember our players are experiencing a situation that is unique, and they're young, prone to rash statements. I would ask that you give them the opportunity to restate their responses sometimes."

"Rephrase?"

Coach Rascon smiles and nods. "I have twelve daughters, eight of whom lived below the poverty line before coming here to be middle class for a few years and are not sophisticated with the press. I doubt if any of them have ever been asked to comment on the politics of the nation. When a microphone is in their face, it's always been to get a response to the game that just ended or the one about to occur. I want you to write about their feelings, because that's an important part of this story you want to write but be gentle as you always have been. In the end, it's the athletes who are the story."

The meeting moves on. Coach Jakino asks if she can contact recruits via text or cell. Molly says to put everything on hold. "Make one more call today and explain the circumstances and that we are still interested. Tell them that there will be coaches from other universities who will not follow the rule, but that won't mean we want them less. It simply means we will follow the NCAA directives, but we'll monitor that closely."

Coach Powell laughs out loud and looks at Davidson. "We don't have any 5-star recruits in tow, Ken. One of our recruiting targets is 2-star from Utah. She's not getting bombarded from South Carolina or Baylor. Utah State is our chief competitor for her."

"Next up," says Molly. "I asked the ladies if they felt okay, but I neglected to ask you all. If you have or get any flu-like symptoms, let me know and quarantine. Don't brush it off."

Mose stirs. "Coach, my wife asked if you were still going to pay me my massive salary during the pandemic. Can you afford me?"

The others laugh. "I don't know," says Molly. "Not sure I can come up with the gas and meal money I've been providing you with. Tell Sally she might have to go back to work to support you during this crisis."

Coach Aikins hadn't considered not being paid. "Is that really something I should worry about? I haven't heard anything about it."

"Nicole, I haven't heard anything about that either for the four of you. Don't let Mose's warped sense of reality alarm you. Anyway, Coach Robinson has a trust fund that he can draw upon to pay yours and Jackie's salaries." Molly looks to Mose and wags her finger.

Davidson breaks in while looking at his phone. "Coach, it looks like electronic recruiting contacts are still permissible. Calls, emails, DMs, texts. All okay. No face-to-face meetings, so no camps, visits, surreptitious meetings at McDonalds."

Molly thanks Ken and the meeting moves to lodging for spring break for the players who can't get home. After thinking at least six of the team would be able to get to their California residence, that number has dropped to just four. Emerson, Joyce, Greta, and Keilani. Coach Aikins volunteers to ensure that those who remain will be at the cafeteria for each meal. Coach Powell says she'll oversee individual training and study tables.

"Those who are staying are really vulnerable. We need to be on guard," says Molly.

∿

Agriculture and Basketball. Blog, March 13, 2020.

Spring break for The Tribe was going to be a week at an NCAA site, the first weekend of the Big Dance. Can't get more exciting than that if you're a 20-year-old basketball player who has dreamed of such a thing since junior high. Oops, just showed my age. It's middle school. Spoke with Maria Sanchez and Sylvia Castro this afternoon before dinner. Half-sisters from El Paso, Texas, who had hoped the NCAA would send them to a Texas campus so their family might have a chance to watch them play, something they have never done. A distance of 973 miles. This is Sylvia's third year at SJV; she's been the starting power forward since the fifth game of her freshman year. Maria joined her sister this season, and both are on full scholarships, but the family could never afford to fly out. Sylvia sends video of every game, but the thrill of seeing the sisters in person in Dallas or Waco or San Antonio would have been unbelievable. "Mom would pee her pants," says Maria.

The disappointment of the tournament's cancellation is palpable, and it takes discipline to hold their frustrations inside. Coach Rascon talked to her team about the road they were about to travel over the next several months. She compared it to an unexpected death of a healthy friend or family member, something that seems so unfair in the moment. Coach told the team they were going to get through this and come out stronger on the other end. Her two seniors, Dyani Dehiya and Danelle Weston, will find those words difficult to swallow, since their senior year offered such rewards that are now dashed. At the team meeting this afternoon, the two ladies received their second standing ovation, the first coming yesterday when they left Santa Barbara. Lots of wet eyes. Dyani seems especially downhearted. She is the heart and soul of the Sequoias, has been for two years, the best and most tenacious player in the conference. She's on track to graduate this May, and her plans include returning to the Navajo Reservation in northern Arizona. That way of life is markedly different from the dorm and cafeteria and internet and modern conveniences of SJV. Dyani's grandmother has no electricity in her home. Dyani's biggest supporter is her uncle, Hector Dehiya, who basically raised her. He has been out to watch her play. He just shows up without advance notice, probably hitchhiked, and then leaves after a brief meeting telling her how wonderful she is. Hector plays a key role in Char's life too. Dyani tells me that her uncle might be a shaman, and then she smiles. I'm not sure whether she's kidding me. Hard to imagine not seeing Dyani play against a top-seeded team in the NCAAs. The nation will not see the reason why SJV is in the tournament.

Over the past few days, I've watched the girls and their coaches as the coronavirus news has washed over the nation and now, their season. As they absorbed the latest strands of bad news "out there," they went to practice, study tables, and classes as if they could live in a bubble. I believed that too. The Tournament lay ahead of them. Now, their moods have changed, from the head coach to the non-scholarship Kenti Solorzano. Today, as I watched the president declare the COVID outbreak a national emergency (and joke about handshaking as people begin to die in larger numbers), as Los Angeles closes all its schools for at least the next two weeks, and as I stood in line at the Vallarta Supermarket to buy toilet paper, it finally sunk in to my thick, saggy skin. The Tournament is not going to be played this year, and this special team has played their last game together. And these girls don't live in a bubble.

❧

"Kaori," yells Joyce from the dorm hallway. Only the coaches call Kaori Kay-kay. Kaori rooms with Emerson two rooms down from Joyce and Sylvia, the two juniors on the team. "We're leaving for the Coffee Bean. Emerson is downstairs and says she's not waiting." Team coffee usually occurs on Saturday mornings, but this Friday seems like a Saturday, so Dyani set it up. "Wear your colors. We're still the team."

Kaori apologizes and the three young ladies head down the hallway to the stairs to catch up with the others. "I was on the phone with my father. My Nai-nai can't have visitors."

Dyani sent Char and Esther to the Coffee Bean to reserve three tables in the corner for the twelve girls. None were excused from this team meeting. "No coaches."

Dyani presides. "So, we beat Atascadero last night," clapping, "and of course our opponent tonight is Palm Valley for all the marbles. This is personal to me, so we can't blow it. There's that huge gambling casino on Interstate 10 that sits on the reservation like some kind of Indian monument to greed. Evidently, you can't be a real reservation unless you have gambling casinos." Dyani gave a similar motivational speech during the season when they prepared for an actual game with Palm. Dyani's head starts nodding and she speaks a few Diné phrases for effect, and her teammates giggle. "Win and we're off to the NCAAs; lose and I won't be able to ever show my face on Navajo lands again. I'll be cast into the wilderness to wander until the winds die down. Alone."

"Is it a coincidence that Palm Valley's mascot is The Wind?" asks Danelle feigning seriousness.

"All Native schools should have The Wind as their mascot," replies Dyani without missing a beat. "For it is The Wind that . . ." She stops and looks at the other Navajo on the team. "Little Sister followed me here on The Wind, and she will lead the journey next season when The Wind returns. Danelle and I will retire to The Sacred Mountain to observe."

Danelle stands and spreads her arms. "Mt. Whitney on the edge of Death Valley. And I will freeze to death." The team explodes in laughter as Danelle and Dyani hug.

Dyani has called this meeting to schedule everyone's Spring Break. The four players going home live within three hours of Tulare and have agreed to share their homes with their teammates. Emerson and Keilani live in the Los Angeles suburbs, Greta lives in Oxnard, while Joyce lives "just up the street" in Fresno. Dyani has done the logistics:

house size, number of bedrooms and bathrooms, minor children at each house, internet capabilities. The ladies will be expected to help with meals for the host families they're staying with. Because of the coronavirus, no parties with outsiders will be permitted, even though fewer than 1,000 people in all of California have the virus. The team will leave on Monday. Tonight, they have a date with Palm Valley at 6:00 for the conference championship, and Sunday afternoon, they will meet with the coaches for Selection Sunday.

"We may not be putting on our uniforms tonight, but we are going to be together and imagine," says Dyani. No one argues because they all want to share in whatever excitement they can create. They've earned it.

"I wonder how Mr. Davidson will handle his blog," says Char Betany, Little Sister, the backup point guard and player from a small town on the Navajo Reservation. "Maybe he can make me the star."

"That would take great imagination," kids Kenti.

"Would you settle for getting five assists?" asks Emerson.

Dyani gets the team's attention again. "Okay, next Friday, we Zoom and listen to Mr. Davidson read his blog about our first-round game at The Dance."

✺

In the basketball office across the campus from the dorms, Coaches Rascon, Powell, and Aikins try to make sense of the various "proclamations" about Covid that are coming from President Trump, Governor Newsom, and SJV's president, along with the "recommendations" from the CDC and Dr. Fauci. If classes resume after the break, what will they look like? What measures should individuals be taking to insure their own health? Stay hydrated, get plenty of rest, and social distance doesn't sound like much protection. What if the virus is just like the flu?

"An abundance of caution," says Ryanne. "How many times have we heard that over the past week?"

"Or 'an overabundance of caution,'" adds Nicole. "We don't even have five deaths from the disease out of the millions of people in this state. One car crash on the 5 kills more than that."

"Seems to be centered in nursing homes, hardly any of those on our campus," laments Ryanne.

Molly leans back in her desk chair, clasps her hands behind her head, and breathes out heavily. "It's not what is, but what's coming, at least according to the health experts. These little waves are the precursor to a tsunami, and California may be one of the epicenters, especially if the storm is coming from China." She shifts her hands to rub her face. "You're both right though. Right now, it feels like we've been cheated out of what's rightfully ours, what we earned."

The office returns to the task at hand, the immediate problem, which is making sure their ladies don't go off the rails over the next week to ten days. As if on cue, the team shows up at the office door.

"When's practice?"

"We don't practice on game days. Remember?" answers Ryanne.

"A shoot-around then?"

Coach Rascon smiles broadly. "I guess if we social distance, we could shoot a few hoops." She pauses. "At least until the president issues a new proclamation." The team cheers and leaves for the gym. Molly tilts her head and pulls her keys from her jacket. "Mums the word. If this gets out, we'll plead ignorance, or at least uncertainty. Who knows, it might be our last practice for a while."

Saturday night, San Joaquin Valley defeats Palm Valley to claim the mythical Ring of Fire Conference championship and earn the automatic bid to the NCAA Women's Basketball Tournament. Their record stands at 29-2 with wins over two major conference opponents and the three mythical tournament victories. The four freshmen and Kenti think eating pizza and drinking pops during a game is pretty strange—but cool. Ken Davidson cannot contain his giggles and promises to write a blog fitting this championship team. Reality will set in soon enough.

California reports its sixth death from Covid on Sunday, while Italy is being ravaged by the virus. Nearly 2,000 deaths and soaring.

Governor Newsom orders bars and restaurants to close, and the CDC recommends limiting meetings and gatherings to 50 people. The SJV Sequoias meet in the team room at the arena to find out about their seeding. Ryanne Powell has poured over the rankings and decided that SJV will travel to Chicago, her hometown and one of America's hotbeds of women's basketball, to meet Florida State. An upset win over a power conference team would send SJV into the regional finals against the host school, the DePaul Demon Deacons.

And the first cracks in the wall appear.

Kenti Solorzano didn't attend, texting Coach Rascon that she needed the afternoon to work in the lab.

Danelle Weston's dormant anger surfaces. "If we're going to play make-believe, why not send us to the beach." Her outburst is aimed at Coach Powell, but it's mostly frustration at the way her career is ending.

Maria Sanchez begins crying and leans into the shoulder of her sister. "I just want to go home." Home is El Paso.

The room, instead of bursting with cheers that would have accompanied an actual seeding event, turns quiet. It's Dyani Dehiya who gently asks. "It's really over, isn't it?" Her season, this season, her life in Tulare, her time with this team. Her basketball dreams.

Molly has been standing off to one side, near a small refrigerator. She has allowed her assistant coaches to play out the tournament scenario . . . the tournament fantasy, hoping it would ease the team's transition into grieving. Coach Rascon walks to the front of the room but pauses next to Dyani to give her a hug. Molly remembers a hug she received from her high school coach 25 years ago, a one-armed hug after he had suffered a stroke and was sitting in a wheelchair, and she realized that he was no longer going to be physically able to be her coach anymore. But in that hug, he told his seventeen-year-old point guard that he would always be her coach, just in a different arena. Molly hopes her hug is telling Dyani the same thing. The rest of the team waits.

Molly Rascon now speaks in a whisper. "This is cruel." She hears muffled cries and stifles her own tears. "Hey, hey," she says a little louder but so gently. "Give me your eyes." She waits until every girl lifts her head. "This fantasy wasn't meant to add to the hurt; it was meant to give you a sense of what might have been, of what you earned." She emphasizes the word *earned*. "I'm sorry if it caused greater disappointment." Off to one side, Coach Powell lays a hand over Danelle's shoulder, unseen by the rest of the room. Danelle tilts her head into Coach Powell's side. The adult and the not-quite-yet adult. Molly dabs her eye. "To answer Dyani's question, yes, it really is over. Our season has come to a close. In a sudden, incomprehensible way. We're going to have to face that." Again, the head coach pauses, measuring each word. "The basketball part, but not The Tribe part." Molly steps to Dyani, takes her hand, and gently pulls Dyani to the front of the room where the coach continues to hug her star player. "Do you know what you brought to this program, what you mean to all of us?" Molly looks to Ryanne. "Remind me later tonight to call Coach Todd and thank him for sending me the best player I ever coached. And the best teammate a team could ask for." Molly kisses Dyani on the cheek and sends her back to her chair.

Moses Robinson leans into Ken Davidson's ear and says, "And now it begins. This is where your story really starts.

Chapter 5

Agriculture and Basketball. Blog, by Ken Davidson

Seniors across the nation are done. Many of the women's tournaments are over, so those ladies had already faced a predictable ending, but for the Ivy League, the Ring of Fire, and a few others, cancellation was a shock. As gently as this old geezer who made a living prying answers out of athletes could, I asked Dyani Dehiya and Danelle Weston about their feelings. Both came to SJV as junior college alums, so they had some college experiences, and both have been two-year starters for the Sequoias, teams that won the conference championship both years.

Danelle came from Colorado via her two-year stint in Oklahoma. She spoke of her lingering anger over the NCAA decision, coupled with the overwhelming sadness. I asked her about that sadness. "Coach took a big risk on me; she was the only D1 coach who saw something in me to compete at this level. I realized this year that she didn't so much improve my skills as channel my anger into a positive force on the court and then how to sort of shelve that anger off the court. I grew as a person. My hometown just north of Denver has much in common with The Valley, but I never appreciated the farming community in Colorado. Coach made me see these workers. My teammate Greta is a farm laborer, or at least was. Her whole family picks, and I'm no better than her. I was so looking forward to going into battle this last time with my team. I never played on teams with winning records, so I never understood this level of anticipation before." She stopped there to see if I understood her meaning. "Coach played at that level and wants us to experience it, not for just the moment but for our futures." Danelle has no path to future basketball leagues, but she did indicate she might go to graduate school or maybe become a coach herself even though education is not her major. "It wasn't Coach Robinson's either." Danelle made it clear that when she spoke of Coach Rascon, she was also speaking of all the coaches at SJV.

When I first met Dyani nearly two years ago, I thought her name was Dani. She didn't correct me immediately and later told me that she thought I might be getting senile. Just hard of hearing. We had a good laugh over that. Unlike Danelle, as I interviewed Dyani, she fought back tears constantly which surprised me. I gleaned a softness that I have never seen in her. She was always the fiercest competitor in any contest. Coach Robinson once told me that his advice to really talented players was to allow the game to come to them and then seize the moment—except to Dyani. Mose said the game presented itself to her at the opening tip almost as a gift, and she opened that present immediately. "Why wait, Coach?!" Coach Rascon often called her Magic, and I understood why, how she mesmerized the opposition. Asked about her feelings, she replied that she didn't know what to feel at the moment, that it was too raw. "It's like I've been dragged by a horse and all my skin has been scraped off." Her tears started again with this answer. "Coach and me talked about seeing the next stage of my basketball career, maybe playing professionally. I just can't at the moment." We stopped for a moment so she could go to the bathroom and compose herself. I felt like I was intruding on her grieving process. When she returned, she talked without my questions. "Do you know what the softest word in the English language is? It's 'Hey' when Coach says it—or when she texts it. 'Hey, how are you holding up?' and I just melt. She doesn't say 'Hi' often; it's usually 'Hey,' and we know that we're more than just basketball players to her. I'll miss that word from her. The other thing I'll miss is my teammates. I don't know how Covid will allow us to move on. I love them so much!" So much for the unshakable warrior persona.

I didn't get to ask the dozen other questions I had written in my pad, but I had my interview. By the way, we sat eight or ten feet apart.

I considered the distancing afterwards, and it seemed to me that what Danelle and Dyani said they would most miss was the distancing from their coaches and teammates. That was the sadness.

∾

Monday is the travel day, the unanticipated Spring Break, and four groups leave at the same time, three heading south on CA-99 towards Los Angeles, and one heading north on the 99 to Fresno, the shortest drive. Greta's car, a 2003 orange Mazda is a beater with no room for luggage, but Dyani planned for that. Coach Robinson also lives in Oxnard, so he will ferry their travel bags in his truck and drive in tandem with those heading south. All four groups should arrive before noon, and their first task is to go to the local grocery store and stock up. "No mooching!" is Dyani's order. "Buy for the whole family for the entire week!" Not so easy for most of the team; only Kaori, Joyce, and Danelle have extra cash. Moses Robinson slips envelopes to the four hosts. An NCAA violation in normal times. An act not discussed with Coach Rascon.

Tomorrow will be "trip day." The Fresno group will visit Sequoia National Park. The Santa Monica group will go to the pier, of course. The Oxnard group will get a tour of the docks and port in Oxnard, courtesy of Mose and Sally Robinson. The Inglewood group will go to Hollywood. New instructions: social distance. Share goofy photos. Wear your colors.

Mose officially resigns his position as assistant coach before he can be furloughed. Molly's discussions with the AD lead her to conclude that Nicole and Jackie will also be furloughed shortly. Molly and Ryanne will keep their jobs at current salaries. For now. "Fortunately," says Ryanne sarcastically, "Trump says the virus will disappear when summer comes, and we'll be able to hire you back."

In the parking lot as the ladies are preparing to leave, Coach Rascon addresses her girls. "Monitor your symptoms. Fever, cough, headache. If you feel sick, self-quarantine and call me. Remember, Zoom call every night. Check with your professors to see how their classes will be taught next week. If any are online, make sure you know the process and technology." The team wonders aloud how many of their professors are capable of teaching virtually. "And call your family every night too. You know they'll be worried sick." Molly looks at Kaori. "Let me know how your grandmother is doing, if there's anything I can do." Kaori nods.

Ken Davidson hands each player his card.

As the team pulls out, Molly says to Ken, "Good thing they're on their way. Stay-at-home orders are popping up all over. Let's just hope we can get them back at the end of the week." She looks at Nicole. "How are you doing with transportation if school closes?'

Nicole shakes her head. "We may have to drive them all home ourselves. The airlines are cutting flights."

Ex-coach Robinson, his truck loaded with SJV bags, walks over to Molly and puts a long arm around her shoulders, giving her a hug. He doesn't say anything, just looks at the caravan like a grampa. It's Molly who breaks the anxious silence with a question for the two old men.

"Is this what it's like to send your children off to college?"

Since it's Mose whose action has brought out Molly's thoughts, Davidson stays quiet, allowing Mose to respond. Still not taking his eyes off the street where the team has departed, he finally answers. "No, not really." The others know he's going to elaborate, so they wait. In a moment he adds, "I never felt mine were vulnerable like this. Sally and I had eighteen years to prepare them for leaving the house and knew they'd do fine, and that we'd continue to be their parents. You've done wonders for those girls, Coach, taken them giant strides along their growth, but when they return at the end of the week, they'll look to you for answers to new questions that they only just thought of this week. Sending my kids off to college was a proud day. Yeah, Sally and I cried, but your tears this morning are not tears of joy." As always when Mose answers questions about life from an old man's perspective, he doesn't provide the details, he gives a framework.

Molly puts an arm around Mose's waist. "So, you noticed that I cried?"

"You know what's around the corner, and I admire how you've kept that to yourself for now, but you know. They're going to close this campus, probably before the break is over, and you're already preparing for that. I seriously doubt you've been crying at home or in the office.

You've been making lists, detailed lists that change hourly as new edicts are given regarding the virus. 'Like leaving for college?' Hell, no! What was last week is no longer, and I don't really say that just to you. I say it for your staff, because I know you're going to put them to work like never before on a problem that's never existed before." Mose finally removes his arm from Molly's shoulders, turns to the assistants, to whom he's really being addressing, and says, "Hang on, ladies," he says with a grandfatherly smile.

Effective coaching staffs are diverse as opposed to being clone-ish. Additionally, the head coach must have vision. Molly's players believe Coach Rascon has eyes in the back of her head, but what she really possesses are focused high beams. She and her staff walk Mose to his truck and exchange brief hugs to send him down the road. When he pulls out, Ken Davidson excuses himself, leaving the four coaches to themselves. The campus is mostly empty except for professors and staff taking crash courses on technology to teach online. Nationwide, cases and deaths from the coronavirus are exploding, the stock market is in steep decline, losing all of the gains of the past three years, hospitals are pleading for protective gear, especially masks and ventilators, and airlines are cutting back on flights. In California restaurants and bars are closing, elementary and high schools are going on extended breaks. Everyday people are questioning the severity of Covid-19, wanting to believe it's just a severe flu outbreak and will go away soon. College students say it's a problem for the aged but shouldn't disrupt their lives. In a parking lot on the campus of San Joaquin Valley University in Tulare, California, four women have a less expansive view. They're focused on The Tribe.

❧

Kenti Solorzano didn't want to leave campus when Dyani announced the plan. The Farm Laboratory didn't close for spring break and her studies are mostly hands-on work in soil science. Additionally, at 26-years old, she is the semi-outsider on the team, but Keilani told her that Los Angeles has a sizable Guatemalan community that they would visit. Because of the looming shelter-in-place directives sprouting up, Dyani convinced Kenti that this four-day trip might be the last team excursion for The Tribe, that each group of three would return on Thursday to unite as a group and share their experiences. Kenti agreed but took her agronomy notebooks and laptop computer along to monitor soil samples. She is part of another team at SJV.

Kenti and Coach Rascon first met eighteen months earlier when Molly took last year's team on one of her Tulare excursions, this one to the Farm Laboratory, a 500-acre farm just west of the campus but a part of the university. Modeled after Fresno State's larger University Farm, SJV's farm lab focuses on field crops and soil management, which is why Kenti enrolled at SJV to do her graduate work. It was Kenti who acted as the guide for that tour. This season, Kenti has been the "second backup to Dyani," or the third point guard, a role she has relished, but it is a one-year gig and now it's over.

On the team's Tuesday night Zoom call, after everyone has shared the trip experiences, Molly relates the newest edicts about Covid protocols. SJV will go to all virtual instruction on Monday, the first day of classes after the break. Students who went home are asked to stay there and not return to Tulare, which presents a variety of concerns, problems that all colleges are facing. Will the dorms remain open with food services? Without exception, every member of The Tribe wants to return to campus on Thursday, even the four who drove home. Neither SJV nor Tulare County has issued shelter-in-place orders as yet. Ryanne informs the team that student housing will be available with meals for the rest of the semester unless the county's department of public health closes the campus down. That, says Coach Powell, could happen.

For Danelle and Dyani, if they complete their current courses, their degrees will be issued, but commencement has been canceled. The university is working on some kind of virtual celebration but has not come up with one so far. Graduation will occur without any cele-bration of their accomplishment. Both young ladies will be the first in their families to graduate from college, and for Dyani, she's the first to even attend a college. Greta, Char, Maria, Sylvia, Esther, Keilani, and Kenti are also the first in their families to attend college. They understand. Coach Rascon is sick that there will be no commencement ceremony. It has always been the capstone of her players time at SJV, almost a sacred rite.

Molly assures all her girls that their scholarships will be honored for the rest of the semester, so they will have meals and lodging through May if they can't get home and remain on campus. The coaching staff discussed the vulnerability of their young women, that it would be the SJV's most vulnerable who would be left behind, both educationally and physically, unless the school's staff remains vigilant. As a first-generation college student herself once, Molly remembers how valuable in-person learning was for her. She understands how difficult the transition to virtual learning will be for half her girls. As long as Kenti is allowed to remain in California, she will be fine. Joyce's hours on hospital rotations will be increased, and being less than an hour away, she can maintain her studies. Kaori is tech savvy, the guru for the team on all problems regarding computer glitches. She tells her teammates that she will teach them all how to become masters at Canvas or Blackboard, whichever program their professors choose to operate. Half the team grew up with home computers, but even that's not a guarantee of a successful transition.

"I don't know if virtual learning will be temporary, just an emergency measure during the coronavirus epidemic, or whether it will become the norm next semester, but you need to prepare for either outcome," says Coach Rascon. "Don't shy away from it. Ask for help and get comfortable with it now."

When the Zoom call ends, Molly sits in front of her screen, a picture of a path heading into a dense forest, her face supported by both hands. Ryanne asks if she's sad. Molly shakes her head. "No. Angry. I'm going to the gym to do what I've always done to handle my emotions. Would you do me a favor before you go to bed?" Ryanne nods. "Would you jot down those points we talked about concerning the season ending so suddenly. I don't want to forget anything in my letters to anyone who had anything to do with this sudden decision." Ryanne nods again. Molly breathes out heavily.

Upon entering her gym, Molly calls security, turns on the lights over the gym floor, gets a basketball from the storage closet, changes into her basketball shoes, and begins a routine that she first started 25 years ago. It's ingrained in her memory banks, so she can think about other things, like who to blame for denying her kids that chance that she always speaks about. "All I want for them is a chance." Molly pounds her hands against the ball to get the blood flowing. Then, right hand layups, left hand layups, angle jumpers, free throws. Ten minutes into her routine, she screams the f-word at the top of her lungs to the Basketball Gods and hurls the ball up into the seats. "They have the talent; they just need the opportunity," she screams.

Still yelling to an empty arena, Molly vents. "They did everything and more that was asked of them! They came from nowhere and earned everything they got! These are the players you invented the game for! Not a single one of them cut corners; they worked their asses off to get here!" She stops and breathes. Then, she sits down on the floor, apologizes, and talks in a conversational tone. "Okay, I'm done yelling. Just needed to get that out. This game has always been fair to me. Whatever I worked for I got. Just want you to know that. Thanks. Still, this won't be easy for them, and I'm going to need your help to get them through this." She stops and whispers just to herself so the Gods can't hear. "Going to need help to get myself through this." Molly stands, climbs the stairs to retrieve her basketball, and returns to the floor to shoot a few more shots. As she finally walks off the court, she turns. "One more thing, it's not just my ladies. It's all the players everywhere."

Returning home, Molly checks on Frankie before sliding into bed with Frank.

"What time is it?" asks her husband.

"Late, my dear. Really late."

"Did you make any threes?"

Wednesday night's Zoom gathering is filled with laughter as Greta tells of her group's day in the Oxnard strawberry fields. Greta's family are pickers, or at least were until *madre y padre* moved over to the docks. Greta took Maria and Char to the fields to meet some of her former classmates. It seems as if the easiest way to get comfortable was to join in the picking. Char jokes that she's found her profession after college. Maria tells her teammates that 6'2" women are not meant to bend over for that long. Her sister Sylvia reminds the team that her younger sister is always the pampered one in the family and has never done manual labor in her life, hence her softness on the court. Coach Rascon reminds her team to get an early start in the morning to arrive back on campus before noon. She also reminds them to strip the sheets and do the dishes before leaving, "and give the family hugs before you leave!"

∽

"I've missed them," says Ryanne.

Molly laughs ironically. "You know, Ry, we're old enough now for them to be our children, at least the freshmen are." Molly remembers that her mother was just seventeen when she gave birth to her. If Molly had started at seventeen, she is old enough now to be every girl's mother except Kenti's. "I didn't have that feeling about our players when I first started doing this. Heck, I was just four or five years older than my first team when I assisted, about Nikki's age. The good old days."

It's Ryanne's turn to smile and shake her head. "Are you going to start singing that song? Who sang it anyway?"

"Several people. I like Gladys Knight's version the best. I think the problems we were worried about last month won't be of much concern if this virus explodes like some doctors are predicting. God, I hope it doesn't!"

"What does Frank think?" asks Ryanne.

"He's not optimistic, especially given the cavalier attitude of you know who. Frank wears a mask at the office and thinks we all should." Molly stretches and yawns. "This whole thing is wearing me out. I'm going to bed."

Ryanne keeps late hours, but she too has noticed how stress tires her out. This is a different kind of stress than games. She's kept herself busy with basketball related topics since the tournament was canceled, but when she's alone at night, her neck and knee joints ache. Old sports injuries. Her parents reside in an apartment complex in Chicago's

Southside, and she worries about them. "Stubborn, stubborn, stubborn," she mutters. "They might like it out here, but no, their home is Chicago." Ryanne's house is large enough for her parents; part of the reason she bought it four years ago, hoping she could convince them to move out.

∾

Emerson Loki was not named after the Transcendental poet of another century. She was named after her grandfather, who was named after Ralph Waldo Emerson. Her mother believed her daughter could be called Emmy, which she was as a young child, but about age ten, she demanded the family call her Emerson, and it's been that way ever since. Emerson Loki is also a dancer, Improv. Tonight, she's dancing in the dark while Dyani and Kaori game in another bedroom. Emerson wears headphones turned up, so while it appears she's dancing in silence, she's actually listening at a noise level unacceptable to audiologists. After the first song is finished, she will remove the headphones and continue dancing to that tune as it plays in her head. Like the Robinson's, Emerson's mother is White, her father African American. She is named after her mother's father, who was somewhat of a Sixties hippie. He owned a small surf shop in Santa Barbara for a time but did not have the discipline to be successful. Emerson, the basketball player, never met Emerson, the grandfather. He died in an anti-war protest near San Francisco in 1969. What Emerson shares with her grandfather is being a free spirit.

Emerson finishes dancing around midnight and checks in with her teammates who are still playing video games. They barely look up when she enters, as Kaori steals another car. Emerson says goodnight, closes the door and goes to bed. She has never played a video game in her life.

∾

Greta, Maria, and Char are the first group to return to SJV on Thursday, with Mose and Sally following in his truck. He informs the coaching staff that since resigning his position as assistant coach, he has taken a new job for the team as equipment manager. Besides, he tells Molly, he still has time on his apartment in Tulare. The three other groups arrive shortly after. Molly tells them to put their bags in their rooms, grab a bite to eat in the cafeteria, and meet at the gym at 1:30.

In the gym two hours later, Coach Rascon asks coaches Aikins and Jakino to give each player the sack with the player's name on it. The ladies are widely spaced. In each SJV bookstore bag is a gold t-shirt, brown baseball cap, and a card. The shirt and cap say, "Undefeated Conference Champs," while the cards are personal notes to each player signed by all five coaches. When each player has adorned the shirt and cap—the cards are to be read later up in their rooms—Coach Rascon gets their attention.

"The governor has just today issued shelter-in-place orders. Only essential travel will be allowed. I'm not sure exactly how that term is going to be defined or enforced, but I'm sure it will further restrict our ability to meet as a team. The most important thing is for all of us to stay safe and healthy. We're getting bombarded by news conference information that changes every day, but I also get advice from my husband about safety precautions. Baby doctor, you know, so he's extra concerned about spreading germs. He's always telling Frankie to wash up, and you guys know how dirty Frankie can get." The ladies laugh. Coach Rascon's little boy is a part of the team. "Anyway, my husband says to take this pandemic seriously, that it's going to get a lot worse in the coming weeks and months. He says to be especially careful about social contacts, mostly large groups. He was, like all of us, really disappointed about having the tournaments canceled, but he believes it was the right thing to do. Unlike us, he's not angry about the decision, just terribly disappointed for you all. He lets Ryanne and me be angry and frustrated."

Coach Ryanne interrupts to address the team. "You gals know how Coach can get when something isn't right." It's a statement cloaked in a question and the team collectively groans and laughs, basically saying, "Oh God, yes, we certainly do!" Ryanne nods and walks a short distance away from the head coach/her best friend. "Well, this past week she's been sorting through all the things that aren't right that have led us to where we are today, i.e., sitting here on our butts missing out on our tournament and wondering if we will be scattered to the four winds in the next few days." Ryanne knows this meeting may be their last as a team for a while. "Coach warns you about your language on the court, and for Keilani her language off the court," the team laughs again, "and she usually walks the talk, but over this past week, I've heard words come out of her mouth directed to the heavens that describe things even animals shouldn't be doing." Off to the side, Molly lowers her head to hide a smile. "Anyway, what I'm getting at is that your *Mama Molly* has been making calls and writing letters to the powers that be trying to get these people to fix this cluster . . ." She stops herself and looks at each young woman sitting on the floor. "Danelle, what's the first rule of practice?"

The whole team laughs because they all know this unwritten rule. Danelle answers. "Don't do anything to make Coach mad."

"Correct-a-mundo! Char, tell us why."

"Because she never allows bad behavior to go unpunished."

"And . . ., Greta"

"And because we will never enjoy the punishment," says the big freshman.

Ryanne nods. "And why does she do this? Dyani."

"Because Coach cares about us beyond the court. We play to win the game, but we're on the team to grow into responsible adults."

Ryanne nods again. "Yeah, well said, Dyani. Ladies, you're going to be tested these next few months; it's going to be hard but remember Coach and all of us will be here to help." Ryanne steps back and returns the stage to Molly.

"Questions?" asks Coach Rascon.

"Can we stay in the dorms if we want?"

"If I drive home, can I come back if I need help with classes?"

"If I get it, will I be sterile and not able to conceive?"

"Did China send it to the U.S. on purpose?"

"What do I do if I get it and can't breathe?"

"How long is this Covid thing going to last?"

"Coach, you said your husband wears a mask at work, and I work at the hospital, and we wear masks, especially with patients who have infectious diseases, and I think maybe we should start wearing masks, at least when we go out in large groups," says Joyce Hensley, who is a third-year nursing student.

Kaori Park piggybacks on Joyce's idea. "Some people in my family always wear masks when they travel, especially on planes. Since my Nai-nai got sick, my parents wear masks to visit her before the hospital said she couldn't have visitors. Masks are kind of an Asian thing." Kaori says that last statement as a joke and giggles a little.

"Masks certainly wouldn't hurt," answers Molly, "especially when you get on a plane, but I'll check with my doctor-husband." She turns to her assistants. "Do you know where we would even get masks?"

"I'm not sure the ones you get at the hardware store would work," says Joyce. "Those are for sawdust, not for microscopic particles. At least that's what they tell us at the hospital."

"You guys are scaring me," says Char Betany. "Part of me wants to stay here with the team, but part of me wants to go home and be with my family. They don't live like the rest of you. I think only Dyani understands." Char looks over to Dyani like a true little sister would look to an older sister for support.

"Her family doesn't have electricity," says Dyani softly.

"Char," says Molly in her motherly voice rather than her coaching voice, "we're all a little scared and very confused." She pauses. "You and Dyani and a couple of others come from homes that were much poorer than the rest of us, and several of us were poor. I don't have many answers at the moment, but we're trying to find out all we can. From early reports, it seems like the virus is affecting the elderly and not so much people our age, especially your age. That's good for you but worrisome for your families. Especially your grandparents, like Kay-kay's grandmother. I'm sure we'll learn more each day, but for now, we just must lean on each other."

Agriculture and Basketball. Blog, by Ken Davidson

When I first met Coach Rascon years ago, I wasn't blogging seriously; I was writing my columns for The Times. I was doing a series on high stakes recruiting at the Division I level, focusing on men's basketball. We were sitting in the stands at a high school game—a boy's game in the Los Angeles area—and she was studying one particular player. I assumed she was an assistant in charge of recruiting for a West Coast team, something like that, and I struck up a conversation about my series at halftime. I asked her what skills she believed the young man possessed that would lead big-time coaches to see potential in him. She laughed and informed me that she wasn't recruiting this boy, but his sister. To show genuine interest in his sister, she wanted to know what the family valued. The boy was self-centered and not a team player, the same traits she had observed but to a lesser degree in his sister. Both were multi-talented, but as she readied herself to leave after just one half of play, she said she was going to pass on the sister, that she didn't feel the girl would fit into her team's culture. We exchanged business cards, stood, and shook hands; she was a little bit of a thing, a young woman in her mid-thirties at the time, but polite and direct. I made a mental note to follow up on her career. I didn't, of course, and didn't meet her again until two years ago after I had retired and returned to my beloved San Joaquin Valley.

When I reminded her of that brief meeting, she said she vaguely remembered it, that there were so many episodes where men assumed women were assistants but not real coaches. Then she laughed. Two years later, she seldom misses an opportunity to tease me about my male perspective, a knee-jerk reaction developed over a lifetime of covering sports. It's difficult to unlearn anything. Once you've been programmed, you're resistant to change even with a mountain of evidence to the contrary.

I spent a good amount of time this morning listening to experts break down the nation's Covid options. No good solutions, just trying to make the best of bad ones. A total quarantine would collapse the economy in less than a month. Doing nothing to move toward herd immunity, in other words, allowing for the "free spread" of the virus seems morally bankrupt, allowing potentially millions to die hoping that the economy would keep running. One doctor said that having millions infected could crush the health care system and would most likely just provide individual incubators for mutations of the virus. It seems the best path is to "flatten the curve" as they say to social distance and wash your hands. The doctors didn't give much hope to the immunocompromised—like me—and the aged—like me again. My wife and I are definitely in the two categories *that need to isolate as best we can. I'm learning more about what "essential travel" means. Pretty sure I won't be allowed to interact with The Tribe for some time, and that hurts.*

I spoke with Coach Rascon by phone to try to get a sense of what the university will allow over the next few weeks. As of this moment, 7:37 on Thursday evening, March 19, she wants to keep them on campus and monitor their studies and health as best she can, but everything may change by morning. A few of her players will go home for the remainder of the semester. They're angry, frustrated, and scared. I can't blame them.

This is nuts and it's going to get nuttier.

∾

Coach Rascon and Coach Powell meet with each player on Friday, individual meetings that once focused on basketball, but now have an additional agenda item. But there is still basketball. Keilani Russell's meeting is mostly about basketball.

"With Dyani graduating," says Coach Rascon, "we're going to be light at the point. Remember our first game against Chula Vista when Dyani rolled her ankle?" Keilani nods. "You did a very good job of filling in. Calm and secure."

Keilani nods again. "Their press wasn't very effective. They got after the first pass in, but after that, they just sorta drifted back."

"Yes, but still, no turnovers." Both coaches notice that Keilani sees where this is going. "We think you could step into that spot next year . . . if you really work hard on your ballhandling skills this spring and summer," says Coach Rascon.

"If I remember, you played some point in high school," adds Coach Powell. "You wouldn't be a Dyani-ish point guard, more of a Kelsey Plum than Sue Bird type point guard. We'd go three out with you, Kaori, and Emerson."

Keilani smiles for a moment. Then, "How will Char take this?"

"Char knows where she stands, but at this moment she has bigger concerns. Basketball-wise, she's feeling some pressure about stepping into Dyani's shoes. She's not ready, and she knows it." Coach Rascon makes a checkmark on her legal pad. "We don't know how much we'll be able to work with you over the next few months on a one-on-one level what with the stay-at-home orders, so you'd be on your own to develop your ballhandling skills. We'll give you some instructional videos and game films."

Keilani jumps right in, almost interrupting her coach. "I would do that, every day, every hour. I'd love to play the point!"

∾

Danelle breaks down during her session. "Don't tell my teammates. They're all being so strong, and I'm just being a wimp." Ryanne hands the 6'4" senior a tissue. Danelle removes her glasses to wipe her eyes and gets semi-control of her outward emotions. She asks for another tissue to blow her nose, and then looks up to her head coach. "You thought I was tough, didn't you?"

Molly smiles kindly. "On the basketball court, you are, but if you were that way all the time, maybe Coach and I wouldn't have recruited you. You're tough so you can protect your teammates, but it's because you have this giant soft spot in your heart for them." Molly pauses to let her words take hold of Danelle. Coach Rascon turns to Coach Powell. "What do you think, Ry, maybe three games over five hundred if Danelle isn't taking care of her teammates; maybe just break even? Certainly not undefeated." Molly turns back to Danelle. "Yeah, you're such a softie." In ladies speak, *softie* is a compliment, while *wimp* is not.

Danelle tears up again. "Thanks. I needed to hear that. It's just that I lost out on the tournament and graduation as well as my teammates. I can do the online work, so I'll get my degree, but I'll probably go back home for the rest of the semester. That way you'll have a smaller group to work with that won't go past the size limits, and I don't get to play next season anyway."

Molly reaches out and takes Danelle's hand. "Hey, stop there," she says gently. "If you've played your last college game, you go out with an undefeated conference season. If we had played in the NCAA, while I believe we could have advanced past the first weekend, we eventually would have run up against a better team and lost. Then, your last collegiate game would have been a loss. And, if I know you like I think I do, you would have stewed about that for years." Molly tugs on Danelle's hand. "So, young lady, get your chin off your chest, and as you always tell me, count your blessings and not the curses."

∾

Ryanne Powell's accomplice, as she jokingly calls him, returns on Friday to beat the stay-at-home order. His plan is to stay with Ryanne for a couple of weeks until the travel ban is lifted. Earl Warren works between Chicago, where he met Ryanne, and Washington, D.C., as a political consultant for various Democrats. Ryanne jokes she wouldn't be with him if he worked for Republicans. Both Earl and Ryanne are Chicago Southsiders: White Sox fans, Bulls fanatics, and children raised by strong mothers. Earl answers more to Junior than Earl, "so as not to be confused with the former Supreme Court Chief Justice." Like Ryanne, Junior could hoop, and neither one is pushing for a formal marriage, "since we both are married to our jobs first," but neither one sees another. They have been together longer than Molly and Frank, and the two couples have grown close over the years. Frank laughs because at every gathering, he is the quiet one. For Frankie, Junior and Ryanne are Uncle Earl and Aunt Ry.

∾

On Saturday afternoon, the remaining and returning students at SJV stage an impromptu goodbye bash in the quad. Loud music, heavy drinking, and rowdy behavior turns destructive in one dorm. The police are called to assist the campus cops who seem unwilling to arrest students for rioting, instead labeling the event a protest. None of The Tribe are involved, although five are in the quad having a beer and dancing. Molly receives a text from Sylvia Castro alerting Coach about the vandalism. Molly tells Sylvia to round up her teammates and get them away from the scene.

"Evidently, the frustration of the moment spilled over into a near riot," says Ryanne. She and Junior are serving dinner to Molly and Frank and Frankie.

"I imagine there's lots of frustration for college students," responds Junior. "Some will be graduating into a recession and see this as completely unfair. Four years of study and the job market is collapsing."

"So much for social distancing," adds Frank. Frankie slides off his chair and leaves the room.

Molly shakes her head from side to side. "For those kids who don't have a team or group to give support, I can imagine they're more than just frustrated, more like lost and persecuted. The virus doesn't seem to be affecting them, and yet they're being asked to give up their immediate future." She turns to Junior. "How are your political friends going to handle this pandemic?"

"Friends might be too strong a word, Molly. It's a toxic atmosphere back there and Trump has certainly exacerbated that. I'd like to think this Covid crisis would unite the two parties, but it hasn't. Like every other issue these days, somehow, they'll come down on opposite sides. Molly, your degree is in poly sci, you could answer this." Molly puts up both hands and passes. Junior looks at Frank. "Any chance this virus will ease with the summer months like the president says?"

"No," answers Frank. "None at all. Until the nation gets a handle on behavior, especially in crowds, and until we get a vaccine, this thing will accelerate. What we need, what the entire country needs, is a plan for workplace safety, a clear and direct plan from the federal government, from the very top, on best medical practices on how we all are supposed to behave. Lots of people who show no symptoms will think they're being put upon by having to follow the medical guidelines, but like with other diseases, they can be asymptomatic spreaders. I know that's a pessimistic outlook, but I think that's what we need to prepare for. I've already spoken with our parents about their behaviors, and I know Ry has pleaded with her mother to come live with you guys."

Molly lays a hand on her husband's arm. "I've already been warned, and today's campus party sort of tells us how difficult the coming months could be. When I went over to see the demonstration, . . ." She makes air quotes with her fingers for "the demonstration." She continues with her observation. "I heard one boy yell at a campus policeman that he didn't care if he got 'the Rona,' that he was young and was going to celebrate his spring break regardless of any official orders to stay home. I was sure proud of Sylvia and our ladies though."

Junior raises his glass to toast. "I think this is the longest conversation we've ever had that didn't mention basketball." The four clink glasses. "Will that be the legacy of this virus?"

Molly takes a sip of her wine. "I hope that's the legacy and not a huge death toll. Frank seems to think tens of thousands will die over the coming year. That's tragic if it comes to pass. We're ramping up for an ungodly election campaign. I remember my first vote, 2000 for Gore. Nothing like this."

Junior looks around the table. "I think that was all of ours and we all voted for Gore." He looks at Molly again. "What was your main issue?"

"The environment, but you know us minorities always vote Democratic." She smiles sarcastically. "Especially you Blacks."

Ryanne puts an arm around Junior's shoulder and pulls him closer for a hug. "If I remember correctly, isn't that when we first met, around 2000? Then we reconnected in '08." She looks to the ceiling as if her memory is stored there. "In 2000, it was at some party in the neighborhood. In '08, at least I'm sure of that, it was working for the Obama campaign." Junior agrees.

"Who did you like this year, I mean at the start?" asks Frank to both Ryanne and Junior.

Ryanne goes first. "Well, Bernie and Warren can't beat Trump, so not them. Junior thought Booker was a decent guy, but he's done. Kamala was okay, but as Junior knows, and being the math person I was in college, I kinda liked Yang."

Junior is succinct. "Booker at first, but I'm all in for Joe now. You?"

Frank nods. "Castro and then Bernie, but like you, I'm backing Biden in the Whoever Can Beat Trump campaign."

Molly smiles. "Inslee. Every day I breathe this air in the Valley, I think about the environment. I guess my old ideas stay with me. I knew he had no chance, but I want that issue front and center. Maybe if Biden wins, he'll appoint Inslee as his environmental secretary."

Frankie wanders into the room carrying his iPad, and Junior asks him who he wants to be the next president. Frankie squints as if it's a nonsensical question and leans up against his dad. Frankie clicks his screen on to reveal an image of Steph Curry. "Him," he says.

❧

Kenti Solorzano's professors have put in place strict guidelines for interaction at the university farm regarding social distancing. On the bus ride to the farm this Saturday, Kenti observes the farmworkers in the private fields. Ninety percent are Latin, and probably half of those are undocumented. Social distancing will be nearly impossible given their lifestyles. Work, substandard housing, transportation to and from the fields; shelter in place? Kenti knows that won't happen. And when they get sick, they'll put off going to the doctor. The unseen underbelly of America's food chain. The majority of Kenti's classmates are Latin, but on this day, she sees them as different from the field-workers and feels a tinge of resentment at their *poor me* attitudes.

Most of the team is religious, about half being Catholic. Dyani reminds her teammates with a devious smile that she and Char are more spiritual than religious. Emerson kids that she's Transcendental, so she doesn't have to go to church as long as she reads poetry frequently. Keilani is a communications major and has never gone to church. Danelle is Baptist and Joyce is Episcopalian. Kaori teases that she's Shinto when she needs to be. On Sunday, however, they all agree to attend the non-denominational Valley Church near the campus as a team and then go to Coach's house for a late breakfast on the patio. Dyani texts Coach Rascon warning her of their imminent arrival.

Molly's husband is working this Sunday morning, so the team is met by Frankie at the door, who tells them to walk around the side to the backyard where Coach has set out a soft breakfast with coffee and juice. Paper plates and cups, sit on the lawn, "social distance." The last words are orders from Frankie.

"So, whose idea was it to attend church together" asks Coach Rascon.

The team points at Danelle. "Then she got Dyani to go in on it, and like she usually does, Dyani took over," says Emerson. "But it's all good."

"Pretty laid back, I assume," says Molly who is a twice a month Catholic during the season.

"You can say that again," says Sylvia, "not at all like my church in El

Paso, which, by the way, is given in Spanish."

The ladies chatter about the differences in this service and their own church while they eat Molly's pancakes and yogurt. Danelle comments that one of the reasons she thought of the idea of attending together is that no official has yet suggested that churches be shuttered. Bars and restaurants and basketball games, but not churches.

Molly changes to her Coach Rascon voice. "The gym hasn't been declared off limits either, and I think if we stay spread out, the school will allow us to practice. I'll need to structure our time in there a bit differently but working on individual skills can be done. Lots of shooting and footwork drills, which is never wasted time. Also, Coach Powell and I will wear masks, so when we're up in your faces, you'll be safer." She smiles at that last remark. Coach has been known to get into her ladies' mugs.

"Should we be wearing masks, Coach?" asks Esther Santiago. "President Trump said young people are immune, so when we're just with each other, maybe we don't have to."

"My husband thinks we should, especially indoors or if you travel. Anywhere where you're in breathing space, as he calls it. Regardless, it won't hurt is what he says. The president doesn't seem to be following his own experts' advice on best practices. I know that's confusing." Molly sees that several of her ladies are apprehensive. She chooses one. "Maria, what is it that scares you?"

"Coach, there's just so much. At church I prayed for all our health, and I think we all did, but every day it's something new. Now, you're saying you and Coach Powell will wear masks, so, should we? Is this gathering safe?" Some of Maria's teammates nod their heads in agreement.

Molly steps off her patio and sits on the edge. She changes back to her Mama Molly voice. "I've relied on my husband's expertise on being safe so far, and he says that meeting like this is safe. We're all spread out and that's good. Practicing with just us in the big gym is okay too. Doctor Frank is staying on top of the conflicting reports, and I know he's concerned about your health. He thinks masks are good, especially when you're in close contact with others. He's convinced that the reason masks aren't being pushed more is that there's a shortage and they're so desperately needed in the hospitals. Also, masks are sort of like a badge that says, 'I care about your health.'" Coach Robinson and Mr. Davidson are searching for masks for us all. Because they're both in their seventies, they're in the high-risk group which is why they're not going to be around others much. Mr. Davidson has some other health issues, so he and his wife are staying home as much as possible."

Char Betany has her hand in the air. Molly nods at her. "Coach, I gotta get home to my family. They don't know all this stuff, and the reservation always is last to get any news or help. The medical facilities there aren't very good. Can you help me?"

Molly's biggest concern has been for Char and Dyani. For that reason, she reached out to Dyani's uncle, Hector Dehiya, when the team returned from Santa Barbara. The team knows Mr. Dehiya as Hector and respects his spiritual presence. "Char, let me answer your question in two ways. First, yes, if you finally decide that you must get back to your family, we'll get you there, even if one of the coaches has to drive you home, which is what we talked about. Secondly, Hector wants you to stay here at school for now. He wants you near Dyani and your teammates and continuing with your studies."

"You talked with Hector?"

"Yes, Char. I've talked with him a couple of times." Molly looks at the whole team. "Ry and I have spoken to someone in each of your families except Kenti's."

Esther Santiago blurts out. "You talked with my mother?"

Molly nods. "I'm breaking a bit of a confidence because she doesn't want you to worry about her, but since you already do and this is a unique situation, I'll tell you. She's struggling but no worse than usual. She's proud of you, but you know that."

"Is she in San Diego?"

"No, but she's trying to get back."

"How did you find her?"

"Coach's magic, Esther." Molly smiles, "and knowing old men with lots of contacts. Coach Robinson has an old friend who's worked on border issues all his life. You can ask Coach next time you see him about it."

∾

In the 1960s Ken Davidson played guard on the Tulare Union High School basketball team and led the conference in scoring. Moses Robinson played for Oxnard High School and was one of the outstanding players in all of California. He went on to play college basketball at the University of Colorado and then had a brief but productive career in the NBA. Davidson played small college ball and then became a sports journalist. Mose says that he was a better player than Ken, but that Ken soared past him in the post-basketball years. Ken calls bullshit on Mose, saying that being a teacher, especially a successful junior high teacher, is as valuable as it gets. Mose says that coaching kids is just coaching kids, regardless of their age, except that one gets paid more the older the players are.

Ken is now blogging from home and making contacts via his cell phone. Mose slow jogs daily along the beach, texts his children and grandchildren, and sits in his lounger next to his wife after dinner and reads. Both men are ponderers, and America in 2020 has much to be considered. While both see the bigger picture, these are two men who focus on community. On Sunday, March 22, Ken Davidson and his wife drive the back roads of Tulare County observing the workers in the fields, fields that he never worked but came to love. Moses Robinson and his wife walk the fields in Oxnard and converse with the pickers in Spanish.

∾

Coach Aikins, Coach Nikki to the players because of her young age, paces the War Room re-reading her notes on the whiteboard one more time before sitting down at her computer. She has crunched numbers from the season for the San Joaquin Valley University Sequoias and for the Florida State Seminoles and DePaul Blue Demons. She's looking for that analytical edge to win the hypothetical game, just as she would look for the statistical edge if the tournament was proceeding as once scheduled. Florida State crushed opponents with lesser talent and played the ACC's best straight up. A tough first round for SJV. Still, their bigness, meaning height, hides their lack of quickness, if a team from the ACC can ever be considered un-quick. She laughs at her choice of adjectives and adverbs.

Nicole's role on the staff, besides the analytics, is inbounds plays, especially out-of-bounds plays under the offensive basket. She has compiled a notebook with over 100 plays that she updates weekly depending on SJV's opponent. She knows how many possessions are successful on these plays as compared to regular offensive possessions, which she also knows. She knows that over the past four years, when point guards are the triggers, SJV is much more likely to score. With Dyani as the trigger, these plays resulted in 1.5 points per possession, a full .4 points better than regular possessions. Nicole has statistics on the effectiveness of each player on her screens, who should get shots where, and where any missed shots are likely to fall.

While this imaginary tournament crashed at an earlier team meeting, Nicole noticed that some of the team still wanted to play the contest, almost like a video game. When SJV played USC in an early season non-conference game, her analytics indicated that SJV had a real chance to defeat the high-profile opponent. It would be close, but Nicole determined that, statistically, there were avenues to victory. Coach Rascon traveled those roads in practice, emphasizing USC's weaknesses that played into SJV's strengths, and the result was a four-point win. Collect the data, analyze the data, apply the findings, stay the course. Florida State was weaker defensively when teams attacked from the left side and vulnerable on the right-side boards. Those two combined give SJV that opportunity.

Nicole pulls her fingers off the keyboard and leans back in her chair with a grin. "Luck occurs at the intersection of preparation and opportunity!" Nicole spins her chair to scan the whiteboards. All her numbers coalesce in her mind into one thought. *Coach Rascon can get you ladies good shots, now it's up to you to make them.* In Nicole's mind at this moment, it isn't an imaginary game any longer.

Chapter 6

It's official. Classes restart virtually at all University of California colleges and universities with few exceptions. San Joaquin Valley seems deserted. About 70 percent of the students either didn't return from spring break or have packed up and left. Those who remain keep their distance on the sidewalks and public areas but not so much in private; most of them will be leaving campus over the next few days. As of this Monday, eleven of the twelve members of the women's basketball team remain housed in the dorms. Only Kenti lives in a different dorm. Danelle will leave on Tuesday, driving home to Colorado, not knowing if she will return to Tulare anytime soon, and still crying privately. Greta, like many of SJV's students, lost her university job, and plans to drive home to Oxnard and work part-time in the fields, work she knows well. She teases Coach Rascon that in addition to being tutored by Coach Robinson and his wife Sally, she will simply be continuing her studies in agribusiness with hands-on labs. Keilani leaves Wednesday for Inglewood, Emerson back to Santa Monica, and Joyce just up the 99 to Fresno. Each one intends to return to Tulare weekly to check in with Coach Rascon and her professors if travel is not further restricted. Essential travel is an elusive concept. The two other California Girls are staying, Kaori only until her parents tell her Nai-nai is non-contagious. Esther doesn't have a California address to return to at the moment. Five players plan to stay, and Molly is searching for temporary housing, temporary meaning for the remainder of the semester for these five plus two.

❧

The team meets for one last practice at 3:00 in the gym. Coach Rascon and her three assistants all wear masks, purchased by Mr. Davidson at the Visalia Walmart. As it turns out, this Walmart has a huge supply of workshop masks because of the demand in the San Joaquin Valley due to the polluted air. Doctor Martinez, Dr. Frank to the team, is not sure how effective they might be to halt microscopic virus particles, but he tells Molly they can't hurt. Coach Jakino jokes that she will serve as the manager today and walks around with a towel draped over her shoulder giggling with the team. Coach Rascon blows her whistle and yells, "zig-zag," and twelve ladies begin a full-court drill to teach defensive footwork, just like on the first day of practice six months earlier.

And maybe this is a new Day One.

Purposely, Molly has not included any contact drills, but contact still occurs, especially on "Rez-ball." The enthusiasm and joy are apparent. Molly tells Ryanne and Nikki that this practice reminds her of high school. No one is filming it for later critiques, the clock isn't running down the time remaining for each drill, and no player needs to be reminded to step it up. Just the coaches and the players enjoying being a family again. They are not preparing for another game; they are entirely in the moment.

An hour into practice, Coach Rascon sends them to six baskets to shoot free throws and to run their misses. As always, they come together after that for a small evaluation, and then it's back to another drill, skip passes leading to three-point shots. Today, even Danelle and Sylvia get to shoot them. And it goes on, drill after drill: encouragement, laughter, fist bumps, and banter.

At this Last Practice of the 2019-2020 season, Coach Rascon avoids pure contact drills in the face of limited information about the danger of spreading a potentially life-threatening virus. In the face of an unfolding human drama fueled by so much information and yet so little information, in an arena with no spectators or media lights, one team—in the truest sense of the term—runs, jumps, and embraces physical activity to hold off the pandemic tide that threatens their very existence.

It's a sweaty bunch that sits on the floor at mid-court at 5:00 to listen to the words of their coaches. Joyce Hensley, one of two juniors on the team and along with Sylvia Castro the only girl who has been in the program for three years, yells "Yeesss" at the top of her lungs and pirouettes into her sitting position. Months later, she will remember that she won the last game of "knockout," and thus made the last shot of the season for The Tribe. No one else will remember that except Coach Rascon, but every girl will fondly remember this practice.

As Coach Nikki hands out towels to each player, Coach Powell speaks. "Remember your spacing, and I don't mean offensively. Social distance!" She looks sternly at the team. "I loved your spirit and energy out there today. We got a little better. Char, your passes were much crisper in shell drill. Very good! Greta, Coach Robinson would have been happy with your footwork on the low block. In the coming months, keep working on it. All of you, really, really nice job out there." She steps back toward Molly and whispers something into her friend's ear and then smiles.

Coach Rascon nods to Kaori Park who stands. "Kaori has a bit of news, some very good news. Kay-kay."

Kaori puts her hands together as if she's about to pray. "My mother called this morning to tell me that they released my Nai-nai from the hospital. It was the coronavirus, but she's doing well enough to come home. She's too tough, and except for her age, didn't have any other conditions. She's going to be fine, and I can go see her." Her teammates all clap as Kaori shakes her whole body happily.

Coach Rascon's huge grin settles into a warm smile. "This is bitter-sweet, but what a wonderful practice this was. Tomorrow, the first wave of you will leave campus and head home. Danelle, Coach Nikki has you booked at a motel in southern Utah, a non-smoking room." The team laughs. "It's a long two-day drive for Danelle," says Molly to the entire team, "about eight hours both days. Danelle, come into my office after dinner, and we'll go over your itinerary like we talked about this afternoon." She nods to Danelle. "Joyce, Keilani, Emerson, Greta, and now Kay-kay all leave sometime tomorrow. You guys make sure you pick up your packets too. It's all stuff that we've been talking about. For the rest of you, we're still working on housing for the next week or longer." She smiles at her team. "None of you will be living in the concrete tubes," a reference to the huge construction pipes along the path of the bullet train project that many of the truly homeless have adopted for their sleeping quarters. "Piggybacking on what Coach Powell just said, I want you all to consider your behavior around others, that you could be a spreader and never even know you have Covid. Act like you have it to protect others, especially your family as you return home." Molly nods to Coach Jakino for her to say a few words.

"I will be texting each of you daily, nagging you to log in to your classes and get your homework done. I will expect a response to each and every one of my texts." Coach Jakino lowers her head and looks as stern as she can. "If the technology gives you problems, text me and I'll see that it's corrected. Some of the professors are more confused about online teaching than you are about online learning, so hang in there, but don't let a problem fester. Let me know!" She steps back turning the floor over to Coach Aikins.

Coach Aikins smiles deviously, and the team giggles. She continues her silence, looking over a notecard and nodding her head, almost as if trying to solve a riddle. Finally, she speaks. "Help me here," she says as if she's truly confused. "In the two games we lost this season, we were outrebounded." She pauses again and looks at her notecard. "The only two times we were outrebounded all season." Again, she pauses. "Wouldn't it stand to reason that if we were outrebounded against Florida State, we would lose?" A rhetorical question and a few of the girls begin to see where Coach Nikki is going. "I've analyzed these stats until my eyes are blurry. Florida State outrebounded us by eight boards, 37-29, and yet," she pauses again. The entire team gets it, knows now that Coach Nikki wrote a scenario for the imaginary first round of the NCAA tournament even though it stung when she first mentioned it. She has chosen the perfect time to deliver the results. "Wouldn't that determine the outcome?" She looks up.

Kaori, the math major, answers. "Stats can be misleading, you know."

Danelle picks up the thread. "It's not always the number of rebounds but getting the important ones. Offensive rebounds are often key."

Coach Nikki nods.

"Doesn't Coach look at other statistics," asks Emerson, "like shooting percentages and turnovers?"

Dyani closes the loop. "I'll bet if you factor in those other statistics, put those into your precious computer, you might find that there was a big differential in those statistics, almost as if a team with grit maybe made up for lack of size with guts." Char giggles. Dyani asks, "How many turnovers did we cause?"

"Eighteen."

Dyani asks again, "How many turnovers did we commit?"

"Seven."

Dyani again. "Offensive rebounds?"

Coach Nikki plays this game like Bobby Fisher might close out an exhibition chess match, allowing a young protegee to win against the master. "Hmm. Sylvia and Danelle got four each, and the rest of the team added five more. Yeah, that might make a difference."

It's Maria Sanchez who finally asks for the outcome, even though The Tribe already knows. Coach Nikki smiles now. "61-56. We're in the round of 32. Possible spot in the Sweet Sixteen. The girls erupt in cheers and laughter. For a moment, all is well among the trees in Sequoiaville. A seemingly healthy forest.

"Okay, everyone up but stay in your spot." The ladies rise and raise their fists, pointed slightly toward their coach. "Who are we?" asks Molly.

"SEQUOIAS!" the team yells in unison.

"THE TRIBE!" yells Dyani.

If this is The Last Practice, it ends on a high note. The cancellations can't be changed, school won't be called back in session with in-person learning, the team will not play any more games, they will not collect again as a team of twelve. But they believe they could have advanced had they been given the opportunity. Often, it's that verification that sustains the dream and nurtures the soul.

Danelle Weston bends over at center court and gently touches General Sherman before she leaves for the last time.

∽

Coach Rascon is not the most important person in any of her play-ers' lives, although this role Molly plays in their lives is critical. What outsiders do not realize is that the role she plays as a basketball coach is not her primary one. Teacher, counselor, mother, big sister—those are her primary roles. Universities pay big money for Xs and Os, and not enough money for teachers. Molly will be the first to admit she isn't perfect, but she is grounded, and she experienced poverty like many of the students at SJV. She was never as poor as Greta or Char and Dyani, and the gradations of poverty are important, a caste system within The Caste System. The years between age seventeen and twenty-two maybe are the transition between old kids and young adults. In Latin culture, there is the quinceañera, the celebration that marks a girl's passage from childhood to womanhood, but Molly knows from her own experience that's way too young. Of the members on her squad, she thinks Sylvia Castro and maybe Kaori Park took on womanhood at age fifteen, but none of the others. Sylvia because she had to raise younger sisters when her father was away serving the country, Kaori because her family raised her to take responsibility from a young age. Most of The Tribe held jobs when they were in their teens, and most of their wages went to the family upkeep, not for frivolous spending money. Molly knows, and as she prepares to send most of her team home in the next few days, she hurts because the process is incomplete.

Frankie Martinez is mostly an indoor kid. Basketball, when played at his elementary school or in the SJV gym, is his sport. Frankie has allergies which are exacerbated by the poor air quality of the San Joaquin Valley. When he does play, and he is a non-stop kid, he carries his inhaler. He is not a child of poverty but of modest wealth. His mother is a university basketball coach, and his father is a pediatri-cian. Their clients, i.e., players and patients, are mostly poor though. Frankie's parents insist that he understands his privilege; they insist he attend Tulare's public schools. There is a Montessori school and a few Christian academies, all rated higher in academics than the public schools, but Frankie does not and will not attend those. He will not be segregated from his community; his parents will not allow that.

Now, however, a virus has a different agenda.

❧

Molly returns home just before Frankie's bedtime. He's doing homework on what he calls "the big computer" rather than his iPad. That way, he gets to work in his dad's office. Big boy stuff. "Did you eat?" asks Frank to his wife.

"Jackie brought some pizza in."

"I want your job," teases Frankie. "Pizza every night." Molly kisses her son on the top of his head and her husband on his cheek.

"Did you find lodging for all your girls?" asks Frank.

"I think so, but we might have a guest or two for a few days. The dorms may stay open though. Hopefully."

"Let me guess," says Frank, "Dyani and Char, Maria and Sylvia, and Esther?"

"They can have my room," volunteers Frankie. "I'll sleep in the tent out back."

"Thanks, but no. We'll find a spot for anyone who stays for a few days." Molly squeezes her son's arm and breathes out heavily. "Maybe you can help put up sheets in the den and the upstairs bedroom."

Molly's husband closes his journal. "Your most vulnerable, huh?"

Molly nods her head. "Dyani's uncle," she looks at Frankie. "Hector Dehiya. He's been wonderful. So gentle and knowing. He calls Dyani and Char every day and settles them down, tells them to stay here for now, that they're better served here than back in Arizona."

Frankie interrupts. "I got a text from Hector today. He said that I can be Char's little brother and tease her since she can't be home with her real brothers."

Molly smiles. "Don't get too excited yet. They can stay in their dorm rooms for now and maybe for the rest of the semester. We'll just have to see how things unfold. For now, it's your bedtime. Go pick a story."

❧

Lying in bed an hour after Frankie has fallen asleep, Molly apologizes. "I know we can't house all of them, but I just feel responsible. You've warned me about crowded dorms, and now I want to move them here."

"No, don't worry. California has 40 million people and there's been fewer than five thousand cases reported, and as far as I know, none have been on college campuses. There will be some later this spring, but as long as we take precautions, we'll be fine. What you're doing is what you should be doing. Get back on the phone tomorrow and keep searching for places for the girls. We live in a generous community. And I may have a line on one or two places for a couple of your kids."

Molly curls up into her husband's arms. "Maybe this is God's way of telling us we've had it too good."

"Oh, and when did He start infecting the older folks to send us a message?" He laughs, but only for a moment. Molly pulls the hair on his chest, and he winces. They go silent for a few minutes before Molly speaks again.

"Do you think I ought to bring in guys to practice against my gals? All the big schools do it."

∽

Kenti Solorzano accepts a room on Mr. Fuchigami's farm, a casita really, with a small kitchen. And high-speed internet. "Not like my family's farm in Guatemala!" Now she says she's a real farmer and not a student.

Kaori Park and her mother are pushed down on a sidewalk in San Francisco coming out of the grocery store. The man shouts, "Go back to China! Take your China virus with you! Get out of my country!" Neither are hurt except for a few scratches, but now they are frightened of something more than Covid.

Danelle Weston arrives safely at her home in Brighton, Colorado, after a two-day drive. She texts Coach Rascon and then Coach Robinson telling them she will be okay and for them not to worry, that she'll call in a few days.

Keilani Russell begins a conscientious program to improve her ball-handling skills in preparation for taking over the point guard position. She avoids the local courts as a safety precaution, instead practicing on the cracked driveway at her parents' rented house in Inglewood.

Joyce Hensley gets a part-time job as a quasi-nurse in the Fresno hospital which is in dire need of nurses and has relaxed some of its licensing requirements. Her professor tells her she can count these hours toward her rotation at the Tulare hospital. Paid work. "Essential work!"

Greta Espinoza takes a break around lunch to sit with Coach Robinson and his wife Sally at a table near the strawberry field where she started working again. This is just two days after returning to Oxnard. She explains to the Robinsons how the strawberry is the only fruit that carries its seeds on the outside, and she laughs when Coach Robinson begins counting the number of seeds on one strawberry. "About 200," she tells her coach.

Emerson Loki divides her day into three parts. In the morning she gets online to complete her school assignments. After lunch, she shoots baskets, lots and lots of baskets, but tells herself, "It's not how many shots I take each day, it's how many I make." She begins her first full day back with a goal of 300. Makes. In the evening she dances. She begins creating an improvisational score to identify her own work. Emerson will not hang out on the Santa Monica pier this spring.

San Joaquin Valley decides to keep one dorm open for those students who can't get home. Char, Dyani, Maria, Sylvia, and Esther all get their own rooms in the new dorm and have to move their stuff, and their rooms are on the same floor. The cafeteria stays open, but the menu is sparse and pre-wrapped, "boring," as Sylvia puts it. Molly and Ryanne create routines for these remaining players and sees them daily in the basketball office one at a time. Not only Coach Rascon and her assistants, but nearly the entire SJV staff steps up to provide support for the remaining students. SJV was created to serve the underserved, students from poor backgrounds, and they do not intend to allow a virus to derail that original mission, to postpone the harvest. Everyone is on the tightrope: they have to comply with university, county, state, national, and NCAA regulations—and these change almost daily.

On Saturday, March 28, 2020, Tulare County records its first death from the coronavirus, while California approaches its first 100 deaths. The Grim Reaper will harvest tens of thousands more.

Chapter 7

Agriculture and Basketball. Blog, by Ken Davidson

I had a good laugh with Mose Robinson yesterday. As most of my readers know, Mose is a former NBA player who retired to teach and coach middle school kids in the mid- Seventies. I still wonder about his sanity. Regardless, we were talking about the impact of Covid news on our daily lives, especially for us geezers. Every time one of us or our wife coughs, we wonder if we've contracted the virus, and yet, I don't know anyone who has Covid. If the numbers continue to rise, I soon will.

This blog began with the dual purpose of linking sports with the economic base of my beloved Central California Valley. Nothing moves me more than the green fields at harvest time. Not so much the dairy farms. Many of us who were raised in this valley moved away to get an education or begin a career, but few move back. Tulare, Visalia, Corcoran, Fresno, and the towns up and down the valley are not retirement destinations, so when I gave up my professional career and returned, I didn't meet any of my old friends or family. My sister and her husband retired to southern Arizona. A fellow columnist for The Times has taken up pickleball in Florida. These are communities that cater to the old-timers where the weather is nice all year long and the 20th century remains. My wife and I considered it, but we're both from this valley and it drew us back. No regrets.

Enough of my melancholia.

The virus has impacted my two threads differently. The farms continue as might be expected; we need to produce and eat. Sports, though, have shut down completely, not even a pickup game of workup on the ball fields. No kid shooting baskets at the outdoor courts in the park in the evening. My new favorite team in my retirement, the university's women's basketball team has scattered with the winds. Only five or six members of the team remain in Tulare. They can't practice together, but Coach Rascon and her staff work with the players on their individual skills one at a time. It seems as if her work now is less about coaching basketball and more about caring for her girls' health and welfare. Then I realized that that's what coaches do behind the scenes all the time.

Rumors, but my sources are pretty good, indicate that several colleges and universities are considering cuts to their athletic departments in response to the sudden collapse of revenue. Certainly, assistant coaches will be furloughed in the days ahead, but my sources are saying that entire programs could be on the chopping block. These probably don't include football or basketball programs but will focus on so-called minor sports. SJV doesn't have a football team, and the two basketball teams are not revenue positive. SJV athletic programs exist to enhance the entertainment and cultural climate of the campus. Sports have traditionally been a path for the underrepresented; hence the mission of SJV and the other schools in the Ring of Fire Conference. California regents and individual university administrators will be making difficult decisions in the months ahead. These decisions will have huge impacts on students from poor families who attend school on scholarship.

In the days and months ahead, Covid is going to reveal much about our communities and about our nation, about the people who we can rely on and about those who we can't. It could be The Great Teacher for America, but I fear in our current political climate, it will only further divide us.

❧

The university tells students the school is closing to in-person learning and that with few exceptions they have to vacate the dorms. It feels like eviction orders; a gut-punch that forces air out of the lungs of the campus in a community where poor air quality already makes breathing difficult. The order also leaves essential campus workers gasping for air. Within 48 hours it becomes apparent that the orders are unsustainable at face value, and members of the SJV community recognize that they need to be amended. Just as the basketball coaching staff circles the wagons to protect their team, professors and sponsors organize to provide support for their specific groups, both students and staff. Up and down The Valley, families who had sent their children to SJV volunteer to house students, provide meals, give temporary storage space for belongings, and provide transportation when possible. While many around the country ridicule the stringent measures being taken to prevent the spread of a potentially deadly virus, The Valley knows that those most at risk are the underserved, and that these are the people who will be most affected by this virus.

☙

Coach Jakino answers the phone in the coaches' office, a landline that seldom rings. "Coach Rascon's office. This is Coach Jakino."

"Coach, this is Stephanie Borges, and I'm a graduate of SJV, class of '81. I played basketball back when we always lost." There is a slight laugh from Stephanie. "Anyway, my friend Janet and I are wondering if there is anything we can do for your girls right now."

Coach Jakino jots Stephanie's name on the pad that sits next to this phone. "Is it Borges with a B?" Stephanie spells it for Jackie. "Thank you for your offer. Yes, there are a thousand things that they need at this moment, none of which are basketball related."

Again, Stephanie chuckles. "Coach, judging from your record over the past four years, there is nothing Janet and I need to help you with on that end. We're just fans and alumni with some extra money and would like to help."

The friendly call turns serious with the mention of the word *money*. "Ms. Borges, can I get your cell number and have Molly, ah, Coach Rascon, call you back?"

☙

Out jogging, Molly Rascon receives a different type of call. "Molly, it's Bianca. Queenie is sick. She's in the hospital in Denver, and Mercedes says it's really serious."

"Is it Covid?"

"Yes."

Three pictures adorn Molly's desk in her coaching office, the official office of San Joaquin Valley Women's Basketball. On the left, Frank and Baby Frankie sit on a horse on a beach near Thousand Oaks from six years ago. On the right, Molly's high school basketball coach and his wife sit on chairs in front of six women Molly refers to as the Mountain Matrons. One of the women is a large Black woman, Queenie Roberts, a lawyer of considerable skills, a bit of money, and a generous heart. Sitting cross-legged in front of the adults are ten girls wearing letter jackets and holding a banner that reads 1997 STATE CHAMPIONS. Just to the side of that photo is one of Molly's brother Alex in his Army uniform, taken in 2006 at the conclusion of basic training.

Molly sends a group text.

❧

Eleven of the twelve members of Coach Rascon's team shelter in California. Danelle Weston, however, has returned to Colorado, 1,100 miles east of the SJV campus by car. Two long, long driving days. She's isolated from her team. Upon arriving at her house, she finds that her parents have moved her bedroom furniture into the garage for her pandemic residence out of extreme concern that she not spread the virus, since "California is where the coronavirus is all over." Danelle is isolated on a second level now. Wednesday morning, she calls Coach Rascon.

"Coach, this is Danelle," something Molly already knows since Danelle's name appears on her screen when "We Are the Champions" begins. "I'm sorry I didn't return your calls last week when I first got here, but I'm settling in."

"Moving is time consuming. I understand. How was the drive? Any problems?"

"Not really. I had to drive through some snow at the end, on Vail Pass and the tunnels."

Molly knows this area well. Her hometown, Oro Hills, sits about halfway between the Eisenhower tunnels and Denver. "Were your tires adequate?"

"Sort of, but the roads were pretty much okay, and I drove slow."

"I imagine your parents are glad to see you."

Danelle hesitates slightly. "Yeah. Parents are always happy to see their children, aren't they? Anyway, things are fine here. Did the others make it home all right?"

"Those that went, yes. So far, SJV is keeping open one dorm for those students who can't get home, so Dyani, Char, Maria and Sylvia, and Esther have their rooms, and they seem pretty happy. They're all worried for their families, of course, but for now, everyone has a place."

"Will you have a practice this afternoon?"

"No. The university put an end to that, but I do get to let one in the gym at a time. A little shooting and running. I can check up on each of them at that time, and I think that's healthy. It's more about sociality than practicing basketball. I'm not sure how long that will be allowed though. I've been warned by the AD that the gym will be closed completely soon. Wish I had somewhere else to meet. Have you spoken with Coach Robinson yet?" Molly knows Danelle has not called Mose.

"No, but maybe later today I will."

"Hang on, Danelle. Frankie wants to say hi." Molly hands her phone to Frankie and leans back in her desk chair. Since Frankie's school closed, he's been spending most of his time with his mother.

"Hi D-West," Frankie screams into the phone.

"Hey, Frankie. Good to hear your voice. You must be happy with no school."

"Dad and mom make me do my homework, and then I get to shoot lots of baskets, but I miss my friends."

"Tell me about it. I can't believe I'm here and you all are still there."

"When are you coming back?" asks Frankie.

"I'm not sure. Good talking with you. Put Coach back on the phone, okay." Danelle waits while Frankie returns the phone to his mother. When Molly is on, Danelle asks, "Is the cafeteria still open?" It seems like a peculiar question to Molly but there are a lot of odd questions these days.

∾

Esther Santiago came to California from Mexico City when she was three, in 2003, with her mother and brother. The family lived in San Diego with an aunt. Her mother worked in sales and always had a job, reminding her daughter that jobs were the path to a better life, and that education and jobs were her daughter's path. Esther worked all her life too. Her brother returned to Mexico City when he entered junior high and never returned. Esther became a "Dreamer" in 2012 and reapplies every two years. While she was a good high school student, she had no plans to attend college, but all that changed as she grew to over six feet and excelled in basketball. A few small California colleges offered her partial scholarships, but the demographics of SJV and the persuasiveness of Coach Rascon convinced her to become a Sequoia. Since Trump became president, Esther has worried about her future. The coronavirus has simply added to that stress.

"Esther, it's Coach. Hey, I think I've found you a new job," With the closing of campus, Esther lost her student job at the bookstore, extra money that has been needed to supplement her scholarship. Much of it, she sends back to her mother, or at least to her aunt's address.

"I didn't think the college was offering any anymore."

SJV isn't hiring, and the jobs that are available in Tulare are mostly "essential," which during the pandemic means "risky." Molly is aware of this but understands the need that Esther and some of her teammates have for jobs to supplement their scholarships. It's a fine line. Molly answers Esther's concern. "They aren't, but it's close. Stocking across the street at the grocery store."

"Is there more than one available? Sylvia and Maria need jobs too."

"No, just the one across the street, but I think we may have leads for jobs for them too."

There's a pause. "Coach, can I ask you something?"

"Of course, Esther. What is it?"

"Are all these jobs that we can get," Esther pauses again, "dangerous?"

Molly feels a bit guilty. "I talked with Dr. Frank, and he thinks there probably is a heightened risk, at least for what is known now. He also says the real infections seem to be focused on the elderly. He doesn't know why, but that's the evidence at the moment. He wants you to wear a mask at any job you take now and keep your distance as best you can."

Esther laughs slightly. "You know we all giggle when you call your husband *Dr. Frank*. It's cute." The two women smile on each end of the call. "I'll go over this morning and apply. I speak English, so they may consider me." She laughs again, a sarcastic chuckle.

Esther Santiago did not go directly to college after high school, because she did not know how to get through the paperwork, the bureaucracy. She doesn't have a Social Security number, so she lived in the shadows. When university coaches scout one player, they are often attracted to another who's playing in the same game or at the same camp. Coach Rascon was scouting a 3-star player at a Nike camp in San Diego who eventually rejected SJV, but Molly's time was not wasted. She noticed a "camp filler player" who seemed to be in the right place at the right time in the scrimmages. Esther didn't seek the spotlight; she just made the stars look better, and the team to which she was assigned always won. Always. Molly's staff worked Esther through the bureaucratic red tape showing her that living in the shadows limited opportunities for one's future. At SJV Esther could explore those opportunities, play in the spotlight.

The virus tears through Italy, especially northern Italy, and that nation registers over 13,000 deaths by the first of April. Spain and the UK are not far behind. Nor is the United States. Two weeks later, the U.S. total will surpass Italy's grim numbers. Frank notes that over 100 doctors have died from Covid so far. He searches for information about nurses and other healthcare workers.

Agriculture and Basketball. Blog, Ken Davidson

I have Covid. I've been having trouble breathing over the past few days along with a headache, so I went to the doctor's office for a test. Positive. Just to be on the safe side, he's putting me in the hospital for a few days. I go in tomorrow up in Fresno. The missus won't be able to visit, but it will give her time to catch up on her reading pile.

❧

Molly and Ryanne talk constantly by phone but less in person. They each go to the office but are seldom there together. Often, one will call the other from the office. Texting is ongoing. Coach Nikki does all her charting from home, and Coach Jackie is living with her parents in Corcoran as she manages the crowded recruiting boulevard. Cell phones and laptops. Facetime and Zoom. The coaches text the players trying to make contact with every player daily. Some of these messages are about basketball but most deal with mental health. "How are you doing? Are you eating well? Are you exercising? How's your energy level?" Or school. "Are you keeping up? Is your professor giving you what you need? Do you need a tutor?" Or family. "Tell me about your little brothers. Did your father recover from his fall? Is your family practicing safe measures? Social distancing?" Every text ends with the initials ALYHI. *Act Like You Have It*. Most of the players' homes have multiple family members, including small children. Molly knows these aren't ideal conditions for coping with an airborne pandemic. She worries about her own family.

Molly has a love/hate relationship with her cellphone.

Mose Robinson calls to inquire about Ken Davidson since Ken's wife hasn't returned his calls.

Dyani's uncle Hector Dehiya doesn't only call; but he shows up unexpectedly to meet with Dyani and Char, almost as if teleported. He's done that since Char arrived on campus a year ago. Dyani and Char are not sisters but act like it. Char came to SJV because of Dyani and hopes to fill her shoes one day. Dyani holds hero status on the Navajo Reservation, maybe the best basketball player ever to leave. When she graduates, her plan is to return to teach and coach or work as a sociologist.

Maria Sanchez is Sylvia Castro's half-sister. "There's no such thing," insists Sylvia. "She's my sister. Period." As a high school senior, the University of Texas at El Paso offered Sylvia a partial scholarship, but Coach Rascon went all in with her, and Sylvia enthusiastically signed. Both schools are majority Hispanic, but SJV is only about half the size and would pay for her education. Coach Rascon told her that the Sequoias needed a *Big Stallion* to win consistently. Sylvia took this as a challenge. The UTEP coach offered limited playing time.

Maria's father is Sylvia's dad, but her mother is not. Sylvia's mother raised Maria, nonetheless. It was never complicated. Maria's mother left to somewhere and never returned. Their father serves in the Army, usually at Ft. Bliss, his home base. When he has been deployed elsewhere, life goes on with his wife, five kids, and three dogs all living on the base. Coach Rascon knows the names of all three dogs. Why Maria's last name isn't the same as Sylvia's is another story, says Sylvia. Much like Char, Maria followed her sister to SJV and hasn't regretted it. Both sisters began as education majors, but Sylvia sees additional opportunities for her life instead of simply returning to El Paso to teach eight-year-olds. Maria hasn't thought that far ahead, too busy dating without Papa supervising.

Wearing masks, Molly and Ryanne pace the War Room and add notes to the already busy white boards. The gym is off limits for even individual practice time. The information is not about basketball games, but about the physical and educational health of their players. "A giant list," kids Ryanne. Each player has a section of one of the boards. A flip chart/poster pad sits in one corner with notes for each day. To-dos and dones. Check marks. Today is Monday, April 20, and all hell has broken out.

Ken Davidson has been put on a ventilator, and Char Betany bought a bus ticket and is going home. She told no one, just left a note that Dyani found this morning when she went to pick up Little Sister for breakfast.

"At least we saw it coming," says Ryanne. "She's fallen behind on her classwork and is listless."

Molly starts to respond but Freddie Mercury interrupts her. It's Dyani.

"The bus left at 6:10 and she was on it," says Dyani in her angry voice. "I tried to call my uncle, but he hasn't picked up. I can't believe she just left."

"What's the final destination and where'd she get the money?" asks Molly.

"Phoenix. I checked and the ticket cost $90. I don't know where she got the money, but if she's only going to Phoenix, I'll bet one of her brothers sent it to her. They want her back, have been telling her that she's needed back on the rez. My uncle's been trying to get them to stop encouraging her."

Ryanne tells Molly to ask Dyani if she knows when the bus is due in Phoenix.

"Tonight about 9:00. I'll bet one of her brothers will be there to pick her up and drive her home. Stupid, stupid, stupid!"

"Don't be too hard on her, Dyani. She's been struggling and is the youngest on the team," says Molly.

"I'm not talking about Char. I'm talking about me. How did I not see this? I'm supposed to be looking out for her."

"It's not your fault, Dyani. Come back here. Coach Ry and I are in the War Room with coffee and scones. Bring your computer and you can work out of my office. Use the service entrance door. Are you wearing your mask?" asks Molly.

"Yeah, I'm about the only one who is here at the station."

The conversation ends and Molly fakes throwing her phone against the wall. Both coaches remain quiet for a moment. Ryanne writes notes in Char's space on the white board, while Molly writes on the flip chart. She puts the cap on her sharpie and turns to her assistant coach.

"Covid sure has a way of exposing our weaknesses, doesn't it." It's a statement and not a question.

Ryanne nods and lays her marker on the tray. "It sure does." She picks up her marker again and taps on a word in Char's box. *Withdrawal.* "I feel terrible for Dyani. She'll hold herself responsible."

"Not much we can do for now. Dyani says Char didn't take her computer. She'll lose all her credits if she stays away." Molly shakes her head, taps Coach Jakino's number, and waits. "Jackie. Hey, can you get me a list of Char's professors asap? When you come in at noon will be soon enough. Ry and I are in the War Room, and Dyani will probably be studying in the office when you arrive." Molly breathes out heavily. "Okay. Next?"

Ryanne walks away from the whiteboard to get her coffee cup from the small desk. "Nobody's returning calls this morning. Ken's wife has an excuse though. My guess is she's at the hospital just sitting in the waiting room in a panic. She'll call later if she remembered to take her phone with her. Being on a ventilator can't be fun. Yesterday, she said the doctors indicated he might be on it for a week. Not good, but you knew that. I'll stay on that. I think one of Ken's daughters is coming into town later today."

Freddie Mercury alerts Molly that Sylvia wants to talk with her. "Hey, Sylvia, are you still in the house?"

"Yeah, but I need to get online with my bio class. Is it okay if Frankie works by himself for a few minutes until my sister arrives?"

"Yes. He has his phone if he needs anything. Make sure you get something to eat after your lecture. Thanks for sitting him. Did he beat you in horse?"

Ryanne smiles. "Those two are doing well. Maria said it's because of their military upbringing. See a problem, solve a problem."

Molly smiles back. "Sylvia attributes it to her Apache ancestry. Mescalero." Molly shakes her head. "We have the most mixed-team possible. Half this, half that, and it begins with you and me and Mose."

"Who's next?" asks Ryanne.

Molly turns a page on the flip chart to a clean sheet. "Kaori."

Dyani arrives at the basketball office after a fifteen-minute walk from the bus stop, plops her purse on Coach Ryanne's desk by the door, takes out her computer and plugs it in. She takes her special Grand Canyon cup from the cabinet and fills it with Molly's strong coffee. From her purse, Dyani takes out a small bag of toasted flour and mixes in three spoons to her coffee and stirs it until the consistency resembles a pudding. She doesn't drink her coffee; she eats it with a spoon, a habit that her teammates think is hilarious.

Dyani logs onto SOC 189S: *Engaging Underrepresented Populations as Volunteers*, an upper-level sociology course in her major. Her semester thesis focuses on young adults who grew up under foster care. Before starting her class, she checks her phone for any messages from Char or Uncle Hector. There are none. She lays her phone next to her computer, takes a spoonful of coffee, and begins her studies.

The Kubler-Ross Model seems to fit this first few weeks of the pandemic shutdown, denial and anger being obvious signs for herself and her teammates, with depression beginning to show up. Dyani talked to her coaches about Char's signs just last week. Dyani hasn't moved past the anger stage yet. Interesting, she thinks. Char went from the cancellation of the tournament right to depression, while she is stuck in anger. "Well, what else would you expect from a Navajo warrior," she asks aloud to herself.

Coach Jakino enters and, noticing Dyani, puts on a cloth mask she made for herself. "Hi Dyani."

Dyani slips on a mask. "Hi Coach. What's Coach having you do?"

"Contacting Char's professors to see if we can get her extensions. I think they'll be reasonable. Any word yet?"

"No, the little turd. You don't abandon The Tribe!" Kubler-Ross's anger stage rears its head.

"Are you okay if I sit at Molly's desk?"

"Yeah. I'm starving for company anyway. It's a good thing that I have this team, or I'd be a complete hermit," answers Dyani.

Coach Jakino arranges her stuff on Molly's desk, allowing a moment for Dyani's frustration at Char to settle. She hums a Beach Boys tune as she pulls up a page of high school players that she's in contact with, then asks. "You knew Char as a kid, didn't you?"

"Yeah, a little. I coached little kids during the summer, and she was one of the best, maybe the best. I think maybe as a freshman she could have made the varsity with me, but the coach already had a pretty good rotation, so Char played on the jayvees. We didn't hang around together. She wasn't originally from the rez. Came from New Mexico up near Shiprock. She moved closer to Chinle to play basketball."

"I envy your people, having your own reservation, even though things are hard. We Yakuts don't have our own land, and we're not very many anymore. I think it would have been amazing to have our own basketball team with the whole nation in the stands like your tribe." Coach Jakino is heading somewhere.

"There was nothing like those games, nothing." Dyani pauses to remember. "As much as I've loved my college career, having 6,000 people in our arena screaming their hearts out can't be replicated. And they know the game. Here, we've never played to a crowd of more than a thousand or so, and that was this year when we were undefeated. Now, we circle the wagons and play for each other."

"Isn't that what the White Man did when you attacked them?" Both women laugh at the bad metaphor. Coach Jakino continues. "You talk about those games, and I'm just in awe. When we scheduled Arizona State in your gym, that was as good a day as I've ever had. We lost a close one and then beat Arizona two days later in the consolation game. You know Coach did that for you, don't you?"

Dyani nods. "Growing up, I wanted to play at Northern Arizona, but they never recruited me, so I went to community college and had a pretty good run. I hoped NAU would recruit me then, but they just said I could walk on. I was so disappointed. Then Coach Rascon showed up at my house, and here I am."

"By the way, the ASU coach, Coach Turner Thorne, had already made feelers out about a game on the rez, so she deserves a bunch of credit for that game. I respect her for that. I guess she's been working with your people for years. She gets it. Her whole team signed autographs and toured the reservation." Jakino raises her eyebrows to Dyani. "When we recruit, we watch tons of film. Being a small D1, we have to be sure. With you, we didn't. Well, Coach Rascon didn't. She maybe watched two games and was convinced that you were the real deal. It's strange how recruiting works. We obviously had never heard of you until we got a call from your college coach. Asked if he could send a tape. How he knew about SJV and Molly's style, I don't remember. He was looking out for you though."

"Coach Rascon yells louder than he ever did. He had that look though that made me do whatever was needed."

"Maybe," Coach Jakino pauses, "maybe, Char didn't abandon the team. Mama Molly thinks Char is just so scared and lost and that she needs to be with her brothers and grandma. Her clan. Remember that first year when you needed to go home for a week, just to feel their love. Your uncle came and got you."

"Message delivered. I'll go easy on Char. Did Coach Rascon send you in here?"

Jackie Jakino raises her palms and tilts her head. "Would she do that?"

∾

Coach Robinson is angry this Monday, but it's not stage one of Kubler-Ross's chart; he's not grieving. He's upset at the president's poor response to the coronavirus crisis, especially in light of Ken Davidson's rapidly deteriorating health and the second physical attack on Kaori Park in San Francisco. On his near weekly Sunday night call with his dearest friend, Paul Garrity, Mose sees the president's attack on China for sending the virus as a smokescreen to avoid responsibility for his incompetence. The Republicans will run with that.

"Clearly, Sal, the buck stopped somewhere else than his desk," says Mose in an elevated voice, used only for politics. "His words caused the attack on Kaori and so many others. Every time he speaks about the virus, he's stoking the fires of anti-Chinese hatred which leads to these assaults on Americans. Good people just trying to do what's right, and Trump's hateful words unleashes violence on them. He's an uncaring bastard."

"Want to go for a walk?" asks Sally.

"I think our neighbors might be getting a bit tired of me ranting and gesturing as I walk down the street."

"We can drive down to the beach and walk. The porpoises always enjoy your political rants."

Fifteen minutes later, Mose and Sally are walking barefoot in the sand. "The protests this week . . . unimaginable before," says Mose in a calm voice. "Fire Fauci?! Do these people have any common sense left?"

Sally takes his hand as they stroll. "This from the guy who used to caution Paul to settle down after he attended anti-war rallies in Boulder in the late-Sixties?"

"Yep, the same. Guilty." They walk in silence on a warm sunny day at the beach.

After a few minutes of allowing her husband to go inside himself, Sally asks, "Is this about Ken?"

"It's all connected. Ken and Kaori."

Sally squeezes her old man's hand and bumps her head against his shoulder but stays quiet.

"Ken may not make it. All that press room smoking over the years. Even though he quit years ago, this virus seems to find any avenue to attack us old folks. Naomi can't even sit with him in his hospital room. Not just sad, but tragic. And not once has Trump shown any empathy for anyone with Covid or with their families." Mose's voice rises again.

∞

Mama Rascon spends a good deal more time at home these days, something her son appreciates. Her workload hasn't changed; if anything it's increased. Fewer Xs and Os, however. Frankie sits with her on his iPad while she works her phone messages, not just in the evenings but also in the afternoons. No school, no daycare, fewer excursions to Dad's office, and no time in the university gym. The stay-at-home orders curtailed that.

"That's not basketball," Frankie says pointing to the book she's perusing.

She smiles. "No, it's an old college text."

"That's not a text, it's a book."

Molly smiles again. "No, not a text, but a textbook," she replies emphasizing the *book*. "Once upon a time I was interested in things beyond basketball, at least my teachers made me interested in other things. This one is a political science textbook, a book about government, our government."

"The one you and papa are always angry with?"

Again, Molly smiles at her son, as well as to herself. "Yeah, that one, although it doesn't seem these days like the one that I studied while I was in college." She bookmarks her text and lays it on the end table. "What are you reading about?"

For the next quarter-hour, Molly and Frankie talk about news that pops up on his screen or that he googles. For an eight-year-old boy, he has an unusual interest in current events. Their time is interrupted by Dr. Frank at 6:00 with a sack of hamburgers and fries.

"Because I felt like burgers, that's why," is his response when Molly raises her eyebrows at him. He kisses her on the top of her head.

"Come on, Frankie, help me set the table."

Frankie jumps up and follows his dad into the kitchen. Frank removes his tie and dress shirt, so that he is down to a white tee shirt. Frankie sets the table for the feast, and they call for Molly. Frank lets out a loud "Aah" when he sits down, and the family holds hands while he says a quick prayer. In unison, they say "Amen" and dig in.

"Any news today?" asks Frank to Molly after he has listened to his son relate his day's events.

Coach Rascon returns to the table, sitting in the same chair that Mama Rascon also occupies. "The university will furlough most of the assistant coaches, which for me means Jackie and Nikki. I took a voluntary ten percent pay cut. The finances of this shutdown are going to be hurtful beyond what we first thought. It's not like my salary matches Coach Auriemma's where a pay cut could help fund my assistants' salaries." Coach Rascon breathes out. "Kay-kay wants to come back to school to live in the dorms. She's so afraid in San Fran because of her two episodes. I can't blame her. I checked with the dorm managers, and they said it might be possible. They have extra rooms. Char called. We talked for over an hour. I see why she's home; she seemed so, I don't know, relaxed. Maybe safe would be a better word. She wasn't making it here. Then I spoke with Dyani, and she felt the same way as I do, so we'll try to help her with her studies as best we can, but I doubt if she'll complete any of her spring courses. Kenti called to tell me she loves being a farmer, which means living on Mr. Fuchigami's farm. When the university reopens, she wants to give the team a tour of his farm. She says he's working on climate stability, which she explained to mean that the farm and those around it are working with new methods to meet the demands of climate change, new ways to make the Valley's soil more productive and retain moisture better. She was giddy about it all. Oh, more good news, Joyce got Sylvia a job as a nurses' aide at the Fresno hospital. Joyce says she's been given real nursing responsibilities. I think that's the direction Sylvia may take for her last few semesters. That fits her, I think." Molly stops and looks at her husband, who is smiling. Then, she says, "You asked."

Frank looks over at his son. "Did she leave anything out?"

"Ask her about the recruit." Frank Sr. looks back at his wife.

"I got a text from the girl in Tucson. She's crossing us off her list. And I guess I might have expressed myself in a not so ladylike manner that Frankie might have heard."

"Mom said the s-word over and over," adds Frankie.

"Well, if she would have given a reason, I could have accepted it, but she just said SJV wasn't a good fit, and that we were not to communicate with her any longer."

Frank looks at his son. "Oh, then I understand. Your mama doesn't take rejection well, and especially when she doesn't know why. Why is kind of important to her."

"But she said a naughty word!"

Frank looks at his wife. "Do you want me to explain when naughty words are sort of acceptable?" It's a rhetorical question. He has passed the ball to his wife.

Molly leans into the table and places her chin in her hands, looking intently at her son. "Sometimes, not very often, but sometimes, just saying darn or heck or shoot just doesn't convey a person's feelings adequately."

Frankie interrupts. "What does convey mean?"

"It means express." Frankie nods and waits. "Anyway, naughty words aren't to be used until a person has gained experience in communicating at an adult level, which is why you are not allowed to use them. You haven't had that experience yet. Maybe when you're in college, or possibly for a few things in high school, but not before then." Molly raises her eyebrows. "Understand."

Frankie smiles. "I think dad would probably put his hand up to his forehead with the "L" shape and call you on that."

Molly looks over at her husband. "We've raised a precocious child, you know."

Frank nods. "Certainly an insightful one."

"Your phone's ringing, mom." Frankie shifts between calling her mom, mama, coach, and Molly daily. There is a NO PHONES AT THE TABLE rule in this house, broken only for Dr. Martinez's medical emergency tone.

"We're done here. You can go get it," says Frank. "We'll get the dishes." Molly gives him a face. Carry out with paper plates. Finger food.

Molly retrieves her phone from the living room and checks the caller. Bianca Acero, her best friend from high school and still one of her dearest friends. The message: "Call. It's Queenie. They put her on a ventilator."

Chapter 8

"Coach, I got a tattoo!" says Keilani in an elevated voice.

Coach Rascon smiles into her cellphone. "You mean another tattoo, don't you, Lani? What this time?"

"It's another basketball; on my right bicep with my number inside. When I do my lifting, it appears to be bouncing."

Molly laughs to herself imagining what that might look like. "I can't wait to see it."

"Do you have any idea when that might be yet?" asks Keilani. "I want to show how much I've improved with my ball-handling skills."

"No idea yet, Lani. The NCAA is being bombarded with demands disguised as requests to restart everything, especially football which is the money machine for all other sports."

"We don't have a football team," says Keilani. "What funds our team?"

"California taxpayers," responds Molly flippantly. "That's a bit of a simplification, Lani. We get money from several sources like donors, student fees, state appropriations, but we're not a revenue generating sport, so we rely on outside sources."

Keilani lowers her tone. "I got Coach Nikki's text. She got laid off?"

Molly breathes out quietly, but it is probably audible to Keilani. "Furloughed. Coach Jakino too. Beginning May 10. They'll go on unemployment." Keilani knows what that means. "Lani, how are your parents doing?"

"We're okay. Neither of them will lose their job. *Essential workers,* you know. We got the stimulus checks, which helped a little. They won't let me work; they tell me to get back out onto the driveway and practice and don't want me breaking the stay-at-home. My older brother moved back in. He lost his job at the nice restaurant but got another one at In-N-Out. We're managing." Keilani pauses only briefly. "Coach, I didn't have to pay anything for the tattoo. My uncle did it; said I could pay him back when I get drafted."

Molly hears in Keilani's voice a hint of guilt about the cost of a tattoo. Most of her teammates have at least one tattoo. Keilani, Emerson, and Greta have multiples. Urban West Coast girls. All streetwise, although Greta is modest, while Emerson and Keilani can be . . . loud. For a moment, Molly envisions next season's lineup: Lani at the point, Emerson and Kaori on the wings, Sylvia and Greta or Esther inside. Maybe the most athletic of any team she ever coached at any stop. But no Dyani, the motor. Lani's growth will be the key. Keilani's voice interrupts her thought.

"Coach, how is everyone doing? They all put on a smiley face on the Zoom calls."

"I think, Lani, mostly okay. Like you, they miss being here as a team, and the stay-at-home makes it that much worse. So far, no one has gotten sick except Mr. Davidson, but Joyce is able to keep me up to date with his progress. Did Sylvia tell you that she got a part-time job at the same hospital in Fresno? Only Char has quit her classes, but Dyani and her Uncle Hector are helping her."

Lani breaks in. "She and Danelle are the most vulnerable, you know."

Molly is surprised by Keilani's comment. Of course, Char is the youngest and least stable, but to hear one of her players include Danelle is surprising. Molly and Frank—in his capacity as Dr. Martinez—have spoken about Danelle, but in confidence, and Ryanne knows. "Why do you say that about Danelle, Lani?"

"She couldn't hide her crying before we all left, and she misses some of the team calls. Besides, the rest of the team have all lived below the line, but she never has." Molly knows what "below the line" means; she lived there once herself. "Coach, most of us are fine and will be back raring to go when we can. Even Dyani will figure it out or at least go back to the reservation and be someone. She's so tough, but Char and Danelle, I don't know."

☙

Californians—and the rest of the nation—interpret "essential travel" differently. Living in a single dwelling with a yard allows for different associations than living in a high-rise in Los Angeles or a rental in Inglewood or on a farm in The Valley. On Wednesday, April 7, Mama Rascon and Frankie drive out to Mr. Fuchigami's farm to see Kenti Solorzano. Masks and social distance, but a walk-around. Molly has never been to Kenti's home in Central America. Kenti wasn't recruited; she simply walked into the gym and asked for a tryout, explaining that she didn't care if she ever got into a game, but that she wanted to work out with the team to keep her athletic skills toned. Competitive practices would be enough. As Molly remembers that first conversation, Kenti said, "tuned." Also, Molly's recruiting budget doesn't include trips to Guatemala. Her out-of-state players were all recommended to her by a coach who believed one of theirs was being overlooked. Dyani is the prime example, but Molly and Ryanne have been to the reservation. They have also been to Danelle's home in Colorado.

Kenti is waiting for Molly and Frankie by a field covered in plastic. She introduces her coach to several men and women in flannel shirts, none of whom appear to be a boss or supervisor. She is proud to do that. Molly wonders how many of these workers are getting tested for Covid, wonders how many of them have ever been to a doctor, how many were born in the United States. Frankie has none of those thoughts. He's able to converse politely with them in Spanish, and while Molly explained the social distance requirements again, he holds Kenti's hand frequently as they move through the fields. His papa told him that would be okay so long as he wore his latex gloves and kept his mask on. Molly walks with a plastic container of wipes.

At a picnic table under a beach umbrella emblazoned with a beer logo, Kenti has drinks and sandwiches waiting for her coach and the little boy.

"Coach, I wanted to have you here to show you I'm doing good, and you don't have to worry about this member." Molly understands. "I'm happy and learning. It's ironic that I left Guatemala to get schooling but end up just being a field worker again to get that education. I never told you about my home, about my town. I tell the school that I'm from the capital and am part Maya to get admitted. The Maya part is true, but I come from Nabaj in the mountains. It's a beautiful town." Kenti gives Frankie a plastic sack of carrots and motions for a worker to show him the horses. When he leaves the table, Kenti continues. "You have been so good to me, Coach, and I want you to know my family, but you can't because of the travel restrictions. My family wants to meet you too but can't. They are nice people who work hard to send me here." Kenti is stalling.

Molly picks up on Kenti's hesitancy. "What is it you want to tell me, Kenti?"

"You always listen." Kenti looks deeply at her coach. "I don't have grandparents. All of them were murdered in the civil war in 1982. My town is, was, considered to be communist and against the government back then, and everyone was suspected of helping the guerillas. Not the animals but the rebels. My parents lived because they hid in the jungle when the government soldiers came and burned the town down. They weren't married then. They were teenagers." Kenti stops as if she is checking Molly for permission to continue.

"I know only a little about this, that my government helped the Guatemalan military government in this civil war, that many atrocities were committed by the Guatemalan government and my government looked the other way."

Kenti smiles slightly. "You surprise me that you know that much. How is this so?"

"I studied political science and history in college. I wasn't the best student, but I learned about America's foreign policy during that time. It's not something we are proud of now, at least for some of us. Why are you telling me this?" asks Molly.

"I have told my family very much about you and your team and that you let me practice with you and be one of the team. They think very much of you." Kenti pauses; Molly waits. "They want to come meet you, but never will. My parents still fear your country and especially during Mr. Trump's reign. They will never come to America. I just want you to know that they are appreciative of you for what you give me. Not the basketball but the love. And the security."

Molly tears up and doesn't hide it. She wants to hug Kenti but follows her husband's orders and simply puts her hands over her heart. Kenti reciprocates. Kenti looks over to the corral and waves for Frankie to come back to the table. When he sits next to his mother, he takes a big swig from his soda.

"How would you like to visit Kenti's country one day?" Mama Rascon asks her son. She looks up to Kenti. "This travel restriction won't last forever, and when it's lifted, I'll come visit your family and eat everything your family puts in front of me. And I'll bring Frankie and Dr. Frank.

Kenti gives her coach and Frankie an extended tour of the farm. Again, Molly realizes how lucky she is to have players like Kenti, to be able to walk around a farm during the pandemic and to be healthy. She hopes to return to this farm frequently during the coming months and tell Kenti about her family, and when the restrictions are lifted and basketball is once again played, Coach Rascon will bring her team here to learn more about The Valley and keep Kenti as a teammate.

As Molly and Frankie prepare to leave, Kenti loads five crates of vegetables into the back of Molly's SUV. "These are for Maria and the store. Molly understands that this food is for the school's free pantry, that Maria just works there part time, that Mr. Fuchigami is giving back to The Valley, doing what he can.

Over dinner Frankie tells his papa all about the day on the farm, even though it lasted only about an hour. When he finishes and leaves the table, Frank asks Molly who won the Wisconsin Democratic Primary.

"Won't know for sure for a week because of some goofy Wisconsin court order, but rumor has it that Bernie's dropping out tomorrow. So, we get Biden to run against Trump. Two old men; old, old men." Molly shakes her head.

Frank smiles. "A Bernie-Trump campaign would have been fun, but the Trumplicans would have skewered Bernie as a communist, way beyond a socialist. Maybe Joe has the best chance to win the election.

If so, then I'm all in."

"As I said, old men. Makes me sad. Now, Joe will become a socialist in Republican ads." Molly makes a thoughtful sound. "If Trump shows a little bit of sympathy for the victims of Covid or their families, he'll win."

For the next two weeks, Coach Rascon lives with her cell permanently attached to her ear. In addition to twelve Sequoias, she has six high school girls that she is trying to persuade to join The Tribe, a dozen small donors who need reassurances, and nine members on her seasonal staff with whom she has had no personal contact in over two weeks. Molly has three scholarships to give if things stay the same. Dyani's, Danelle's, and one vacant scholarship. Kenti did not have one; her schooling was being paid for by an anonymous Guatemalan. Of the six recruits, Molly thinks she has a better than even chance to sign two of them, but one is a point guard, SJV's shallowest position. The restrictions on recruiting put in place by the NCAA have so far not hindered the SJV staff in their efforts, since most of the spring communications have always been by phone, text, videos, and emails. The one exception has been not being able to entertain the recruits on campus, although as Coach Powell thinks, that may hinder other schools more since they have more impressive facilities, something that high school kids first notice. SJV has a recent history of winning, a pace of play that kids love, and a young staff of women all eager to serve the needs of the recruit. Additionally, the SJV student body represents most of Molly's targeted players, another plus.

Coach Rascon works in the War Room, talking with Ryanne while she studies the notes on the white boards, both of their phones on speaker. "The rumor still persists that seniors are going to get an extra year of eligibility," says Ryanne. "If that happens, we can shift our focus to the Merced forward. We'll be secure at the point."

"We can't count on that, and I really don't believe it will happen. I think we both agree that Keilani can be our answer at point, but she needs a backup, and the one we count on is Char. It would be so good for her development if she had time to grow, but we both know she's not likely to return. No, Ry, I think we need to lean hard on Claudia." Molly laughs loudly enough for Ryanne to hear. "I think we have the inside track on Claudia, and that isn't the case with Ms. Prissy Merced. A one in four chance there. We could end up losing both if we relax our efforts with Claudia." Molly vows to keep Nikki focused on Claudia. "They seem to have bonded a bit."

Ryanne nods on her end and then teases. "Claudia probably believes that her growth would be better under the direction of a former All-American point guard."

Molly continues to stare at the notes on Claudia but responds. "I didn't know you were an All-American back in Chicago. Seems like on the tapes I watched of you, you were just standing on the wing waiting for a teammate to throw you the ball so you could shoot." Molly chuckles.

"Well, yeah, that, and I didn't particularly care to play defense unless it meant knocking someone down. Maybe some tiny point guard with a big ego who thought she owned the paint."

Molly sneers. "You were never quick enough, and yes, I did own the paint."

If they were working in the same office, the banter might continue, but while they are on the same page this day, Covid has them physically separate, so they hug from different locations and get on with recruiting.

≈

On the first of April, the U.S. registered its 4,000[th] death from Covid. Italy has recorded three times that number. At the end of the month, the U.S. total surpasses 70,000, about three times Italy's. Ventilators keep Ken Davidson and Queenie Roberts alive.

The end is not in sight . . .

. . . despite assurances from Vice President Pence that the country will have the "coronavirus epidemic behind us" by Memorial Day.

. . . despite President Trump's flippancy over mask wearing and social distancing.

≈

On the first of May, frustration over stay-at-home orders boils over in Michigan. Right-wing armed protesters march on the state capital, threatening physical violence against the governor. It continues the movement toward violent responses against those whose beliefs and attempts to stem the spread of the coronavirus threaten "constitutional rights." Dr. Martinez vaccinates children for other diseases on a regular basis and wears a mask at the office. Joyce Hensley wears a mask throughout her long shifts at the Fresno hospital out of safety for both her and the patients. Their masks are N-95s, and Dr. Martinez worries that most people's masks are inefficient in halting the spread of the virus.

⌇

Molly sets aside Monday, May 4 to return messages that she has put on the back burner. Normally, she returns calls within 24 hours of the day they were received, but Covid has disrupted her routine. On this day, she rises early to cook breakfast for Frank while Frankie sleeps. Generally, her husband will fix himself a yogurt and fruit bowl, toast, and juice, but this morning, she will cook huevos rancheros and sit with him and help him eat them. Molly promises not to divide her attention. She keeps this promise. At the door, Frank kisses Molly with enthusiasm as if he's making a promise of undivided attention later. The stress of Covid has disrupted that part of their lives too. Covid has sent its tentacles into every facet of life.

Waiting for Frankie to wake and demand his plate of huevos, Molly sips a coffee and makes her list. "Catchups" will be first after Frankie is fed and settled into his schoolwork, although he'll participate on the Facetime calls with the grandmas. Next, Molly will call former teammates and coaches from her college days. Because of Covid, these friends should be available to take her calls on a weekday. No video for these, just voices—warm voices from a different time. This is when Molly loves her cell phone. Then, three of her dearest friends: Bianca, Izzy, and Stevie. Bianca will talk horses and kids and update Molly on the Mountain Matrons. That part of the conversation will be difficult. The Matrons are down to four, and Queenie is in critical condition with Covid. Izzy and Molly will talk basketball. Izzy has a couple of State Championships and was charging toward a third when Colorado canceled its tournament in early March, but Izzy will put the most optimistic face on the situation. Molly envies Izzy in many ways. Izzy stayed connected with basketball but has never let it consume her life. She teaches, raises her two kids, travels a bit during the summers, and wins. Molly will save Stevie for last because no one makes her laugh more than Stevie. The ADD, loud, and off the wall Stevie. The "I just can't sit still" Stevie. Molly will begin with the same question she always asks. "Have you learned how to make a layup yet?" and the giggling will begin. Molly sets no time limits for these calls.

At 10:30 Molly ends her call with Stevie. It's time for recess, so she takes Frankie to the driveway to shoot baskets. He has a routine too that is like the one she developed in her high school years. Fifteen minutes and then juice time and a walk around the block. When they return, Frankie sits at the piano to do his scales. Molly sits on the bench with her son, marveling at one more thing he does well. At noon, Maria arrives to entertain Frankie. The weather is warm, and Maria is Frankie's favorite babysitter, more of a playmate than a sitter.

Molly now tackles the second part of her list, to return the calls of boosters and administration. These calls won't be from Molly, but from Coach Rascon. The one administrator that she talks with daily is Dr. Calhoun, the athletic director and her direct line to everything NCAA related. He is SJV's compliance officer making sure every sport follows the NCAA guidelines to the letter. SJV competes in eighteen sports at the Division I level, and there have been rumors that some of them may have to be eliminated due to budget concerns exacerbated by Covid. Since Molly speaks with Dr. Calhoun so frequently, he is not on her list for today, but if he calls her, she picks up.

Coach Rascon makes her first call. Coach Jakino's note lists two names with the word *money* underlined with an exclamation point below the names.

"Hello?"

"Hello, this is Coach Molly Rascon. I need to apologize for being tardy with this call. Is this Ms. Borges?"

"This is, but please call me Stephanie. No need to apologize. I fully understand how busy you must be trying to get all your ladies taken care of these past weeks. I'm so sorry."

"It has been hectic, that's for sure. You'll have to excuse me again, but I don't know what you called about. The note my assistant left me just has the word *money* on it, which doesn't give me much to go on."

Stephanie laughs on her end. "I've found that throwing that word around gets people's attention. As a bit of an introduction, I'm an SJV alum, class of '81, two-year starting forward for the Sequoias, and now an attorney living in Santa Barbara with two teenage grandchildren, one of whom plays on her middle school team." Stephanie laughs again. "I don't think my team won as many games during my whole career as your teams do every season."

"Is your granddaughter any good? I'm always looking for young talent." It's an icebreaker line that Molly has used before.

Stephanie doesn't miss a beat. "She'd better be, or her grandma won't be happy after all the money I've spent sending her to basketball camps and that AAU stuff. But that's not why I called. My best friend, who never played college basketball but is a geek about it none-the-less, and I were talking about how we missed not having the tournaments this year." Stephanie pauses. Then, "I hope you're getting a picture of two 60-year-old women having lattes at Starbucks in Montecito discussing March Madness, lamenting its cancellation."

Molly laughs. "I can see that, but it would be two men at a bar over beers."

"Beers are a part of our diets, as well as wine, but in this instance, it was lattes. Anyway, Janet, my friend, had just finished reading a book about a Native American girl in Montana who played basketball, which led to the connection to your team. Another friend had recommended it to her. As I'm sure you're aware, a man named Ken Davidson writes a basketball blog about my alma mater, and one of those blogs was about one of your players, Dyani Dehiya, and about what a unique player she is."

Molly interrupts. "I don't know if you know, but Ken is in the hospital in Fresno with Covid. It's serious."

"Oh, my God!"

Molly speaks softly. "Ken is on a ventilator. He's been following our team closely over the past two years, since he retired, and he knows all my ladies very well, but he's probably closest to Dyani. I wouldn't be surprised if Dyani hasn't also read that book."

"I'm so sorry. Please send along my regards." Stephanie pauses. "Back to my call. Janet and I and our husbands would like to become financial supporters of your program. No strings attached. Janet runs a non-profit, so she understands the value of donations." Stephanie pauses and giggles. "I assume your basketball team isn't turning a profit each year?" It's a rhetorical question and Molly laughs. Stephanie continues. "Both our husbands are SJV grads, so that makes three of us who already donate a small amount to the school, but after beers and wines a few nights later, we decided we'd like to do more. So, what I'd like from you is a list of things your program needs that we could help you with and the name of SJV's person who we might contact to make our donation."

"That is so generous of you. Thank you so much. We are in need of a few new basketballs."

Stephanie understands the joke and laughs politely. "Maybe new practice jerseys too? Actually, we were thinking in terms of a large upfront donation and then a continuing contribution. The donation would stipulate that a part of our contribution would endow you and your staff at a higher and more stable salary. When the pandemic restrictions are lifted, we would like to meet you, maybe for some of those beers."

Molly knows how to be quiet when the situation requires it, but at this moment she is stunned. While Stephanie waits, Molly collects herself. "You're not just talking about meal money, are you?"

"No, Sweetheart." Molly smiles a big smile when she hears that term on this day. Queenie's word. Stephanie continues. "This will be a substantial gift that will be managed by an investment firm. We're thinking in terms of an initial amount of a half-million dollars with sustaining amounts yearly. We want this to be a reliable revenue stream that you have access to . . . in perpetuity. All we would ask in return for ourselves would be season tickets at the end of your bench, so we could hear your words of wisdom for your players." Quickly, Stephanie amends her last sentence. "I hope you know I'm kidding about the seats. Also, this gift is to be anonymous. You can thank Mr. Davidson for publicizing what you do so well. We are proud of you. You make our university proud."

A hundred thoughts pass through Molly's brain at this moment. "I think I can find you some pretty good seats. We don't sell out often."

The two women converse for another half-hour as Stephanie asks about every player, about the assistant coaches, about Molly's family. While they talk, Molly begins a list of wants. When Stephanie ends the talk, Molly sits alone in silence interrupted only by Frankie's reappearance. After a quick sandwich with Maria and Frankie, Molly texts her husband.

"Boy, do I have a surprise for you when you get home tonight!"

Stephanie Borges calls her friend Janet Caldwell to relate her call with the SJV coach. "She's poised, that's for sure. I think she was a bit stunned when I mentioned the dollar amount, but she quickly recovered."

"I'm meeting my husband at the golf course this afternoon. Just nine, but I'll tell him to talk with the board again. I'm excited about this." Janet clicks off her cell but keeps it in her hand as she sips a warm coffee. She didn't go to college, but she now feels a sense of ownership with a school she would never have attended forty years ago, a university that she never considered for her two children, both of whom attended UC Santa Barbara. After working with environmental organizations in her twenties, Janet switched to helping people more directly, more specifically teenage girls. The roundball geek in her sent her to watch a high school basketball game between Santa Barbara High School and Oxnard a year earlier with her granddaughter. Watching the Oxnard girls ferociously competing against the Santa Barbara Dons, she was impressed by the tenacity of Oxnard, especially that one girl, Greta Espinoza. When she later read that Greta had accepted a scholarship to play at SJV, the alma mater of Stephanie and the husbands, Janet's generous mind began to whirl.

Molly Rascon charts her life as BF/SF. Before Frank/Since Frank. BF was compartmentalized. There was basketball and then the "other things," things that should have been given a more important place in daily affairs. Coaches tend to do that, to place people in their lives on hold. Molly's immediate family was her players, her ladies, which meant that her mother, father, and brother didn't receive phone calls or texts on a regular basis. When her brother Alex was killed in Afghanistan in '06, she hadn't communicated with him in nearly four months. She was devastated. She vowed to be better with her mother, but even that slid for a time. When Frank proposed to Molly, she warned him about her priorities, and Frank verbally committed to her quest for a head coaching job at a D1 school, but he made a vow to himself that he wouldn't take a backseat to basketball, and he has kept that vow. To himself and to her and now for Frankie. Frank keeps lists too, and he checks off Molly's call to her mother every Sunday, her attendance at Frankie's school events, and regular nights "going to bed on time," although Frank doesn't need to note that on his list.

Dr. Frank arrives home around 7:00. Frankie has finished dinner and is now texting with his grandmother, making plans for a Disneyland trip later in the summer. Molly hands Frank a beer and leads him to the dinner table where a plate of spaghetti sits covered with a plastic plate. As he eats, she tells him about her call with Stephanie Borges and her discussion with her athletic director.

"Dr. Calhoun went over the basics about a coaching endowment, how it's set up and all. I asked him if it was specific to me, that say if I didn't win the NCAA tournament next year and he fired me, would the endowment continue for the next coach. He assured me that my job wasn't on the line and that having the money was neither a reason for keeping a coach or releasing a coach."

"I'm pretty sure your job isn't on the line."

"Calhoun was joking about that. Anyway, Ms. Borges and I hit it off on the phone, but I told her that any endowment could not be tied to me specifically, but to the SJV coach, whoever that might be. She understood that but told me they had done their research about donating money and knew that before offering this gift. She told me their organization has made endowments before, so she knows the money doesn't flow overnight."

Frank has several questions. Dealing with young children, however, has taught him to be patient, to listen to their stories all the way to completion. It's a habit that he now carries over to adult conversations; he almost never interrupts, often to the point of seemingly withdrawing. But he hasn't; he's patient. Frankie, however, does interrupt one of his parents frequently. His conversation with his grandmother over, he comes bounding back to the table. Since this grandma is his papa's mother, most of Frankie's comments are directed to his dad. Molly excuses herself to call another one of her coaches.

"Hey, Mose, it's Molly. Am I interrupting anything?"

"No. Sally and me are just contemplating retirement again." Sally must be sitting next to her husband, because she speaks into his cell, telling Molly that Mose was taking an after-dinner nap. Mose corrects Sally. "That's how I do some of my best contemplating. What's up?"

"I just wanted to tell you about a conversation I had today, but I guess I need to warn you that it may impact your retirement a bit." Mose makes an old-man noise on his end. "I spoke at length with a woman from Santa Barbara, you know, your rich neighbors up the coast. Nice lady. A lawyer. She and her husband and another couple want to make a generous gift to the university."

"Why would a few people donating money to UCSB matter to me? It happens all the time."

"No, Mose. They want to donate money to SJV, to us, to endow our basketball program." Molly goes on to relate parts of the conversation and how those parts might affect him, that she wants to hire him back, this year at a regular salary."

Mose responds to the pay part. "What you paid me before is just fine. If I'm making too much, I might feel like I'd have to do more, you know, like watching lots more film." It's a standard line that Mose uses with Coach Rascon, that some aspects of coaching might be a bit overdone, like film sessions. "I still want to be able to get up from some of your extended meetings and come home to Sally."

Molly nods on her end and lets out a soft laugh. She loves this old man who reminds her in so many ways of her high school coach, understated but so insightful about the game and the personalities of her players. Mose has been the perfect complement to her staff, the grandfather that every young woman needs at times. Molly knows that she is the fire, but fire sometimes can get too hot for a hormonal twenty-year-old playing an emotional game. Molly's fire can sometimes be too hot for herself. Mose can soften her voice, not her enthusiasm, but her tone.

"Coach, can I ask you something, something that I've asked you before, but I want you to give me a more serious answer? How did you just walk away from the NBA, from the biggest stage? Don't tell me that your body just wore out again, tell me the real reasons."

In Oxnard Mose straightens his body on the couch and clears his voice. He looks at his wife who has been listening to Molly's account of more money about to be infused into her program. "Well, Coach, okay. Having my body ache most of the time during the season had some part of my decision, but I won't use that. I had walked away before. I learned how to walk away; some might call it quitting, but I never sealed the deal. I didn't want to play my senior year in high school. I just wanted the recruiting drama to go away, and my mom wasn't feeling well, doing too much for me so I could play. My high school coach, who I respected so much, and my mom sat me down and talked some sense into me, so I continued and got a scholarship, but one that was far away from California. I wanted to remove myself from my neighborhood adulation. Could have gone to UCSB myself. Then, I walked away after my freshman year at Colorado. My coach there was a screamer, and you can guess how I responded to that. My roommate talked me through that episode. I love basketball, but I hate the animosity that is sometimes required, or at least that some people think is required to play at high levels."

"But the NBA?" asks Molly.

"It was a long time ago, so I can't give you the exact moment, but at some point, I saw a different path. First, and since she's sitting here, I'll get bonus points for saying this, but it's true; I really missed Sally during the season. She's kind of important to me, you know. I also had a good friend who needed my support."

"Aww, Mose, you old softie," says Molly.

"No shit." He laughs. "We also wanted to start a family, and I wasn't going to have Sally raise the kid alone, or as it turned out, kids. We talked about it all during my last season, and I inquired about teaching here in Oxnard, and they basically offered me a job if I came back." Mose pauses and smiles to his wife. "You know, 'two roads diverged in a yellow wood, . . .'"

Molly finishes the poem, ". . .'and I took the one less traveled by, and that has made all the difference.'"

"There you go again," says Mose, "You continue to surprise me."

"That I've read something other than a scouting report?"

"Yeah."

"Anyway, getting back to the purpose of my call. If this money actually does appear, I want you back on staff, and I want Sally up here as support too."

∾

Tulare and Visalia do not hold their traditional Cinco de Maya celebrations in 2020, canceling at the last moment because of stay-at-home orders. Music and food, necessary for successful gatherings, go missing in the downtown streets and parks. Frank remarks that it is as if the French had won the Battle of Puebla 158 years earlier, and that General Zaragoza had been captured and hanged. The stay-at-home directives are causing a severe economic hit on Tulare's businesses.

Molly and her AD Dr. Calhoun discuss again the endowment offer, specifically how quickly a gift like this could be used. Dr. Calhoun teases Molly that she cannot start drawing from it this week. "Wait at least until we see a bank statement."

Coach Rascon's call with Char brings some optimism to Molly. Char reminds her coach that she can just say Natives instead of the cumbersome Native Americans, or better yet just say Indian. "We do most of the time." While Char has not completed most of her assignments, she at least contacted her professors, and Coach Jakino's efforts as a tutor/facilitator seem to be helping. Char and Dyani are talking daily and texting almost hourly.

Molly tells Char that she will continue to say Native or Diné and avoid the old term Indian. "I get the same thing with *my people*. Am I

Latina, Latinx, Hispanic, or Chicana?"

Char laughs. "Chicana. Definitely Chicana. Don't tell Sylvia and Maria that I told you this, but sometimes after we've had a tough practice where you've been hard on us, they'll call you that, meaning a hard-ass chick."

Molly can't stop laughing at this.

☙

Dr. Frank says goodbye to his last patient, does a bit of paperwork, shares the last work with his nurse and receptionist, locks the office and goes to his car where he sits reading a text from a friend, a fellow pediatrician who works in Los Angeles. Frank is stunned. As of May 6, more than 260 nurses have died of Covid. Two … hundred … sixty. He wanted to know, and now he doesn't. The front lines are taking a terrible hit, but he knows the nurses will return tomorrow and the next day and the next.

☙

Forty-five miles north on CA 99, Joyce Hensley and Sylvia Castro begin their shift at the Fresno hospital. Joyce dons the PPE over her coveralls: gown, hood, gloves, mask, goggles, and face shield. Sylvia does not have personal contact with patients, so she only wears a mask and gloves around the hospital and is told to reuse these protections throughout the day due to shortages. Sylvia already has a rash near her nose where the metal clip rubs. When their shifts end in the morning, Joyce will go to her parents' house and fall into bed exhausted. Sylvia will return to the dorm in Tulare, spend three hours in front of her computer with classes, and then fall into bed exhausted. Before doing it all over again that evening, Sylvia will call Coach Rascon and tell her she's doing fine, "learning a lot real fast. We're really trying to stay ahead."

Molly checks to determine when the team that is still in Tulare has a free afternoon. As it turns out, that will be Sunday. Mothers' Day.

☙

Frankie wants a dog, always has, but his parents won't allow it because of his asthma. It showed up early when the family moved to

117

Tulare in the spring of 2015 when his mother was hired as the head basketball coach at San Joaquin Valley University. On this Sunday morning, as his parents set up the backyard for a social-distancing late lunch, Frankie plays frisbee with the neighbor's border collie. There is no fence between the two yards. To his father, the dog seems to be living up to its name and babysitting Frankie by keeping him within the boundaries of the yards. When the dog retrieves the frisbee, she always brings it to the patio so that Frankie is herded back to home base. Frankie's asthma seems to ease in the summer months, and Dr. Frank knows that the Valley's air is bad all year round, but that the winter particulates are more dangerous. In every season, Frankie carries his inhaler.

In preparation for this gathering, Frank buys ten folding chairs all equipped with a cup holder. Easy to store when not in use, and easy to set up on the lawn at safe distances during the pandemic. Seven players will arrive around 1:00 along with three assistant coaches. Molly and Frank will sit on the deck in patio chairs, along with Frankie, if he ever sits. All will wear masks. Molly remarks that the team seems more like a band of outlaws than a tribe, but she says this not as a complaint.

Kaori arrives first, driving down from Sunnyvale. She will be moving back into a dorm room after the gathering. She brings a dish of shrimp numbering nearly 100 along with a San Francisco cocktail sauce. Kaori has the nicest car of all the ladies, a two-year old SUV which now is packed with her clothes and accoutrements for moving back into a dorm room. The university granted her an exemption due to the physical attacks on her.

"I can't tell you how nice this is to be back," Kaori says to her coach. "I can't wait to see everyone."

Maria and Sylvia arrive together, walking over from the campus. Both are wearing their SJV Champions caps that Molly gave them when the season was canceled. Kenti drives from Mr. Fuchigami's farm in one of the pickups that has the farm name on both doors. Dyani dribbles up for effect, reminding her coach that while the season may have been halted, basketball is a lifestyle choice, and she has made hers. Dyani spent an hour prior to this gathering at the Kappa Sigma frat house two blocks away shooting baskets. She dated a Kappa Sig for a time, a guy who played intramurals and was pretty good. The Kappa Sig house has a private court behind their house. Joyce drives from Fresno and brings two buckets of chicken for the picnic. Esther is the last of the players to arrive. She sports a pink baseball cap tilted off to the side with San Diego embossed on the front. The three assistant coaches, Ryanne, Nicole, and Jackie arrive shortly after. Nicole and Jackie will officially be furloughed on Monday.

It's a sunny day in The Valley, not too hot and little wind. Coach Rascon has a brief introductory welcome, saying how good it is to see them together again, but mostly she just serves food from the patio. At 2:00, Ryanne instructs everyone to take out their cellphones and call their mothers. Just as Molly reaches for her phone that sits on the grill, it rings. It's Frankie, and from his chair ten feet away, he giggles. Kenti, Dyani, and Esther aren't' able to make this call, so they call Keilani, Emerson, and Greta instead.

The picnic lasts for two hours, the length of time the university recommends for such a gathering, and the players all take leftovers. Ryanne, Nikki, and Jackie help clean up—at a distance—before they too head out. Frank has Frankie help fold up the chairs and put them away in the back shed. Molly tries to contact Danelle, but she doesn't pick up. Then, Molly calls Hector Dehiya to ask about Char.

Hector can always be counted on in moments of crises. "She's much better now. I think we've got her doing her studies again. One of her brothers is taking her to the library so she can get a regular internet connection, and she has to meet with me daily. Dyani really has a calming effect on her since you spoke with Dyani. It's a difficult time and The Nation is struggling with new cases daily. The People don't have much trust in the government, as one might expect, but we're trying to get the word out. Char is saying she wants to return to school once the campus opens back up. That's a positive sign. Still, . . ."

"The team asked about her, wishes she was here."

❧

In bed Molly and Frank talk.
"Interesting day, to say the least," says Frank.
"The picnic was so good for us all."

"Lots of smiles. Good vibes. Nice to see Kaori again. She's been through it."

Molly kisses her husband. "I think most of the gals are managing pretty well. If we can just get through this semester, maybe things will settle down. The university is making dual plans for the fall, but if the students have some confidence in themselves and what's to be expected, I think they can do this," Molly pauses. "By the way, did you hear Kenti say she might want to play again next season if we had a spot, if we even have a next season?"

"No, I didn't hear that. She's such a wonderful young lady. Really enjoying her stay on the farm."

The monitor that Molly and Frank use to be alerted to Frankie's breathing beeps, and Molly gets up to check on him. She returns mostly unconcerned. "He had a busy day mostly outside. Damn pollution." Molly slides into her husband's body again.

"He beat Sylvia in horse, you know."

"She lets him. Notice that Kay-kay beat him though."

This Mothers' Day has been one of the best days since the tournament was canceled; not perfect, but very good.

∞

But then Monday comes. In Denver, an old, Black woman dies alone in the hospital, her wife coming every day to the parking lot to wave and hope the nursing staff will relay that love to her. Queenie Roberts is Colorado's seventeenth death. It is Bianca Acero who calls.

"Hey, Molly, it's me. Bad news. Queenie passed this morning. I just got off the phone with Mercedes." Bianca chokes up, and the call goes silent for a few moments as Molly begins to cry also. "Mercedes told me to be prepared last week." Bianca goes quiet again.

When Molly and Bianca were juniors in high school, a group of eight women in their poor town of Oro Hills, Colorado, raised money and provided unconditional love for a team that had never won a game. Two seasons later, that team won a State Championship, and a life-long bond developed. Now, only three of the Mountain Matrons survive, all in their eighties, Queenie was the heart of the Matrons, the loudest, huggiest, biggest hearted, most generous, the fighter who taught the girls that poverty was just an obstacle, not a sentence. For every event, college graduations to weddings, Queenie Roberts and Mercedes Spinelli were there. They are Frankie's godparents, and Bianca's daughter's godparents, and Izzy's daughters' godparents, and Stevie's. Queenie found Penny Mathews and breathed air into her damaged life and provided a line to recovery. Penny is now a nurse in Colorado Springs.

Molly finally finds her voice. "When will the funeral be?"

"There won't be for now. Covid kills those too."

"Was Mercedes able to talk much?"

"You know Mercedes; she'll carry on, go back to the ranch and work."

Molly knows. It was Mercedes who taught Bianca to ride horses and then gave her a horse when she went off to college. It was Queenie and Mercedes who paid for Bianca's graduate studies in veterinary medicine. It was Queenie who paid for Ryanne's legal fees nine years ago.

Bianca speaks through her tears. "I have to call the others, but I want to talk tonight, even if we just hold our cells to our ears and cry. Okay?"

"Yeah," Molly gets out. "I love ya, Big Stallion." Molly closes the call, lays her cell on the table, puts her head in her hands and sobs.

That magic time in her life is taking a hit.

Frankie is at the gym with Maria or Sylvia, but Molly is thankful he doesn't have to see his mama at this moment. She wants to call Frank, but she won't be able to talk, and he will be with a patient. She texts him, telling him Queenie has died and that she will tell him all about it when he gets home for dinner. Molly knows that any call with an old high school teammate will be impossible at this moment. Too raw. Molly calls Ryanne.

"Can I come over?"

෨

"Have you eaten this morning?"

Molly nods. "Yeah."

Ryanne pours two cups of coffee and leads her best friend to a cushioned bay window overlooking a small back yard. They sit without speaking for several minutes, each with one leg tucked beneath the other, mostly not drinking their coffee, just holding it like a precious stone. While Molly stares out the window, Ryanne looks at Molly. A time to speak, a time for silence. Tears stream down Molly's cheeks. She takes another tissue, blows her nose hard, wipes her cheeks and then looks at Ryanne.

"She called all of us 'sweetheart.'" Molly opens her eyes wide in an effort to stem the tears. "The daughters she never had. I can't imagine her dying in a hospital bed alone. Imagine is the wrong word. I can imagine it; I just can't comprehend it. Covid." Molly says the word with such disdain, almost with hatred. She steels her jaw. Ryanne reaches over to take one of Molly's hands. Molly curls both lips into her mouth and looks out the window again. "She was such a force," says Molly softly. She turns back to Ryanne with questioning eyes. "If Covid can take Queenie, it can run over this whole country. It's going to be bad."

The two women sit like this for another hour, Molly speaking in broken sentences with Ryanne listening gently. A text from Sylvia reminds Molly that Frankie will be needing lunch soon. Only then does Molly stir. At the door, she hugs Ryanne despite protocols, thanks her for listening—an unnecessary gesture—and leaves. Ryanne watches Molly drive away but doesn't move away from the door. "A force." Nine years ago, Queenie said with conviction, "We will not allow that man to win!" One Black woman to another Black woman. "We will not allow that man to win!"

Molly and Bianca speak through their tears for nearly a half hour, and then Bianca suggests they expand the call to include Izzy, Stevie, Rosa, and Cindy. Therapeutic. Finally, laughter begins to creep through the cracks of their grief, and the old teammates from a different time provide Queenie with the goodbye she deserves. Queenie would have reprimanded the team if they wallowed in sadness. Lives are led to be celebrated, she would have told them, so they tell stories and build upon those. "I remember that one time when she . . .," and another girl adds to it.

In Molly's home, Frank and Frankie sit close and listen in. Frankie giggles constantly, so hard at times that his papa has to take him into the kitchen so the women can continue. Queenie wasn't happy with Molly's first husband, but she adored Frank Martinez. When Molly told Queenie about Frank's proposal, she flew out to meet him, to put her stamp of approval on him. Gold Star, A+. Queenie read people, liked most of them, and loved the special ones—unconditionally.

Damn Covid-19. Damn, damn, damn. Amid all the stories worth telling in 2020, it interjects itself into everyone—in the worst way.

Two days later, Frankie has a difficult time breathing, and it scares him and his mother. Molly calls her husband, who immediately comes home. It turns out to be an asthma attack probably brought on by the air pollution, and Frank has a spare inhaler for his son. Not Covid.

"Why didn't you use your inhaler?" asks Frank.

"I couldn't find it."

Frank looks to Molly who is holding it. "It was under your pillow." She holds it up and lowers her chin, a reminder that whenever he goes outside, he's to take his inhaler.

Dr. Frank tells the patient and his mother that Frankie is to stay indoors for the rest of the day, and if he continues to wheeze, then she is to take him to his clinic for extra treatment. He's been there before for this same thing. "Work on your math this afternoon and a little Spanish." Frank taps his son on his thigh, stands and hugs his wife. "I'll be home early; light patient load today."

When Frank leaves, Molly fixes Frankie lunch and sits with him. He finishes, and then lays down on the couch for a nap. Molly sits close by and texts her players. Then she googles *Seattle, Washington, air pollution*.

Chapter 9

Dyani and Coach Rascon text daily. Dyani is one of those rare great players who responded to every coaching style along the way. She respected her coaches, and they respected her. Molly knows that her own style is different from Dyani's high school coach and her junior college coach.

Dyani sends the first text. "Coach, can I get paid for all the coaching stuff I'm doing for you? I think I've convinced Claudia to come here and take my place."

Molly laughs. She knows that Dyani has had extensive conversations with the high school senior about signing with SJV. "Just consider this an independent study or on-the-job training for your next career. You can combine this with your sociology degree and be an outstanding coach. Your recommendation will also include notes about your dances at practices and your demands that teammates buy you coffee on the weekends."

"LOL!!!!!! What's today's memo about playing games next season?"

"All rumors still. AD Calhoun doesn't think so, but tomorrow's news could say something different."

"My Uncle Hector says to say hi. I pray he's got Char on the path."

"I think you've done wonders for her too. You're her rock. You're my rock."

Dyani texts a heart emoji. "Thinking about staying here in the dorm for summer school. Better AC than at my house in Chinle."

Molly smiles at Dyani's humor. Molly knows that Dyani's life is basketball, probably from the time she began grade school, but Molly senses that the isolation of the pandemic is both a crisis moment for Dyani and a time for introspection. Growth. "What about your boyfriend back home?"

"Over. No ambition."

"When?"

"Couple of weeks ago. No biggie. How's Frankie?"

"Comes and goes. His last episode scared me a bit. I need to hang his inhaler around his neck."

"Tulare needs a dome." Very quickly, Dyani adds a second text. "Mind if I give Danelle some guidance?"

∾

As the semester ends and the ladies receive their grades, it's apparent that eleven of the twelve will earn all their credits. Only Char receives incompletes with credit withheld for now. To receive all-academic honors in the Ring of Fire Conference, an athlete must earn a 3.2 gpa. Based on preliminary reports, and a call from her AD, Molly thinks seven of her players will be honored. Kaori leads the way with her fourth consecutive semester at 4.0. Emerson receives one B, and if Sylvia scored well on her last final, she might be the eighth all-academic honoree. The four freshmen are not eligible but, except for Char, pass all their classes. Online learning was not easy, but Molly is so proud of her team's grit. San Joaquin Valley has just over 11,000 students with just a 50-percent graduation rate. The majority of the students come from poor homes that must come up with $6,000 in tuition after grants to send their sons and daughters to college, plus the rest of what college costs. Molly's ladies are all on scholarship, and she insists that they produce not only on the court but in the classroom. Unknown donors and taxpayers deserve a return on their investments in the ladies' futures. Since her second year as head coach of the Sequoias, every eligible senior has graduated. Every recruit hears that promise: "If you come to SJV, you will graduate." A handful of players haven't made it, have dropped out before their senior year, each one hurting Coach Rascon, but the goal remains the same.

Coach Aikins interviewed for a high school coaching job in a middle-class Los Angeles neighborhood, and on May 22 is informed that she has won the position. She will also teach mathematics and statistics. She had applied back in January while the season was still in progress. Now, Ryanne, Jackie, and Molly want to give her a small celebratory party. They want to give her a big sendoff, but protocols prevent that, so they meet in Molly's backyard. A banner hangs over the patio and champagne flows. A Zoom call allows nine of The Tribe to wish Coach Nikki well, to thank her for everything.

Later that night, Dyani asks Coach Rascon about her path into coaching; how she ended up in Tulare at SJV.

"I know you were a good college player, but did you need any coaching classes?"

"No, D, I just moved from the player end of the bench to the coaching end. I became my coach's assistant.

"How long did you stay there? I mean, like, did you have a plan in your head to become a D1 coach?"

Molly thinks. "I guess I did, but there was no timetable, and D1 didn't seem like a possibility. I considered being a high school coach, but never applied since I was having so much fun as an assistant. It was like my hair was on fire."

Dyani laughs out loud into her cell. "That's a goofy phrase! I only know what you mean because my uncle uses it. How long did you stay at your college before you got the job in California?"

"Let's see. I stayed at State Tech for three seasons and then went with another one of the assistants to Cal Irvine. She was my coach's head assistant, and I liked her a lot, and she asked me to come with her. I think I stayed there for four more seasons and then got the head job in Thousand Oaks. Cal Coastal."

Dyani interrupts. "That was a good job, wasn't it?"

"Yes," answers Molly with a bit of hesitancy.

"Then, why?"

"Selfishly, I wanted to coach better players, players like you and Emerson. I really did see myself in this scenario. True D1 players. Coastal inspired this confidence in myself that I could do that. And I like recruiting and then teaching. I also like having players like you who didn't get offers from the UCLAs of the world and have something to prove."

"Since Coach Aikins is leaving, would you consider me for her position?" It's the question Dyani called to ask.

Molly knows the difficulty that Native Americans have completing a four-year degree. She knows the percentages, which is the reason she is so proud of Dyani and why she is so concerned about Char. Molly can't take all the credit for Dyani; there were special people in her life from the moment she left the reservation, people who refused to allow her to fail: coaches, counselors, professors, and always her Uncle Hector. In a sense, these people sent Dyani to Coach Rascon to carry the torch for this special young lady.

Molly sits quietly still holding her phone as Dyani clicks off. She thinks about the end of her own basketball playing career at State Tech nearly 20 years ago, the apprehension of moving forward without a basketball in her hands. Then, a coaching position opened allowing her to remain at her university for a few more years. Molly had people along the way too, not so much to teach her basketball skills, but to teach her the one life skill so important for girls/young ladies of color: perseverance. Molly has drawn a line through Coach Aikens' name, and now beside it, she writes Dyani Dehiya.

It's Memorial Day, May 25, and a video of the murder of George Floyd surfaces. Protests erupt in Minneapolis, protests that will most assuredly spread across the land. Molly and Frank watch in horror and will not allow Frankie to watch. Coach Rascon decides to hold a Zoom conference with her team in the evening. They held one on Sunday night, a celebratory call at the end of the semester. This one won't be.

"I'm guessing that all of you have seen the video by now," says Coach Rascon. Nine players and Coach Powell are listening. Only Char, Kenti, and Joyce, who is working a hospital shift, are not present. "It's a terrible thing to witness."

"It's just a terrible thing!" says Keilani forcefully. "Cell phones bring these things into the light, but they've been happening forever. That cop won't be held responsible. Already, the police department is saying terrible things about George Floyd, like it's his fault."

Sylvia piggybacks. "My dad is always warning Maria and me to stay away from the downtown police in El Paso, that they're not our friends. The police on the base, the MPs are okay, but not the city cops. They think they're above the law." Her voice shakes.

Words like *angry, disgusted, shocked* are voiced by the ladies as Molly and Ryanne listen. They want their team to vent, to get out their feelings. The two coaches have "the talk" with the team every fall.

Esther speaks softly. "My mom used to tell me that we came to America to get away from this type of policing. In Mexico City, it's worse, I guess, but I was too young to see it, but she tells me the same thing. When I'm out, I need to be on my best behavior and not do anything that will give the police a reason to arrest me."

"The only reason we give them is that our skin is black," says Emerson. "Mostly, they don't need any other reason."

Molly is not surprised that it's Keilani and Emerson who are the most vocal. City girls. Mixed race, but in America, that means Black. There is a lull in the conversation, and then Coach Powell speaks.

"Los Angeles, Minneapolis, El Paso, or in my case, Chicago. The city. Any city. People of color know." Ryanne stops for a moment, measuring her words for The Tribe. "Only Coach knows my story. In Chicago," she takes a deep breath, "I was an angry teenager, not openly afraid of anyone. Inside, scared to death. Like all you gals, I could hoop, and that alone got me out of my neighborhood. Good thing because I might be dead by now. I have scars from my fighting. Like some of you, I don't trust the cops. From Chicago, I made it to California. Irvine. That's where Coach and I met, as assistant coaches. One night I was out on the town and got into a heated argument with a couple of cops, and you gals know what happens when a Black woman confronts a cop. The charge later was *resisting arrest,* and I spent a night in jail before Coach bailed me out. What I resisted was being pushed to the ground and trying to get up. Three cops laying their hands on me because I was leaning against a nice car. I was waiting outside a restaurant while my friends paid the bill inside. It was my birthday, but there was no explaining to the cops. Finally, I hit one—after I had been pushed up against the wall." Ryanne pauses again.

Keilani asks, "I'm jumping ahead here, but how did you get a job coaching if you have a felony on your record? I mean, this is a state university, and that kinda goes against the rules, doesn't it?"

Ryanne and Molly laugh lightly. Ryanne continues, "As I said, Coach was inside paying for our group's dinner and came out to find me on my stomach handcuffed. No, I didn't have a cop on my neck, but he did have his hand on my back. I thought they might arrest Coach too, but she managed to settle me down, at least enough to get me off the ground and into the cop car. To make a long story short, the university vouched for my character, and Coach's friend Queenie, who was a lawyer, got some of her California lawyer friends to help me out. I got off with a misdemeanor, thank God. Without Coach, I'd be in prison now." She ends her story without providing "the moral of the story."

Greta has her own story but tells it generically. "Oxnard is mostly a Latin city, but when my parents were kids and some of the LA gangs moved in, there were lots of conflicts. Protecting our turf, you know. My dad has a record; so many of the men and boys do and a few of the women. A person can stand up against other minorities but not against the cops. They always win."

"I don't have any of your experiences," says Danelle. "I've heard about it, but never experienced it. The police have always treated me with respect. I'm sorry."

"All of us except maybe you, Danelle, are Black Lives Matter in some way," says Keilani. "Coach knows and supports us.

Dyani jumps in. "Not me. I'm still on the warpath with Russell Means." The team doesn't know who he is, but Coach Rascon explains and tells the gals that Dyani is slightly kidding, her way of telling her sisters that she supports them. Dyani continues. "America is just so racist. When it confronts a person of color, it just goes brain dead, especially if we act out of place."

"I can vouch for that. I've been pushed down and yelled at twice since the pandemic hit," says Kaori. "And I don't think I have it as bad as the rest of you guys."

As her players vent, Molly recalls events in her life. Her last name put her into a certain category, but her looks did not. She mostly took her mother's features, the Anderson side of the marriage. She believes that Cal Coastal considered her ethnicity in a positive way when they offered her the head coaching position. She knows SJV did, that the university linked her ethnicity to the demographics of the student body. Molly also uses her ethnicity in recruiting. "I understand. I can relate." Molly does understand, and bringing these players to SJV has provided them with a haven for a few years and allows her the incubator needed to mold them into incredible women. *Mold*. It's the word her husband uses, both as a compliment and as a tease. "Your mama molds—and wins games," Frank tells Frankie.

Keilani brings Coach Rascon back to the discussion. "Coach, I know you don't want us to join the crowds and protest, but it's something I need to do."

"No. Why would you think I wouldn't want you to protest? I would be proud of you. I want you to always stand up for what's right and protect all that you are."

Ryanne jumps in. "No slapping policemen but wear your Black Lives Matter shirts." She laughs. "Don't force Coach to come bail you out of jail."

The call ends on what Molly feels is a note of optimism, that the ladies feel there is something they can do after nearly three months of having little control of their lives. She gets up from the kitchen table, walks to the living room where her boys are working with their iPads, and sits with them. She is conflicted; her little universe has been turned upside down, Covid by itself is a severe health threat that will wreak havoc, but to Molly it seems like a messenger exposing the fundamental inequalities of the Disunited States of America. She fears for her young ladies, but it goes beyond that. Maybe for the first time in her life, except for Frank and Frankie, Molly prioritizes something above basketball.

༄

"Coach, do you want some good news for a change?" It's Joyce Hensley.

"Always."

"Mr. Davidson was taken off the ventilator this morning. He's doing well. A little confused, but he's going to make it. We don't yet know what problems he'll have coming off the ventilator, but his life isn't in danger anymore. I thought you might know."

"Thank you, Joyce. That's wonderful! How are you holding up?" asks Molly.

"I think better than most of the nurses. I don't have to take care of my own family like most of them do. I can just go home and collapse. I kind of self-quarantine away from the hospital. Sleep, homework, eat, shoot hoops on my driveway. Coach, could you call Coach Robinson and tell him. He's called either Mrs. Davidson or the hospital nearly every day."

"I will right away. Thank you, Joyce. Be safe."

Coach and player end the call. The player changes out her protective garb, writes up a report, and then redons new protective wear and moves on to another patient. The coach texts her husband with the good news and then calls Mose Robinson.

"Hey, Coach, I already heard the good news; just got off the phone with Naomi. She couldn't talk much, but obviously is relieved." Mose's voice indicates he's relieved too.

The two coaches talk of problems that Ken Davidson may still face, the lingering effects of being on a ventilator for a few weeks. Frank has explained this to Molly, but today is a day for gratitude to the doctors and nurses who have cared for their friend. "We'll pray for the best," adds Molly. The conversation moves to the team.

"I had an outdoor session with Greta yesterday. She came over after work for a bite to eat and to work on her baby hooks. She's getting better. That girl has no fear. Somehow, she finds time to practice her skill work." Mose laughs. "She works me harder than I work her. I had to take a nap after she left."

The rumors are true, and in early June the NCAA ends the rigid restrictions for teams about social distancing, opening up campuses to allow for interaction between coaches and their players on a voluntary basis. As some athletes return to campus, they must avoid large gatherings to some extent, but face-to-face interactions can occur as long as masks are worn. Additionally, university actions must comply with local and state policies, and California's are more restrictive than football crazy Alabama's. Coach Rascon tentatively schedules workouts with the five players living on campus plus Kenti who is living just a few miles away. Joyce asks for a schedule so she can try to work around her hours at the hospital. Keilani and Emerson tell Coach that they want to return to campus for the summer, and both register for online classes. Greta wants to return but doesn't know if it's feasible. Neither Char nor Danelle will return for the summer.

Molly has a Zoom meeting with the AD and several SJV coaches to get precise information about the NCAA guidelines. *Precise* is a relative term these days. Dr. Calhoun believes the easing of restrictions was meant to accommodate the D1 football programs, but it has to apply to all sports. SJV has no football team, something Dr. Calhoun notes makes his job easier during the pandemic. A hundred players plus all the coaches and managers and assorted personnel that surround college football would nearly double his caseload. The largest program at SJV is track, but its numbers and expenses are dwarfed by football programs. SJV's athletic finances, while stretched, are not in dire shape like UC Riverside's, which is contemplating ending its entire athletic program to save money during the pandemic restraints. Molly hears the rumors that some of SJV's programs are being considered for the cutting block, in particular the golf and tennis teams, sports which don't fit into the culture of The Valley. Tulare and the surrounding towns and cities are soccer, track/cross country, baseball/softball, and basketball mad. Dr. Calhoun assures the coaches that SJV will not be eliminating any of its programs. He tells them that indoor facilities are still not open for use. All "practices" must be held outdoors.

Coach Rascon's cell beeps, the new number in her bank, but she has a funny feeling. Rather than let it go to message, she steps into the hall and answers.

"Hello, Coach? This is Janet Caldwell. Could I buy you a coffee?"

❧

What Janet meant was could they talk the next morning. She drives over from Santa Barbara, covering the distance in just under

132

three hours arriving at Coach Rascon's at 9:30. "I kind of just ignore the speed limits." Because of Covid restrictions, Molly suggests they meet on her patio, and Janet insists that she bring flavored drinks from Starbucks along with scones. Typical June weather in The Valley: 76 degrees by mid-morning with heavily polluted air. Janet comments on the size of Molly's yard, that it would be a wonderful space for her dogs, chocolate labs.

"It's been wonderful for Frankie during the lockdown. I can't imagine living in a high-rise apartment during all of this." What Molly discovers is that Janet Caldwell possesses the interpersonal skills necessary to be a successful fundraiser.

"Tell me a little about your family, Coach." Janet listens intently while adding bits about her own adult children.

"Any hobbies?" Molly smiles as she relates her failed attempts at gardening. Janet adds that gardening is a full-time job even in the best of conditions.

"I understand you coached at Cal Coastal before you moved over here. Bigger stage, huh?" Janet rubs her eyes while she listens.

"Where in Colorado did you grow up? Must be beautiful there."

Molly laughs slightly as she recalls her life in Oro Hills. "I wasn't a mountain kid or a small-town kid or any of that. I was simply a gym rat. Oro Hills has a beautiful river just outside of town, and I never set foot in it, but I knew every dead spot on my high school gym floor. At least when I went to college, I began to see a bigger picture of the world." Molly pauses to take a bite of her scone before continuing. She wonders why Janet has made the trip to Tulare this morning. "I think getting a little involved in local issues in the South during college pushed me to explore the job here. At least a little."

Janet smiles. "So, your official college major wasn't basketball?"

"No," smiling back, "political science and history. Once I learned to read better in high school, I kind of got hooked on it."

"Oh, what are you reading just now?" asks Janet.

"I'm working through books by Luis Urrea. Border stuff. I have a couple of players who grew up with that."

Janet nods, almost as if she has connected. "So, you don't just watch game tapes at night?"

"During the season, I'm kind of addicted to game film." Molly leans forward. "So, what is it you came up here for?"

"My friends tell me I'm anal." She smiles back when Molly smiles. "No, Coach, type A personality. Impatient, overly organized, competitive, highly focused. I think you know." Janet reaches into her purse for an envelope. "I'm meeting with my husband's accountant later today about the endowment. He's a bit concerned about the health of the company, about whether giving money to university sports teams is prudent at this time. He's a bit on the financial conservative side, so I'll need to reassure him about this. We made a commitment, and we'll see it through. Don't worry about that. I wanted to assure you that what we talked about earlier is still a go."

"It's a generous amount," says Molly. "Very generous."

"Yes, it is," adds Janet quickly. "I could have told you all of this over the phone, but I want to get a better feel about you. When my husband and Stephanie and her husband began talking about donating to your school, it was about being alumni. I think Stephanie was being bombarded with letters from your school about donating. For me, there's no emotional attachment, and they certainly could donate without me, but my husband never likes to make financial decisions by himself. I can be awful to live with if I'm not on board." Janet's eyes are squinted. "Coach, can I call you Molly?" Molly nods. "Molly, what has attracted me to this venture is that your program is a winner. That's important to me. I don't want to watch a game and not see my investment winning on the scoreboard. Selfish, huh, but it's the way I'm wired. Type A, remember."

Molly sees that Janet is not done yet. There is more.

"So, I went to see a couple of experts on basketball, which I admittedly am not. I asked them to look into a crystal ball and predict the future of your program. They analyzed your roster, looked into your history, and studied your coaching style. All three said you're a 21st-century coach, that you get it. In effect, they said an endowment in the way I envision things is a good investment." Janet stops there but isn't done. Molly stays quiet, waiting for the *but*.

"Molly, public employee salaries are just that. Public. San Joaquin Valley doesn't pay you what you're worth, at least in comparison to other D1 coaches with your track record. Universities that demand winning programs are willing to pay big money for a coach who can get them there. My guess is that San Joaquin doesn't demand that you win. They like it, of course, but your job here is secure because of who you are. But, in the near future, some schools are going to waive that big money offer in your face. I wonder how long you'll stay here."

∾

On Wednesday, June 3, Minneapolis files charges against three officers in the death of George Floyd. Former Secretary of Defense James Mattis says President Trump is simply trying to divide the country for political gain. Protests spread around the country, mostly peaceful, but some become violent. Coach Powell watches the evening news with her partner, Junior Warren.

"No shit!" she says with intensity. "Just say it, Trump. 'Gas the Blacks!'" Ryanne swears again.

Junior shakes his head. "Those are mostly White protesters. He always plays to his base, and we aren't it."

"Unbelievable," says Ryanne. She watches the loops again of the murder of George Floyd and President Trump marching to St. John's Church in D.C. carrying a Bible that Ryanne thinks he's never read. "What kind of people believe his schtick?"

"They've always been out there, it's just that now he's given them license to come out from their closets." Junior knows he's preaching to the choir. "Not all Republicans are MAGAs, of course, but those far-right crazies have been unleashed. Old-style Republicans don't know what to do." Junior pauses. "I need to get back to Washington."

"I know they're there, but why is the whole Republican Party buying into all this?" She puts up her palms. "I know; you don't have to answer." She turns off Lester Holt.

∾

Ken Davidson's wife bought the used Sony tape recorder at her husband's request, and from his hospital bed, he speaks into it, a throwback to the previous century. He told her that his mind is too cloudy to recall how to record into his phone, but he wants to restart his blog, **Agriculture and Basketball.**

"I've lost nearly a month of my life. Seems like the last thing I remember is riding up here to Fresno through the Tule Fog, and now my brain is denser than that fog that causes major pileups on the highway. The doctors tell me I'm lucky to be alive and to expect some difficulties with my health in the months to come. Hopefully, I'll be out of here soon, but I don't want to have my wife do all the nursing things that I need help with now. For now, she'll be transcribing my recorded words. Bless her heart; I certainly won the lottery all those years ago.

"My throat is sore, a result of the ventilator tube. No mind. This morning, my thoughts returned to that enigma who goes by the moniker of Coach Molly Rascon. Evidently, she's been writing words of encouragement to me nearly every day and then sending them with one of her players who works here at the hospital. One of the nurses, I'm told it's either Joyce or Sylvia, reads these words to me off the three-by-five card and then passes the card on to my wife. She's been reading these to me, so I guess I'm hearing them for a second time. Coach called me a "rat" in the note my wife read after breakfast, not in a bad way. Coach said I was a sports-junkie rat like she was a gym rat. I guess I am. Since I was in high school, I've written about sports; began while I was a player. Three sports in high school but only basketball in college. I was a better athlete in ink than I ever was on the court. I can't imagine America without its sports. It certainly has been my obsession.

"I asked what day it was this morning, evidently once to my wife and once to a nurse. June 6, 2020, three months since sports shut down because of the virus. What do these gym rats do to replace the hours missed on the court? What does a coach do to fill her life when her team is taken from her? Maybe those are not the important questions as people are dying, but they are still important. Since God seems to have granted me a few more minutes on this earth, I intend to probe these questions, to grapple with these issues, hopefully in the larger context of the pandemic.

"I suspect this first day with oral recording has been somewhat rambling. My wife will be the ghost writer for these blogs, trying to make sense of the intent and not just the words. I think she's been doing that my whole life. Tired now, so I'll turn this machine off and take a nap."

❧

"Is anyone feeling sick today?" is the first question Coach Rascon asks of her players on Zoom calls or at social distance meetings at the ball field. She sits in the bleachers as four of her players jog around the field, all spaced by at least twenty yards. When Kaori laps her team-mates, she gives them a wide berth. Maria, Sylvia, and Esther keep their spacing throughout the afternoon. When the running is complete, the four girls stretch on the outfield grass and do pushups, sit-ups, and burpees. Coach Rascon and Coach Powell will run with the girls on Mondays, Wednesdays, and Fridays, but today is Sunday. No church services due to virus restrictions. When Dyani left for Arizona earlier, her Uncle Hector procured a pickup truck off the reservation and came to get her for a couple of weeks. Since she graduated, along with Danelle, Coach Rascon isn't sure Dyani will return to Tulare, even though Dyani assured her she will. Molly thinks Dyani promised to return so as not to have a sloppy goodbye.

Frank and Frankie arrive at the field for batting practice just as the players are finishing their exercises. Molly climbs down to greet "the boys" and say goodbye to her ladies. Kaori stays, along with Molly, to shag Frankie's hits. Papa Martinez pitches. Kay-kay seems happy in every way now that she has the protection of the campus from verbal assaults on her "Asian-ism." SJV's summer classes begin Monday, five weeks of online learning. Kaori has decided not to take any courses in her major—mathematics—but instead will take art history and music appreciation. They both seem to be online friendly, looking at art and listening to music. She plays the violin, lessons since she was in kindergarten but not concert level. She practiced her shooting more than her scales, methods for coming off a screen more than the Suzuki Method.

Papa teaches Frankie to hit to all fields, so Molly and Kaori play opposite fields, social distancing by necessity. In time the hitting stops, and the fielding practice begins, Frankie at short, Kaori at first, with Papa hitting grounders and Mama catching. There is no Little League this summer in The Valley, another casualty of Covid. Frankie calls timeout to get drinks, and Kaori tells Coach Rascon that Emerson went to a Black Lives Matter protest in Pasadena on Thursday and was taunted and pushed by protest protesters. Emerson called Kaori to tell her and then have Kaori tell Coach so that Coach wouldn't lecture her. Kaori assures Molly that Emerson wasn't hurt. Sitting on the grass with a sports drink and snacks, they talk.

"It's natural, Coach, Emerson is Black. Besides, it shouldn't matter. Police brutality shouldn't be accepted by anyone."

Molly nods. "Remember our Zoom talks that week when the tournament was canceled? How everyone said they were partially a minority except Joyce and Danelle?"

Kaori laughs lightly. "I'm like one-sixteenth Irish. Coach Powell said she wasn't mixed, that she was all Black. We laughed because she's the darkest Black I've ever seen." They both laugh again when Kaori mentions the colorful clothes Coach Powell always wears. "None of her outfits are subtle, that's for sure. In the dorm my first year, Sylvia said Coach Powell was your alter ego. I didn't understand that then, but I do now. Sisters."

Molly smiles. "I'd be lost without her. She's the loud me." Molly sighs. "I miss us all being together, and I know you all do."

"Coach, when do you think things will get back to normal again. I don't just mean we start playing hoops again, but just everyday life?"

Molly doesn't want to answer Kaori's question with total honesty, because she doesn't think they ever will. Certain lines have been drawn and much of the nation will not back down. The middle ground is evaporating daily. "Kay-kay, it's hard to say. We need the vaccine, and when everybody has taken it, that will help a lot, but the day-to-day interactions seem to have been," she pauses searching for the correct word. "We don't accept the normal behaviors with those who don't believe the same . . . political ideas that we do. Ryanne and Frank and I were talking the other evening, and we agreed that while the virus is terrible and getting worse in so many ways, it isn't society's worst problem in the long run. America seems to be marching head-long into a crisis of character. Covid is revealing this crisis." Molly stops there to get Kaori's reaction.

"You're telling me." She gently shakes her head. "The Chinese in the San Francisco area have swung over to the Democratic Party during my lifetime. I think most Asians have. My parents and grand-parents were Republicans before I was born, but they're not just dissatisfied Republicans now, they're active in the Democratic Party. Trump's words have pushed them even further to the left. We see him as dangerous on a personal level. Our representative in Congress is a Progressive. Here in Tulare, it's Nunes, and he's so far in Trump's camp." Kaori pauses. "Are you a Democrat, Coach? I assume you are."

"I am, but when I was your age, I sure wasn't very political." Molly smiles. "I was just a basketball player. As a history/poly sci major, my professors made me get involved in campus and local politics in the South. Opened my eyes. They also made me write a paper on a current issue. I chose the environment. Maybe it was fate that I ended up here in the San Joaquin Valley where the environment is taking a beating, both the air and groundwater."

Kaori nods. "That one series that Mr. Davidson wrote on The Valley's pollution that you made us read opened all our eyes. I never told you this, but when you recruited me, that you weren't a man was important, that sounds funny and it's not what I mean, but I really didn't want a male coach like I had in high school. Sort of why I hoped I could play at Stanford under Coach VanDerveer." Kaori smiles to herself. "Kinda got off track there."

"That's okay," says Molly. "And for the record, you can play at that level."

"I'm happy here; no regrets. Maybe I'll do my graduate studies at Stanford, so I can have that prestigious diploma on the wall of my den." Kaori smiles. "Or I'll sign a pro contract and play in the WNBA for a decade. Coach, did you have a chance to go pro?"

Molly shakes her head. "Not when I graduated. My body was shot for a few years. Dallas offered me a trial, no guaranteed money, but my ankles and back said no. It was the right decision, but I did consider it." She looks over to her husband and son. "I've got them, and you gals, and the backing of the university. Pretty fortunate for a small-town girl who once hoped to simply graduate from high school and maybe join the military to get away."

Kaori raises up onto her knees. "Close your eyes and hold your breath." Molly gives her a puzzled look. "Just do it," orders Kaori.

When Molly's eyes close, Kaori crawls over to her coach and gives her a hug. "Thank you, Coach."

⁓

After dinner Mama Rascon transforms into Coach Rascon for her contacts with her players, especially those not living in Tulare. More like Counselor/Big Sis Rascon. As always, her notepad is close-by. When she finishes and reads Frankie his bedtime story, after she has spent a few minutes with Frank, tucking him in also, Molly returns to her notes. Dyani mentioned that the outdoor court in Chinle isn't as nice as the Kappa Sig court. "It's hard on my shoes."

⁓

Molly is a little surprised that the house still has a landline.

"Kappa Sigma House, this is Mrs. Goodman."

"Hi. This is Molly Rascon. I'm the women's basketball coach here at SJV."

"I know who you are. What can I do for you?'

"I was wondering if I could come over to look at your basketball court."

⁓

Keilani Russell enrolls in summer classes to be on campus for workouts. She rents a room across the street from the student center since she can't get a room in the dorm, and she begins driving for Grubhub. "Flexible schedule. I'm here to be the second coming of Diana Taurasi." Two days later, Emerson Loki walks around the side of the Kappa Sigma house where Kaori, Keilani, Maria, Sylvia, and Esther are working with Coach Rascon and Coach Powell. Outdoor gatherings fewer than fifteen; Dr. Martinez wants fewer than a dozen.

"I heard you needed an even number to do the drills correctly," she announces as she drops her gym bag and throws her arms up in the air like a soaring eagle. She turns to Coach Rascon. "Anyway, if I'm here, you won't worry about me leading a riot in LA."

Molly conceals her grin. "Well, don't just stand there prancing. Do you have a good mask?" Emerson pulls one out of her pocket and waves it over her head.

Now, the SJV Sequoias have six players, the core of the next season, if there is a next season, three returning starters, two who will battle for the other big to compliment Sylvia down low, and the heir apparent for Dyani's point guard slot. Not enough to scrimmage, but enough to drill and drill and drill. Besides, says Ryanne, basketball was meant to be a three-on-three game like it's played on the parks in Chicago. "Lace 'em up and get after it!"

No fans.

No NCAA monitors.

No politics.

Just pure basketball on a private outdoor court behind a deserted frat house, out of sight from the world, approved by Dr. Calhoun and Dr. Martinez, in compliance with NCAA guidelines and county regulations.

An atmosphere of absolute trust.

And trash talk.

Chapter 10

Another list. The six players of The Tribe who are in Tulare. Coach Powell. Maybe Kenti at the farm that one afternoon. The short trip to the grocery store; but it was just a pickup. Certainly, Frank and Frankie. Her AD, Dr. Calhoun.

Contact tracing.

It started with the "How are you feeling?" query that Molly begins each call she has with a player on the daily basis. Joyce Hensley, who as a nurse is super sensitive about her contacts, turned the question on her coach. "How are you feeling, Coach?" When Molly joked that she was tired and her eyes were watery because of the air pollution in the Valley, Joyce went full-on nurse mode. "Headache? Cough? Fever? Difficulty breathing? Sore Throat? Diarrhea? Any muscle aches?"

"No. No. No. No. No. No." Pause.

Nurse Hensley again. "Runny nose or sniffles."

As Molly answered, a fear arose in her chest, not for herself, but for Frankie. She has been a picture of health her entire life, but her son has asthma, a pre-existing condition. Joyce told Molly not to worry, but to get tested immediately. "And wear a mask even in the house."

Three tests. One for her, one for Frankie, one for Frank. One positive result. Molly.

Now that the public health worker has collected the contact information, Molly will go into quarantine at her house. Protocols. Her biggest worry is giving it to Frankie.

Frank puts up plastic in the hallway leading to the master bedroom, and he moves into the third bedroom and uses the same bathroom as

Frankie. Molly stays isolated in the morning until her husband and son have had their breakfast and left, Dr. Frank to his clinic and Frankie to Ryanne's house. He will still go to the "outdoor" gym to be with the team as they do their workouts, but he will not have his mother. She will miss his ninth birthday during this first week of her isolation.

The first days feel like the flu or a bad cold, but at no time does Molly have trouble breathing. She experiences muscle aches and a lack of appetite and is tired. Mostly though, she feels unproductive, and to a workaholic, that is severe. From bed she texts her team, stays in touch with recruits, reassures her donors, consults with Dr. Calhoun, and checks in on her old teammates from college and high school. Fifty to seventy messages each day. So far, she's the only one who has contracted Covid. Her most frequent contact is Ryanne, both by text and phone.

"Hey, substitute mom, how's Frankie?"

"He's napping just now, Mol. He misses his mama." Ryanne details Frankie's activities before he tuckered out and fell asleep on her couch. "The girls gave him a little birthday party at practice. Sylvia had the grocery store make him a cake." While Coach Rascon generally refers to her team as ladies, Ryanne usually calls them girls. "He's shown no indication of being sick; I know you want to know that again. He's like his mama, tough and resilient." She asks Molly how she's feeling.

"About the same. Certainly, no worse, but it lingers." Molly coughs. "Ry, this week has made me think of every scenario, and you know how I am with down time. Anyway, if Covid were to, you know, get me, would you take over the program, take care of our ladies?"

"It's not going to kill you, Mol, so don't worry about it. Another week and you'll be back yelling at Maria to toughen up."

"You're probably right but promise me you would."

"You're delirious, but okay, sure, if it makes you feel better, yeah, I'll become the girls' first mama." Ryanne laughs into the phone. "That also assumes SJV would hire me. Remember, this is mostly a brown school, and this Black lady has a police record."

The conversation switches to recruiting, to point guards, to pace of play without Dyani, to how lucky they are to have such players as they do. Ryanne listens to her best friend worry, something Molly almost never does, and then reassures Molly that Covid won't last forever, and that they will pick up the program at that point and keep moving forward, but Molly worries about "sustainability."

They talk for an hour before ending the conversation. Both coaches have taken notes on various topics and will review them before they speak on the phone again but will text comments whenever a tangent arises. Frankie wakes from his nap, and Ryanne feeds him a pre-dinner. Dr. Frank arrives just after 6:00 to pick him up. He doesn't come into Ryanne's house out of safety, just honks for his son to come running. Frankie does not hug Ryanne when he leaves. Both are masked all day long, and that is what Ryanne considers, the lack of physical touching for a boy who is being raised in a touchy-feely home.

By mid-June it's clear that Tulare County and the San Joaquin Valley are hot spots for the coronavirus. California Covid restrictions are tougher than most states. Field workers and essential workers are particularly hard hit, as they are closely bunched because of the work they do. Packing sheds, harvesting and processing, stocking groceries, working to keep the economy moving. In one of the most productive agricultural counties in the world, one in four residents lives below the poverty line. With no N-95 masks available, these workers mostly use bandanas to cover their breathing, something they have always done to protect against air pollution.

Kenti Solorzono feels sick, tests positive, and goes into quarantine. Back on the Navajo reservation, Char's extended family has an outbreak. Hector Dehiya informs Coach Rascon that Char probably has Covid but isn't showing any symptoms. Danelle Weston calls Coach Rascon to tell her that she has enlisted in the Army with the promise of working in their criminal justice system. Danelle assures Coach that all is okay, that her parents weren't going to help her with college expenses any longer, and that the military will pay for lots of educational advancements. She will report in August.

None of the members of the team who are staying in the dorms or just off campus have Covid. They continue to practice with Coach Powell, working on fundamentals mostly, but playing a little three-on-three. It's clear that Keilani's ten weeks of self-drills have paid off. Her defense still needs work, but on the other side of the ball, she is becoming a terror. Coach Ryanne's text messages to Coach Rascon speak of "head up, eyes up, vision, and quality of passes. Keilani can be our answer. It will be her decision-making and game management that will take time." Coach Rascon reminds Coach Powell that great point guards are more than ball skills. "It's that leadership component that's key."

Since the NCAA lifted some restrictions on player/coach interactions, Moses Robinson has been working daily with Greta Espinoza after her field work. Greta loves to bang; she's not a pretty player or one who wants to hang out on the three-point line like Maria. Still, outside shooting is an important part of her workouts. Coach Robinson sees a transitional player in Greta. Mose texts Molly, "Tell Sylvia that she'd better be ready for a new battle this fall and an entirely different teammate than Danelle."

In Chinle, Arizona, on the Navajo reservation, Dyani Dehiya holds her first little kid clinic. Seven girls and eight boys attend at an outdoor court at the high school. Afterwards, she signs autographs.

On Thursday, June 18, the Supreme Court rules that DACA can remain in place, a decision that goes against the Trump Administration. But the decision is met with whoops of joy and a bit of dancing by Esther Santiago and a dozen other DACA students who still remain at SJV. For these students, it means that they will have two more years of protection and won't be deported for now. They know it's temporary and that the president, if re-elected, will try again to cancel the program, but for today, it's a victory. Esther calls Coach Rascon in the early afternoon.

"Coach, did you hear the news about DACA? We won!"

With the past few days as a couch potato, Molly has watched lots of television news, mostly CNN and MSNBC, and she is fully apprised of the verdict. "I'm so happy for you Esther, and for all of the DACA kids." She pauses to correct herself. "I guess most of you are not kids any longer."

"I hoped the Court would rule for us, but I was so worried. I've been here all my life, since I was a baby really. America is my home. Besides, with Covid so bad, we've been doing a lot of the essential work. It would be pretty hard to deport 650,000 of us. You guys would starve." Esther laughs at her little jab.

"Selfishly, I get to have you for the rest of your college years. You know, the coach in me."

"Well, at least through my junior year anyway, but I'm not going to worry about it today. Just going to celebrate. How are you feeling today? Any better?"

Unseen by Esther, Molly nods. "Much better. Still a little achy, but some of the worst aspects that other people have been going through seem to have missed me. Keep your fingers crossed."

"I texted Coach Powell and told her I wouldn't be at the court today. Some of us are getting together downstairs and then marching through campus. Celebrating."

Molly smiles. "I understand. Wear your masks!" admonishes Molly.

Molly does feel better, and so far, neither Frank nor Frankie have shown any symptoms of being infected. The family has followed strict procedures about distancing, and Frankie has bought in to Zoom calls with his mama from two rooms away. The bonus for Frankie has been lots of pizza and home delivered Mexican food from Mariscos or Taqueria's. Molly circles June 30 on the calendar as her "clear" date, her return to family and coaching date, but her husband thinks it could be sooner if her symptoms disappear.

As bad as the Covid pandemic is in Tulare County, Molly knows that the numbers are much worse on the Navajo reservation. After getting a bite to eat, a late lunch, and doing a bit of housecleaning, Molly texts Dyani in Arizona.

"Good news from Esther. DACA in place for a while. How are you and Char?"

There is no immediate reply.

☙

San Joaquin Valley's AD Dr. Calhoun returns Coach Rascon's call. "Hi, Coach. How are you feeling today?"

"Much better, thanks. Having my own personal doctor helps immensely. He's a good nurse too. I guess I'm through the worst of it, and even that wasn't too bad. I'm lucky." She asks about the general health of the SJV staff and whether the student body has avoided any serious cases. Assured that, by and large, SJV has fared well, Molly gets to the reason for her call. "Dr. Calhoun, I keep hearing rumors from my coaching colleagues, especially the ones back east, that the NCAA is considering plans that would allow every athlete to have an extra year of eligibility. I know that's for spring athletes, but are they considering it for winter athletes also?"

Dr. Calhoun has heard those same rumors, and they seem to be getting louder. "Still nothing official, but, yes, that idea is floating around. I know having your two seniors come back would bolster your team again." He pauses. "I wouldn't count on it though, since they played most of their season."

"Well, Danelle won't be returning under any circumstances. She enlisted in the Army and will be reporting in two months. She has her diploma in hand. Dyani would most likely return for graduate work, and I am considering hiring her as a grad assistant, but if she has another year, that changes many things. My number one recruit is a point guard. Part of my presentation is that I'm losing Dyani, and she would have an opportunity to play extra minutes right away."

"Coach, I wish I could give you a definitive answer on this, but I can't." The AD gives Molly new information regarding contact hours during the summer and what the tentative return-to-action schedule looks like. "First practice around mid-October with the first game that last week in November." He pauses. "Tentatively. Covid makes every plan tentative."

Molly nods. "Well, it is the NCAA, and they won't act until they get the blessing of the big schools and major conferences. Their vast money resources might be in jeopardy. Oh, heavens." Dr. Calhoun understands her sarcasm.

❧

Molly is alerted to the text by the ping of her phone.

"Coach, my Uncle Hector has the rona and is missing. Gone off to use his shaman powers to heal himself. More later. Can't talk now."

Molly is stunned. Hector Dehiya is a mystical man, someone who has always seemed to live above the stresses of those who live mortal lives. Dyani once told Coach that her uncle might be a hundred years old or older. Then Dyani laughed and said that Hector was probably in his sixties. Dyani told Molly about a coffee can that he keeps on his mantle, and that he puts a pinch of dirt in it when someone on the reservation dies so that the tribe can continue to stay together in spirit. Coach replied that she hoped he didn't fill the can this year with the Covid deaths. It wasn't meant to be funny, but Dyani laughed anyway.

Molly wants to get in her car and drive to the reservation, to give both Dyani and Char hugs. Molly knows the data. The Covid infection rates on the Navajo reservation are as high as any location in America. Sad, because the Navajo locked down and did everything right, but once it hit, it exploded. Frank and Joyce both explained; Frank to his wife and Joyce to the ladies who were still in Tulare. Damaged immune systems, especially obesity and diabetes. A social people living in extended households with frequent clan gatherings. Poor or no health insurance compounded by fewer medical personnel. Lack of infrastructure, with nearly a third of the Diné living without electricity or running water which forces many to congregate unsafely. Joyce laid it out starkly. "If you think Tulare has a poverty problem, I guess it's nothing compared to Dyani's home. What's more, our campus pantry continues to give out fresh fruits and vegetables, but the reservation is a food desert." Joyce said this while she shook her head side-to-side. Molly had been there to recruit Dyani and Char and when the team played ASU and Arizona in the reservation celebration. It was as poor and desperate as Joyce had said, ignored by the rest of Arizona and the federal government, and now, a virus not of their own making is devastating the reservation.

Molly texts both her husband and Ryanne, pours herself a cup of coffee—and waits. A roster lies on the end table, a proposed roster for next season with notes scribbled all over it. Molly tucks one leg under her butt and picks up the roster. Name, height, class, hometown: the information that was listed on the tournament roster for the tournament that was canceled. Molly has listed each player's major. Char's is undecided. Keilani's is communications. Molly smiles thinking Lani will need to refine her vocabulary in that field. The f-word is quite communicative but not acceptable in most public venues. Emerson's is dance. Of course, Joyce's is nursing, and Kaori's is math. Greta's is agribusiness. Greta, who spends six hours a day in the fields of Oxnard and then two hours on Coach Robinson's driveway shooting baby hooks and 22-foot jumpers. Greta, the most secure young lady on the team. Greta, who must make the jump to starter if SJV is to repeat as conference champs. An arrow goes from Greta's name up to Keilani's name, because Lani must also make that jump. Lani, who will replace Dyani at the point and will no doubt use the f-word in practice to communicate her frustrations or exhilarations and then be repri-manded by Coach and then apologize. Sylvia and Maria, the sisters from El Paso, Texas. Army brats with no brat in either of them. Well, maybe a little in Maria. Respectful, hard-working, quality teammates. Sylvia, whom a coach builds around, the rock in the middle. Maria, who plays basketball completely for fun, who is more athletic than her sister but less driven. A sub for the next season and the one player Molly has had the safe sex talk with more than once. Esther Santiago. The Dreamer. Esther, who showed Coach a photo of two teammates from an Ivy League school who were all smiles after an important win and told Coach that's what she wants for the team. Esther, who once lived in the shadows and now lives on the edge, who has been given a reprieve on her immigration status but understands how tenuous that status is. Esther, who doesn't know where her family lives week to week. Kenti's name is penciled in at the bottom. Agronomy. "How do I get home?" Molly's cell pings. It's Frank.

"Hector's missing?"

"Just got a text from Dyani. No details."

"Sorry. Keep me informed. I'll be home late. I texted Ryanne. She'll feed F."

Freddie Mercury interrupts the texting.

"Hey. How's Frankie?"

"He's reading," says Ryanne. "So, what's this about Hector?"

Molly tells Ryanne what she knows, which isn't much, but her concern comes through the airways loud and clear. Hector is Dyani's and Char's protector, the closest thing the girls have to a guardian angel—and Dyani says he has Covid. Evidently, Hector has gone into the desert to self-heal. "I'm waiting for Dyani to call with more."

A thought hits Ryanne. "I think Frankie was texting with Hector yesterday. Let me see if I can bring it up on his cell." She goes quiet as she walks into the guest bedroom to retrieve Frankie's phone. It's on the nightstand, and Ryanne quietly takes it back into the kitchen. "Hang on, Mol." Ryanne finds the text conversation and begins reading it aloud.

"I'm looking for dinosaurs in the painted desert."

"Who painted the desert?"

"Mother Nature many years ago. Before my people came. Sorry I missed your birthday."

"Mom's team gave me a party. We had cake."

"How's your mama feeling?"

"She's getting better. Still behind the plastic."

"She's tough. She'll be fine soon. I promise. Now, you need to be. I'm sure your papa is tired too, so you need to do all you can around the house. Wash the dishes, clean the toilets, vacuum."

"I wash the dishes with dad."

"Good boy. I may not be texting for a few weeks, but don't worry. We all just need to be careful with the virus going around."

"I wear a mask when I go anywhere and around my house."

"That's good. Say hi to everyone and that we'll all get together when this pandemic ends."

"I will."

Ryanne sniffles. "That's all there is. God, I hope Hector's all right."

Molly curls her lips inward and runs her left hand through her hair. "I'll read it when Frankie gets home. Seems like Hector is speaking in generalities. Such a unique man." The coaches talk for a few more minutes. Molly returns to her roster. On the back, she has scribbled other notes. Details about DACA, phone numbers for two high school players, NCAA information, the names "Paul/Abby Garrity-refugee workers" circled with a phone number that relates to Esther's border dilemma. Molly turns it back over to the roster names. Ten players. Dyani's and Danelle's names are absent. At the bottom are the coaches. Jackie Jakino has a question mark behind her name. Nicole Aikins is crossed off. Below the coaches' names is one word in all caps. "UNDERSERVED!" Molly bobbleheads herself. So much undecided. Covid questions. "Outsiders, college years in the middle class."

∾

June turns to July and Covid cases are lower in some states, although the nation registers 50,000 new cases in one day. Tulare businesses begin cautiously opening again. Still, Major League Baseball cancels the All-Star game scheduled for July 14. Europe excludes the United States when it opens its borders to "safe countries." Covid concerns alter presidential primaries, and President Trump insists on Fox News and at his rallies that the only way he can lose the election is if it is rigged. Junior Warren warns Ryanne that Trump's setting the stage for a dangerous ploy. Uncle Hector Dehiya remains missing, Ken Davidson leaves the Fresno hospital, and Frank Martinez removes the plastic barrier he hung in the hallway. Molly Rascon hugs him and her son and begins working with her team again. SJV AD Dr. Calhoun calls his women's basketball coach on July 2 to check on her health and to see if she's feeling good enough to meet briefly about her contract.

∾

On the morning of July 6, a masked Molly Rascon meets with Dr. Calhoun in his office for "a brief conference about her future plans." Handing Molly a cup of coffee, Calhoun says, "Well, you don't look any worse for the wear." He moves behind his desk and sits.

"It really wasn't so bad, just the isolation. I think I may have worn out my phone though. After the first few days, I was able to talk and text with my ladies. Then, I set up a Zoom schedule for all our coaches. We're all isolated now, and I thought that might be a way to share our concerns. The first meeting, I think we had over twenty coaches. I'm hoping more of the assistants join since they're the ones most left out of the loop now. We'll see."

"You do have this reputation as a workaholic, you know. Let me know about the Zoom meetings; sounds like a positive thing."

Molly smiles. "You should talk."

The AD lifts his cup to his coach. "Coach, I wanted to have this meeting to keep abreast of your plans and to assure you that you're a part of the university's long-term plans. You are the face of our athletic program." Molly squints her eyes, but Calhoun ignores the gesture. "One of my talents is squelching rumors, or at least addressing them before they start fires. I can't tell you where I heard this, but there's some talk about you being hired away from us. More money, you know."

Molly repositions her body in the leather chair. "I think I may know where that rumor started, but I haven't officially been contacted by any other university. I'm happy here."

"Well, I want you to know we feel the same way. SJV is a better place because of you. You're in the second year of your second contract, but I've had some discussions with my boss about tearing it up and writing a new one, specifically to pay you more. Your team's success would justify a pay raise." Molly starts to speak, but Calhoun raises his hand. "No, no. Because of budgetary issues during this Covid pandemic, you took a ten percent pay reduction, voluntary, and SJV's athletic budget keeps your pay in the lower half of the conference. Because of your value to the university and our community, I'm trying to convince the boss that you're worth an additional investment." Again, Molly starts to speak and is stopped by Calhoun. "Hang on just a minute, Coach. In the past two weeks, while you were under the weather so to speak, I've been contacted by two Pac-12 universities about getting permission to speak with you about upcoming openings. My guess is that these two openings will not occur this coming season, the pandemic keeps everything in a state of flux, but soon. I don't have to tell you that what they can offer you far exceeds anything SJV can afford, and I wouldn't blame you for jumping at that kind of money. What I would like to have you consider, however, is that if you are contacted and some offer is proposed, you sit down with us before accepting." Calhoun stops here to give Molly a chance to respond.

"There's always rumors. I assumed you were referring to the two women who have offered the endowment." She hesitates to check Calhoun's acknowledgment. "I fully intend to honor my contract."

"I appreciate your loyalty, not just to the university but to your team. Still, contracts are complicated things, and there are clauses that allow you to end this association, clauses that foresee another university offering you three to four times what we pay you. When this pandemic ends and you get back to coaching games, if your team continues to win at the level we're accustomed to, someone will give you a call. What I'm asking is that you keep us apprised of your thinking."

Three times what we pay you. Molly does a quick calculation about what she makes now compared to what her own mother made each year when Molly was growing up. She remembers working late into the evenings at the laundromat during high school to bring a few extra dollars into the family's coffers, about her little brother's paper routes. "I assure you that if I'm contacted, I'll keep you informed." Molly wants to say more, to reassure Dr. Calhoun about her plans, but she holds her thoughts. She thanks the AD for his time and confidence in her and leaves. Exiting the Ad Building, she doesn't return to her car; instead, she strolls the sidewalks of SJV, the mostly empty pathways of her university.

Near the library, she finds a bench under a tree, and texts her husband. "Would you ever want to leave Tulare?" Moments later, she receives a text, not from Frank but from Dyani.

"Coach, no word about my uncle, but the Los Angeles Sparks just called to offer me a tryout."

"Oh, D! What a wonderful opportunity! When?"

"It's all kinda fuzzy, what with the league on hold, but they said as soon as things open up. Maybe I'll have to go to Florida or maybe wait until the shortened season is over. Anyway, it's exciting."

"Another award for my Navajo warrior!!!!!"

"Thanks Coach."

When Dr. Frank returns from Visalia, after ten minutes of backyard catch and another ten rebounding for Frankie on the driveway, he asks Molly about her text, about moving from Tulare. Tulare, he reminds her, is just one of a dozen towns in The Valley that stretches from Sacramento to Bakersfield. "Did I say a dozen? I meant a hundred."

He tells her that he's happy in Tulare, that he loves the community and their neighborhood, and that Frankie is involved in everything available, the pandemic aside. Five years in, he reminds her, his medical clinic in Visalia is prosperous, well-respected, and needed. What Frank doesn't say is that he knows where this conversation originated and where it's going.

Over dinner, Monday's dinner which generally is Molly's night to cook, Frankie informs his parents about a new family in the neighborhood with a bunch of kids. Papa laughs when he asks what they look like, and Frankie responds with a shrug. "I don't know; they all wear masks."

"I don't recall a For Sale sign in the yard," says Molly when she finds out which house it is, the largest one at the end of the block.

"It was only on the market for a few days, and you were in quarantine," says Frank. "Good buy. Cheap. Less than what we paid for ours." He tells Molly that both parents will be employed at one of the larger dairy farms in the county, but since there's more than 300 of them, he can't recall which one they said. "Seemed like nice people when I met them briefly. From up north past Fresno. I guess they were hired away from another dairy farm, so they must bring certain skills that were in demand."

Frankie takes over the conversation, telling his parents about how he's better than any of the kids at basketball, but they are still pretty good, especially the boy a year older than him. "He's going to be in fifth grade."

"How many are there?" asks Molly. Frankie says six, but Frank thinks only five. Molly shakes her head, rolls some spaghetti around her fork, and goes quiet. Eventually, she points to her son's glass of milk, his still full glass. "Drink that. We have to do our part at supporting the dairy farmers, and they're some of our biggest donors. They're having a tough time these days. The schools and restaurants used to buy a lot of milk, but they closed, remember, and so lots of the farms can't sell the milk that the cows produce." She explains that the drought has forced many dairy farms to sell their cows and grow crops instead.

"Then, why aren't you and dad drinking milk?" asks Frankie.

Molly nods, gets up and goes to the refrigerator for the milk, gets two glasses from the cupboard, and fills them. "You're right, we should." She puts one glass in front of her husband and takes the other to her place. She raises hers and waits for Frank and Frankie to raise theirs. "To our dairy farms," she toasts, and Frankie giggles, but he does finish his glass.

"A nice compliment to the chianti and pasta," says Frank. "I guess we'll be having milk with everything now."

When Frankie finishes dinner, he asks to be excused, kisses his mama, and heads to the driveway. Frank reaches for the carafe to refill his wine glass and offers more to Molly.

"You know," says Molly, "we just became part of the pollution problem in the Valley, consumers of products created by massive industries, and that was a problem before the pandemic hit."

"Cow poop?" asks Frank.

"More aptly called 'manure lagoons.'" She wrinkles her nose at the thought. "This valley's pollution problems run deep through nearly every enterprise."

Frank recognizes that "Molly, the environmentalist" is making an appearance. He kids her. "We'll stop eating beef to compensate for our new milk addiction."

"Yeah, the Rascon-Martinez family's individual action single hand-edly halts the local pollution crises. No more methane gas." She smiles lovingly at her husband, stands, and walks behind him wrapping her arms around his chest from behind. "Can we put Frankie to bed early tonight?"

❧

Agriculture and Basketball. Blog, by Ken Davidson.

It's late, but I just heard about the death of a good friend, a man I played sports against as a kid, not on the same team but in our confer-ence. Not Covid, but suicide. Eddie was a dairy farmer over in the next county. Married a farm girl from Tulare from my class. That's how I knew him. One of those men who never retired, and as things spiraled down in The Valley because of the long drought and now the Covid anvil, he probably couldn't see a way out. Eddie and his sons had to dump much of their milk a few months ago, and they sold some of their cows for slaughter. That had to have hurt him to the core. A decade of unrelenting obstacles after a lifetime of success.

This Valley prospered because of water, first from the rivers and more recently from below the ground. So much is taken from the aquifers to maintain the farms, the most productive farms in the world, that the ground in The Valley sinks. Faster in some areas than others, sort of like men's spirits. This land has a carrying capacity just like human endurance. Farming asks much of a person, of a family. They aren't like the rest of us, and that's to America's everlasting benefit.

Tulare long ago passed its carrying capacity. This homey, quiet, wonderful town where I grew up, that I chose to come back to for my remaining years, lost the battle years ago when I was writing in LA. Being the "Dairy Capital of the World" requires great sacrifices. Maintaining that status broke it and broke a hard man like Eddie. What was good for the state's agricultural economy wasn't good for the local communities. As our town and all the smaller towns in the county shifted from pasture-based feeding to confinement feeding systems, as family-owned farms were bought out by corporations, as cows were nourished by imported feed, and as the manure from a million cows overwhelmed the lands' ability to use it or dispose of it, The Valley has become an environmental nightmare. Still, it has to keep producing to feed the nation. The residents, the little people, be damned.

It's been happening before our very eyes, but it's taken a pandemic to make us see. Maybe it was Covid that killed Eddie after all. I won't remember him from high school sports or as a farmer. My memories will be of playing town-team basketball against him when I would drive to Fresno to compete in their leagues. Eddie could ball and was tough as nails.

✧

Frank cradles Molly's head in the crook of his shoulder after making love. "By my calculations this has been the longest interval between sex we've ever had." They both smile unseen by the other in the darkness. "I'll bet the CDC isn't keeping statistics on that."

"We'll have to make sure it never happens again. I'll try not to get a contagious disease again."

"I'm glad Frankie's beeper didn't go off; not sure I would have heard it with all the noise you were making. You wear me out." Doctor and Coach go quiet for a moment, slowing their breathing before Frank speaks again. "This afternoon you texted me about leaving Tulare. Want to go there now?"

10:30 is not late for Molly. Basketball has kept her up late for decades. The AC kicks in trying to keep the house cool as the outside temperature remains in the 90s. "Calhoun wants me to tell him if I get offers from other schools. He said that when this hiatus ends, he'll repay the cut and renegotiate my contract to the highest level, but he said it would never approach what Pac-12 schools could pay. I told him I hadn't been contacted and I hadn't reached out to any other university. I think Janet or Stephanie may have talked with him."

"If you took a job with one of those schools, I could retire and be a stay-at-home papa."

Molly gently knees him. She knows he's as committed to his medical profession as she is to coaching, and she wouldn't want him to give it up. "Because of basketball, I've been in four different places, and each one of them was where I should have been at that time. The thought of someone paying me the going rate at a major basketball factory is unimaginable."

"Unimaginable until Ms. Borges suggested it to you. I googled it when you told me last month: Four hundred thousand plus bonuses with a guaranteed four years." Frank pauses. "Who'd have thought a little girl from the mountains of Colorado . . ."

"That's what I can't imagine. I can dream about coaching that kind of talent, but then I realize I already have it here, and I get to recruit girls who are overlooked by bigtime schools. Girls like Dyani and Sylvia."

"You're skirting the issue, I think," says Frank.

"Maybe. I'm . . . I'm happy here . . .and challenged. There are no expectations of me beyond what I put on myself. The university, the alumni, you and Frankie, you all think I've exceeded expectations and are content. But for me, I'm chasing something. I thought I had a chance this season to get to the Sweet Sixteen. We'll never know, but that's my yardstick. For myself. What I think now is that I can get there from here . . . on my own. There are coaches who are great recruiters, and there are coaches who can really coach the game. I want to be one of those who can do both, but there's more." The beeper from Frankie's room goes off. "I'll get it," says Molly. "Go to sleep."

Molly lays with her nine-year-old son until his breathing returns to normal. She once told Ryanne that she had never seen an inhaler in Oro Hills, that she only became aware of them at college. Now, they are a part of everyday life, sort of like her cellphone. When she returns to her bedroom, Frank is sound asleep. She slides in next to him, knowing his days are always stressful, more so with the pandemic, and lets him sleep.

San Joaquin Valley University, she thinks. *This damaged, flawed town away from the big lights of Los Angeles and San Francisco, away from the centers of women's basketball, but representative of the new America.* In the dark, Molly smiles. *You ought to write fiction, girl, this is a romantic novel you're painting. Still, there is that other consideration.*

Molly thinks pediatrics is exactly the medical profession her husband was born to practice. Gentle, persistent, soft-spoken, and physically flexible—the latter in order to constantly bend at the knees to be at eye level with small children. Three times each week, Frank gets up at 4 am to work out in the gym, but the pandemic requires extra hours, so his schedule has been compromised. Down to two days each week. Because of the limits on practice hours, Molly is home more to do the cooking, a task Frank generally did from October through March. Neither parent is a world-class chef, but they are well-known at Watson's where ready-made dinners are superb. And at the pizza restaurants. And Guadalajara's meat market. Frank admits to adding to Tulare's air pollution problem by barbequing frequently. It's a skill he wants to pass on to his son, but Frankie doesn't understand the concept of ageing one's meat. Molly laughs and says she does.

Ryanne comes to Sunday dinner on July 12. Junior remains in Washington, even though he's basically doing his consulting over the phone. Because of the heat and air pollution, supper is served inside. Ryanne brings ice cream for dessert.

"I think we'll have eight scholarship players tomorrow for practice if Joyce can rearrange her schedule. That young lady has been one of the heroes during this shit," says Molly. "Greta's supposed to text me tonight when she gets in. Your campus flyer got us one walk-on, and we can use Martina too." Martina will be in her third year as manager, but she played in high school and has been a fill-in for drills through-out her tenure."

"Have you even seen the walk-on play?" asks Frank.

"Briefly. On Thursday. She's pretty good and athletic. Madison. Maddie. Maddie Martin. A freshman. A guard."

Ryanne interrupts. "How'd she see my flyer?"

"She was up with her dad touring the campus."

"Where did she go to high school?" asks Ryanne.

"Bakersfield. She knows about us and said she was going to contact us about walking on. I kind of wonder how we missed her, being so close and all. Her team wasn't good, and that tends to mute any press or awards. She'll be interesting."

Frank collects the ice cream bowls and puts them in the sink. "Any word from Dyani or Char on Hector?"

"I got texts from both today. That's the good news. Still nothing about their uncle, but Char said the rez isn't too concerned about him, that evidently, he's always had a reputation for wandering. I guess since he was a boy he's been known to take off into the wilderness for weeks and then return as if nothing happened. The only difference is that he left with Covid symptoms this time." Molly shakes her head.

"What's Dyani's take?" asks Ryanne.

"Scared. I asked her about coming back if the NCAA lets seniors have an extra year. She surprised me a bit by saying she wasn't sure."

"That tells me she's scared," says Ryanne. "What will she do if she's not here helping us coach or playing?'

"She doesn't know, just says things like she could help on the reservation. The offer to play pro ball is still out there, sort of, but like everything, it's on hold. My guess is that she's like thousands of seniors around the country who don't know what next year looks like. It just so happens that our senior is a Navajo with a sociology degree."

Frank hangs a dish towel on the refrigerator and sits at the table. "I worry about her because I'm sure she's back on the reservation mixing with her clan, helping where she can. From what little I know, and you two know her much better, she just assumes the leadership role in any environment, and with her status as a basketball player, she'll be in demand. Right in the middle of a terrible outbreak of a highly contagious disease."

With every conversation that circles back to Covid, there is no silver lining.

Ryanne leans forward. "Let's assume we don't have Dyani back, or Char. Keilani becomes our girl, and we must sign Claudia. Then we work like hell to keep everyone else here and healthy. That's the cold, hard facts if we want to be champions again.

"Well, if Lani is our point guard, I'll have someone to battle with," says Molly. "Or we can always show film of me getting frustrated with Char in practice."

"Keilani knows how to push your buttons, that's for sure. Every time she apologizes and says, 'My bad, Coach,' your face turns crimson. I think she says it just get a rise."

Molly punches Ryanne in the arm. "My least favorite phrase, and to think, I'll be giving her the ball on every possession."

Frank sits with his arms folded, amused by the two friends working through next season's lineup. "Molly tells me she never yells in practice, that she learned that from her high school coach."

Ryanne rolls her eyes. "You might want to attend a practice before she retires or ask some of the girls."

Molly touches her hair and lifts her chin. "I raise my voice; I don't yell." She looks over to Frankie who has returned to the room and is sitting on the floor against the wall with his iPad. "Tell papa how Coach Rascon behaves at practice, sweetie."

Without looking up from his computer, Frankie says, "Commander-in-chief," and the adults break out in laughter.

∾

Greta can't get to Tulare on Monday for practice. Family needs come first, especially since she isn't taking classes. Her text asks Coach Rascon to give the practice schedule to Coach Robinson so the two of them can work on the drills for Bigs. That leaves just four ladies—Sylvia, Esther, Joyce, and Maria—to bang in the paint. The coaches know that Maria will not like matching up against her sister, and as coaches are prone to do, they smirk at Maria's dilemma. Kenti will now become Keilani's nemesis, using her perfect footwork to impede Lani's path to the basket. Maddie from Bakersfield will get the opportunity to showcase her talents as a backup point guard on offense and a defender of Emerson on defense. Good luck with that. Kaori will be defended by Martina, the manager, or Coach Powell if Martina isn't capable of providing any resistance.

The vision of having a full team for the first time in almost four months is exciting to Molly and Ryanne. Molly plans practice being mostly scrimmaging with small breaks for shooting. She and Ryanne just "want to see." If Keilani can be the point guard her talents indicate she can be, then the Sequoias can challenge for the championship again, if next season is played. Always the goal of repeating as champions.

The Kappa Sigma court has been a godsend, a gift from a successful alum, a high-performance court, full-sized halfcourt with a main plexiglass basket and two similar hoops at the sides, premium surface. Fenced in and secluded. No wonder the Kappa Sigs have been the intramural champs for the past three years. Molly laughs to herself. *No wonder Dyani dated a frat boy from this house.*

Molly arrives early and finds Martina already there with the bag of balls. Since she will be scrimmaging, she has bought herself a new pair of kicks, three-striped Adidas. Martina Smith from Las Vegas and as big a basketball geek as any of the players and their biggest cheerleader from the bench. Martina, alone at the court for at least a half-hour, is wearing a mask.

Practice will be a gathering of thirteen women, all of whom have heard about the risks and volunteered to be here, eager to return. Not one feels as though she has been pressured, but Coach Rascon knows she has stretched the university's guidelines to the maximum limit for a gathering. While Covid numbers eased some in June when the new guidelines were established by the NCAA, preliminary July numbers are rising. Dr. Frank has concerns and reviewed best practices for Molly's practice.

After a few words, Martina asks what else Coach needs. Molly tells her manager that she is not the manager for today's practice, that she is a player, so she should get a ball and start warming up. Martina beams, gets a ball, and begins dribbling at a casual pace. She knows the pre-practice routine. Molly watches for a second, then gets a ball for herself, but not to dribble, just to carry as she walks the court's perimeter. She's nervous, almost giddy. Today's practice is a restart to her life's chosen profession. What she's been doing since the tournament was abruptly canceled can't be called coaching in the athletic sense; rather, a counselor maybe, a big sister, or an older friend with experiences to guide her ladies through this tsunami. Molly stops at a side basket and shoots a few easy shots, making them all, and then walks again. Maybe she's become the female version of Hector Dehiya, not always there in the physical sense but present in each lady's soul. Whatever Molly is, she knows more about each lady and their personal struggles than she did as their basketball coach. She also has learned more about herself.

"Coach!" screams Keilani Russell from just inside the gate. Keilani high-fives Martina as she jogs over to Molly. It's obvious Keilani wants to hug her coach, but she pulls up and fist-bumps her. "Shit! Point guards are supposed to be the first to arrive at practice and Martina beat me. Won't happen again." It's a rehearsed line that needed tweaked because the manager was shooting baskets.

"Martina's going to be scrimmaging with us because of numbers. Any Covid symptoms?" Keilani shakes her head, her hidden smile behind her mask radiating into her eyes. The old point guard involuntarily shivers. She's about to restart the journey with a new point guard, and Molly likes the first few minutes of the trek. She reaches into her back pocket for the folded practice plan and hands it to Keilani. "Look this over and see if it seems okay for a first day."

The women stand in silence for a few moments as Keilani scans the detailed schedule. Without looking up, Keilani asks, "Who's this Maddie opposite my name? A fill-in or a walk-on?"

"Walk-on from Bakersfield. Ryanne and I missed her because she played on a bad team. Got a tape from her coach last week. She can hoop a bit. You'll have to work with her as we go. Not sure what her confidence level will be."

"Little like you or big like me?" asks Keilani.

"In between, but athletic. She's only seventeen. Young."

Keilani nods and hands the plan back to Molly. "Any word from Dyani? She hasn't answered my texts except to say Char's struggling with her classes and may not return to school."

Molly shakes her head and flips the basketball to Keilani. "Go shoot with Martina and make her feel comfortable."

It's still twenty minutes before pre-practice is to begin. Ryanne and Coach Jakino enter the court. Coach Jakino continues to work without a contract. After briefly speaking with Molly, they move to rebound for Martina and Keilani. Molly keeps walking, inspecting. She protects this new practice court like a curator guards her art museum. It's not the university arena, but it's now her gym.

Kenti arrives alone, taking time off from the farm, recovered from her bout with Covid. Maddie walks in with her dad and is greeted by Keilani who escorts her away from papa and tells him that Covid restrictions prevent him from staying. The rest of the ladies arrive together walking over from the one dorm that still houses students. They know the routine. Arranged in a wide circle, they stretch and socialize. Lots of catching up to do. Lots of bantering. Martina is accepted as an equal. Keilani sits with Maddie. Coach Nikki and Coach Robinson are missing, one permanently and one hopefully temporarily. Ken Davidson is not sitting along the fence with his note-pad. It's just thirteen women going to work on the first day back.

In time, the half-court scrimmage begins.

"Lani, you can't throw that pass to where Sylvia is going! Throw it where she is. She's going to get bumped and her progress will be impeded. Throw it hard and direct. Don't lead!"

"My bad, Sylvia."

"Maddie, you need to hedge to help. You can do it."

"Actually," whispers Ryanne to Molly, "she can't yet. Emerson and Kaori are way too quick and experienced, but it's the right advice."

Maddie has that deer in the headlights look much of the time, always with a goofy, kid-like smile though.

"Keilani looks great. Large and in charge, as the saying goes," says Molly. "Your suggestion was spot on."

The big surprise of the practice, however, is the performance of Maria who seems to have transformed into Cheyenne Parker overnight. Her sister and Esther both hit the deck when trying to cut through the lane." Bump all cutters! Harder when they come through the lane." *Somewhere*, thinks Molly, *Moses Robinson is beaming*. It's clear to the coaches that Martina will continue to be a manager next season, that Kenti will simply see Keilani as Dyani, the Second, and make her better by harassing her in practice, and that Maddie can make the team. A small gift. With Greta, Coach Rascon has a solid ten. Reel in the two top recruits and SJV can repeat. It would be nice to have Char, but it's likely she would be ineligible even if she returns to SJV. Hell, it would be best if they had Dyani, but that seems remote.

Scrimmaging while wearing masks is challenging, but the ladies follow the rules for the most part. Every so often, the mask will be pulled down for a good deep breath. Martina laid out a box of masks to be exchanged during practice if one got sweaty or torn. Joyce brings her own N-95 and reminds her teammates to pinch the nose guard. When Coach Rascon informed Joyce about practice, she balked but then agreed since so few young people were showing up at the hospital, and this practice was outside. Of all the players, Joyce seems most ready for a break from her current life. She has tended patients on ventilators and watched them die alone, cut off from the family. She was the last to touch three patients. Joyce will return to Fresno to work the night shift, but for two hours, she's only a Sequoia. A giant tree amid the forest.

Molly blows her whistle ending practice and the team sits in that wide circle to stretch. "Ladies," Coach Rascon pauses. "Ladies, that was a good practice." Her ladies know that "good" in Rascon-speak means "great." As Molly critiques the practice, a man enters the gate and watches. Ryanne sees him, but he is behind Molly, and the assistant coach sighs. Coach Rascon finishes; the team raises their fists and yells "Sequoias," and heads out. Martina returns to her manager status, putting balls in the bag and collecting the unused masks. She has no illusions. This practice gig is going to be a blast, but she will not earn a uniform because of some magic. Her role is to be Molly's and Ryanne's aide, and that's more than okay.

Ryanne curls her lips inward and tilts her head to the man on the edge of the court.

"Oh, shit," mumbles Molly barely audible under her mask. "Well, let's go get the new monitor-and-adjust directive." The two coaches meet Dr. Calhoun at the free throw line.

The AD sees by the coaches' demeanor that they are prepared for the bad news. "How did it go?" he asks, but he doesn't wait for an answer. "I could have told you before you started, but I felt you all needed this. Dr. Trevino put out the revised policy this morning. Because of the rising numbers here in Tulare County, we're going on time-out again, especially with teams and organizations. You can still meet one-on-one but no full practices for now. I'm sorry."

Molly swears and then apologizes to her supervisor. "Thanks for the two-hour window. It was good for us. I'm assuming we can still hold individual workouts."

"Yeah, for now. Dr. Trevino and I met with the public health officials early this morning. Told me I could stroll over here. Our numbers on campus are pretty good, but the county's are terrible. We've seen this since the beginning. Field workers, the prison, the nursing homes. Incubators."

Martina calls out from the opposite end of the court. "I'm leaving now, Coach. I think I got everything. Thanks. That was so much fun."

Molly waves for Martina to join her. The manager jogs over, still wearing her mask. "Dr. Calhoun, this is our all-conference manager, Martina Smith."

"Nice to meet you, Martina. So, you're the person who oils this machine, keeps it running smoothly, huh."

Martina smiles beneath her masks. "I try."

Molly gives Martina the news. "Practices need to go on hold again. I'll text you later. Kaori and Emerson are pretty hard to guard, aren't they?" It's a rhetorical question.

Martina nods and leaves.

Dr. Calhoun speaks again. "Dr. Trevino is on Zoom with the NCAA as we speak, informing them, making sure we're in full compliance. I expect the line will be the same. 'We will exhaust every avenue to get back to competition. We will remain vigilant in our efforts to protect the health and well-being of our student athletes.' I have it memorized; I've said it so many times." There is a hint of fatigue in his voice.

❧

Late dinner. Dr. Frank works late and picks up the Mexican that Frankie ordered. Most of the county's restaurants have gone to delivery only, no in-house meals, although several are fighting the governor's orders just to stay financially above water. The town seems to be drowning, and to the small businesses, the continued restrictions are adding water to the pool rather than providing life preservers. Molly says grace as the family holds hands, and she keeps a grip on her two boys after saying "Amen." Her husband doesn't know that practices have been put on hold again, but he expressed his concerns to Molly about their restart last night.

"Good practice?" he asks.

"Too good," answers Molly taking a burrito from the sack and unwrapping it for Frank. She pushes the jar of hot sauce to his plate and then takes two tacos from the sack for herself. "Are you seeing many more kids with the virus this week?"

"Not really, but a lot of concerned mothers. Most of the sniffling is allergies from playing outside in the summer with our air pollution. A lot like Frankie. Big demand for inhalers. Tell me about practice." There is an awkward silence.

Molly finishes a bite of her taco and wipes her mouth. Finally, "One and done. Our county and the conference put a hold on things again. The prez and Dr. Calhoun could have prevented me from holding practice, but they hesitated telling me the bad news, sort of a gift." She pauses. "A one-day gift."

"Have you told your girls yet?"

"Yeah. Quick text about an hour after practice ended. We're

Zooming tonight. It just makes me so angry, and I don't know who to direct my anger towards. I keep coming back to either the NCAA or our conference. I don't think many of the conferences back east or in the southern states are pausing, just California. Tighter restrictions in blue states."

Frankie puts on his "arbitrator face." Is this politics talk?" he asks. "No politics at the dinner table."

Papa Martinez lays his hand on his son's forearm. "No, this is therapy talk. Sometimes a person needs to talk out really bad frustrations rather than hold those feelings in. The tone may sound like politics, but it's not tonight." Papa looks for his son's understanding, and the arbitrator's face eases. Frank turns back to Molly. "California is seeing a rapid rise in cases, and the nursing homes are not the hot spots this time. California might be taking the right action."

Molly needs to hear this. But she also needs to talk.

"For two hours today, I was fooled into thinking it was all going to be okay, that I could be in control. It's how I wanted it to be." Her husband keeps his hand on Frankie's forearm. "The only problem is that I'm naïve. Dyani and Char, Greta, and Danelle weren't there. Maybe I can rationalize them away, but that's all it would be. The truth is that I'm not in control; none of us are. The virus is and will be for the foreseeable future. Dr. Calhoun slapped me in the face again with that truth. The virus is insidious; it sneaks into every facet of our lives and makes us compromise our actions and our principles." Molly realizes that her mood is too threatening to Frankie. She takes her eyes from Frank and smiles at Frankie.

"It's a good thing you're here to keep mama laughing and happy and to keep papa entertained. What did you do this afternoon?"

"I was at dad's clinic, don't you remember? I played games on my computer in one of the rooms. Mrs. Monroe sat with me when she wasn't at her desk with a patient."

Frank moves his hand from Frankie's arm to his shoulder. "He's teaching Margret Spanish." He smiles proudly at his son. "You probably didn't realize The Valley had another air pollution warning day, so he had to stay indoors."

Frankie jumps in. "Mrs. Monroe calls them poopie air days."

Molly rises quickly from her chair. "Ice cream time," and moves to the refrigerator.

∿

The family watches a movie about a squirrel before bed. Mama Molly says, "No computers tonight for any of us," and after the movie, they play a board game. When Frankie is tucked away, Coach Rascon Zooms with her team, explaining the reason for calling the halt to tomorrow's practice and practices in the near future. Afterward, she pens a few notes on her legal pad stopping only when Frank takes her pen and escorts her to bed.

"You can pick up where you left off now, Coach," says Frank.

"Sometimes, I'm selfish. I have it so good with you and Frankie and a yard. I forget that so many people are living in close quarters like high-rise apartments or farm-workers housing."

"Or nursing homes," adds Frank.

"Yeah. I got Covid and it's an inconvenience. In other parts of the county, it's raging, and I only think that I can't hold practice tomorrow. So selfish."

Frank knows this Molly and pulls her closer into his body. "You might be the only person in the world who would describe you as selfish."

"You warned me about holding practice."

"No, I cautioned you about wearing masks and taking Frankie with you."

"I hate it that he has to spend so much time indoors. Not just the virus but the poopie air."

"We're handling that. He has a full childhood," says Frank. "Wearing a mask now probably prevents him from getting other diseases."

"Still, it would be wonderful to just send him outside like we did when we lived by the coast."

"Poopie air there too. Most places have it." Frank laughs slightly. "Do I have to say that word with a high-pitched voice like you do?"

Molly returns to the virus. "It's not going away soon, is it, Doc?'

"No. Not until we get a vaccine and get everyone vaccinated. It's on the horizon. The pharmaceutical companies have been working on it for years, so I expect them to produce one shortly. That's good news."

"So, it's not being created out of nothing at Trump Laboratories at Mar-a-Lago?"

Frank mostly ignores his wife's snide comment. "We've already seen the division that's developed over mask wearing and closing businesses and the anger that has erupted on social media. Parents come to the clinic and get irate over wearing masks. Margret tells them that to enter they need to mask up. I've never heard the language they use before this. Pediatrics is supposed to be gentle. Part of the ugly political divisions that divide our country."

"I'm sorry I'm so self-centered about all this."

"Mol, we operate in different spheres just now. You need to protect your team, and they're a vulnerable group in so many ways. The problem you have, that high school and university sports have, is that your clients are healthy and seemingly immune to the ravages of Covid, so why should they be having to make the sacrifices. I guess I'm one of those who believes that if they weren't bringing it home to their families, then I would keep them playing, but they are. Your team is living in a semi-bubble and is mostly safe. Covid is highly contagious, Period."

"Invisible, huh?"

"Only until you go to the hospital and see people on ventilators, then it's starkly visible. So many people don't know anyone who's died yet or lost a family member and seen the struggle. Just the flu, you know." There is anger in Frank's last sentence.

Molly squeezes her husband. "Enough of this for tonight. We'll talk about moving to the South Pacific another time."

"I doubt if they have a college basketball team there anyway."

❧

Tuesday will be a hot one in Tulare County, well over 100 degrees, so the morning is already uncomfortable. There is almost no breeze, and the pollution hangs on the town like limp banners leftover from one of the many agricultural festivals. The AC runs constantly during the summer, its hum serves as white noise to drown out the highway traffic. Frankie eats a pancake while reading from his iPad. Molly sits across the table with her coffee scanning various websites for bits of information about other university programs. The doorbell surprises her, but it's Frankie who bolts out of his chair to answer it.

"Mask!" yells Molly.

Frankie doesn't recognize the masked man who has stepped back eight or ten feet from the door and is holding a box. The man realizes this, slips his mask down, and smiles. "Good morning, Frankie. I hope you didn't fill up on healthy food this morning. I brought donuts."

Molly appears behind Frankie and smiles brightly. How long has it been since she last was with the journalist? She invites him in, but Ken Davidson refuses.

"I'll walk around and meet you on the back porch. I would like a cup of joe, however."

At the patio table, Ken opens the box to reveal six unhealthy donuts and motions with his eyes for Frankie to dig in. "Don't you get really tired of texts," he says rhetorically. "I heard you held a practice yesterday and then were instructed not to do it again. Must be hard on your girls."

Molly breathes out heavily as if she has been holding air in her lungs for days. She exhales heavily again. "So hard. For two hours, all was right with the universe, and then it imploded instantly. At least it felt like it. I Zoomed with the ladies last night, and we talked it out, but it's just so hard on them. Most of the team are here at the university, but a couple of them drove over just to do this. They're staying with Coach Powell who has extra rooms, but they'll head home in a few days unless we get new information and permission to start up again."

Davidson shakes his head. "Not going to happen, is it?"

Molly purses her lips and shakes her head in time with her guest. "No, not with the surge in cases." She alters her expression and genuinely asks, "How are you feeling, Ken?"

"All things considered, pretty good. Didn't think I was going to make it there for a while, but those young doctors and nurses up in Fresno just wouldn't accept me dying. Those people are amazing, doing a helluva job, putting their own health in jeopardy every day."

He takes a drink and brushes some powdered sugar from his shirt. "How's your husband? I'll bet he's tired at the end of each day."

"Long hours, but you know him. Never complains, unlike his spouse who thinks the whole world is conspiring to keep her from holding a practice."

"Sort of why I'm here, other than to see Frankie. These donuts are a bribe. I'd like to write a few sentences about what it's like to press on during this bullshit."

Frankie looks up at his mama. He's heard her use this profanity before, and she always apologizes, but Mr. Davidson doesn't. Molly cocks her head and directs her son back to his donut.

"Here's my problem though, sort of what you just alluded to. Old people, sick people, doctors and nurses," Davidson pauses. "They're dying, but university athletes and their coaches aren't. You got it, and evidently, it was like the flu except you had to quarantine. Asymmetric."

Molly laughs. "I think you mean asymptomatic."

"Nope. Asymmetric." Davidson puts his donut on the paper plate and lays the side of his hand on the table moving it back and forth. "This virus seems to have a central line that divides just about everything. It shouldn't, but it does. Old versus young, rich versus poor, healthy versus those with immune deficiencies." As he talks, he jumps his hand back and forth over his imaginary central line. "And then it mutates into politics. "Who's wearing the mask? Who's not? I have to tell you, it makes absolutely no sense to this old man. Covid is becoming the Great Revealer."

Frankie is listening intently and speaks. "My dad calls it the divider."

Davidson looks at Frankie. "Are you sure you're just nine years old?" Frankie doesn't understand. "Anyway, even though the virus attacks some people and simply annoys others or doesn't affect many at all, its insidious nature is that both groups are connected as if by an invisible thread." He pauses. "Sort of like offense and defense." He smiles coyly, and Molly knows why the journalist has brought donuts.

When Molly Rascon was growing up in the 1990s, her hometown, Oro Hills, Colorado, was nothing like the mountain ski towns, as if I-70 was that central dividing line Davidson referred to, but that interstate certainly connected them. Oro Hills was where the poor lived.

They would get up in the morning, drive or be bused to a resort town, serve the rich, and return at night to sleep away from the wealthy. Molly wasn't one of the kids who grew up resentful of her condition; after all, she had basketball, and that sent her to a comfortable life. The Land of Opportunity. She didn't recognize gender inequality, political correctness, or societal conditioning. She worked, her mother worked, her friends worked, their parents worked, and when they could, they played basketball.

When Ken left, she and Frankie went out to the driveway to shoot baskets. She can't stop thinking about Ken Davidson's thoughts. "The Great Revealer." His request. "I want to write an incomplete account of Covid's effect on a single team, a successful team."

Molly asked why since all teams seemed to be in it together.

"In my mind, it has to be a successful team, a team on the cusp of something great, a team tracking a championship, and a team that hasn't sniffed that rare air before."

"I had that sniff, and almost all my ladies played on winning teams in high school."

"I know you did, but high school is the small stage, an important stage, but when you're seventeen, you don't know. Those girls have never been cut from a team. All the best players on their high school team. The Tribe had just one best player and eleven teammates. The air is thinning."

Davidson's words echo in her ears as she chases down one of Frankie's misses. He has advanced to the ten-foot baskets this season, up from the adjustable seven-footer, and he has the touch.

On Thursday, July 17, Congressman John Lewis dies. Ryanne, Molly, and Frankie sit in the coaches' office watching the television coverage. Molly listens while Ryanne describes her actions campaigning for Obama in 2008 in the neighborhoods of south Chicago. "Congressman Lewis first supported Hillary but switched mid-campaign. It was a big deal. Junior was more involved than me. I think he met him a few times that year. I just walked the projects trying to register voters. It was right after that when I moved to California to coach." Ryanne addresses Frankie. "That's when I met your mama, and we became best friends."

Molly smiles at her son and Ryanne at the same time. "Aunt Ryanne was the original *good trouble* for me." Molly sees that her son doesn't understand. "Congressman Lewis had a motto, 'Good Trouble,' which meant that sometimes a person needs to cause trouble for a good cause, that if something is really wrong, a person needs to stand up to it. Being silent doesn't improve the bad condition." She nods. "He was a brave man."

Ryanne uses the remote to turn down the sound. "Do you remember a couple of years ago when your mama got written up in the newspapers for standing with the farm workers when they protested the use of pesticides in the fields, that those chemicals were harming their children. Some people wrote letters saying Coach Rascon should stick to basketball, that she hadn't lived in The Valley long enough to know. She was taking a brave stand about something that was hurting the people in our county, and she spoke out even though many people criticized her. That's what *good trouble* means."

"Mama got her picture in the paper," says Frankie.

Molly waves as if to minimize her actions. "Some of the kids who were affected went to your school. Remember Luisa and Bernard? It seemed to me that the farms were hurting the environment, that maybe fertilizing the crops could be done more safely and not damage the soils, and thus the health of the people who worked in those fields."

"Dad took me to watch," remembers Frankie. "That one man yelled at you."

In the afternoon, Coach Rascon and Coach Powell work with individuals at the Kappa Sig court. Maximum of four on the court at any one time, all masked and widely spaced. Half-hour sessions, position specific. Molly works Keilani hard; 30 minutes of dribbling skills with her head up, always with the goal of getting into the paint. Coach has set orange cones at various spots, toss-backs in both corners, and a cardboard Draymond Green waits in the lane eight feet in front of the basket ready to take a charge or deflect any weak pass.

The practice number gets bumped up to six again. Coach Rascon has Keilani, Emerson, and Kaori, while Coach Powell works with Maria, Sylvia, and Esther, all individually. Three hours away, Coach Robinson works with Greta. Seven hundred miles to the east, Dyani works with Char. Joyce Hensley is too tired for basketball. Kenti Solorzano chooses to be a full-time farmer. Danelle Weston exercises to prepare for her induction into the military in August, a 6′4″ recruit—again.

Former assistant coach Nicole Aikins moves into an apartment in a Los Angeles suburb in anticipation of becoming a high school head coach. Furloughed assistant coach Jackie Jakino begins her first week as the recreation sports coordinator for her people, the Yokuts, north of Fresno. Manager Martina Smith finagles a paying job in the registrar's office at SJV. Ken Davidson buys a new notebook, desk lamp, and a box of pens.

Much like sports teams across the country, the San Joaquin Valley Sequoias carry on as best they can. Coach Rascon holds another Zoom call for the SJV coaches, reaching out to ease the isolation of the pandemic.

Back east, the Ivy League suspends all individual and team workouts. Their institutional criteria differ from most other conferences, including California's Ring of Fire. The Ivy League's official position on Covid is that there are no gray areas, that the nation is clearly in the midst of a deadly airborne pandemic and until three conditions are met, athletic competition will be treated exactly like classroom attendance. In addition to a vaccine and better therapies, the public needs to step up to better compliance behavior, something that hasn't been done. The Ivy League has, however, floated the idea of allowing for an extra year of eligibility for some sports. Vague.

The Covid surge in the East is surpassed by the surge in the San Joaquin Valley. The statistics aren't merely numbers to Molly. Frank brings home his cases each night, not deaths of any of his young patients, but unnecessary illnesses to them and to their parents and grandparents. His face reveals his fatigue. Joyce Hensley brings the deaths to the Zoom calls when she has the energy to participate, but more, Joyce tells of the suffering that goes on day after day in the hospital, people like Ken Davidson who linger near death for days before recovering. And Queenie was real, is real. As much as Molly wants to restart her program, she isn't misled by figures saying college athletes are safe. The universities in SJV's conference are her opponents, but Covid is the enemy. Its transmission is invisible, but its casualties are not.

America desperately wants to return to normal, whatever that was, because this pandemic is another sword dividing the country. One side's facts are the other side's disinformation. Willful ignorance is Covid's ally, and social media its chief propagandist. Into every aspect of life, Covid injects itself. A nation without sports. That can't happen.

The text is brief. "Coach, M and me are going home." Its brevity doesn't bother Molly; Sylvia has never been wordy in her correspondence. She opens up in face-to-face meetings. Molly responds. "We'll talk at our session this morning." Sylvia's time is 10 am, Maria follows at 10:45. *Today*, thinks Molly, *we won't work on footwork.*

Molly texts Ryanne asking if she knows anything about this. Ryanne says she doesn't, but with the first summer session ending and Sylvia's work at the Fresno hospital exhausting for a candy striper, it makes sense. Molly wonders about transportation costs. Once they get home, they should be fine. Ft. Bliss, El Paso, Texas. Army brats from a stable home. Frankie will lose his babysitters too. Keilani, Emerson, Kaori, and Esther will all take classes online for the second five-week session. Four months ago, twelve players prepared for the conference tournament. Today, the team is down to four, a solid four, but four, nevertheless. Molly makes a quick call to Dr. Calhoun.

Molly receives a text from her husband. "Britain just announced that they have a vaccine." She texts back, "Thank God!!!!!"

"Frankie, honey, time to go. Grab your gym bag and computer." Molly takes the small cooler from the counter, and they head for the car.

Precisely at 10:00 and already dressed for their workout, Sylvia and Maria arrive at the outdoor court, and their agenda does include one last practice session. Together. While the sisters have their own dorm room, they fudge and share just one. Having them workout together shouldn't be less safe. For 30 minutes, they bump, push, bang, and laugh as Coach Rascon instructs, encourages, and compliments their work. When they finish, the three ladies sit in plastic chairs near the gate in the shade and towel off. All are sweating profusely.

"Have you noticed how Sylvia fouls me every time I go up for a shot?" kids Maria.

"Crybaby," answers Sylvia. "Toughen up."

After a quick critique of the basketball part, Molly listens to the sisters explain their decision. "It really wasn't that hard," says Sylvia. They need a break, just as they would have under normal conditions, and they would like to spend some time with the family. "Dad is being deployed overseas for six months."

Maria adds, "Mom handles his deployments fine, but she stresses the first few weeks until she settles into her routine. We know the pattern."

The sisters assure Coach that they will return in the fall if the team gets to play games. Molly tells them that their scholarship will pay the plane fare and that they can leave their things in one of the rooms for now. "I'll drive you to Fresno to catch the plane. You said you wanted to leave on Thursday, so the school will make the flight arrangements." They talk for another half-hour, and Maria and Sylvia both want to practice again on Tuesday and Wednesday, bonus practices. Maria will watch Frankie on both afternoons to free up Coach for other practices and duties. Sylvia is scheduled to work one more shift at the hospital.

Army brats, thinks Molly. *Loyalty and responsibility.*

Ryanne arrives at noon for the afternoon session just a few minutes after Sylvia and Maria have left. Junior has been away for weeks now, and every room in her house has been repainted. She sits in one of the plastic chairs, unscrews her water bottle, taps her phone to retrieve a message, and sighs. That one number has left another message.

Molly tosses a ball back to Frankie and takes a seat next to Ryanne. Molly takes a relaxation breath. "I had a good session with Sylvia and Maria. If we can keep this together, we can still be really good."

Ryanne jots a quick note and puts her pen down. "Yeah, maybe for one season, but if we lose all our recruits, the program will take a tumble, so keep hustling, Mol."

"Twenty-four hours each day, 365 days a year. With Greta and Esther, our front line is solid even with Danelle gone. I can't lose sight of what we have right now."

"Worst case scenario?" poses Ryanne.

"How about most realistic scenario as of July. We lose Char—at least for a year—but Kenti returns to harass Keilani. Our seniors are gone, and we lose Joyce to full-time nursing—she seems to have gone full-in to her chosen profession—but the rest of our ladies return. We'd be light in the backcourt, especially at point guard, but at least the nucleus will be really good."

"What if you were to lose your whole coaching staff?"

"What are you saying, Ry?" Molly reaches down for her water.

"UIC keeps calling. You know, 'off the record, but we know about your success as an assistant, and you're from Chicago, and blah, blah, blah.' But it's home and Junior would be there more, and my family." Ryanne pauses.

"Worst case scenario. I'd have to play you in the Sweet Sixteen in four or five years." Molly purses her lips. "No harm in talking," She would be devastated to lose her best friend, but she would be so happy for Ryanne. She also knows Ryanne makes her more effective, knows that SJV's defense relies on Ryanne's demand for physical play.

The two women stare at each other for a moment before the assistant speaks. "The job hasn't been officially posted, more of an 'if it was open, would you be interested' sort of conversation."

"Ry," says Molly in her Head Coach tone. "If it does open, you go after it! It's time and you've earned your chance." Molly softens. "You wouldn't have to carry me around letting me get all the credit and big money."

Ryanne smiles and nods. "Well, there's that too, but right now we have two girls coming around the house."

❧

The announcement of a vaccine has Dr. Frank Martinez optimistic for the first time since the first cases were revealed. "Finally, something we can all get behind." The news comes to him via text from a colleague in Los Angeles. Frank dons his mask, walks to the examination room where one of his nurses is cleaning up after a five-year-old vomited, and tells her to stop for a moment. He tells her the news as much for himself as for her; he wants to say it aloud. "It took four years to develop the polio vaccine, and that was the fastest reveal ever. This one could be out at the beginning of next year. That would be amazing." His voice inflection sounds like a high school boy who is relating his first kiss to his friends or how he juked an opposing linebacker to score a touchdown. Dr. Martinez grabs a sponge and begins helping the nurse as if when the vomit is removed, so will the virus.

July 23, 2020. The United States surpasses 143,000 dead from Covid. The NCAA seems to be putting profits over the welfare of the athletes as it moves to restart the football season. President Trump threatens to send federal agents to Portland to suppress the violent protests. Junior Warren arrives in Tulare to spend a week with Ryanne. The Dreamer, Esther Santiago, officially changes her major from art to medical technology and takes a job at the Tulare medical center aiding in Covid testing.

The next day, Sylvia Castro and Maria Sanchez don masks and plastic shields and board a plane in Fresno bound for home, for El Paso. They each carry a plastic sack of cookies baked by their coach.

Chapter 11

Even though her team is down to four players remaining in town, Coach Rascon believes it's improving significantly. Keilani, Kaori, Emerson, and Esther are enrolled in the second five-week summer session at SJV, and all are tech-savvy, so online courses present no obstacles. Every workout focuses on skill improvement. The "Fab Four," as Emerson has dubbed them, are tight. They push each other to excel academically as well as on the court and their conditioning. Dr. Frank Martinez tells them that there have been no deaths in the county for women under the age of 25, and since none of the Fab Four have an underlying health condition, they are mostly safe. Mostly, as they completely avoid the social scene in Tulare and Visalia where Covid cases continue to rise, and they test frequently. They are on a mission to retain the conference championship next season and advance to the NCAAs. When their teammates return, The Tribe will pick up where it left off in March.

Workouts include lots of one-on-one. N-95 masks don't restrict the play, and when it's Keilani versus Kaori, Kaori versus Emerson, or Emerson versus Keilani, it's an evenly matched contest that often goes past eleven, win by two. Keilani's improved ball-handling skills seem to be lifting her into "first place." She's keeping a record. Emerson says it's "bullshit," that Keilani's data is flawed. Esther is at a disadvantage, but she leads "the league" in punishing blows. Her advantage is that the "pretty girls" have to shoot from the perimeter because they fear driving to the basket that she so fiercely defends. Coach Rascon has Esther working on her three-point shooting, an important tool in modern basketball. Esther shot no threes in her freshman season, but as Emerson sings to her, "for the times, they are a changin'."

Coach Rascon, in her private moments, alone with her legal pad, lists various starting fives for the upcoming season, the one that might or might not occur. Always, there is the "worst case scenario" list. Keilani, Emerson, Kaori, Esther, and Greta, whom Mose Robinson assures her is getting taller, stronger, and more skilled back in Oxnard. The problem would be a weak bench to practice against, but if that's the worst-case scenario, SJV will field a better starting five than any other team in the conference. Coach Rascon leans toward having men to practice against in this scenario. She believes Sylvia will return, Maddie Martin has enrolled, and Kenti will find time to practice and make Keilani better.

And then she lists the others. Char, Dyani, Joyce, Maria, Danelle. Danelle has her degree and will be inducted into the military in the next few weeks. She should be fine, but her texts and emails have been few and brief. Hopefully, Maria will return with her sister. Joyce will be a senior and will get her degree, but probably won't find time to play basketball. She's fully invested in the fight against Covid, a true hero in this war. Char dropped all her classes and has not re-enrolled. Molly taps her pen against her lower lip. Char needs this team for her emotional health, needs to see beyond the pandemic and the current difficulty. Her family wants her home and that's the primary tug in her young heart.

Dyani. Dyani Dehiya. Molly lays her pen on the pad and puts her hands together in front of her lips as if she is praying. Her amazing point guard, the best player she has ever coached, once told her that her name means "beautiful deer, fast and smart." *Yes, Dyani, you are,* thinks Molly, *and strong, carrying the hopes of much of your people and the championship dreams of The Tribe.* Dyani completed her degree in the spring but had no ceremony. Now, she's taken on the task of healing Char. Coach Rascon is an enthusiastic hugger of her players, but Dyani was a reluctant hugger. Coach was persistent and broke Dyani's resistance down, but they didn't get to hug before Dyani left for the reservation with her degree in hand. Molly reaches for her phone.

"Hi, Coach. What's happening?"

"Same ol', making lists, contacting donors for another pledge, worrying about Frankie, fighting with Dr. Calhoun for more money, texting high school girls trying to sell our program. I just called to see how you're doing."

"Oh, Coach, it's awful here on the rez. Everything's closed and, I don't know if you know, but we've got the highest rate of infection and deaths in the country. It's like 400 of my people have died already. So far, my family hasn't got it, but we know it's coming. There's just this cloud hanging over our heads. Some asshole posted on Facebook that everyone on the rez was infected, and the government should kill us all to protect the rest of the country. It's not true, but things like that make us even more suspicious of the government. Even the masks that they sent us weren't the right kind and defective." Dyani pauses to take a deep breath. "Sorry, Coach, I didn't mean to burden you with all that."

"No, no. I'm here for you. Dr. Frank keeps me up to date on some of that, so we pray for you and Char every night. So does Frankie."

"Pray hard, Coach, we need it. One of Char's aunts died, but at least she's wearing her mask." Dyani makes a sound that seems like a sarcastic laugh to Molly. "Did you know that Char is one stubborn Indian?"

Molly knows, knows that it's based in insecurity and a lack of trust of non-Native Americans. Molly knows that the pandemic has only enhanced those fears. "Is there anything I can do, Dyani?"

"No, not right now. She won't do anything to get back in school, so I just kind of have to hold her hand through this. She thinks she flunked every class and threw away her chance."

"I'm pretty sure the school will be very forgiving about all this, that she can get re-enrolled when she's ready. SJV gets it—most of the time." Molly pauses. "How are you doing, Captain?"

Softly, Dyani answers. "Okay, Coach. Just really tired."

Molly taps off and shakes her head. "Yeah," she whispers, "really really tired."

❧

As he waits for his phone to ring, Dr. Calhoun knows that SJV athletics are not about winning national championships, that they are about participation and the experience of competition at the highest level. He also has the revenue figures in front of him, and his budget is now in shambles. He has been working the phones with his donors, but most of them fear a coming recession and are not willing to commit additional monies. Over half of the university's assistant coaches have been furloughed and every head coach stepped up to take a voluntary ten percent pay cut. The furloughing of talented, usually young assistants hurts him, throwing these people out into the cold, as he sees it. When the pandemic eases, he'll be able to rehire some of them, but he can't promise them a date. This season? Next?

There is talk of tuition hikes, but that wouldn't kick in for a couple of years. Dr. Calhoun's concern is 2020-2021. His 3500 regular donors have already indicated that their contributions will be less this coming year. Thank goodness for the dairy association; its donation amount seems to be safe. Oh, for a television contract for the Ring of Fire! He understands the figures, but he is the athletic director, charged with operating SJV sports, and he does not want to cut any program, and he wants to remain competitive within the conference. SJV serves the underserved, a university for students from families below the poverty line, and he is proud of his school. Serving these students is written in the school's mission statement, promoting opportunities without reservations. SJV is a public university set in central California, not a private university aligned with the Ivy League. Many of his students have already spent two years at a community college to save money and are now trying to complete a four-year degree, and extra-curricular sports help so many of them with purpose and financial aid. He looks at his cell that sits silent on his desk.

Dr. Calhoun swears, gets up to pace, but stops in front of his second-floor window that looks out over a grassy area of the campus. Mostly empty, but he notices four masked coeds walking toward the one open dorm, one of them dribbling a basketball. Coach Rascon's players he surmises. If he had to cut programs, her sport would not be one of them. The promised donation from the Santa Barbara families will ensure the health of that program and allow SJV to divert funds to other sports. He returns to his desk and pulls out the data. Five hundred students participating in eighteen sports. Five hundred out of the 11,000 students. *How am I going to protect each one during this pandemic*, he thinks.

The university's president announced in mid-May that the university would not discontinue its entire athletic program but added that not all the programs would be kept. Find a way, she said, to fund golf and tennis, or they'll have to go. What she meant was find a revenue source. Dr. Calhoun wonders if he has found enough money over the last three months. His cell buzzes. He breathes in heavily.

A summer without Little League baseball or youth soccer, a summer without hide-and-go-seek. Covid intrudes on every facet of life. Frankie is luckier than most of the children in Tulare because he has several big sisters who understand best practices to hold Covid at bay. Still, he doesn't play with kids his own age. His iPad gets lots of time. As he sits watching his mama direct Keilani through a complicated two-ball dribbling drill, her phone buzzes. It's not Freddie Mercury's tune, but a familiar name pops up. "Mom," screams Frankie. His tone startles Molly, and she immediately stops the drill to attend to his concern. Frankie holds up her phone and waves her over. As she starts over, he answers her phone.

"This isn't Coach Rascon; it's Frankie. Where have you been?"

"I had the virus and didn't want to infect my people, so I went up to Doko'oosliid to heal myself. Besides, I'm good at being by myself. Remember when I told you I search for dinosaurs?"

"Did you find any?"

"No, but I'll keep looking?"

Molly stands next to her son as he talks, tilting her head with that "Who's that?" look. Frankie holds up his hand telling her to be patient. He smiles at something the caller says, then giggles. Shortly, he hands the phone to his mother. "It's Hector."

"Oh my God, Hector! Are you okay? Where are you?"

Hector explains that he has been existing in the sacred mountains north of Flagstaff fighting with the virus. "It had much to teach me. At first, I thought it was all evil, but anything that can teach me a truth can't be all evil." Molly sits on the plastic chair that Frankie had been sitting on when her phone rang and listens. "The virus revealed how lazy I was becoming, how much I was excusing that laziness as old age. It scorned me for my pride, reminding me that yesterday was yesterday, and it is no longer yesterday, that I can't live off that. For several days I was weak and lingered, but finally it let loose of its grip. I stayed in the mountains to recover and exercise, and now I am returning to Chinle."

"Have you spoken with Dyani or Char?"

"I will shortly. I want to hold my families with my eyes and arms first. Voices can be deceiving."

"Oh, Hector, I'm so glad you're okay. You had us all so worried."

"We must take care of ourselves before we can help others. Would you put your son back on the phone please?" Molly hands Frankie the phone. "Frankie, would you do me a favor and text Char and tell her she will be getting a surprise very soon? Don't tell her that you spoke with me or anything about me. I just want her to get a message from you, so she has that connection to Tulare again."

When the call ends, Frankie asks his mama several questions about Mr. Dehiya, the most thoughtful, "Mama, why did Mr. Dehiya call us first?"

❧

Coach Robinson drives Greta Espinoza to SJV on Monday, August 3, so she can meet with her agribusiness advisor before the fall semester begins in three weeks and he can talk with his staff too. Her major is one of the few that will be allowing for in-person gatherings although even hers will mostly be virtual. Mose, who has never taken an online course in his life, jokes that he now understands the term "virtual reality." In addition to her academic meeting, Greta will practice—for that precious half-hour allowance—with Coaches Rascon and Powell to demonstrate how far her skills have developed. It's the practice time that she really desired more than a face meeting with her advisor. She has grown another half inch and now stands six three and a half. With the graduation of Danelle, Greta will be the tallest player on the squad, and she has dreams. Being Coach

Robinson's only charge, she has worked hard with a mentor who understands what it takes to reach the highest levels of the game. Greta hasn't lifted a pound of artificial weight over the summer but has hoisted hundreds of fifty-pound crates from the fields onto trucks. Throughout the summer, she covered her face with the traditional bandana of the strawberry fields, but under her bandana, so as not to stand out, she also wore a secondary N 95 mask given to her by Sally Robinson.

Coach Robinson parks his truck at the arena. Greta texted Coach Rascon ten minutes earlier to tell them of the arrival time. Molly and Ryanne are standing in the lot waiting for them. All are wearing masks. Greta's hug envelops Coach Rascon, that new sinewy body bending over to embrace her five foot-maybe-five-inch coach. Geta releases her head coach and steps to Coach Powell who takes a step back. They bump fists and nod. The meeting is brief; Greta's academic conference is scheduled first, before lunch. Lunch is planned after that with the Fab Four. These five young women make up what Coach Rascon calls her "for sures."

"Oh my God, Greta, you look amazing," crows Coach Rascon. The recently turned twenty-year-old beams. "Your teammates will be surprised."

"No," says Greta. "They know. We have Instagram, unlike you old people." Molly feigns hurt but the group laughs at Greta's truth. "Any more news about the season?"

"Everything I'm hearing is that somehow we're going to play, but it's all rumor. My guess is that we will but with restrictions. My AD thinks we'll be delayed, but how long we'll have to see."

"I'm so excited, but it's just so frustrating not knowing." It's the emotion that Molly deals with most with her team. Looking toward the tall old man standing next to Ryanne, Greta says, "Coach keeps me positive though. He thinks I should only get one day off a week to rest." She smiles warmly, and Mose looks back at her like he doesn't know what she's talking about, but of course he does.

The gathering breaks up so that Greta can go to her academic appointment. She takes a shoulder bag from Coach Robinson's truck and sets off on her own, while the three coaches sit near the arena entrance on wooden benches. Molly and Ryanne gush over Greta's physical appearance.

"Nice work, Coach," says Ryanne.

"I had very little to do with that physical specimen. She did it all on her own, but when you see her on the court after lunch, then you can double my salary. I challenged her to be a Breanna Stewart-type player and she ran with it. Never once missed a session despite working in the fields every day. Amazing kid."

Ryanne pops the lid of a cola. "So, she's not the post-up center we recruited?"

Mose shakes his head and looks to the head coach. "You may want to rethink your offense. Five out at times, especially when Sylvia isn't on the court. You'll certainly have options. Any word on her and her sister?"

"So far, they're telling me they're returning. Pretty sure about Sylvia, but a little iffy about Maria, but Ryanne's been working on her."

Ryanne nods. "She'll be back. Molly just likes to worry."

The coaches talk about the remaining team members, about recruits, about other teams in the conference, and about NCAA rumors before turning to non-basketball matters. Molly asks about Ken Davidson, since Mose is in frequent phone contact with the old journalist.

"Not doing well. I wouldn't count on him covering the team if we have a season. He has several stories bouncing around his skull, but he just can't shake the aftereffects of the ventilator. You don't hear about that, but even when a vulnerable person survives Covid, he can still be really sick. We talk every few days, but he just doesn't have the energy or desire to write. He's going to therapy and Naomi gets him there, but it's going to be a long slog."

"What about you and Sally?" asks Ryanne.

"So far so good. We're careful and we've never had health problems, knock on wood." Mose raps the back of the bench. "How about you, Coach?" he asks, looking at Molly.

"It was just an inconvenience for a week. Little longer. Mostly achy, but it went away, and the boys never got it. My husband is living in it daily and tests frequently but so far so good."

Lunch is, of course, pizza. Coach Rascon ordered it, and Kaori picked it up and brought it to the Kappa Sig court. It's over 90 degrees and Tulare's air is dirty as usual, but the court is partially shaded, an oasis in so many ways. Each girl loads up her paper plate and sits on the court as do Molly and Ryanne. Mose's knees don't allow for that, so he sits awkwardly on one of the plastic chairs. Throughout the chatter, Molly's basketball mind analyzes lineups and styles of play. The five ladies about to practice are not just basketball skilled, they are run and jump athletes. She remembers a high school team like that 25 years ago, a team that beat people defensively because of their quickness and lack of fear and trust for one another and in their coach. She is brought back to the present by Keilani.

"Hey Coach. Greta's going to stay with us in the dorm for a few days. Send Coach Robinson home and Kaori will drive her back at the end of the week."

Molly looks first to Greta and then to Mose. Both are shaking their heads from side-to-side. "Nice try, Lani, but protocols, remember. Besides, the entire strawberry industry would collapse if Greta didn't show up for work tomorrow."

No girl eats more than three slices of pizza knowing they will be practicing in twenty minutes. Four of them are eager to see the fifth show them her new talents. They giggle, unconcerned about the ever-present virus, even though their social distancing seating has become ingrained in their daily interactions.

Paired shooting at the three baskets. Kaori with Emerson. Coach Robinson works with Esther. Keilani with Greta. Coach Rascon has seen the growth of her new point guard; now she gets to see the development of her other X-factor. Coach Robinson keeps Esther focused on her drills, but Kaori and Emerson are drawn to the exhibition at the main hoop. Shoot and move. Target hands. Finish high. Move. Keilani rebounds most of Greta's shots from the net. Receive the pass, one dribble step backs. Receive the pass, head lift and drive. Shoot and move. Smiles take over the faces of Kaori, Emerson, Molly, and Ryanne. Coach Robinson holds his ball and directs Esther's eyes to another basket. Seven straight makes later,

Greta holds up her hands for a break.

"Fuuuck," says Keilani. "I may never get to shoot again, but I will lead the nation in assists."

Molly shakes her finger at Keilani's language, but she understands. *If this is the future*, thinks the head coach, *bring it on!*

After a water break, Molly puts the ladies into five out motion. "No screening; all pass and cut. Step to your pass and then make a deep cut. Remember, every drill is a passing drill. No shots for now." The players know this drill, but never in Coach Rascon's coaching life, not even at State Tech when she played on a Final Four team, has she seen it executed with five such athletes. With Keilani, Kaori, Emerson, and Greta moving like Arab show horses, Esther seems to rise to the occasion. Molly alters the drill after thirty passes with only one flub. "Now, pass and screen away. Yell out 'pop, pop, pop' when you don't curl off the screen. Be loud." Again, the ladies are sharp. Mose stands off to the side grinning like a Cheshire cat. He remains quiet, arms folded across his chest.

Molly's practice plan for the five masked players calls for a little one-on-one, but she doesn't go there. This short practice is all about togetherness, not competition against each other. There will be time for that in the fall, but on this summer day, this beautiful summer day, it is all five acting as one. She wishes she had five additional players so that this group could demonstrate how good they will be defensively. *Oh please, let there be a season!*

Ryanne reads her head coach. "Free throws!"

☙

Tulare County records the highest rate of infection in California for the first week in August. Governor Newsom moves toward lessening the restrictions for his state, but some counties are problematic. For Tulare, it's not just the food industry and nursing homes, but it's across all sectors, ages, and occupations. For the San Joaquin Valley, the stay-at-home directive remains in place.

Staying at home is no problem for Ken and Naomi Davidson this summer. Ken's balance prevents him from doing any activity that doesn't require a walker, but on Wednesday morning, with Naomi at the grocery store, he decides that he no longer wants to be so limited, so dependent on his wife. He turns off the television, stands, grabs his cane instead of his walker, and moves gingerly to the kitchen nook where his computer sits gathering dust. Breathing hard, he arranges his workspace in order to read his notes while he types. "Nice going, Kenny-boy," he says aloud. "Keep it going now." **Basketball and Agriculture**, he types.

It's mid-summer, 2020, and the United States of America has just gone through the opening stage of a pandemic that has shut down the economy and the social life of most of its citizens and further divided my beloved country. Medical professionals tell us that Covid is far from over, that until we get the vaccine, it will attack us again in waves with greater energy further adding to our already too tragic death toll. America may surpass 300,000 before it's over. It is especially transmissible because of our POLITICAL PANDEMIC, the continuing melodrama over wearing a simple mask to protect one another and avoiding large gatherings. Did I say "melodrama"? That's being too gentle with my country. Covid is a pandemic, but poisoned politics is a juggernaut, an invisible, destructive force that bears no resemblance to the principles of a democratic republic as established by the Constitution. It has been an imperfect course, for sure, but in these times, when we need to be working together, we can't find the compassion, the patriotism, the small-town self-sacrifice to work together to combat our shared troubles. Patriotism and liberty are empty words these days used to cover willful ignorance of facts. This blind devotion to goofy conspiracies and those who spin these crazy deceptions confounds me. My country is racing at warp speed to deny democracy and the republic, racing toward autocracy, and those who promote this seem to be winning. I am equal parts angry and sad, that at the end of my life, I may not again see a UNITED States of America striving to live up to the promise of liberty and justice for all.

I had to get that off my chest. I suspect my readers who have bought into some of these conspiracy theories will now stop reading my blog and start a campaign to discredit me or send vulgar texts. So be it.

Coach Rascon and Coach Powell came by yesterday to update me on the progress of their team. Fits and starts, although I think they chose Tuesday to visit because of all the good things that have occurred over the past few days. They cautioned me that it could all come apart in the blink of an eye, or as in the case of The Valley, in the rise of Covid cases. As she spoke, Coach Rascon kept fiddling with the gold chain she wears, the one with the small cross. Her top two recruits have now enrolled. The fog in my head keeps me from understanding the details of the NCAA's recruiting exceptions. These two players will replace SJV's two graduating seniors, Dyani Dehiya and Danelle Weston. These were two of my favorites. Coach Rascon told me that Danelle will be inducted into the military later this week. She certainly was a warrior on the court, under the boards. Dyani is back on the Arizona reservation, and her status is up in the air. There are rumors of giving seniors an additional year of eligibility to make up for the abrupt end to last season, but those are just vacant hopes for now. I would love for the whole country to see Dyani compete one more time in her quest for a championship.

Champions without a championship. All is relative, I suppose. It's a pipe dream to think that SJV could capture an NCAA championship, so advancing into the tournament is a sort of championship, but not in Coach Rascon's mind. Maybe advancing into the Sweet 16 would give her satisfaction, but I doubt it. Covid robbed her team of that deep run last year, but she hasn't blinked. As she spoke glowingly of her girls, I could see that she is primed to challenge again. Think about that, little ol' SJV versus Connecticut for all the marbles.

An old man can dream, can't he? Blind people can scale Mt. Everest now.

The coaches are concerned about a couple of their players, however. These are girls raised, for the most part, in poverty, and we all know that poverty takes its toll. It can be humiliating, even brutal. Poverty is a form of punishment for crimes never committed. Still, each one was thriving at SJV before Covid struck. A couple of the girls have lost relatives to the virus. The isolation has also been a hardship. Esther, The Dreamer, still hasn't spoken with her family, but she remains in school, working to achieve that dream, while many in our disjointed nation erect new barriers that Esther must scale.

My bout with Covid has kept me from sharing beers with my friend Moses Robinson, but Coach Rascon assures me he is doing well. Isolation is in his bones, so the stay-at-home shouldn't bother him much. Coach says he works out daily with another of the players, Greta Espinoza, and that she has made amazing progress in her offensive skills. Mose and I talk on the phone, but my wife says that because of my fog and Mose's penchant for silence, there's not much talking that goes on. A minute of conversation in a ten-minute call. Still, it's the connection that counts.

Coach Rascon and Coach Powell exude optimism in the face of this continuing crisis, but Coach Rascon shows new wrinkles around her eyes. She fights through her fatigue. Coach Powell's behavior reveals what her role has always been; she is Coach Rascon's KC Jones. Now there's a reference that none of my young readers will get. KC was the great Bill Russell's best friend, his teammate for most of his championships, the friend in the shadows who always had Russ's back. That's Coach Powell to Coach Rascon. My professional experience is sports, mostly male sports, so I apologize for using two old guys rather than the friendship of two female athletes.

It's bean harvesting season in The Valley, all kinds of beans. The dairy farmers continue to struggle. The air is thick with dust and pollutants. Construction on the high-speed rail continues with hopes of completion before I die, which means I must stay on the planet until at least 2025. My visit with the two coaches of my favorite sport has buoyed my spirits, seeing their love for their ladies, putting basketball on the back burner just to get their girls through this pandemic.

My wife will need to clean this blog up, but at least I've started again. Naomi is my KC Jones.

∾

With the end of the summer sessions, Emerson, Kaori, and Keilani return home for two weeks leaving only Esther in the dorms, while Kenti Solorzano continues to live at the farm. When school starts for the fall semester, virtual learning will not require on-campus living for some of the team, but those who don't return by August 24 will show up shortly after to begin workouts. Again, rumors abound about when that can be, but the pressure to restart football gives credibility to these rumors. Major conference football directs most NCAA policies. Molly thinks SJV and the Ring of Fire Conference will give the go-ahead for some kind of pre-season gatherings beginning in mid- to late-September with full practice a month later. At least, that's the schedule that she will prepare for. She's light on the number of players firmly committed to playing, seven returnees, two recruits, and a walk-on, but she is comfortable with her game numbers. It's practices that concern Coach Rascon. Kenti would be a wonderful addition to harass Keilani, but Kenti's doctoral studies are intense. Joyce hedges on her plans; she has grown into responsibility, leaving little time for basketball. Hector Dehiya took Char to Durango, Colorado, to tour the small college there, to see if it would be a better fit, and she will enroll there. Closer to home and family; a better fit, but that leaves SJV shallow at the point guard position. Keilani will need to stay healthy, and Claudia will need to be a quick study. Danelle left for Ft. Leonard Wood for a three-year Army commitment.

Freddie Mercury sings to Coach Rascon. It's Dyani.

"Hey, Coach. Is that coaching offer still open?"

Molly smiles to herself. "Well, that depends. Would you be willing to dress out and scrimmage against Lani?" Molly knows the answer.

Dyani makes a sound that sounds like "pashish." "Since the Char dilemma is settled, I won't need to babysit her any longer, and I thought I could begin graduate work this semester."

Molly decides not to pretend coy. "The short answer is yes. The details are that my line is just two at the moment, just Ryanne and me. That will change for the season, but I can't get you an immediate salary, maybe for as long as two months. When would you be able to get here?"

"Well..." It's Dyani's turn to be coy. "I registered for classes online, so I don't have to be there for that, and you aren't having practices just now. Without my scholarship or a paycheck, I may need to find alternative housing. I think I can get my tuition paid for. Why don't I just come in and talk about it."

Molly is confused by Dyani's last sentience. The doorbell rings, but before Molly can get to it, Ryanne and Dyani walk in. "Mornin' Coach."

∽

AD Calhoun tells Coach Rascon that the university will now allow for a third coach for her program immediately and a fourth line soon. The team manager, Martina Smith, will receive aid in addition to her part-time job. Calhoun assures Molly that her staff will never be funded like UCLA's or Duke's. Molly admits that she wouldn't know how to use that kind of staff. "Last two years I had five, and that was plenty." Jackie Jakino decides to remain at her current job and not return to SJV. Calhoun also reminds Coach Rascon that the NCAA is reviewing the number of scholarships allowable, but that it remains the prerogative of the member schools to restrict that number depending on their finances. Molly again commits to no more than twelve full scholarships, that currently she has ten ladies on full, wants to give partial money to Maddie and Kenti if she practices and suits up, which would leave one full scholarship available. Molly asks AD Calhoun about his concerns if she was to bring in male students to practice against her team. He has no problems with this and says the university's insurance would cover it. "Might be safer not to have those extra bodies though."

Finally, Calhoun advises his women's basketball coach that the Tulare County public health office may shut down gatherings again if the county's numbers continue to rise. Molly knows what that means for her team. However, the Kappa Sigma court remains available for gatherings fewer than twelve. Covid restrictions will keep the fraternity empty throughout the fall semester with only one occupant—Mrs. Goodman—and she bakes wonderful brownies for the team. She needs company too and often sits at the edge of the court watching.

After this meeting, Molly meets with Ryanne and Dyani over coffee to plan the dead period, the days between the end of summer school and the middle of September when the NCAA allows for limited hours for practice to begin again. "Roster management," is what Molly calls these few weeks, but under Covid this becomes much more than just massaging class schedules, preparing individualized workouts, and arranging transportation for players whose families can't afford airline tickets. Mental and emotional health are the "management" issues on the front burner.

"I wonder," says Molly, "how we would navigate through all of this if our ladies came from other backgrounds."

"Do you mean wealthier?" asks Dyani.

Ryanne gently shoves Dyani's arm. "Yeah, players who owned a car in high school, a new car."

"Yeah, economically secure." Molly laughs at her phrase. "I wonder what my reaction would be to all of this had I grown up at least middle class."

"You know we can't save every team," reminds Ryanne. "We do our best with our girls, and so far, I think we're keeping their heads above water. With Char enrolling at, what's that southern Colorado school, oh yeah, Ft. Lewis, she'll make it too. We haven't lost anyone."

"I've had multiple talks with other coaches, and they seem to be faring about like us. We're all frustrated about things we can't control, but we try to keep our ladies close." Molly sips her coffee with a faraway look in her eyes. Ryanne plays with the point guard line on her roster list as she waits for Molly to come back to the present. Keilani-Claudia-Maddie. A converted off-guard, a 2+-star recruit with lots of upside potential, and a walk-on who may surprise given the opportunity. Dyani looks over Ryanne's shoulder. Molly returns. "What word do you want this year?"

Ryanne knows what Molly means. Each year, she has the university paint a word in front of the team's bench as a motivational reminder. Last season, it was *Scrum*, a subtle reminder to be the most physical team on the floor, to win the 50-50 balls. The Tribe bought into that word. Ryanne nods. "Haven't given it much thought what with everything else going on. What do you think, Dyani?"

Dyani shrugs. "I'd just leave it as it is." She stands and excuses herself for a meeting with her academic adviser.

"I think we need to put lids on our coffees and walk over to the gym, take out our cushioned chairs, and stare at the floor. You know, ponder on it," says Molly.

Fifteen minutes later, Ryanne and Molly are doing just that, staring at *Scrum* and wondering what to replace it with.

"That was a good word," says Ryanne. "Our Bigs sure loved it. The little ones liked it when they were diving on balls against other teams; not so much in practice against Danelle and Sylvia." She laughs a bit. "We could keep it for another year."

"Dyani sure liked it. I remember that once against Palm when she came from halfway across the court and made a swan dive on the top of the scrum. Sort of put the capstone on that game. Palm waived the white flag after that. When the refs cleared the bodies, Dyani had that huge smile and pointed to the word."

"She said she'd join us when she finished with her advisor and financial aid supervisors." Ryanne is talking to Molly but still pondering the floor.

On cue, both coaches lean back in their chairs and look across the floor as if surveying the arena. *Consolidated Dairies Arena*, named after the most prominent agricultural enterprise in The Valley. Dairy farming. Hence the statue of a dairy cow with a swollen udder at the front entrance. A Holstein donated by one of the dairy farms north of Tulare that once stood where the new railroad is being built. On one wall, the wall with the smallest set of retractable bleachers, *Consolidated Dairies* is painted with a list below of seven dairies that contributed substantially to renovate a Division II arena that seated about 2200 into a D1 arena with a capacity of 3400. It's never been filled for an athletic contest, something that disappoints Molly and was cause for Dyani to always comment about during every pregame warmup. "I never played a high school game in Chinle that had fewer than 5000 fans, Coach. Maybe we need to bus them over to watch." A giant redwood modeled after General Sherman, the world's largest tree, graces the center of the court, hence the Sequoias nickname.

"We could paint *COVID* as a reminder of who owned the court at the end of last year," says Molly disdainfully.

"Or *Queenie* as a reminder of why you and I are here," says Ryanne almost in a whisper.

"I'd have to include a half-dozen other names too." The two friends go quiet for a moment before Molly speaks again. "God, I'm melancholy this morning. Let's go over to the court and play horse?" Ten minutes later, two former college players way past their prime smack talk through three games of horse on an outdoor court hidden from the view of every other person in America.

Chapter 12

Stanford Coach Tara VanDerveer probably never drove to San Francisco International Airport to pick up any of her players returning to college, but Molly and Ryanne use an SJV extended van to get Sylvia and Maria in Fresno on the seventeenth, a week before the fall semester is to begin. Most classes remain online, but it's quite difficult to practice basketball that way, especially in the team sense. Most students will not be returning to Tulare for classes, but by the middle of the week, the entire Sequoia roster has returned. Again, it's a roster that looks like the demographics of the university and is comprised mostly of Californians. Sylvia and Maria are Texans and Kenti is Guatemalan, but seven live up and down the coast. Joyce and Maddie come from The Valley. Dyani's move from the team to the coaching staff alters the makeup of both, but not the overall complexion. Moses Robinson has signed on again but won't be joining the staff until the season begins, at the moment in mid-September. He'll receive half pay. Danelle is at boot camp and Char didn't return to SJV, deciding to stay closer to home at a smaller college. Coach Rascon hopes to add two or three walk-ons for practices unless she goes in the direction of male practice partners. A part of her is still uncomfortable with that change. Extra bodies, however, increase the chances of contracting Covid.

The Democratic Convention opens on Tuesday, mostly online, as Covid continues to infect millions of Americans. The visual format originates from Milwaukee. The nomination of Joe Biden will occur later in the week. He has already tabbed Kamala Harris as his vice-presidential running mate. While California is a strong blue state, Tulare

County is a Republican legislative district represented by Devon Nunes, a former dairy farmer and a rabid supporter of President Trump. Nunes wrote a book in which he claimed that environmentalists are socialists, and that climate change is a hoax. Now, during the pandemic, Nunes is telling the people in his district that if they're healthy, go out to restaurants and bars, that the media is exaggerating the danger. Needless to say, Molly and Frank and Ryanne are not supporters of Nunes. Neither is Joyce Hensley.

Coach Powell itches to walk her old Chicago neighborhood to campaign against Republicans. She wishes she could frame her politics as being for the Democrats, and she has been a Democrat all her life, but in 2020 her politics are primarily anti-Trump. "There are dozens of issues I'm passionate about, but if that man is re-elected, those issues will be denied even a fair discussion. This election is about America's historic promise. If these last four years have taught me anything, it's that a third of my country holds the views that Trump holds, that they are what he is, and that not only disappoints me, but it angers the hell out of me."

Molly listens each time Ryanne goes off on Trump. Both coaches worked the phones for the 2016 election, and neither one felt much backlash from the community for their political participation. But the climate has changed, and now, each one has received phone messages to stick to coaching and stay out of politics, that being a winning coach doesn't give them the right to talk politics. "Stay in your lane!" Ryanne acknowledges her tendency to comment every time she hears a Trump commercial or sees the flag decorated with Trump attachments. "It's not a damn Republican flag, it's supposed to be the flag of the *United* States of America. United my ass!"

Molly and Frank are quieter in their political views, but as Frank often comments, "We didn't grow up in Chicago's projects." Since college, Molly has become politically aware, has studied the issues, and has done local campaigning every two years, but she doesn't wear her politics on her sleeve as Ryanne does. Molly has never had to. Still, those around her know where she stands. Her inner circle also sees a pessimistic Molly Rascon when it comes to her view of the future of America regarding liberty and the march of freedom. "*That man* idolizes dictators like he wants their power. Rule of law is not something he respects. The Constitution just gets in his way. I just have to assume that after four years of watching him behave the way he does, the people who support him hold his values, and those values are not my values."

Coach Rascon set limits to the political discussions she and Coach Powell have. "At our homes, okay. In our cars, okay. In the gym or in the basketball office, no." That edict has forced them both to bite their tongues, but they have stuck to it. "If our ladies ask us, we'll be honest about our positions, but we won't stand on the soapbox and rant to them." With the TV coverage of the Democratic Convention, however, talking points abound.

The 2020 summer is one of the hottest on record for California. The Valley's F-rating for clean air has been exacerbated by the multiple wildfires burning throughout California. Frankie's pediatric asthma requires that he stay indoors most of the time. Just as he befriended Hector Dehiya two seasons ago, he became friends with the arena's custodial staff over his mother's tenure. They became his babysitters as he roamed freely in every part of the building. Before the arena was closed in early April, he didn't have to wear a mask since he was the only person shooting baskets or kicking a soccer ball or sitting against a wall reading his iPad. For the fall semester, the university has opened the arena to staff members, with limited access for athletes using strict protocols.

Coach Rascon often sits at the highest level of the bleachers when she is meditating on life at her workplace. A filming platform above the last row at mid-court is large enough for two cushioned chairs, and it is there that Molly claimed as her semi-private get-away place. Frankie and Dr. Frank are welcome, although her husband has only sat with her a handful of times there over the years. Ryanne is frequently a partner, and Dr. Calhoun climbed the stairs to discuss personnel issues there a few times before the virus hit. Players are not allowed; Coach will descend and speak with them on the gym floor or in her office.

On Wednesday evening after dinner, Molly goes to the arena to finish paperwork for her ladies. Frank and Frankie need time together. Dr. Frank has been bombarded with extra cases due to the heatwave and hasn't had the time to spend with his son, at least the quality time that he desires. Molly called Ryanne to see if she would join her. Dyani is staying with Ryanne for now, but has a date, so Ryanne agrees. She finds Molly in her nest nursing a flask.

"This would be a good place to smoke cigars," says Ryanne.

"If we smoked," says Molly. The two women sit quietly relaxing after a day that began at seven, thirteen hours earlier.

Eventually, Ryanne asks, "Did you hear about the new fire in the park?"

"No. Another one?"

"Yeah. Lots of worries about some of the oldest sequoias. This fire season is going to be the worst." The friends go quiet again. A custodian flashes his flashlight at the two women, a signal that he will be leaving soon and will dim some more lights.

"Johnnie's a good man," says Molly.

"You know, Mol, I never thought much about the environment when we came here, when we took the jobs. Actually, I didn't think about it at all. This was just the D1 offer we'd been moving toward. Kinda hard not to think about it these days though."

Molly nods, takes a sip from her flask, and lets out a deep breath. "Me neither. Sure do now though. It's about the only drawback to this place. We were dealt a good hand."

"Calhoun called me this afternoon, a little before dinner. He's worried he's going to lose you." Ryanne lets that sentence hover.

"Tulare needs giant fans like those wind turbines. These fans wouldn't catch the wind though, they would create winds to blow the pollution out to the ocean." Molly pauses. "Or giant vacuum cleaners to suck it all in." She scoots forward in her chair and lifts her feet onto the railing. "America is being hit by a tsunami. Covid isn't going away anytime soon. Frank tells me to hang on since we both work in contagious environments. He worries without showing it openly. The political campaigning will be so ugly. We've turned on each other, and the divide is so entrenched that I fear it can't ever be bridged." Molly pauses again.

Ryanne waits but eventually asks, "And . . ."

"Frankie's attack. It wasn't as bad as some others, but it's always a punch in the gut. I talk climate change, but I can't do anything about it . . . except bitch."

In a few moments, Ryanne asks, "What's in the flask?"

"Cranberry juice. I have a bladder infection. That's why I didn't offer to share. And the Covid protocols too." She smirks.

"Yeah, I wondered."

Molly sits up. "We've got a good bunch, especially if Keilani stays injury free and Claudia grows like we think she will. Greta's improvement really sets us up. Nobody can gang up on Kay-kay and Emerson now. And they're all underclassmen."

Ryanne reaches over and lays her hand on Molly's forearm. "U-Dub?"

Molly nods.

"I thought they were a year away."

"They are."

"So, when were you going to tell me?" asks Ryanne.

"Tonight. But there hasn't been an offer and I don't know if we would accept it and a thousand things."

"We?"

"Yeah." Molly turns to look at Ryanne. "Let's for just now assume they offer me the job after this upcoming season. Big assumption because everything right now is back channel. Agent. But let's assume. I wouldn't leave our ladies without knowing they would be in good hands, and I wouldn't leave the university with an empty cupboard. So that means I need you to be on board."

☙

Keilani's half-hour session on Friday is not spent on ball skills at the court. Instead, she sits with her coach watching film, dissecting decision-making. "When you get a three-on-one fastbreak, turn it into a two-on-one and send Kaori to the corner for the three. That keeps you out of a charge situation and improves the passing angles. Here, watch Dyani on this break. The defender has size and stays at the hoop, so the pass goes to Emerson for the three. Even though she missed, we rebound." Coach Rascon rewinds and points out angles. Keilani soaks it in. What Molly is learning is that her new point guard is cerebral.

Molly has loved watching film since she and her high school coach would stay up late analyzing opportunities. Twenty-five years ago. Molly laments the loss of Coach Aikins and her ability to break down numbers into analytics.

"Did you do this with Dyani too?" asks Keilani. Coach Rascon nods her head. "It wasn't a crash course though, was it?" Coach shakes her head.

"You'll get it, but remember, Dyani has had the ball in her hands all her life. You're not Dyani, you'll make your own dimension."

Keilani gives her coach a funny look. "Dimension?"

Molly laughs. "I don't know where that came from. Anyway, Dyani was a pass-first guard. I don't see you quite like that. You just be Keilani Russell. Take care of the ball and get us good shots. Lots of those will be your own."

The record-breaking heat continues, and Governor Newsom declares a state of emergency as over 25 fires burn thousands of acres of California forests. Two major fires burn in the Sequoia and Kings Canyon National Parks just to the northeast of Tulare, putting some of the oldest and most revered trees at risk. Frankie asks if the gym floor would have to be repainted if General Sherman burned up. Tularians are told to stay inside, if possible, to avoid the F-rated air, an option not available for the thousands of field and dairy workers or their children. Dr. Frank treats more and more children with lung disorders. The county continues to register the highest rate of Covid infections in California. Joyce Hensley confesses to Coach Rascon that she is worn out from her overtime work at the Fresno hospital and looks forward to school and practice as a respite. She'll gladly exchange her PPE for basketball gear, gladly start giving high-fives instead of holding a dying patient's hand, gladly look forward to her computer screen revealing course information rather than patient charts. She admits that her commitment to working through the pandemic has been lessened because of so many people's stubborn refusal to wear a simple mask to protect their families and friends. "My God, it's a contagious airborne virus. The mask is trying to keep us all healthy." Joyce lobbies

SJV to do a better job at testing students and staff.

On Saturday afternoon, August 22, the last weekend before classes begin, the team gathers in Coach Rascon's back yard, the first meeting of the entire 2020-2021 squad. Although the temperature is in the 90s, the yard is shady and the drinks are cold, so the heat inconvenience is the price they pay for a social gathering. Twelve players, one manager, and three coaches all masked and spaced at least six feet apart gather to what Molly says is "the restart." It's the first time some of the returnees have met Claudia, Maddie, and Adriana, the freshmen recruits. Dyani promises that as a coach she will be even more animated and demanding than she was as their leader over the past two seasons. Sylvia responds that she's not sure that's possible. "Am I supposed to call you Coach now?"

A half-hour into the gathering, SJV's Athletic Director, Dr. Calhoun, arrives to formally greet them and provide them with the best information he has about the season and the safety requirements. Molly introduces him to the new players as "her boss," the person who has the responsibility of translating the ever-changing NCAA guidelines for competition in the age of Covid. "He's the guy responsible for our frustrations and trauma." Funny—but not funny. His best guess as of this Saturday is that official practice can begin in mid-October, but that there are still several variables that could change that date. "The season will be played, but exactly when the first game will be scheduled is not yet determined. Whenever that occurs, I expect this team to pick up where it left off last season, to once again claim the Ring of Fire championship and advance to the NCAA tournament." His statement is greeted with a round of cheers and clapping. Dr. Calhoun answers a few questions, apologizes for not being able to be more personable, takes a mask from a small box, and holds it up. "These were made especially for you all. I had enough printed so that each of you can take three." The mask reads, *The Tribe. Ring of Fire Champions.* "Wear these over your N95s at special events."

Shortly after Calhoun leaves, the university's trainer stops by to greet the team and update them on Covid rules for the upcoming term. More structure and social distancing, more appointments, and less casualness. She leaves and the coach for weight training and conditioning speaks next. Same message. Because many of the spring athletes won't be on campus during the fall, the facilities might be less crowded, but the rules will still be enforced. They both leave the ladies with the same sentiment as the AD gave: "You're the defending champions and we expect you to repeat. We're here to help you succeed."

Ryanne steps to the front of the patio, which acts as a slightly raised platform, and gets the team's attention. "Another consequence of the pandemic is that our university's budget is strained." She lets that information settle over the team for a moment. "For the past couple of years, we've had fifteen scholarships at our disposal, but we didn't use them all last season for a variety of reasons. If you remember at the start of last season, we lost Margie and Keisha and never filled their scholarships. This year, we have been limited to twelve total, which doesn't seem to you to make any difference. But since Kenti isn't on one—her expenses are covered elsewhere—we have two left over. We'll save one just in case, but the other one," Ryanne pauses again and looks to the youngest lady in the yard, "Maddie, stand up." Maddie Martin stands and, realizing what is about to happen, puts her hands over her mouth. "As of this morning, you are now on full scholarship like the other girls. We want to honor your commitment to us with our commitment to you." From the side of the house, Maddie's father appears wearing a mask and an SJV ballcap.

Not surprisingly, the 2020-2021 SJV website features Molly Rascon's photograph since her team was the lone league champion last season. What is surprising, however, is that the photo is not of her in a coaching pose, but a professional studio head shot. Subdued makeup highlights her brown eyes and accompanying wrinkles, her few freckles, and her dark hair. Small, silver hoop earrings and a matching necklace holding a small cross accent the pose. It is her confident smile that allows the image to suggest the serious caption beneath the photo. *The Sequoias want you.* There is no subtlety that the photo's intended audience is Latin women.

"When did you sign the modeling contract and give up coaching?" teases Frank. "You are one beautiful woman." Molly is slightly embarrassed by it all but proud of the photograph none-the-less. Bianca Acero was the beautiful one in high school, and other teammates in college held that distinction. Now, at age 41, she feels a bit humbled by the picture. AD Calhoun has given Frank the proofs, and he has had one framed, and it now adorns his office wall at the clinic in Visalia. A slightly different proof sits on the bookshelf in their living room.

Sitting in Molly's living room in the high-backed chair directly in front of the photo, Ryanne seems to be studying it. Frank is having an after-dinner coffee while Molly sits on the floor with Frankie with her back against the sofa.

"You look taller," says Ryanne.

"It's just a portrait of mama's head," responds Frankie, as if in defense of his mother.

"Still," says Ryanne, "if I didn't know your mama, I'd see this picture and think she was tall."

"That makes no sense," says Frankie.

Ryanne continues. "When you first saw the picture, what did you think?"

Frankie puts down his book and looks at the picture again. The three adults wait. "I didn't know it was mama." The adults laugh. "I didn't know who it was, so I don't think I paid much attention to it."

Pretending seriousness, Ryanne asks. "What do you see now?"

Frankie stands, retrieves the photo, studies it, and then puts it back. "A Sunday school teacher."

Frank laughs, Ryanne laughs, and Molly says, "What?" incredulously.

When she stops laughing, Ryanne asks Frank the same question.

"I see my Molly. Most of the time, Molly is everyone else's Molly, but in this photo, she's my Molly. When she first showed me the proofs, she said she wasn't going to allow the university to use them, that they weren't appropriate for that, whatever that is. We talked and she consented. I think they capture what the university wanted."

Molly helps Frankie find his place in the book he was just reading. "The university should've used a picture of Sylvia or Emerson or Greta. They're the real faces of our success."

∾

Childcare is expensive. Frankie hasn't been sent to any facility for his entire life; he's always had babysitters, usually one of Molly's players. Covid has made things trickier. Between Aunt Ryanne and Dr. Frank's receptionist and the Kappa Sig court, he's had supervision, but with the start of the school year and public restrictions still in place, Frankie's parents are looking for an in-house tutor who can be with him "during the school day." Because of NCAA regulations regarding coaches paying their players, Coach Rascon doesn't think she can use Maria and Sylvia in that role. They insist that they will be with Frankie for free, that they enjoy joining Ryanne as Tia Sylvia and Tia Maria.

"Can I tap into the endowment to pay my players to watch Frankie," Molly jokingly asks AD Calhoun. He shakes his head. "My girls need jobs, but I hate to put them out in grocery stores or some such during the pandemic."

Dr. Calhoun, always precise in his preparation, leans forward. "What Maria and Sylvia do is quite a bit more than babysitting. These are strange times, so I contacted an NCAA official to see about, how should I say this, . . . exceptions. Childcare runs about $800 per month in Tulare, something that in yours and Frank's economic station is affordable."

Molly interrupts, "I can't imagine how so many families do this. Two jobs are a necessity."

"My NCAA contact is anal but offered some guidance. He didn't just deny this out of hand. I know what this entails, but you will need to extensively detail the conditions of employment. Tutoring, transportation, food preparation, and so on. Next, he said to pay the childcare person with transfers or checks, definitely not in cash. Make sure there is an official accounting just as if you were dropping Frankie off at a daycare center. For this, have your husband make the payments using his doctor checks and have them deposited into a local account that is easily accessed by the provider." Dr. Calhoun stops there.

"So, you're saying I can hire Sylvia and Maria? How secret do you want this to be?"

"I want no secrecy at all. I will report this to the NCAA to maintain compliance. One of the things you have going for you is that both ladies are education majors; they're both here to become elementary school teachers. Online education requires at home classes. This is a win-win situation for Frankie and Maria and Sylvia. Let them know that it's a job and not a favor, that if they choose not to accept the conditions, they won't be used as babysitters either. They need to have lesson plans and keep records. They aren't to go around telling their friends that they're getting paid, but they're not to lie about it if asked."

Molly ponders this only for a moment. "Can they also get college credit for this?"

"No," smiles Dr. Calhoun. "That would sort of be like double-dipping."

"Do they both get paid if they're together?"

"Nope. It's an hourly rate whether it's one sitter or two. Excuse me, one tutor or two. I know your son. He really does need to be taught; Frankie's an exceptional boy, a gifted boy."

Molly laughs openly. She pulls her mask down to wipe the corners of her mouth. "Frank and I use the word precocious."

"I'll have one of my assistants create a legal contract. Have them sign it and get a copy back to me."

∽

In response to Ryanne's query, her significant other Junior Warren responds that Devon Nunes' re-election is secure. Her desire to get involved in the 2020 campaign might best be focused on local contests. "I know you, Ry, it'll just piss you off to walk the neighbor-hoods and then lose decisively. Fight a battle you can win." For those who invest significant time on political contests, losing is worse than losing a basketball game and more long-lasting. Ryanne believes the Democrats' position that this election is the most important of her lifetime and that she's fighting for "the soul of America." California will overwhelmingly vote for Joe Biden, but Tulare County will go against the state and re-elect a Republican. She feels her contribution in this election will be minimized, and that hurts her.

Sitting with Molly and Frank on Sunday night, she talks about her political journey. "Chicago loved Bill Clinton. I couldn't vote in '96, but I walked my neighborhood passing out literature. When I could vote, Al Gore didn't really inspire me, but I campaigned anyway. It's funny, though, because when the Supreme Court decided the outcome, I stomped around my dorm room raging about it. For all my life, Blacks have talked about voting rights, but that was the first time it was visceral to me. Somehow, votes were being skewed or stolen."

Molly sips her wine. "You . . . angry . . .politics?" She pauses and looks to Frank. "Who would have guessed?" The trio laughs at Molly's sarcasm. "For the record, Ry, and you've heard this before, I liked Gore. It was my first dip into the political deep end. Remember, my professors assigned me to get involved, so my issue was the environment. Growing up in my little town, what I remember was that politics wasn't a big issue to me. The grunt work of getting people registered and out to vote hasn't been imbedded in my DNA like it has in yours. I admire that about you." Molly smiles at a memory. "Remember when you got stopped by the police in Thousand Oaks because you were *in the wrong neighborhoods?*"

Ryanne purposely puts on her best stereotypical Black voice. "Honey, if you ain't in your own neighborhood, you in the wrong neighborhood." She looks into her glass of wine like it's a crystal ball to the past. "Here I sit drinking semi-expensive wine in a nice house in a nice neighborhood with a really good job, and yet I can't wrap my head around the fact that America is still trying to limit the vote for us of color. Yeah, it angers me, but it disappoints me mostly."

"Careful not to broad-brush America. Yeah, lots of people are trying to limit the vote for us, but not the majority," says Frank, "but I do know that right now, the momentum seems to be on the side of those who want to restrict the vote."

"So, what are you going to do about this election, Ry?" asks Molly.

"I bought myself a plane ticket to Atlanta for a week from now. Gonna put on my mask and face shield and get on that plane and go down and work with Stacey Abrams to register voters. I love that woman. Toughest lady I've ever seen. Talk about voter suppression. She would've won the governor's race if not for what we're talking about right here."

"How long are you staying?" asks Frank.

"It's our down time here, and your wife keeps promising me a vacation, but after the ten years or so I've been working with her, she's never left me alone. Almost like she'd be lost without me." Ryanne laughs.

"I would be, you know." Molly smiles at her assistant coach like a mother would to her oldest daughter.

The three freshmen additions to the team, Maddie Martin, Claudia Simpson, and Adriana Galvan, receive special attention from Molly during their first days at college. Each girl is assigned to an upper-class team member, a big sister in a way, although Molly stresses that once on the team, they are all sisters. Greta Espinoza asks to be Adriana's big sister, Claudia is paired with Kaori, and Maddie with Keilani. Coach Dehiya receives her first assignment, to be the liaison for the three recruits for academic progress. Dyani struggled during her first semester before learning the routine to succeed at a university that sometimes seemed impersonal, unlike her high school and community college. With fewer students on campus because of Covid, Claudia, Adriana, and Maddie all are housed on the same dorm floor as the returning players, and they all have separate rooms.

"The dog days," says Coach Rascon to her new assistant.

Coach Dyani Dehiya gives her boss a questioning look.

"The time from the end of summer school until we can get after it again as a team. Lots of administrative things to do, important stuff to be sure, but not basketball. Dr Frank tells me this is the time when I'm most antsy. How are the freshmen settling in?"

Dyani laughs. "They all have more stuff than I ever had. Not sure they're rich, but they're okay. Adriana wants to be called Addie, so we have Addie and Maddie. Claudia brought a few of her trophies with her."

"Any problems that you've noticed so far?"

"No. They're all excited. They do ask lots of questions about what to expect from you. I just tell them you're gentle and sweet. Maddie said you were loud and demanding that one practice we had, sort of like she was the experienced one."

"Yeah," says Molly, "that's me. Gentle and sweet. I'll need to correct that impression on the first day of practice." Molly shifts her focus. "How's living with Ryanne going?"

"What's not to like? Free rent. She cooks and is clean, and she has a sense about privacy. It's a quiet house unless either one of us wants to talk. I've never lived in such a place, dorms or my place back home. This is nice. She seems to be all in with her campaigning in Georgia. She texted this morning, just said her feet are tired from all the walking."

"Don't know if you ever noticed, but she and I text constantly. She's a political junkie, always has been. It's in her blood. Junior works in politics. Did you know that?"

Dyani nods slightly. "You probably told me, but I didn't remember. I've only met him a few times. Is he rich?"

Molly adjusts her mask so she can rub her nose. "He's paid well as a consultant. Just so you know, he owns half of the house you're living in. Even though they aren't officially married, they really are."

President Trump visits Kenosha, Wisconsin, in early September to support the police officer who shot Jacob Blake. He campaigns to his base about the BLM protests in Portland, suggesting that he may send federal troops to quell the riots. Dr. Frank Martinez notes in his journal that healthcare worker deaths in the United States have surpassed 1000 and says a silent prayer for the vaccine. The temperature in Los Angeles hits 121 degrees, an all-time high, and wildfires continue to burn, blanketing the northern California coast in smoke. Ryanne texts that she will be staying a little longer in Atlanta and to give Dyani more responsibilities.

Moses Robinson rents the same apartment that he's had the past two seasons and tells Molly that he will be available beginning September 21, the first day of the Transition Period. "Pre-practice," he jokes. His wife, Sally, will live between Tulare and Oxnard. After unpacking, he goes for a slow jog around campus, then has an early dinner with Molly, Frank, Frankie, and Dyani.

"Are you spending the night or are you heading home after dinner?" asks Frank.

"Staying. Your wife wants me to meet with the new kids in the morning." Mose looks over to Molly. "I'll leave after lunch. That way I can say hi to all the girls, remind them who's really the head coach, despite what my pay stub looks like."

Dyani is drinking her thick coffee mix as a pre-dinner drink. "I got my first check today. Seems like a million dollars. I've never made so much in one month."

"What will you do with it?" asks Mose.

"I opened accounts at the bank today and then bought groceries. Don't know why I need a checking account though. Checks seem so last century. I've sort of been sponging off Ryanne. Before she left, we went to the store and stocked up. You coaches live like royalty."

"Yeah, kings and queens," says Molly. She stops herself. "Actually, when I got my first check from State Tech after I became an assistant, I felt the same way. To be honest now, even though SJV pays at the lower level, I feel pretty fortunate. I'm doing what I love and getting paid for it. Maybe that's in your future, Dyani. Speaking of money," says Molly, "Ryanne says the Georgia senate races are awash in money."

"I don't understand politics," says Dyani. "By that, I mean I don't understand the big money and the hate-filled campaigns. Every day on television, it's just nastiness to the extreme. The lies that even local politicians spread are disgusting. On the rez, we have a history of not trusting outsiders, especially politicians from Phoenix, but here in California, the money seems to be collected just to tell lies. Television is just a vast wasteland with all the commercials. On the rez, we don't get all the cable channels, so we aren't subjected to all this. Ryanne watches news channels all the time, so I've been watching too. I have to laugh, because she says she has to watch Fox News for at least a half hour every night just to know what the Republicans believe. She swears at the night hosts, then she switches back to that liberal channel. She still swears, but for a different reason."

"We have a no politics rule at dinner," pipes in Frankie.

"That's a good rule," says Mose.

"We ought to have no 24-hour news channels rules too," says Molly.

Mose makes one of his old-man noises and stretches out his arms. "In all the time I played ball, I never hated other teams. I'd have moments when the competition was intense and physical, not like today's NBA where tough defense isn't allowed, but for me it never meant war. Part of my personality according to Sally. Politics is war though. Our games with Palm Desert can get nasty, but never on the level of politics. First rule of politics is win at any cost, and if you can destroy your opponent, so much the better."

Molly has had enough politics and not enough basketball. "Who were some of the best players you played against or with, Mose?"

"None of you were born yet, so they're just names."

Dyani slides up in her chair. "We're geeks here. We know some of them, so don't dodge the question. Who were they?"

"All right, but this is going to require dusting off the cobwebs in my head—and another beer." Frankie jumps up and runs to the kitchen to get Uncle Mose another one. When he returns, Mose begins. "Remember, I was a six-six small forward who never had to guard Kareem or Elvin Hayes. Mostly, I guarded big guards and other small forwards. The impossible ones first, the ones you've heard of. Dr. J. He was the best, and just like Char couldn't guard you, Dyani, I couldn't guard him. George Gervin was the same. Unguardable." He takes a drink of his beer. "But a couple you might not have heard of, but you can google them. Bob Dandridge. Dave Bing. Yeah, google Dave Bing. And Havilcek. That mother just had a constant motor; kept coming at you. Like I said, I didn't really have to guard George McGinnis or Spencer Haywood too much; they'd just overpower me. And I didn't have to guard Frazier or Tiny Archibald. Mostly, I sat on a bench and watched guys who had that drive."

Molly shakes her head. "You were so lucky to have been on the court with those guys. Who'd you like to play with most, your best teammate?"

Mose smiles at a long-forgotten memory. "Ahh, you never heard of the guy." He pauses again, and the others wait. "Like you, Coach, I love point guards. I would have enjoyed playing on your team or teaming with you, Dyani. Point guards who knew how to deliver the ball at the right moment. Point guards who didn't turn it over trying to be cute, who just want to win and make their teammates look good."

"Come on, Coach. Give us a name," demands Molly.

"Gordie Thorne. My teammate at CU. He was from California too. A year behind me, but, man, he understood the game. Loved playing with him." He looks at the faces around him, and they aren't disappointed as he thought they might be. The two celebrated college point guards recognize the compliment that has been paid to them. Molly lifts her glass first, and then Dyani lifts hers. Then Mose. When Frankie lifts his juice, it's unanimous.

"Well, it's late," says Mose as he stands. "Thanks for dinner. Come on, Dyani, I'll drive you home." He places his huge hand on Frankie's head and ruffles his hair. "I'll see you at the gym in the morning."

Mama and Papa put Frankie to bed and return to the living room to listen to music and finish their wine, to slow down. Frank prefers beer or margaritas but drinks wine because his wife pours it. He does lots of things to please his wife since he now lives the life he once dreamed about. He's a pediatrician with a professional wife and a happy son. He holds his wine up for inspection.

"We've been pretty insulated and fortunate so far with Covid," he says. "Your little bout was mild, and you were nice enough not to pass it on."

"You're welcome." She leans in and kisses her husband on the cheek. "Frankie asked me today if we were ever going to move. We were at the gym with Ry between sessions with the new girls just talking about job openings, about the salaries some of the bigger universities are paying now. Multi-year contracts for millions of dollars." She goes silent for a moment. Frank knows this is not so much about Frankie. "How much is too much?" asks Molly softly.

NCAA guidelines for the Transition Period, which will begin on September 21, allow for twelve hours per week of strength and conditioning and meetings along with eight hours of skill instruction. Athletes are to be given two days off each week. These first days of the fall semester before then, Molly limits her contact, especially with her returning ladies. She and Dyani want to guide the three freshmen into productive schedules and get them acclimated to university demands. What Molly knows, has discovered, is that scheduled exercise is the best defense against the mental and emotional ravages of Covid, for both her ladies and herself. Before Coach Aikins left for the high school job, Molly had her make up workout schedules, both online and with paper handouts, and these needed to be filled out. Away from Tulare, Molly believed the scheduled workouts were being followed. Three weeks into the semester, Coach Rascon feels confident about the progress of her team. She would liked to have captured the tall high school girl from Utah, a project for sure, but an athlete whom Molly believed had the potential to round out her squad in a year or two. For the upcoming season, however, Molly visions another championship, a year equal to the past one.

Hiring Sylvia and Maria as Frankie's tutors and for childcare has eliminated a major concern. Bringing Dyani on board as an assistant coach has been a treat. Dyani's sense of humor makes Molly laugh daily, and her non-traditional perspective of the game coupled with her confidence forces Coach Rascon to see her team through a different lens.

"If you want to shake up your lineup sometimes, play the new girl, Claudia, with Keilani, Kaori, and Emerson. They all have ball-handling skills and like to run and defend, and then throw in either Greta or Esther for a little size. Both of them are more athletic than Sylvia. Nobody in the conference can match our athleticism." Dyani will say things like this daily.

"Maria?" asks Molly.

"Still wants to play the soft corner. Unless she's matched up against her sister, she's not tough enough. A good sub for our tres amigas." Dyani is referring to Keilani, Kaori, and Emerson. "Claudia's not a starter and over the long run, Sylvia is our enforcer, but in certain situations, playing those five antelopes would be fun to watch, almost like rez ball. I'd sure enjoy being their point guard."

"A year from now maybe?" asks Molly again.

"Accelerated learning, six months from now. I'm going to take Claudia under my wing and make her work with Keilani every drill."

Molly changes the focus of the conversation. "The university is going to allow me to hire again, to bring two more part-time coaches on board. I'm not looking for teaching coaches so much as stat and film experts, sort of like Coach Aikins with her analytics. Graduate assistants."

Dyani smiles almost sarcastically. "So, you want someone who can chart the number of corner threes Kaori makes on the break as opposed to the number of times Keilani shoots a contested left-hand layup in a two-on-one situation?"

Molly cracks up. "Well, what I really want to know is how often we rebound the missed corner three as compared to the three up top."

∾

On Friday, September 18, Justice Ruth Bader Ginsburg dies.

∾

Ryanne calls from Georgia that evening. "You know what's coming now, don't you." It's not a question, but a statement of disgust, and Molly understands. "The Republicans will ram a nomination through in record time, Merrick Garland be damned."

Molly paces in the kitchen, away from Frankie and Frank. "It will certainly be a part of the presidential campaign. "Who's going to be the next justice?" It's always a major issue for the Republicans, as if that, abortion, and gun rights are the only things that should be considered. If they get to put another so-called conservative on the bench, they'll control the court for decades to come." Molly is interrupted by an incoming call. "I'll call back later, Ry, I've got another call."

It's Esther Santiago. "Coach, Justice Ginsburg died." Esther sounds distraught. "My Dreamer status will go away. I'll get deported."

"Slow down, Esther. Nobody's going to get deported. The vacancy won't be filled for a while, and then another challenge would have to work its way up to the court. Yeah, it's something to watch, but you're going to be fine."

"Coach, I'm an American. Can't they just see that?"

"It's hard, but the majority of the people appreciate the Dreamers and want you to stay and prosper; they do see. The loud voices of the Right just make it seem like it's the whole country. Dreamers like you challenge us to do the right thing, to welcome you into America and keep you safe. You're so valuable for us."

"Sometimes, we don't feel that. We have to live in the shadows and keep our situation secret. My high school boyfriend didn't even know I was illegal. He always asked me why I wasn't applying for college. I broke up with him rather than tell him about my status."

Molly shakes her head in her kitchen. She thinks she hears Esther crying. "Esther," says Molly in her gentle motherly voice, "as little girls, you and I both grew up without our fathers, but your situation was harder because once he went back to Mexico City, you lost touch with him, and he took your brother with him. Mine checked in on me on rare occasions, and my little brother was with me. We were raised by our mothers for the most part. I can't even comprehend not knowing how my mother is doing like you. When I last spoke with your mom, she sounded sad and a little lost. Remember when you and I talked about it?" Esther makes a sound of affirmation. "Coach Robinson's friend is still trying to arrange for her to return to California, to get across the border, but Covid is making it so hard."

Esther interrupts. "Yeah, and the president hates Mexicans." She sniffles hard. "Coach, I know, and I try to do all that I can, but it's never enough. I work in the grocery store even though that's dangerous. I help at the testing center. But if they could, they'd send me back to Mexico." She stops herself. "I know, Coach, it's not everyone, but sometimes it feels like it. My records say I'm Mexican, but I don't even know Mexico; I don't remember it at all. I was so young when I left. In every way, I'm American." She sniffles again. "I'm sorry, Coach, I'm just having a little pity-party with myself and wanted to share it."

Molly has had this conversation with Esther before, and she knows that it's born partly out of loneliness. Esther's family in September of 2020 is The Tribe, but all its members are struggling with home and heart, with their inability to control their lives during the pandemic.

"Remember what Keilani talked about last month when it was just the four of you here working out, when everyone else was home?" Molly lets Esther move from pity to her friends. When Molly gets a positive sound from Esther, she proceeds. "Leaving out Kailani's expletives, she said being with the three of you made her feel lucky compared to the rest of the country. She said playing two-on-two with her sisters was as good as it gets. Remember?"

Esther lets out a short laugh as she recalls several of the things Keilani said. "Keilani can't complete a single sentence without the f-word. She's always striking a pose with her guns to make a point. She'll be the perfect replacement for Dyani at point guard."

"She's in the weight room every day they allow it. She likes working on her beach muscles."

"You know we cheated the social distance rules in the dorm, don't you? We paired up at night, so we didn't have to sleep alone to. Keilani was with me. She moved her mattress into my room. Kaori moved hers in with Emerson."

"I know. You're all such rebels," says Molly gently.

Esther shakes her head in disagreement. "Not me, Coach. I'm just trying to survive. I don't know what I'd do without you and my teammates."

"Well, girl, you'll always have us in your life. That's kind of what Keilani was saying in her picturesque language. 'Life-long f-ing sisters.' I know these days with Covid are really hard, more difficult for you than maybe any of the others, but you do have us, and if there are times when it gets like now, just walk over here and ring the doorbell. This house is your house."

"Mi casa, su casa, huh?"

"Yeah."

"I need to stop whining. I don't have it as bad as Char does, or Danelle. She felt so bad she joined the Army. Ran away. Did you know her parents made her sleep in the garage they were so scared of getting Covid?"

Molly makes a short gasp. She did not know that. "What do you mean?"

"Her parents put all her stuff in the garage, and she ate all her meals out there. She could only come into the house to go to the bathroom. That's why she joined. She wanted to come back here, but since she graduated, she didn't feel like that was an option. I guess she has a friend back there who enlisted with her. She told us not to tell you, because she didn't want you to think she was letting you down. Sort of like she wanted you to think the Army was a great opportunity, but it was really an escape." Esther pauses. "Covid sucks, Coach."

On Saturday, September 19, one day after Justice Ginsburg's death, President Trump tells FOX News that he will nominate a conservative woman to fill her seat and that Senator McConnell will get a vote on confirmation before the next Senate is convened.

Molly picks up Ryanne from the Fresno airport, and no sooner is she in the car when she explodes. "One day!" she yells. "One damn day after Ginsburg's death! Oh, we can't confirm Obama's nominee before the election because that wouldn't be fair to the voters. Eight months before the election! Hypocrites!" Molly knows the last months of the 2020 campaigns will feature more and more vitriol, that the airways will be filled with ads of half-truths and outright lies, that in households and workspaces throughout the nation will become battlefields. There will be fewer and fewer civil discussions. Given the makeup of her team and her university, she knows what side she is on.

Arriving in Tulare, Molly drops Ryanne at her house before going to the gym to check on emails and texts. At the door of her office, Molly squirts her hands with sanitizer from a newly installed dispenser. Moses Robinson and his wife have settled into their apartment, so the coaching staff is mostly intact. On Monday, Coach Rascon and her staff will hold its first meeting with twelve young ladies in practice gear, unless Dr. Calhoun or some public health official from the county calls with bad news. It will be the re-opening of the arena to formal practices. At least that bad news doesn't show up on her phone. Molly doesn't sit down. Instead, she stands in front of one of the whiteboards and stares at names. It's an experienced and balanced roster. It's solid at every position except one, the most important one. So much will depend on Keilani, her firebrand replacement for Dyani, but Molly isn't worried about that. She can coach that concern; it's what she can't coach that troubles her. The players' names go blurry. Molly walks to her desk and sits in her chair, and for the first time, she cries because she is worn out.

Ken Davidson felt he was lucky when he left the hospital after his serious bout with Covid. Now, he's not so sure. Recovery seems more like two steps forward and one step back. He's tired most of the time; he doesn't have the energy to get back in shape or to even open his computer to write. Worst of all, Naomi is worn out from being his caregiver. He put off Coach Rascon's invitation to watch her opening practice on Monday, and this Sunday he and Naomi wait for the professional home care representative to arrive. Meals, running errands, a little housecleaning, grocery shopping, someone else in the house who might converse about topics not related to the coronavirus. That damned microscopic devil consumes Ken's life. Naomi gingerly rises from her recliner to answer the doorbell, while Ken remains seated in his. He turns off the TV, slips his mask over his mouth and nose, and picks up the homecare contract.

"Mose, honey, you have a visitor." Naomi steps back to allow space for the guest to enter.

"Don't get up, Mr. Davidson. All the regulations tell me I can only stay a couple of minutes." Dyani Dehiya slips her mask down and smiles and then immediately covers up again. "Coach wants you to have our practice schedule and new roster. You won't have to write any more words about me. Not much more to say about that. You're going to like the new girls, but mostly I think you'll find Keilani interesting to quote. She uses colorful language." Dyani holds up a folder and then places it on the coffee table in front of the recliners. "Anyway, our practice begins at 3:00 tomorrow, and we'll have your spot all sanitized."

Ken wipes a tear from his weepy eye. "Nice to see you, Dyani. I'm going to miss watching you play, but Coach told me you were going to hang around and assist her. I'd ask you to sit for a spell and have an iced tea, but we have a professional coming by, and the governor probably wouldn't approve of your visit."

"If you need anything, I left my new business card in the folder so you can call. Coach Robinson said hi and said to get off your butt and come see him over at the gym." Dyani smiles under her mask, waves, and departs.

∾

Twelve masked ladies jog slowly around the court, each bouncing a basketball, each staying at least six feet away from her teammates.

Molly warned them that an NCAA monitored drone would be observing their behavior. "Now, it begins," is what she told them. "Relish every second." New family members joining the established family. Minutes are precious in the Transition Period, so the ladies move quickly between drills, mostly oriented toward recovering lost offensive skills. Martina Smith supervises three additional student managers, and the four coaches teach their specialties. The idea of using male practice players has been tabled for another year. The conversations center on repeating last year's success, of building on what has already been achieved, of adding to the SJV women's legacy. Coach Rascon tells her team while they jog that she will countenance no talk about the pandemic, about the problems of the world outside the gym. Coach Rascon moves to every station making precise adjustments to every girl, offering praise frequently. Dyani coaches quieter than she played but no less demanding. The two freshmen recruits are good and eager, but clearly Keilani will lead the team. Dyani understands the faith Coach Rascon has bestowed on her, and she vows that every bit of knowledge and experience she has will be passed along to Keilani and the rookies. Dyani will challenge them at every turn; they will need strong backs. Kenti Solorzano smiles constantly as she works with this group. Six months earlier, she believed her playing days had ended and she was satisfied with that. Of all the team members, she was least concerned about the cancellation of the tournament. On this Monday, she practices as she always did, with joy. Her only question for Coach Rascon was who she was to guard this year and make miserable in practice. Molly wanted to hug her. Kenti knows who she's going to torment.

As practice unfolds, Molly begins to see her lineup. At SJV's pace, she needs nine, and eight of those show themselves. It's that ninth that she needs to find. It won't be Kenti or Maddie, and Joyce hasn't improved her skills over the summer, but for good reasons. Joyce has been working extended shifts at the Fresno hospital caring for Covid patients. What Molly needs is a reliable sub for Emerson and Kaori. Molly leans in on Adriana. Adriana will most likely begin below Maria on the depth chart, but Maria doesn't fit the mold of the racehorses that Molly uses at the two and three spots.

Molly catches herself. It's mid-September, the first day of The Restart. Games aren't even scheduled yet, but a coach's mind works that way. Ryanne is the one who wants position players, because that's the way she grew up. Two guards, two forwards, one center. Molly learned from her high school coach that there was a leader, the point, and everyone else. Hell, thinks Molly, with Dyani last season, she employed a dozen different lineups. Dyani knew the strengths and weaknesses of her teammates, and most of all, Dyani knew the mind of her coach. Symbiosis. Basketball players may not need algebra, but they need science.

The gym's water fountains are shut down. All water is consumed through individual bottles clearly marked. The ladies are instructed to drink quickly between drills and move forward. Always forward. Coach Robinson's presence with the Bigs picks up from last season. Quiet instruction, precise instructions, an NBA history, a belief that "his girls" hear best when they lean in to hear his words. "That was good, Sylvia, but I think your arm bar could be carried higher." "Joyce, find Esther before you turn to block out, otherwise she'll just slip past you." "Esther, watch Greta on her inside pivot. See how she rakes the ball from her left hip to her right." "Gang, what's the rule on offense?" Greta answers. "Rule number one is knock someone down, but I think you mean for us to create space."

Ryanne works with the off guards, Kaori, Emerson, Adriana, and sometimes Maria. She yells, or as she calls it, "Punctuates!" She expects Emerson and Kaori to be the leading scorers on the team this season. Their job is to put the ball in the hole, to finish. These two players are confident and relentless. They can run all practice effortlessly in spite of Ryanne's demanding drills which require constant movement. Maria takes the brunt of Ryanne's criticism because she is not the worker her sister is, and she isn't the athlete that Kaori and Emerson are. Ryanne does not want any of Maria to rub off on Adriana. Addie now. Ryanne sees a hidden gem in Addie who goes through the drills as quiet as the proverbial church mouse.

At the close of most practices over the past two seasons, it was Dyani who raised her voice to send the team to the showers, to inspire them. She stands at the center circle with twelve sweaty ladies well-spaced doing mild stretching. Coach Rascon has given Dyani the privilege on this first day to pass the baton, the leadership, on to one of the players. Dyani considered Sylvia, but the tough senior is too quiet off the court to take on that responsibility. No problem on the court, but mannerly off it. So, Dyani tells Emerson and Keilani to stand up.

"There will be no Navajo war dances this season. This year, you need to forge a new identity, something with rap, so you two will need to come up with some kind of ditty to bring each practice to a close, to get us out of here. Some kind of LA hip-hop with dancing. Make it good." The team, including the managers and coaches, clap and hoot.

Molly silently nods. *We're moving on.* She turns to the second level stands behind her to where Ken Davidson sits and salutes.

The team leaves to shower in their dorm rooms. The managers collect the balls, store the clock, and sweep the floor before leaving. The coaches retreat to the War Room to critique practice. There, sitting in comfortable, padded seats with Coach Rascon at the front desk, they sip colas and unwind.

Dyani surprises Molly with her first remark. "Claudia is a better prospect than Char. A little rough, but she has good instincts. Ball security and good vision."

The others add their observations. "Esther and Greta are bigger and stronger; more athletic than Danelle was. The Bigs can dominate the conference."

"We need to find Maria's on-off switch."

"Maddie likes contact. We saw a little of that on that one day this summer, but it was on display today. Not sure she can become game-ready this season what with Keilani and Claudia, but she's a good one. We got lucky."

"Joyce seemed both tired and relieved. She loves practice. I imagine it's a gift for her after the hospital work. A good teammate for sure. She and Sylvia worked well together, and they like playing against Greta and Esther."

Molly asks if any of her assistants noticed that the masks were a problem for the team. "I just kept reminding a few of them to pull it up over their noses." There's a consensus on that point, that practices won't be compromised because of the masks. Molly nods,

"That's good, because non-compliance could lead to a shut-down. Dr. Calhoun is adamant about that. California has certain standards, certain benchmarks, but Tulare County is fighting the statistics. The sheriff is vowing not to enforce closures no matter what the state mandates. We just have to keep our heads down, our masks up, and hope to God nobody tests positive."

Ryanne laughs in her "Oh, Ry," manner. "And then there's the NCAA guidelines," she says. "Let's hope one of the major conferences doesn't shut down, or we all could go through this again."

Molly looks at Dyani. "What's the latest on the rez?"

"Same. Bad." She doesn't elaborate, but the others know.

Sitting three chairs away, Mose leans over far enough to give Dyani a touch. 2020, the year hugging ended, replaced by nods and fist bumps.

Molly returns to basketball. "More of the same tomorrow. I don't plan to go five-on-five this week. I still want to monitor their emotional condition as much as anything. Keep an eye on that. Mose, I think I'll want Maria to move in with the gunners. Her personality just isn't one of banging with your Bigs. You'll still have four. Nice work with Greta this summer. If we had a game today, she'd be the other starter. Ryanne, that means you'll have Maria. We can talk about how to use her. Maybe she just wants to be pretty like Emerson and Kaori. Make her run. All the time. Get on her. I will too." Coach Rascon stops there. "It's good to be back, isn't it?"

Mose straightens up in his chair. "I just want to say I'm proud of this group for taking the high road over the past months. Not once have I heard any of you complain about what you couldn't do, just how to accomplish what you could do."

Ryanne interrupts. "Oh, we've complained. You just can't hear us from your lounge chair in Oxnard." Molly and Dyani laugh.

Mose accepts that but continues. "Okay, but Coach, you're down a staff member, and you've all taken a pay cut, at least for now, and made a pretty good hire here in Dyani. Not sure of your judgement in bringing me back, but maybe that's just as well I don't over-analyze that."

He's interrupted again by Ryanne. "She got my pay reinstated to last year's level."

Mose looks sternly to Ryanne. "Is this how it's going to be? You just gonna jump in and correct everything I say now?" He's kidding, and the group pretends like they've been reprimanded properly. Ryanne puts both hands up in a pose of surrender. Mose nods. "I know I've been out of the loop, which is good because I'm only here to coach, not to be bothered by the bureaucracy of all this. When I was talking with Ken before practice, he said you've been in touch with another university about a job with big benefits. Just wondering if I'm going to have a job next season." Mose stops there and waits.

Molly pulls her lips together as she measures her next words. She takes a deep breath through her nose, her chest rising. Her nod says yes before her words do. "Ken has good sources. University of Washington." She pauses, steps away from the front of the room, and takes a seat in one of the plush chairs with her assistants. Ryanne knows, but Dyani doesn't. Until now. "All of this is confidential. Dr. Calhoun knows and wants to build a package to entice me to stay, but he's up front that SJV can't come close to matching the money that Washington is suggesting." Molly laughs slightly. "Suggesting. Funny word. Anyway, there's no offer, just preliminary talks. Obviously, not for this season, but for next year. There might not even be a *this season*, and the talks are just that. Unofficial talks."

Dyani leans forward in her chair to see around Coach Robinson. "Are you at liberty to say how much money?"

Molly's tongue plays with the inside of her mouth. She takes that deep breath again before answering. "About three times what I make here." She allows that to settle over Dyani and Mose, who laughs.

"So, NBA money, huh?"

"It's all just talk."

Ryanne tries to ease her friend's discomfort. "It'll all go away if we don't repeat as Ring of Fire champions and don't get to go to the Big Dance next spring."

"I'm not the only coach on their radar. I suspect I'm way down on their list, so please don't share any of this with anyone outside this room, and certainly not any of our ladies. I really have no intention of going anywhere."

Chapter 13

Agriculture and Basketball. Blog, by Ken Davidson

Coach Molly Rascon, San Joaquin Valley's women's basketball coach of whom I've written much about, at least a lot about her team and her ladies, is a master at deflecting questions about her life off the court. She will pivot and talk about one of her athletes, about the work that Joyce Hensley does at the Fresno hospital caring for Covid patients, about Emerson Loki's original dance score, or Greta Espinoza's work this past summer with migrant children in Oxnard. Coach Rascon's success is never because she devised a last possession play to score, but because Dyani Dehiya split two defenders and dished off to Sylvia Castro for an easy layup. I respect that. It's refreshing in the age of ego-driven sports figures. Still, my job has always been to peel back the layers and get a glimpse of these people. I find they usually have interesting back stories, much like successful people in other professions.

Last season, I wrote a little about her husband, Dr. Frank Martinez, a pediatrician whose clinic is in Visalia, who never misses an SJV home game. Dr. Martinez carries himself like the stereotypical children's doctor, soft-spoken, gentle, mannerly. His son, Frankie, bounced nearby when I interviewed him, an active eight-year-old. Dr. Martinez told me that medicine was his second job, that making sure Molly had what she needed was his primary role. The talent for deflection seems to run in the family. I saw them in Visalia last year, and it was clear that Dr. Martinez was the leading figure, known to every family in the grocery store. Molly shopped, i.e., pushed the cart and compared labels, while Dr. Martinez made conversation with the other shoppers, especially the young families who were with children. No one asked this highly successful coach for an autograph, and she seemed to enjoy her anonymity.

Over the past couple of years of covering her team, I have uncovered her basketball background. She has a pedigree: two-time all-state in high school and Colorado player of the year back in the 90s, four-year starter in college leading her team to four deep runs in the NCAA tournament. No question about it, the lady could hoop. After college she became an assistant for two stints before taking the head job at Cal Coastal in Thousand Oaks, a D3 college. When SJV made the jump to D1, she became its first, and so far, only head coach. After that first season, her teams have pretty much dominated the conference. Her teams play fast, she always has a dynamite point guard leading the show, and they knock people down. What's not to like for a sportswriter?

One of the places sportswriters turn to for background information is other sportswriters. Molly's success at State Tech is well-documented. Off the court, however, there's scant information. Typical college athlete, study and practice. Another source is Google, and I was able to find two hits for Molly Rascon before she arrived in California, both relating to environmental issues. Seems she led a university project to make her school more aware of the crisis surrounding the loss of nearby wetlands, and then she published a paper connecting that issue with climate change. A sometimes activist in an all-American basketball player's 5'4" body. (Note to myself: Follow that lead, Ken.)

San Joaquin Valley University has an environmental science department, and guess who is a significant financial contributor? The Family of Frankie Martinez, with a tag that requests its donation be focused on air quality studies for the Central Valley. I spoke with the head of the department, Dr. Aldern, and he enthusiastically confirmed that Coach Rascon and Dr. Martinez were financial contributors but would not reveal to what level. He did say that they were both quite interested in the department's research on air pollution and its link to brain disease. When I asked Coach Rascon about this, she gave me that coach's stern look that Coach Tubby Smith made so famous. Basically, back off, no comment. But pre-Covid, back when my brain was sharper, I remember interviewing one of her players, Kaori Park, about her plans after college. Kaori is double majoring in math and, you guessed it, environmental science. I went back to Kaori this week. Kaori knew nothing about any financial donations but did say that Coach Rascon had attended several of the department's presentations.

I attended the opening practice this past week for the women's team, the re-start after their marvelous season ended so abruptly last March and team gatherings were restricted. Watching the ladies fiddle with their masks, I noticed that Coach Rascon never touched hers, never removed it to take an extra breath or make a point. I asked her about it, and she said it was no big deal and that masks probably reduce the effects of other transmissible diseases. I had serious Covid, almost died, so I wear my mask religiously, but watching healthy athletes and coaches who statistically seem to be safe from the virus, I saw none of the players, managers, and assistants complain about the masks. My guess is that Coach Rascon and her husband have done their research. That first practice, with Covid concerns swirling across our nation and how to combat it is quite contentious, this team was having none of that. Every drill, every minute was focused on basketball, but I had the feeling that because of Coach Rascon's concern for environmental concerns, extending that concern to Covid was easy. Deal with it as best you can and get on with your business, as in this case, defending their league championship.

∽

Addendum to Blog.

I'm proud of my county along with the surrounding counties. During this terrible pandemic, Tulare County has launched a program to provide better housing for the essential farmworkers who have been exposed to Covid and need to self-isolate. It's called the Healthy Harvest Program and is available to farmworkers and food-processing workers who need additional services to protect themselves and their families. These are the front-line essential workers who help feed us, so congratulations to those local community organizations who are putting this program together. It looks like the tomato harvest this year will be spectacular given the large number of trucks rumbling through the county. I give thanks to all those men and women who provide them for us.

∾

The official statement from the SJV athletics department gives the needed information but revealed scant details. The university's women's basketball team is pausing all team activities following a positive COVID-19 test result within the team's personnel. NCAA guidelines require team personnel to be tested three times each week, and the second test during this first week of practice revealed two positive members, one player and one team manager.

Coach Rascon's text message to her ladies on Wednesday night expresses her disappointment. After three terrific practices, the season is now on hold, and in accordance with university protocols, the team is to be retested on Thursday morning. Molly tells them that Emerson is the player and Martina is the affected manager, both of whom have been in strict compliance with mask and social distancing requirements. Molly informs her team that both ladies are feeling fine, that neither is suffering any of the symptoms that Joyce or Dr. Frank had warned them about.

Frankie's school is shuttered. He spends his days and nights with his parents and the team. The school superintendent announced early in the summer that the county intended to provide a hybrid model, but with the spike in Covid cases, that is on hold. Public opinion is angrily divided.

"We'll go back to outdoor conditioning at the track and individual workout sessions at the Kappa Sig court on a strict schedule," texts Coach Rascon to her team on Thursday morning. "Even though we are apart for the next days, we will stay united. Consider this interruption a delay and continue to prepare for full-scale practices in two weeks."

Immediately after punching Send, replies begin to arrive. All express disappointment, some frustration, but they also say they will do all they can to be ready. One, however, says, "I don't know if I can do this any longer." Molly is confused, not about the message but about the sender. Before she can reply, her phone rings. It's Ryanne.

"Hey, Mol, since we're going to be on a two-week hiatus, I'm going to fly down to Georgia and work to register voters in Atlanta again. No use sitting at home with my finger up my butt reworking practice plans. Besides, since we're supposed to stay apart, we can text ideas. Can you drive me to the airport in the morning?"

From another part of her house, Molly hears her husband calling to tuck Frankie in bed. "Yeah," she pauses. "Hey, Ry, can I call you right back?" Molly rises from her desk and walks to her son's bedroom. Frank is sitting on the bed holding a book. She leans over to kiss Frankie on the top of his head and says goodnight. Her look tells her husband that she is distracted.

"Anything we can do?" he asks.

"Sorry. Maybe. When you finish here, come talk to me. I'll be at my desk." She kisses Frankie again and leaves.

"Mama's upset because of the stop again, isn't she," says Frankie.

At her desk, Molly looks at the list of players who received her recent text. There it is. Char Betany. She must have been receiving all the team text messages that have gone out over the past six weeks since Char officially transferred to Ft. Lewis in southern Colorado. Molly neglected to remove her name from the team messages. But why would she respond as she did to SJV going into quarantine? Molly taps a response.

"Hey, Char. I got your message." Molly waits.

"I see we got the Covid."

Molly reacts to Char's pronoun. "Yeah. Mild cases. Where are you, hon?"

"Back home sort of. Chinle with my older brother."

"Not Window Creek?"

"No. They don't know."

"Can I call so we can talk?"

"Yeah. I'll be here."

Frank walks in just as Molly clicks out of texting. His look expresses his concern.

"It's Char. She left college and is back on the rez. I need to call her now." Molly holds up a finger indicating to Frank to hold on a minute. She connects with Char.

"Hey, Coach."

"Hey, Char. Your message tells me you're hurting. Tell me about it."

"My coach already has his lineup set, so I'm sort of left out. I just sit in the dorm looking at my computer. All my classes are online."

Molly extends her hand over to Frank. "Lonely then? It takes time even in the best of circumstances, and these days make it doubly hard, huh."

Molly can hear Char sniffling. She waits. "Coach, I just don't know. I didn't want to be there, so I had Arthur come get me. He can keep a secret. Nobody knows I'm here at his house. Don't tell, okay?" Char's last sentence is a plea.

"Does he have room for you?" asks Molly.

"Yeah, for now. It's a trailer." Char goes quiet again.

Molly speaks softly and gently. "I'm giving you a hug right now, you know." Molly pauses to allow her hug to travel through the air to Arizona. "Is Hector in Chinle? Do you know?"

"He might be, but I haven't told him."

"How about if I call him?"

"Do you think he'll be mad at me?"

"No, hon, no. Hector will understand. I think from what little I know about him that he understands loneliness. It's like in his DNA. He intuits things, doesn't he."

Char lets out a soft hmmmm, as if she's giving consent. Molly waits. "Don't tell Dyani. She'll just get mad at me."

"If she did show that, it would only be because she cares about you. It's kind of like how she reacts to things at first, but you know where her heart is." Molly pauses again. "Will you be all right tonight?" Char's response is less than convincing. "Hey, hon. Promise me. You can call me anytime now. Even in the middle of the night."

"Okay. I'll be okay. Coach . . .thanks." Char taps off.

Molly sits looking at her phone. Without looking up, she says to Frank, "I should have Facetimed her so I could see her face."

"You handled that well," says Frank. "Do you have Hector's number? If you don't, Frankie does."

Molly has it and calls. "Hector, this is Coach Rascon in California. Hey, I just got off the phone with Char. She's back in Chinle and not doing well at all. I'm worried."

"I'm driving over from Kayenta. Her mother called and couldn't reach her. She knows Char left school. I should be there in 45 minutes or so. I assume she's at her brother's place."

"That's where she said she's staying. I'll let you drive but let me know if there's anything I can do."

Molly lets out a large sigh, leans over for a hug, and remains there for a moment. "So much pressure on that one; always has been. I should have been more aware. She's fragile. Trying to live up to Dyani."

"No, you've done so much for her. Is Hector going over?"

"He's driving there now." Molly wryly laughs at a thought. "I wonder what kind of rez car he's driving. I don't think he owns one of his own."

"Char will be fine once he gets there."

"I need to call Ry back. She wants to fly to Atlanta for the next two weeks to play politics. Can't say as I blame her."

"Do you need her here?"

"Not really and yes at the same time. We can do all our basketball stuff on the phone. Sort of like practice is a video game. We've had six months of practice for online coaching."

Molly calls Ryanne. "Hey. Just got off the phone with Char. She's depressed and left school. I called Hector to see if he could look in on her. He said he would be there in about 45 minutes. So, you want me to drive you to Fresno in the morning?"

"Yeah. My plane leaves at 10:15. I'll sit in the back with my mask." Ryanne is joking. "The plane ticket was expensive, but I'll just bill the school; tell them it's a recruiting trip."

"That won't fly, so to speak. Send the bill to Junior and have him put it on the Democratic Party's expense account, since you're going to work for them."

"So, what's with Char?"

"I'm worried. She sounded so defeated. The transfer isn't working out. I'm going to check with Admissions tomorrow to see if we can somehow get her back here. Let her practice with the team; she won't be able to play, nor should that be the major concern, but just to get her back with the ladies."

"And away from her brothers."

"Yeah."

"I'll drive over. We can take my car. By the way, you're not mad that

I'm going, are you?"

"Really pissed, but I'll handle it. See you when you get here." Molly laughs and taps off. She looks at Frank. "Maybe when I get back from Fresno tomorrow, I'll just sleep for two weeks."

Frank stands and begins to rub his wife's shoulders. "I can understand that these get pretty tired sometimes with all they have to carry."

"I shouldn't complain. We have it so good. Besides, I get paid well for doing just this." She reaches up to take Frank's hands and squeezes them. "Thank you for my life."

"Let's go and watch a movie on the couch."

∾

Asleep with her head on Frank's lap, her body jerks every so often. Molly's phone rings and lights up. He notices the call is from Hector. Frank rouses his wife and hands her the phone.

"Hi, Hector. How's Char?"

There is a pause. "Coach, she left you a note."

"Huh. What do you mean?"

"The ambulance just left, but I was too late. She hung herself." After a moment of silence, Hector says, "I already called Dyani. Could you see she gets on the bus tomorrow morning with a lunch bag and some water?"

Molly's face tells Frank. He pulls her into his body and holds her while she cries. There is no self-recrimination, just tears. After a few minutes, Molly pulls back and wipes the tears with the palm of her hands. "I need to call Ryanne." Before she can, Ryanne has called her.

"I know. Dyani just told me. Why don't you come over here?"

∾

At Ryanne's Dyani sits at the dinette table drinking her particular style of coffee. Molly and Ryanne sit on opposite sides holding her hands or rubbing her forearms. Maskless. Dyani drifts between anger and guilt but is not shocked or confused. She knows about suicide on the reservation. It's not rare, but it always stings like a scorpion.

"Everyone on the rez has hard lives; that's no excuse," says Dyani accusingly. Molly and Ryanne stay quiet. "I'm not going back there.

231

For what? To hang around with her family who probably all have Covid, to console her brother who might as well have bought her the rope? 'Come on home, Char. We'll get high and everything will be fine!' Fuckers!"

Molly squeezes Dyani's forearm. She's not Coach tonight, just a friend who closets her own grief for the moment. Neither Molly nor Ryanne is angry at Char. Just hurt. Dyani's jaw quivers, she's clenching her teeth so hard. Her eyes narrow as if she's trying to see through the miles to her Little Sister. Suddenly, Dyani releases a guttural cry and pulls her chin down into her chest. She clenches her fists, pulling her forearms from the hands of Molly and Ryanne, drawing her upper body into a ball. Ryanne stands and moves behind Dyani and wraps her arms around the shaking young woman. Molly moves her face closer to Dyani's face searching for an opening.

Six-hundred fifty miles to the east as a crow would fly, an old man looks and feels older. He's lived through other suicides, but each one takes a piece of Hector away. He sits cross-legged on the ground just outside Char's brother's trailer. Hector is wise enough to know this wasn't his fault, that forces beyond his control drove a beautiful young lady to take her own life, but he will collect and carry the guilt of the family, the clan, The People, and The Nation of another senseless death. He tries to channel Dyani, but her shame keeps him away. When he found Char, she was wearing a practice jersey from a summer team a few years back, her shoes removed and sitting near the hanging tree. Expensive Nikes that Char would not have wanted to damage. Hector took them and placed them in his bag before the ambulance arrived. He will pass them on to a younger Navajo girl, but he will not tell that girl where he got them. *The grip that basketball holds on the reservation*, thinks Hector. Fifty years earlier, Hector had a sweet jumper, but the sport didn't captivate his life like it now does to the culture of Native Americans. *Why?* he wonders. *Was it just basketball that led to Char's death?* Hector searches the skies for an answer tonight. The stars tell him there was more, that basketball for Char was a support system.

Papa Frank sits on his son's bed watching his little boy. Events such as suicide make parents see their children in a vulnerable way. Dr.

Frank knows that suicide is born from pain and loneliness, and the pandemic has spread more than just a viral infection across the land. The closing of schools, of playgrounds, of churches . . . of families and clans. He knows that Char's death was not a moral failure, but a result of a collapse of the social network so important to the health of society. Covid has strained society's bonds, and in cultures like Char's, those bonds are based on clan. Frank worries how he will explain to Frankie Char's death. Papa gently lays his hand on his son's head.

In Ryanne's kitchen, Dyani unfurls her upper body, the tenseness evaporating like the morning dew. Her eyes gain focus on the present again. "I could have prevented this." Ryanne utters a soft "Nooo" into Dyani's ear at the same time Molly shakes her head and offers a sympathetic smile. "I could have," says Dyani again. "If I would have stayed back with her . . . at least until she got settled at her new college. I could have been the buffer between her and her family, the compass she needed to stay away from her Hopi boyfriend. Her success was all her family had. Char told me all the time. If I'd have insisted that she stay here. So stubborn."

Dyani talks uninterrupted for another 25 minutes before laying her head on the table and falling asleep. Ryanne brings a blanket from her bedroom and covers Dyani. Molly and Ryanne devise a way to get the word out to her teammates—her sisters—and the others in the community who need to know. Ryanne texts Junior figuring he'll be asleep for another few hours. She reschedules her plane reservation, saying she can leave later in the week if that's still something she wants to do. Molly texts Moses Robinson and Dr. Calhoun giving them the barest information and promises to call them in the morning. Then, she calls her husband telling him she loves him and may not be home for a while.

"They need to hear it in person; we can't just send out a text," says Ryanne.

Molly agrees. "We can tell them to meet us in my backyard around noon, maybe on the pretext of new scheduling and lunch. That way, we can see Dyani off and then pick up something for the ladies to eat."

Dyani lifts her head. "No. I'm not leaving tomorrow. Maybe later in the week, but I'll tell the team. They need to hear it from me."

❧

Dr. Calhoun gives special permission for a masked meeting in Molly's backyard for the members of the team after Coach Rascon has already scheduled it. "Keep it as brief as possible under the circumstances. Schedule another Covid test for those who attend too." Emerson and Martina cannot attend due to the state and the county Covid restrictions. Frank takes Frankie with him to work, and Molly sets up chairs on the lawn as prescribed by health officials. Damn Covid! Ryanne and Dyani arrive just before noon on a warm, late-September day in 2020 to deliver the tragic news. And even though Char Betany does not attend SJV and is no longer a member of team, she is still a member of The Tribe.

Minutes after Dyani and Ryanne arrive, Mose and Sally drive up to the house. They talked about returning to Oxnard for the two-week quarantine period but weren't going to go until the weekend. Their ages place them in the high-risk segment of the population for contracting Covid. Molly had discouraged them from attending the gathering, but Mose insisted they attend.

The team arrives almost as a unit and can tell immediately that something is not right. Molly has facetimed Emerson and Martina so they can be included. Molly gets right to it. "Take a seat and listen up. Dyani needs to tell you something."

Dyani steps to the front of the wooden patio deck, curls her lips inward, and looks up at the ladies who just six months ago were her teammates and who now are her players. Molly wonders if Dyani can hold it together. Dyani swallows hard once more and begins, "Last night, Char took her own life." Several of the ladies make sudden sounds. Molly and Ryanne put their arms around Dyani for support, but Dyani continues. "She hung herself, hanged herself, outside her brother's trailer in Chinle. Hector found her and called me and Coach. She had left her new school on Monday. I guess things weren't working out for her there, but she didn't tell anyone except her older brother." Dyani stops to breathe out of her mouth. She opens her eyes wide to prevent the tears from overwhelming her. "This is hard." She puts her hands up to her mouth as if in prayer but keeps her eyes on her team. "With everything else that's going on, now this. I want to tell you this, . . . she loved you guys." Dyani pauses again. "Coach doesn't know this, but when Char was in high school, she attempted suicide once before over a boy. My town doesn't do good at getting people help who have these kinds of problems. We're supposed to be warriors, even the girls." Dyani looks directly at Keilani. "Char really loved you and your passion and last year's second teamers. She always said that when you sit on the bench so much, you develop a bond. I think you guys kept her alive for an extra year, and I thank you for that. I don't know how we're all going to grieve with all the social distancing shit, but whatever I can do for you, I will."

The ladies cry collectively. Molly looks out on her team and thinks they look lost. News like this before the virus restrictions would have been received with hugs. Molly takes one step forward keeping her arm around Dyani. "I want you all to reach over and take the hand of your teammate while I tell you a story." She waits for a moment. "As you probably know, Dyani attended a community college before coming here. Her first season here, she told me about another Indian player from her rez who might be better than she was. Then, in typical Dyani fashion, she said Char wasn't yet, but might be down the line and that I might want to recruit her. Dyani said that this little phenom would be a project because she didn't have confidence in herself, but that maybe by coming to a D1 school right away might give her that confidence, that if she stayed near home, she would just be another girl from the rez who didn't make it. Because of Dyani and because of you all, Char was making it. The certificate will say one thing, but the real cause of her death was Covid, because Covid took her away from us and left her alone." Molly turns into Dyani and hugs her. Ryanne steps forward as Molly had moments earlier.

"We ask you every day how you're doing. We really mean it, we really do. It's not just about your physical health with Covid, it's about your entire health. So, now, when Coach or I ask you how you're doing and look deep into your eyes, we'll be trying to look into your soul too. It's your souls we're trying to grow." Ryanne tries to project a stern look, but it comes off as something quite different.

Dyani looks out again. "We won't be able to have any kind of open funeral or anything because of you know what, so let's just celebrate her life by being good teammates this coming year." She tries to say, "Take care of each other," but none of the girls hear her words over her weeping and their own, but they understand the meaning.

Sylvia Castro stands and leads the team in a short prayer for Char Betany.

ॐ

On a reservation in a forgotten corner of America, Hector Dehiya and three other men wash a young girl's body. Hector will talk to the body as he performs his work, talking about her journey, about the walk she is about to take.

ॐ

In the middle of the heartbreak, President Trump and his wife test positive for Covid. It is Friday, October 2. The first presidential debate took place just three days earlier, an event that seemed unimportant to the Sequoias amid the emotional distress of Char's passing. In "an abundance of caution," Trump is admitted to the hospital where he begins a regimen of the most advanced and expensive Covid medicines, none of which are available to average Americans.

It's Dr. Frank who states the obvious. "If he tested positive today, then he's been contagious for several days, maybe even during the debate, certainly during his rallies and meetings. No doubt he's put others at risk too." He says this with that "It's just Trump being Trump" tone in his voice—traces of frustration mixed with anger.

Frank and Molly are sitting on the couch by themselves, Frankie already asleep. Molly lays her head back and breathes out heavily. "I don't wish him dead, but I wish he'd just go away. He's worn me out. He's worn us all out."

Frank lays his hand over Molly's. "Everything I'm trying to do at the clinic is made more difficult by his poor behaviors about the virus. His ego is an infection as dangerous as the virus itself. He's made this year . . ." Frank stops. "Preaching to the choir, huh?"

"Yeah. Will God think poorly of me if I wish Trump is put on a ventilator with a tube in his throat for a month?"

"If God does, then there's a whole bunch of people God will think poorly of. I wonder how Trump's people will spin all of this. Evidently, there's a bunch of them that have Covid too."

Without moving her head, Molly continues. "He denied that the virus was going to be a serious problem, then he said it would disappear with the arrival of summer, then he and his followers said not to get caught up in the hype about social distancing and masks. To him, Covid is an inconvenience to his precious legacy." Her last two words are voiced with disdain. "I want him to see how it feels, sort of like what Ken had to endure. I want him to pay for Queenie!"

Frank nods. In time he responds. "Problem is, his soul doesn't react the way ours do. He'll think he's being persecuted by this China virus, that it's unfair."

"The problem is, he doesn't have a soul."

Frank laughs sarcastically. "He's probably not a basketball fan either, certainly not a women's basketball fan."

Molly squeezes her husband's hand and breathes in heavily again. "Not his type as he would say. He's a user and a taker; always about what's in it for him."

∽

Over the next few days, reports conflict as to the gravity of the president's condition, but serious procedures have been used to treat his bout with Covid. It's also clear he has learned nothing during his stay in the hospital and has not had an epiphany about empathy. "Don't be afraid of Covid. Just get out there," he tells America.

In Tulare County, California, a single mother of two of Dr. Martinez's young patients dies, leaving her two boys as orphans. She had been "out there" working in a vulnerable occupation to provide for her family.

∽

Mose and Sally return to Oxnard for six days. Ryanne flies to Georgia to campaign for Raphael Warnock and Jon Ossoff for a couple of days. Dyani does not go back to the reservation but speaks with her Uncle Hector daily by phone. Molly and Frank talk with Frankie about death by suicide in the gentlest terms. In addition to the

30-minute, social distanced, individual workouts at the outdoor court, Coach Rascon facetimes every player every evening. The two-week quarantine passes quickly with no more positive test results, and on Thursday, October 8, at 6 am, the San Joaquin Valley Sequoias begin practice again. It's still the Transition Period, but the ladies are all together on the hardwood. There is a sense of urgency to the team, and Coach Rascon leans on them hard. "Ladies, we have no time to waste! Santa Barbara is two weeks ahead of us, and they won't feel sorry for us, and they won't overlook us, so get your asses down for this drill and slap your hands on the court!" Dyani stands between the two rookie guards, Maddie and Claudia, demanding effort they never experienced. "I won't demand things of you that you can't do!" Coach Robinson bends into a defensive stance in front of the Bigs, who giggle at his lack of flexibility. Coach Powell has the whistle for this drill, blowing it loudly for directional changes. She and Molly want to know if their ladies' conditioning has slipped. It doesn't appear that it has. When the drill ends, they can focus on offensive skills and putting the offense together.

For the allotted 90 minutes of skill instruction as per the NCAA rules during the Transition Period, Coach Rascon seldom gets farther than six feet away from her point guard, Keilani Russell. "Eyes up, Keilani. See your teammates, even over at the side baskets. You're in charge. It's your ball; it's your team. If the team makes a mistake, it's on you. Don't feel sorry for yourself; you asked for this. Do it again. Again. Again." And occasionally, Coach Rascon will walk past her point guard and whisper so that no one else can hear, "Nice job, Lani. You're getting it."

❧

Hector Dehiya shows up in Tulare on Saturday morning, driving a twenty-year-old Ford pickup that he says just showed up at his place, a sign that he was supposed to take a trip. Not wanting to bring "Covid germs" into anyone's house, he rigs up a tent on the back of the truck and sleeps there for two nights. When Dyani is not at practice, she walks with her uncle, mostly at Del Lago Park in town and along the sidewalks of the university. They talk about Char and her family, about the crops and cows in Tulare County, about the difference between playing and coaching basketball. About dinosaurs. He always laughs about that; it's the standard joke on the reservation. Hector apologizes for not seeing Char's pain more clearly and wants Dyani not to feel guilty. If he couldn't see it, there was no way Dyani could have either.

Sunday is a non-contact day for the team, so the coaching staff takes Hector into the national park to picnic and see the giant sequoias. He insists on separation, so he drives the Ford, the third automobile in a three-car caravan. Molly, Frank, and Frankie lead with Ryanne and Dyani next. It's unseasonably warm and the giant trees greet them cordially. Ryanne comments on the difference in temperature between Tulare in the valley and the park. After lunch, Hector, Dyani, Frankie, and Frank hike, while Molly and Ryanne clean up.

"Hector is a unique man," says Molly.

Ryanne agrees. "Remember when we first met Dyani in Chinle?"

"We first met Dyani in Tucson," corrects Molly.

"I know, but I'm referring to when we met her family. Hector was at the house. He's aged since then. Now, I can see that he's an old man. Dyani said something about his role on the reservation, that every death is his death. I guess Char's passing has really affected him."

Molly puts used paper plates in a paper grocery bag to take home for recycling. "It's affected all of us that way. The ladies play through it at practice as you've seen, but every once in a while, a memory hits. Dyani stares out into space sometimes."

"We all keep looking for something that doesn't exist any longer." Ryanne touches Molly's shoulder. "That didn't quite come out the way I meant."

"I know what you mean. It's tough. I watch Dyani for signs. I know you do at home."

Ryanne is twenty years older than Dyani, but they've been good roommates. "We talk a little about Char, but mostly, I think, she's just glad she doesn't have to be alone in her grief. The coaching has really helped. The girls have been so wonderful to Dyani."

"We'll all get through this, but it'll take time. Covid isn't done with us yet."

Frankie is the first to return, sprinting to the picnic table 50 yards ahead of the others. Dyani jogs in, obviously allowing Frankie to win the race. "The trees" are the main topic. Molly serves one last round of drinks allowing Hector to compare the beauty of this park to his part of the world in northeast Arizona.

"Our old trees are petrified." Frankie asks what that means, and Hector tells him that they have turned to stone and taken on wonderful colors. Frankie asks about the leaves, which stumps Hector for a moment. "That's a good question. Maybe when the tree died, the leaves were carried off by the wind to be born again on new trees. I believe, Frankie, that nothing that lives ever really dies; it's just recreated at a different time and maybe in a different form. Life is life, and as long as we remember that life, it continues forever." Hector looks at Dyani and smiles. "When you were a young girl, I gave you a nickname that you didn't like. Little Crow." Dyani nods as she remembers. "Crows are smart and inquisitive and very loyal to the flock. They take care of their own." Hector smiles. "They are also a symbol of transformation. I am very proud of you, Little Crow."

The caravan home splits in Visalia. Hector will take the backroads back to Chinle, take his time as he looks for dinosaurs. The group stops to say goodbye, and Hector hugs Dyani long and tight. He gives Molly an envelope, telling her not to read it until later that night. He musses Frankie's hair, gets in the truck, and heads out.

Dyani watches his path until the truck is out of sight. She turns to the others and says, "That's who he is," and smiles a tight smile with tears in her eyes. "He carries people."

❧

After Frankie has been tucked into bed, Molly sits on the couch with Frank and opens the envelope. It's a letter from Char, a brief note.

Coach,

I'm sorry. I'm just so tired. I know you're disappointed in me that I quit school. I couldn't do the computer thing. I don't have any friends at my new school, and we still have to stay apart. That's why I came home, but we can't hang out together here either. I miss the team. It was the best time of my life. I'm sorry. I love you.

Char

Frank reads the letter at the same time, and when he finishes, he puts his arm around his wife's shoulders and pulls her into his body. The tears that she has been withholding for the past weeks now come, and her chest rises and falls as she tries to catch her breath. Still, Frank senses a release in his wife as if Char's note and Hector's visit have combined to provide an explanation for the unexplainable. Frank strokes the hair on Molly's head slowly. He waits.

After several minutes, Molly pulls away to reach a tissue on the end table. She wipes her eyes first and then blows her nose. "I got your shirt all wet." Frank looks down and nods but remains silent. "What Hector said, that as long as we remember, a life never dies. I will always hold that thought for Char." She pauses. "I blame myself, and I know Dyani feels so much guilt, but I'm going to try hard to get past that guilt and help her do the same." Molly blows her nose again. "When we got Char into Ft. Lewis, I thought that might be the answer, but I also had doubts about it. She had Dyani here to help her overcome her shyness off the reservation. I guess I just hoped."

Frank takes hold of his wife's hand that rests on his chest. "Covid removed so many people's social safety net. For shy people and lonely people, it has been really, really difficult."

"I need to, I don't know, I need to project hope for my ladies as we go forward. It's such a hard time for young people who should be more carefree before heading out into the world."

"Molly, nearly all your players have experienced the cold, hard world at some point. That's their modus operandi. It's one of the reasons you recruited them, to give them that chance. You and this place gave Char that hope, and neither you nor Dyani is responsible for dashing that hope. God knows you both tried."

"Maybe not hard enough."

"No. Covid removed your arms from around her, so do what you just said you were going to do. Remember her. Tell funny stories to your ladies about Char. Laugh and remember."

Dr. Calhoun texts Coach Rascon that he would like to speak with her sometime on Monday or Tuesday when it's convenient for her. At her basketball office on Monday morning, she calls. He offers again his sincere sympathy for her loss. "When I taught back when I was young, losing a student in a car wreck or in any way is so tragic. It sends ripples through the entire school. Char was one of our quieter students, one out of 11,000 students. Her circle was small, but none the less important. Your two benefactors somehow found out about it and want to do something. We brainstormed a little and I offered the university's standard line. Provide scholarship money. I think it was Ms. Caldwell who suggested a different approach. You're operating on a shoestring budget now, and I appreciate that as we move through the pandemic and try to find funds for all our athletic teams. Ms. Caldwell asked if their foundation could provide the funds for another coach for your program. Ms. Borges said that since Dyani is already on staff, they could create some kind of endowment for a First American to be on your staff. California certainly has a history of taking the land of the Native Americans. We talked about that for a while but decided we needed to bring you into the conversation. We left it at that, but I sort of said that if they wanted to fund it, SJV would promise a fourth coach for you."

"We are already four coaches," says Molly.

Dr. Calhoun laughs gently. "Coach Robinson basically works for free, almost as a volunteer assistant. You know that, and he doesn't do any of the things that a full-time assistant would do. He's a presence at practice and valuable, but you and Ryanne carry the workload."

"So, you're saying I could hire another coach? Geez, our bench would begin to look like a typical D1 bench with all the non-players sitting between me and the players. We could all wear matching outfits too." She laughs on her end. "Let me think about it, but I'm inclined to lean toward increasing the salaries of my assistants and letting Dyani be the first recipient of this Native American position. I'm hoping she decides to stick around for several years."

Chapter 14

October 14 is written on the main whiteboard in Coach Rascon's War Room. Beneath that date is written **November 25 vs UCSB.** Then, **6 WEEKS!** The masked team sits widely spaced waiting for their coach to enter the room. While they wait, they read the copious notes entered on the side walls. It's Tuesday evening, October 13, 2020. The afternoon practice was demanding, but short, and then the team was excused for dinner before reassembling at the War Room for this meeting. Martina Smith, the team's head manager sits on a stool just inside the door reading a textbook. Coaches Rascon, Powell, and Dehiya enter before 7:00.

"Vacation's over," says Coach Rascon. "I'm upping your work schedules beginning tomorrow."

There is a collective, sarcastic moan from the team, but they all are anxious to put more time in the gym. It's not as if they must push something off their schedules. The NCAA guidelines now allow for an extra eight hours per week, up to four hours per day, and only one mandatory day off. Only Kenti's time will be scrunched since she continues to live on the farm outside Tulare. She has free use of a farm pickup and a job driver's license, as she calls it. None of the ladies have an 8:00 online class. Morning practices "will get the blood flowing." Skill work. Afternoons will be for team drills and scrimmages.

"I heard on TV that Indio has to pause," says Emerson.

Molly nods. "Yep, both men and women. Oh darn." She smiles. "Don't let your guard down. Several teams around the country are in quarantine, and a few leagues are considering not playing this winter.

America wants its sports, so there's a pushback on that, but it just tells us we need to be super careful." Molly steps to the board. "Santa Barbara. Over there. Especially for you, Emerson. Probably no fans. But a game. The beginning." She's interrupted by Kaori.

"The reason we're still here!" It's both funny and not funny, and the team's response echoes that. Kaori is a little embarrassed. "It just came out, Coach. Sorry."

Molly steps away from the board to her original spot and nods. "Actually, it sort of is, not why you're in college, but why you're here in Tulare. This isn't exactly the garden spot of California, although it surrounds us." She pauses to measure her words. "Every one of you could be somewhere else both to play basketball and to get an education. But you're not. You're here. Ryanne and I recruited every one of you except Kenti and Maddie, and we're fortunate to have the two of you." She nods at both of them. "S . . . J . . . V . . . takes students like you, and coaches like the three of us, and gives us an opportunity. It has a deep understanding of the . . . obstacles that you've overcome to get into college. It's part of the university's mission. I think about that every week. Our campus is beautiful, and if you look out across the fields, if the brown cloud isn't shrouding the area, the county can be beautiful, but when you look carefully, you see poverty and . . . despair. I choose to see SJV as The Valley's beacon of hope, as its symbol of promise." Molly's ladies are quiet and attentive. Her words are not scripted, like so much of the day-to-day living during the pandemic. "I think of you ladies as my responsibility to promote that hope. I hope you feel that responsibility in some way, not just to the university or the county, but to your families, and to that," she pauses and moves her head from side to side, "that mass of young people who live in poverty and despair. Carrying someone else's weight is noble." She stops there and stares out at her team.

Ryanne starts bouncing and sings. "She ain't heavy; she's my sister." The room breaks out in laughter. Dyani high-fives Ryanne who walks over to her best friend and hugs her—against Covid protocols. Into her ear she whispers, "I love you, girl."

Turning back to the team, Coach Rascon says, "These days, people around Tulare don't have a lot to hang on to, so they work because they need to and worry about their families and their own health. Let's be that team that gives them something to cheer for during these dark days. Let's be *The Valley's team*, bigger than just a team at the college in town. We'll be playing for them, and every time a microphone is stuck in your face, remind them of that. Don't let them just see our privilege and comfort compared to theirs, let them see our hard work and commitment."

Molly smiles. She looks to Dyani to see if she would like to say something. Dyani pinches her nose and clears her voice. "We've been The Tribe for the last two seasons, but that doesn't seem to fit going forward. Coach asked me to think about that. Keeping with what she just said, I think I may have something. So many of the workers live in small villages that are not really a part of any of the cities, but they are tightly knit communities. How about when we stack hands at the end of practices or before games, we say, 'La Colonia.'"

Coach Robinson nods in appreciation, holds up both hands to Molly, and shakes his head no, he has nothing to add.

La Colonia has no plodders. This team is stacked with thoroughbreds. Certainly, there are a handful of ladies who are faster and more graceful, but even Coach Rascon's Bigs can run and jump. As the practices proceed, as teammates begin to pair up for drills, Maria Sanchez fosters one of the newbies, Adriana Galvan. Addie practices like the player Molly recruited, all out all the time, and her energy begins to rub off on Maria who sees her playing time could diminish if she doesn't keep up. The two Big slots will be taken by Sylvia, Greta, Esther, and Joyce, although Joyce will only get similar minutes as she did last season. She knows her role. Maria and Addie will back up Emerson and Kaori, and Claudia will be a capable sub for Keilani. Maddie's skills will be tested daily by the constant pressure of Kenti and her soccer feet. La Colonia goes nine deep, "and our three guards won't be able to be contained on either side of the ball."

"Were we this good last year?" asks Dyani as the coaches critique Friday's practice.

Ryanne answers before Molly. "We're better at four spots, more experienced and deeper, but last year we had the X-factor, the best player on the West Coast to lead us."

Molly agrees. "Tough to replace a player like that. Certainly, the best I ever coached. So much will depend on Keilani." Molly pauses. "And on the coaching abilities of her mentor."

Mose pops the tab on a soda. "Last year, Dyani, you took the ball into the paint with your dribble. It's what made us effective. Statistically, you threw about a hundred passes each game. Ninety-seven made it to your teammates. Pretty remarkable. Every scouting report on us said "Get the ball out of Dehiya's hands." They couldn't because you were so good. This year, we won't ask Keilani to do so much. Emerson and Kaori can handle it some. We'll pass ahead more. We'll be a bit different, but still really good."

Ryanne pulls her mask down to scratch her nose. "We need to make sure all our girls are registered to vote. I checked with Sylvia and Maria, and they both are." The two Texas "army brats" and Kenti are the only non-Californians on the roster. Ryanne laughs. "I travel to Georgia to register voters, I'm not going to mess up here, although the outcome of the election here isn't in doubt. Georgia will be close."

Molly laughs lightly. "I neglected to tell you, Dyani, when we were hiring you that Ryanne and I are pretty serious about our politics. Mose too. For Ry, it's in her DNA, and I was infected in college. She's Southside Chicago, and I'm a political science major from a liberal arts university, and as you guys always said, *Chicana*."

"You weren't political growing up?" asks Dyani.

"Gawd no. Isolated and ignorant," says Molly.

"The nineties weren't a time when we had an in-your-face president saying divisive things hourly," says Ryanne.

Molly makes a soft noise. "I just had a thought. I never knew the politics of my high school coach. It never came up whether he was Republican or Democrat. Of course, he couldn't be registering sixteen- and seventeen-year-old players, but I don't recall a single polit-ical conversation. Lots about how to be a decent person, about caring and responsibility, but not about politics." She makes another musing sound.

"Are you registered, Dyani?" asks Ryanne.

"Yeah, now. I sort of tried when I turned eighteen but couldn't. My family didn't have a physical address." Dyani shakes her head and smirks. "The trailer on the left side of the road just past the closed-down gas station. That doesn't work as a physical address. But a bunch of women, sort of like you, Ry, worked hard to get as many of us signed up as possible. I think we'll turn out for this election, but Covid is just running rampant through the rez. I don't know what it will do to voter turnout."

"I assume the rez won't be voting for Trump," says Molly.

"Gosh, no, but I don't know if all our votes will make a difference. Arizona's always voted Republican."

Ryanne tilts her head, "Never know. Arizona is one of the states on the radar. Tell your friends to vote it they can. A legend like you carries a lot of clout among your people."

"Yeah, *my people*. Right." Dyani is dismissive of Ryanne's comment. Dyani stands, spreads her arms, and addresses the invisible multitudes, "Hey, I'm a basketball star, so get out and vote for Joe Biden!"

Her two friends laugh. "It's a start," says Ryanne. "Keep yelling!"

Because of the poor air quality in the county on Friday, Frankie remains inside all day. He reminded his parents that even going to the car was breathing bad air. He scampered from the car into dad's office, so he wasn't completely cut off from the world. Tulare schools closed in the spring and haven't reopened for classroom education. "Distance learning." Frankie calls it "computer learning." Covid complicates every aspect of life, and after dinner, Molly and Frank sit on the couch reading a week's worth of local and state newspapers trying to catch up. Frank reads an article in the *LA Times* and then hands it to his wife. "This won't surprise you," he says.

It doesn't. The article confirms that Democrats are extremely concerned about climate change and Republicans almost not at all. In fact, for Republicans it ranks last on a list of a dozen issues they are asked about when ranking their concerns. Molly finishes the article, tosses the newspaper section off to the side, and leans her head back against the couch. Frank notices but allows Molly her private thoughts for a moment. He knows she'll share them in time.

"We can't talk to each other. We live in separate universes. I'm sure our opposite conversation is being held in millions of red homes, and they're just as cocksure as we are." She rubs the space above her eyebrows with her fingertips and goes silent again. Interlocking her fingers on top of her head, she wonders if there is a college job available where the air is clear, and politics are sane. She allows a tangent of that thought to be expressed aloud, "I wonder if they have basketball in New Zealand's universities?"

"Google it. Pretty sure they don't pay what you make here." Frank knows it's an empty question.

Mama Molly calls to her son. "Frankie, google New Zealand women's basketball for me and then bring me your iPad when you find something." He comes in from the kitchen and hands her his findings. She reads quickly, hands the iPad back to him, and thanks him. "How's the book report coming?" Frankie nods and returns to the kitchen.

"Well?" says Frank.

"Probably not what I'm looking for, and I doubt I could recruit my type of players." Molly leans over against his shoulder, uses one hand to push the newspaper against his lap so he can't read it, and tells him to put his head back. He minds. "I didn't tell you about my talk with Stephanie and Janet today."

"Oh, it's on a first name basis now, huh?"

"They insist. They wanted to know how the team is doing since Char's passing. Nice touch, and it was sincere. They're good people."

Frank lifts his arm and puts it around Molly's shoulders. "And how are you doing?"

"Shitty." She tears up. "Char should be here." Moments pass before she goes on. "We always talk about me. Not fair. I'm a reactor; you're on the front lines every hour of every day. Kind of selfish of me."

"I think we both do what we need to. We take care of each other and the munchkin first."

Molly interrupts. "I don't do a very good job of taking care of you."

"What I do is pretty straight forward. You know that. Not to say I don't have my days or difficult parents; I do what's expected. Once a week, I drive out to another farm and do examinations on kids with no health insurance. You always tell me how much that means to you, and your appreciation of it means so much to me." He hesitates. "Tonight isn't about me. You lost your youngest lady, the baby of the team, and it hurts . . . and you're carrying around a lot of guilt. You're a great coach because everything about your team rests on your shoulders; you wouldn't have it any other way. I'm reminded of Carin Carleton back in Thousand Oaks. She snuck out after curfew; I think at Chico." Molly nods into Frank's shoulder. "What happened to her wasn't your fault or Ryanne's, but you both blame yourself to this day. Some things are out of your control. What you could control with Char, you did. But you couldn't hold her hand every night. She loved you . . . and you loved her back."

Sometimes when Frank tries to console his wife, she blows him off, but not tonight. She stays quiet for a time, unmoving. She doesn't wipe the few tears that trickle down her cheek. *Yes, I did,* she thinks. *Yes, I did love her.* Molly finally stirs, leans up and kisses Frank's cheek, and asks if he'll put Frankie to bed tonight. "I have a phone call to make." She rises from the couch, goes to the kitchen to spend a few minutes with her son, and then walks to the guest bedroom. Sitting in the purple, wingback chair in the corner, she taps a number and waits.

"Hello."

"Hi, Carin. It's Coach. How are you doing?"

Dr. Calhoun informs SJV's coaches of the recent actions of the NCAA, but the basketball teams are directly and immediately affected. "The committee will grant all your players this season an extra year of eligibility and an extra year to complete that eligibility. Not last year's seniors, however."

Molly and Ryanne delay informing their team until further details are revealed, but they do know that this ruling will alter recruiting methods and spiels. Along with the transfer portal, the extra year will change how coaches mold their teams going into the next season. "Every one of our ladies can return next season. We actually could go an entire season without recruiting," says Ryanne as if recruiting was a pain in the ass. "We simply come in each morning and teach."

"Assuming they all opt to stay that extra year. A few of them might get a little tired of us, you know, or a couple of our reserves might choose to transfer to get more playing time." Molly points to Claudia's name on the whiteboard. This new measure will give us Keilani for three more seasons."

Dyani always believed she should never have come out of a game and scowled at Molly when she subbed for her. "Claudia's going to be game ready this season, kinda has to be, and I could see her getting frustrated looking at the future as a permanent sub." Dyani, who now owns the smallest desk in the coaches' office, leans against it and holds her cup with both hands. "If they all improve like we think they will, where will you find playing time for them all?"

"There's an old saying," says Molly, "that's a good problem to have. Deep talent, but it's a double-edged sword. I don't think it'll be a problem this season but throwing out the same starting lineup for three years could be."

"We're definitely top heavy with underclassmen," adds Ryanne. "We'll just have to coach them so well that a couple of them go to the WNBA every year." She knows that's not a reasonable option. "Really, can you imagine having no turnover except Sylvia for three more years?"

"Since we're looking at it this way," says Molly, "I might need to change my practice tone some. They would simply roll their eyes whenever I pretended to be angry. Maria would have nightmares if she thought of listening to me for four more years."

Ryanne turns serious. "You've always maintained that practice has to have the fun element, that we can't always be demanding improvement at every moment. With Covid and all its subsequent baggage, we really will have to be aware of the girls' emotions. It's no longer just the season ahead of us, but years of . . . togetherness."

The coaches all stretch their jaws and go quiet. They lost one player to the pandemic, another joined the military not out of a sense of duty but of a lack of perceived options, and one sits in the room now as an assistant coach. Coach Rascon and Coach Powell will be tested, not for their Xs and Os, but for their interpersonal skills. And their success will ultimately not be measured by wins and championships.

SJV's strength and conditioning coach tests positive for Covid the last week in October putting a scare into every athlete at the university. She has been one of the hardest working employees during the pandemic. A crew dressed in white coveralls, masks, and face shields sanitizes the weight room which is placed off limits for four days. Everyone who was in contact with the strength coach is given another test. Surprisingly, no one tests positive. Molly's Dreamer, Esther Santiago, thought she had Covid because she wasn't feeling well, but it is determined it is just a cold. To be on the safe side, she quarantines herself in her dorm room and has meals left in the hall. Greta brings cafeteria meals to her. Dr. Frank checks on her daily and believes she was sick for several days before the symptoms appeared. She recovers quickly, missing just four days of practice. To be on the safe side, Coach Rascon keeps her out of close contact with the other ladies.

Across the country, university teams are pausing practices and cancelling games as per Covid protocol, and the stress mounts.

Ryanne spends her non-basketball hours in front of her TV watching the Senate hearings on Amy Coney Barrett's nomination to the Supreme Court. Barrett is confirmed on October 27, as expected, and Ryanne's political side is enraged. The outcome of the hearings was never in question, but the finality of a hard right Supreme Court that will be ruling on women's health issues and voting rights terrifies Ryanne. She preaches to the choir: Molly, Frank, Mose, Dyani, and Junior via text and Zoom.

"I LOVE THIS TEAM!" screams Ryanne at the top of her lungs in the gym the next day. It is not yelled with a smile but with a fury in response to the tactics used to confirm a new justice in such a short time after another was denied a hearing years earlier. The ladies don't understand the feelings behind Coach Powell's outburst, but they like her intensity. Keilani high-fives Ryanne moments later after the coach has taken a hard fall demonstrating how to get through high screens. Ryanne's political intensity transfers to basketball intensity, and Wednesday's practice moves the team closer to game ready. Four weeks left before the season opens, before the season might open.

One week before the in-person voting for President and Congress and hundreds of lower political offices takes place, America is a mess.

&

La Colonia gathers on Sunday afternoon for a picnic in Coach Rascon's backyard. Masks, distancing, personal drink bottles are the norm, enforced by Frankie, but a picnic, nonetheless. They arrive on foot in pairs. Three members are missing; Joyce drove home to Fresno for a day with her family, Kaori drove to the Bay area to be with her family, and Kenti needs the day to finish with a lab experiment on soils just after her plot harvested the tomatoes. There are no special announcements, no surprise NCAA directives, just a team with its coaches and lots of food. Molly has the three freshmen give a summary of their first two months of college. They have become best buddies, study mates, dorm partners.

Maddie Martin, the walk-on who now is on scholarship, tells her teammates that it's easier to live under the Covid restrictions in Tulare than at her home in Bakersfield but that living in the dorms might be the reason. "I shared my bedroom with my sister, and she never followed a rule in her life." Sylvia punches her sister in the arm and yells, "Amen."

Addie Galvan agrees with Maddie about coping with the rules is easier in college than it was at home. Maria yells out, "Maddie and Addie, birds of a feather," and everyone laughs. Addie wishes she could attend more of her classes in person but says her online skills are really improving.

Claudia Simpson rises from her chair and spills her paper plate of food but doesn't seem to be embarrassed. "One thing I like is that I can eat all I want since I'm I scholarship, and I like the cafeteria food. My adviser is really nice and always makes time for me. When we had to pause because of the positive tests, I wanted to go home. I was so disappointed, but my dad told me I had to stay. He was right. I'm really happy here." She ends her sentence and quickly bends over to put her food back on her plate.

Molly starts clapping and the others join her, a show of appreciation for the new girls. "We are so lucky to have you, and you have fit in nicely." Coach Rascon tells the team what they already know, that their first game is looming on the horizon, that they must continue to monitor their movements and follow the school's guidelines regarding Covid, that she will be checking on their grades, and if they feel any hint of illness, they are to report to the health clinic immediately.

In the manner that the ladies arrived, they depart, in pairs. Molly sends Ryanne and Dyani home, not allowing them to help with the inside cleanup. The two assistants also are given all the leftovers. While Frank and Frankie put away the folding chairs, Molly does the dishes. It has been a wonderful afternoon, and now she can catch up on the dozens of emails and unanswered calls. She can make one of her famous lists, on one side, the pros, on the other, the cons.

Chapter 15

"We will run! Make or miss, we will run! Wings will sprint the sidelines! The first Big to the ball throws it in; the other Big screens for the Point. Get it in and go!

From the first day of practice, a player will hear some form of this directive. It is non-negotiable. Sylvia Castro played softball growing up in Texas, centerfield, and she knows how to throw a baseball pass. Gather the ball and load the shoulder blades. The difference between softball and basketball is that she keeps her left hand on the bigger ball longer. Her first look is deep right to either Kaori or Emerson. "Don't come up short, Sylvia! Better to overthrow than underthrow." Then Coach Rascon will smile, because she knows her two antelopes will run any long pass down. "Rez Ball." For two seasons, the second option after a made basket was to Dyani who always got open at the precise moment Sylvia was ready. "Come to the ball with target hands!" This year, it will be Keilani. She needs to learn timing, to not come open while Sylvia's eyes are scanning downcourt. "Keilani, pause for a two-count to allow Sylvia to look deep. Then make your break! Keep the defender on your hip."

With Dyani, it was all instinctive, as if she was born to be a point guard, just as Molly was. For two seasons, these two defined point-guard play on the West Coast. Artists consulting one another on how to paint the perfect canvas. Ken Davidson saw it and wrote a blog about how it was not so much a coach-player relationship as a natural affinity of masters. Now these two masters have an apprentice—Keilani Russell— and she is a sponge.

Twenty-five years earlier, an old coach told a high school phenom that the basketball was hers and she was to take care of it. Molly knew what he was actually telling her, that the team was hers and she was to take care of all of its components, all of her teammates. That is the real responsibility of a point guard. "Take care of your teammates. In all situations, they rely on you." Dyani had that quality before she came to SJV; it was what Molly saw in her when she first scouted her. With Keilani, it will be a learned skill, but both Molly and Dyani believe in Keilani, so now it is their responsibility to push her to the limit, to find her best self, both on and off the court.

Monday's practice will be exceedingly challenging because there will be no practice on November 3. Election Day, at least the last day to cast a ballot. All the players and coaches have cast their ballots. By mail. Ryanne made a huge deal of getting the team registered but never once asked who they would be voting for. Both she and Molly bent over backwards to avoid asking. Voters have all kinds of reasons for who they vote for, and as Molly told them, "I trust you have reasons, and I trust you."

It was Emerson Loki dripping with sweat who joked at the end of a tiring practice, "You can have my body, but you can't have my vote." The team broke up as did Molly and Ryanne. Emerson, who had marched over the summer in BLM demonstrations, was the perfect messenger for that thought. Emerson, the impromptu dancer and angry demonstrator; Emerson; the high school all-stater with a chip on her shoulder; Emerson, who never played video games because real life delivered more adrenaline; Emerson, whose grandfather believed in pacifism; Emerson, who always believed "enough was enough," stepped up in practice glistening with perspiration and delivered Coach Rascon's message back to her coach and to her teammates. "It's my vote, and I will decide!"

After telling her team that she didn't want to see them on Tuesday, Coach Rascon fudged by saying they could text at any time to check election results. She and Ryanne would have all the up-to-date information. She reminded them to avoid crowds, "No, you can't go out to celebrate or commiserate. Stay in your dorm rooms."

That evening, Molly and Frank watch TV as the campaigns throw out their last pleas to those citizens who might not have voted. That group is mostly Trump supporters who have been told not to vote by mail but to vote on Tuesday. Those votes in many states will be counted first giving the impression that Trump is the likely winner. Mail-in voting results will be counted more slowly, and it is these votes that have been cast over the previous days and weeks that hold the outcome of the election, despite what Trump is contending. These votes, he tells his base, are illegal, are rigging the outcome.

Trump's top White House Covid adviser Deborah Birx tells the country on Monday that the administration needs to act more aggressively to stem the tide of a new wave. Trump tells his rallies that America has already passed the most dangerous phase, that the recent surge in cases is only due to increased testing. "If only that was true," commented Frank. All the major stations report that the majority of voters have already voted, over 100 million so far. Many said they voted to avoid standing in lines and feared contracting Covid. The networks use extreme caution in predicting the outcome because of the 2016 fiasco in polling.

Junior Warren texts Ryanne that he is getting reports that the Trump campaign is preparing to declare victory as soon as the polls close on Tuesday and are preparing for court challenges in both the states and in the Supreme Court. "It's going to be nasty!!!" Ryanne wanted to be in Georgia tomorrow night, but opted for the Rascon-Martinez household to watch the results come in. She wishes they could bring in their team and all sit on the floor watching.

"It's all about turnout," says Molly to Frank, who already knows that. "Everybody in the whole country who's voting tomorrow have made up their minds."

"I wonder if the Republican strategy of questioning the integrity of the election process will keep some of their base away. I doubt it, but I wouldn't be surprised," offers Frank. "I just worry that Trump will declare victory before the votes are counted."

"So much is riding on the states Hilary lost in '16. The polls are encouraging, but it's just so close," says Molly. "Ahhhh, I need ice cream! Frankie, are you in?"

❧

Molly leaves the house early on Election Day to jog. She promised herself that she would make no basketball calls or texts or emails today, that she would give the day to Frankie and the election. The media has the vote count boards at the ready, lined up political experts for commentary, and created gaudy television sets in anticipation of an extremely close election. Frankie asks what "fact-checkers" do, and Molly explains that they research the available information to correct the statements made by politicians to keep them honest.

"Does it work?"

"Yes and no," answers Molly. "Lots of voters will believe anything and everything their candidate says and not believe anything the other side says."

"Even when the fact-checkers have evidence?"

"Yeah. Doesn't make sense, does it?"

"Why wouldn't people want to know the truth?"

"This is a hard one, hon. In politics, sometimes it's really difficult to determine what's true, because people can honestly disagree on what course of action the country should take to solve a problem. You know how mama and papa pay taxes every year? Should the government spend those tax dollars to improve roads and bridges, or should the money be spent to build new schools, or should it be used to make the military stronger? Not easy choices, and in politics, the two parties will make the strongest possible case for their position, and that sometimes leads to them saying things that aren't true just to persuade the voters."

Frankie ponders his mother's words for a moment. "Aunt Ryanne gets mad when President Trump talks on TV. Sometimes, you and papa get mad too." He hasn't asked a question yet.

"Yeah, we do. We disagree with him on so many things, and he has a way of getting under our skin."

"Will you vote for Joe Biden?"

"We voted early by mail. We won't have to stand in a line this year because that might be dangerous what with Covid being so contagious. And, yes, we voted for Mr. Biden."

"When I grow up, I will too then." Frankie smiles and turns back to his iPad.

Molly watches him, hoping that America will still be the country she loves when he's old enough to vote. She doesn't like the anger and disunity that has enveloped her country. She wishes the country didn't need a fact-checking industry.

∾

Ryanne and Dyani sit with Molly, Frank, and Frankie eating enchiladas off paper plates in front of the television. Ryanne texts continually, mostly with Junior in Washington and with her contacts in Georgia. As the polls begin to close, early voting counts give Trump a sizable lead, but prognosticators from every network but FOX warn that these early vote counts are a mirage, that the early turnouts— those votes that were cast before today—really hold the outcome, and they almost certainly favor Biden.

"What are your sources telling you?" is a question Ryanne gets every fifteen minutes.

Ryanne swears continuously and apologizes frequently to Frankie for her language. "They're telling me that it will appear Trump will be re-elected tonight when the in-person voting tallies come in, so he will run with that and say he won. His base will celebrate like it's a pep rally, but then the mail-in votes will start to be counted, and he will claim voter fraud. Junior is convinced Biden will win, but half the country won't accept it. Trump has been setting up this scenario for the past four months. Voter fraud!"

Frank has made dozens of calls to voters in Tulare County on behalf of the Democratic Party. "I got a lot of that. He's made a point of being a winner, so he won't accept losing to Sleepy Joe. And his base will hang on that. The next two or three days while we wait for the official count to come in will be ugly ugly."

"A disinformation campaign!" adds Ryanne. She stops because of a new text, which she reads. Then, she holds up her phone. "From Georgia. People had to stand in line for over six or seven hours to vote. Disgusting."

"On the reservation, we don't usually vote by mail. Mail delivery takes so long, almost like it's being delivered by Pony Express," says Dyani. "But this year, we'll vote even if we have to stand in line with the coronavirus. Maybe our votes will swing the tide in Arizona."

"That would wake up all those Republicans in Phoenix," says Ryanne. "They'd have a cow."

"We've had some women do amazing work getting people registered," says Dyani.

"Isn't that how it always is," says Ryanne. "Black women are always doing the hard work. That's certainly the case in my Chicago and this year in Georgia."

"If we win, it will be because the Democrats outworked the Republicans. Trump and his people aren't out knocking on doors, they're just holding pep rallies and driving around in their trucks." Molly holds a bottle of beer to her lips but doesn't take a drink. "Sadly, even if he loses, his supporters will continue to think he's the real deal, a real Republican, a real Christian, you know."

As the polls close and the evening slips away, the vote count begins and Trump takes an early lead just as he predicted, just as expected. Ryanne and Dyani leave, and Frank lifts his son from the couch and carries him to bed. Molly sits on the bed and brushes his hair with her hand, saying a silent prayer since Frankie won't be saying his aloud. Frank turns off the light, and they return to the living room arm-in-arm.

"What are you thinking about?" asks Frank.

"Lots of thoughts tonight, I guess. All my girls voted, and probably all voted for Biden and the Democrats, because they're mostly in that category. Grew up poor in California. Not all of them, not Kaori and Joyce, although Joyce isn't wealthy by any means." Molly pauses to evaluate her own statements. "I wonder if Maddie and Claudia did. Doesn't matter. They all voted, and because of where our country is headed, it matters to me. I guess my education off the basketball court has had an effect on me."

"You mean those political science classes at State Tech?" Frank knows they did impact her, that she took them seriously.

"I admire Ryanne's passion for active participation, for walking the neighborhoods." Molly lets out a slight giggle. "I bet she's talking Dyani's ear off right now with the TV still blaring. "Anyway, I'm so worried about the direction of our country."

"It is troubling, isn't it?" says Frank.

"Yeah. We seem to be doubting the concept of democracy, not all of us but a large vocal minority that is well-funded. If they had their way, my ladies wouldn't get to vote, or at least they'd make it much harder for them to vote. Like Dyani was talking about, about how hard it is to vote on the reservation. And it's all so nasty."

"And divisive," adds Frank. "Sort of like this county we live in, huh. Definitely a line between the haves and have-nots, and the politicians who get elected here are backed by the former."

Molly shifts a little so that she's turned toward her husband. "You know, I wouldn't mind it so much, and I'm not talking just about Tulare, I wouldn't mind it if I really believed the Republicans believed in a democratic republic. I view it all through a skewed lens, I know, the lens of my team and my university, but still."

"That adage about two steps forward and one step back. When it comes to the advancement of democratic processes, it seems like we're in the one step back phase just now."

"I know there are good people in the Republican Party, but they are so intimidated by Trump and his base that they've forgotten their principles. If what we're saying tonight was being shared with some of our Republican friends, they'd think we were so wrong, so naïve, but it's how I feel." Molly leans in and kisses Frank on the cheek. "Enough of this for tonight. It's exhausting. Let's go to bed and get ready for tomorrow."

"Gear up for an exhausting next few days as the vote comes in," says Frank.

∾

The texts pour in. Her team, her former teammates, her assistants. "Coach, Biden won!" Ryanne's text makes a plea. "God help us get through the next three months." Molly keeps the television off knowing these texts are still premature. The vote is too close in key states. She makes coffee and sends Frank off to work with a kiss and a smile. She will stay home for the morning making her lists and planning for the afternoon practice after a non-contact day. Back to what she does: coach basketball! She pours herself a cup and takes stock of her team.

It's a bare-bones university squad, something she told Dr. Calhoun she would have for this Covid-infested year. Twelve players; no practice squad. Three assistants instead of four. Three student managers. No support staff near the court. Build a bubble to keep the virus out as best they can. When the team hits the floor at 4:00, there will be nineteen people in that bubble. Well-spaced in the stands might be an analytics director, a media director, the strength and conditioning coach, and an old journalist. They may or may not be in attendance. Of the nineteen on the floor, only two will be male. Coach Robinson and Tommy Cooley, a student manager who has taken the role as Martina's principal assistant. Molly sees him assuming Martina's role as head manager after this season when she graduates.

It's an experienced squad with a lofty goal. Repeat last year's success, including those fictious games that Coach Aikins created after the season was canceled. Lofty goals indeed, especially with an untested point guard replacing the best point guard on the West Coast. But ... better at every other position.

Controlled scrimmages, situational scrimmages. Coach Rascon writes the ladies who will be her starting five—Keilani, Kaori, Emerson, Greta, Sylvia—and the five that will back them up—Claudia, Addie, Maria, Esther, Joyce. Claudia has to grow into her role as backup point guard quickly; it's the one position that is light. Maria will back up Kaori and Emerson. Solid. Esther will be the super-sub, maybe a starter at times, and will back up Greta and Sylvia. Molly schedules time for all the different lineups and smiles. Yep, this team can be champions. Molly realizes that she has made this list several times.

Election Day was all about skepticism; today is all about hope. Hope means looking forward, skepticism glances in the rearview mirror. Ken Davidson texts, asking if he can attend practice. He is always welcome, but he always asks, nevertheless. A sports journalist with scruples. Covid did not erase his manners or curiosity. Mose texts that he spoke with one of the recruits on Molly's radar for next season, and she's excited about coming to SJV. When a team is recruiting a Big, it's nice that one of her contacts played in the NBA. Talk about street cred! Molly texts back to Mose. "Stay in contact daily. She's the one we want."

Private Danelle Weston texts that she has been assigned to paralegal specialist training camp after basic. She's excited, a missing emotion in her texts during basic training. This fits into her college major, criminal justice. Danelle says that there are opportunities for advanced legal training later on, maybe even law school. Molly texts back, "So proud of you!"

Dr. Calhoun texts that he scheduled another game two days after the opener, Cal Riverside at their gym on November 27. An easy bus ride to avoid air travel during the pandemic. "Still looking for another couple of games. Davis has shown interest." Molly has a meeting scheduled with the AD on Thursday to talk contract again. He's worried she'll be offered unbelievable money by the University of Washington and leave SJV. She doesn't know where he's getting his information, but there have been feelers to her about a possible opening if their program doesn't get better this season.

After lunch, Molly and Frankie head for the gym. She still refers to the arena as "the gym." For whatever reason, the men's team likes the practice gym, the old gym near the campus center, to practice leaving the performance gym mostly to the women in the afternoons. The men will come in at 7:00 pm for shoot-arounds to simulate game times. At Cal Coastal and Irvine and State Tech, it was just the opposite. The men's program had priority use despite Title IX. It was just the way it was, and the women had to fight with physical ed classes and intramurals for time and locker rooms. Not at SJV. It has never been an issue.

Dyani works on a graduate class at her desk in the basketball office. When Molly arrives, Dyani hands the head coach a workup for Keilani, Claudia, and Maddie for the post-scrimmage part of practice. "I'll have Kenti to play defense on all my girls today?" says Dyani.

"Yes, but you know she'll send Claudia and Maddie into therapy, don't you?"

"It takes a little crazy to be a good point guard."

"Did you get any sleep last night," asks Molly, "or did you stay up all night with Ry watching election results?"

"I turned in around midnight. Ryanne was on the phone or switching channels trying to get the absolute, latest, up-to-date vote totals.

She's sure Biden will win but kept saying Trump will never accept the outcome. I'm not sure she ever went to bed. This morning, she was fuming over all the reports of Trump's legal challenges. Then, all of a sudden, she began crying over Kamala Harris becoming the vice-president. I think it hit her that a Black woman has made another step."

Molly smiles. "I've known Ry for a long time, and she seldom cries. Gets angry, yeah, but not many tears. She cried when Obama was re-elected; we were together that night too. "

"She didn't cry long. She stopped and said that she needed to wait until it was official, until the networks called it." Dyani tilts her head back just a tad as if she's pondering that thought. "I haven't spoken with anyone on the rez yet."

Molly leans against her desk and looks intently at Dyani. "I'm really glad you're here. How are you doing?" She waits.

"Good. On the rez, I'd be worthless, just hanging around during the lockdown. Here, I'm involved. I know that's not quite what you're asking, but that's my answer. You don't have to worry about me doing what Char did or about me quitting and going back to Arizona. This is good, and I'm good."

"You'll tell me if you're not?"

"Promise."

Molly smiles. "What if the NCAA had said you could play this season?'

Dyani shakes her head. "Nope. My college playing career is over. I'm at peace with that. If the pro offer is real, then maybe, but I'm happy yelling at Kailani. She's your girl now."

Because of the Covid protocols, there are no referees for SJV's first real scrimmage. Molly has Tom Cooley film it so the coaching staff can break it down in the evening, but they already know what they'll see. The starters plus Esther are too good to be challenged by the reserves who are younger, weaker, less skilled, and intimidated. Molly wants to combine Claudia's offensive skills with Kenti's defensive skills to make a competent backup at the point for Keilani. The coaching staff understands that for the first team to improve, practices will need to pit three of the starters against three other starters a lot. Improvisation because of Covid.

It's Dyani who stops the scrimmage during the second quarter. Without asking Molly, Dyani brings Kenti and Claudia to the mid-court line and gives them new instructions. Basically, Kenti will only play on the defensive end, while Claudia runs the second team on the offensive end. They'll make that adjustment in transition. That way, Keilani will be tested. She'll be guarded by Kenti, and she will guard Claudia. It' clunky at first, but as the scrimmage proceeds, it works for Keilani's needs.

Dyani tells Molly, "We'll work on Claudia's defense in three-on-three drills and shell."

Mose builds on Dyani's adjustment and puts the Big who is not scrimmaging in the paint to slow the first unit's fastbreak. Eventually, the scrimmage resembles five on six, at least on the defensive end. For the next three weeks, that's how all scrimmages are run. All twelve ladies on the court at all times. Kenti and Maddie play lots of defense, which means that when the scrimmage is on the opposite end of the court, the rookie receives pointers from a Guatemalan woman who studies tendencies and reads eyes and understands roles, who is on this team because she loves to play and has never concerned herself with game minutes. "Basketball is like futbol; swing the ball and create space." She approached Coach Rascon over a year earlier just to practice with the team and became an integral part of something bigger than herself.

∞

Dr. Calhoun appreciates Molly Rascon. She has no hidden agenda and has been true to her promises made in her initial interview when she was hired. She monitors her athletes and has not once recruited a player who didn't meet her standards for character regardless of the recruit's athletic potential. She has never brought in a 5- or 4-star recruit; those kids don't have SJV on their radar. Tulare isn't Los Angeles or Palo Alto or Seattle. Coach Rascon's recruits don't come in with demands; they arrive asking for a chance. It's the same way Molly Rascon arrived at SJV. "I can do this if you'll give me the opportunity, and I won't let you down."

On Friday morning, Dr. Calhoun's secretary greets Molly outside his office. Mrs. Onorato jokingly warns Molly that her boss ordered his coffee extra strong this morning and wanted no interruptions while Coach Rascon was in his office. Molly holds up a piece of paper as if it's a sword. Mrs. Onorato knocks lightly on Dr. Calhoun's door and shows Coach Rascon in.

"Good morning, Coach. Coffee?

"Please." She sits in a leather chair at the conference table near the window that looks out over the campus. "Did I ever tell you what a nice office you have? My office doesn't have windows."

Dr. Calhoun puts a cup in front of the coach and takes a seat. "If I traded offices with you, could I convince you to stay?" Molly laughs. "You know, Coach, I have these two older ladies who keep pestering me about you. Persuasive as hell too."

"I assume you aren't referring to Ryanne and Dyani."

"No, but I'm pretty sure they hold the same attitude as Janet and Stephanie. And yes, they insist on me calling them by their first names, sort of their way to subtly pressure me." He takes a sip of his coffee. "Strong this morning. Mrs. Onorato makes it this way when she wants something." Molly laughs and waits. "Those two have sources, that's for sure. Last week, they provided me with a list of six universities that most likely will have openings for a head women's basketball coach next season. I told them those are just rumors, that schools with losing records all have disgruntled alumni who are not averse to undermining the current coach. The ladies also listed the salaries of those positions. Damn public records." He takes another sip of coffee. "Covid keeps me from bringing them into my office where I could sit them at this table and show them the trees out there that don't have money growing on them."

Molly plays along. She moves her head off to the side to look past Dr. Calhoun at those trees and then nods her head.

"How's the family?" asks Dr. Calhoun.

"Good, and thanks for allowing the exception in protocol for Frankie to be in the gym with me and the team. Otherwise, I'd have to hire him out to pick tomatoes to keep him out of trouble and make a few extra dollars."

"Would he get paid by the hour or by the box?"

"By the hour mostly. Hey, maybe you could pay me by the hour. That would increase my pay." Molly smiles.

Dr. Calhoun smiles back and nods. "I see you have something for me," he says pointing to Molly's piece of paper.

Molly has two copies, and she slides one over to Dr. Calhoun. "This is an interesting negotiation since I never asked for a restructured contract. You're the one who brought up the whole thing. Yes, I have been in contact with another university, two actually, and these have been unofficial contacts. I mentioned them to you before. The money they're mentioning is way beyond my current salary. I know you can't match it, and it is tempting." She holds up both palms to Dr. Calhoun. "The money aside, I do have a couple of issues with Tulare."

∾

Friday's practice is intense. Sylvia and Maria, the sisters, get into a tussle during a rebounding drill and need to be separated by Coach Robinson. Adriana/Addie takes the next step in being a full-fledged member of the team when she flattens Emerson on a drive to the basket on a fastbreak. Kaori helps Emerson to her feet and then pats Addie on the butt. Joyce decides not to allow any of Keilani's passes into Sylvia go uncontested and takes a Sylvia elbow to the nose, which brings out blood, turning her white mask red. Martina is quick with a towel and then leads Joyce to the training room. Tom Cooley dons the blue gloves and wipes up the floor, and practices continues. Two drills later, Joyce returns to the floor with a cotton swab protruding from one nostril. Sylvia gives her a hug and then bumps her hard on her first rotation in the bump-the-cutter drill.

As practice draws to a close, Dr. Martinez walks with a young woman in a wheelchair into the gym. Molly turns the last minutes of practice over to Dyani, and she and Ryanne go to the young woman and hug her. Covid protocols be damned! The team shoots its free throws, runs their penalties, and then assembles near Coach Rascon and the visitor. Molly tells them to sit.

"I'd like you to meet a former player of mine. Ladies, this is Carin

Carleton. Carin played for me at Cal Coastal before she was injured in a car accident. She's a lawyer now practicing in Ventura." Molly places her hand on Carin's shoulder, a signal for Carin to say a few words.

Carin slips her mask down for a moment to scratch her nose. "Coach tells me you have a chance to maybe be a little better than last season." For the next few minutes, Carin is both funny and insightful about basketball and her own experiences with Molly and Ryanne. Carin teases Ryanne about her weight gain, saying she thinks she could now beat her former coach if she wasn't in the wheelchair. Ryanne disputes Carin's claim. Carin continues. "I play in a wheelchair league in Los Angeles a couple nights each week. I can't get out on the break like I used to, but once I get going, nobody takes a charge," and the team laughs. Carin looks at Joyce who is dabbing her nose, her mask under her chin. "Looks like Coach still demands that you play physical under the basket." She smiles, looks up at Ryanne, and then takes Coach Rascon's hand. "Coach and I talked on the phone a little bit ago, and she told me about Char. That has to be hard." Carin allows that to settle over the team. "I follow you guys, have since Coach moved up here, but I didn't know much about Char since she didn't get much playing time. This morning, Coach Dehiya told me about her. Sounds like she was a great teammate." Carin lets go of Molly's hand and wheels herself closer to the team.

"Fucking Covid makes every hard thing even harder." Carin looks at Keilani. "Coach says you use my word frequently." Keilani laughs and nods. "You lose someone special in your life and you can't even attend her funeral, so you lose a way to pay your respects, not just to your friend but to her family. You blame yourself for not being there, for not doing enough. Don't do that. Covid makes it so you can't be in control of all your actions, like you're helpless in lots of situations. So, what should you do?" Carin pauses for a moment for the team to consider her question. "You grieve forward; you take care of your current teammates." Carin slips her mask down and rubs the back of her hand over her nose before covering up again. She taps her wheelchair with both hands. "What happened in the past can't be changed. You're probably curious about what happened. I got in a car accident during my junior season. Entirely my fault and luckily no one else was injured. Coach Rascon and Coach Powell never blamed me, they just stuck with me through my recovery."

There is a bit of noise by the door where Carin came in, and Dr. Frank walks over. Carin continues. "Evidently, Char's diet included some things that weren't on the proscribed list of health foods for college athletes, so for dinner tonight, so you don't have to endure cafeteria food for one night, I've ordered up some chicken. Regular, crispy, extra crispy, wings, whatever is on the Colonel's menu tonight."

Delivery boys place their sacks loaded with KFC chicken tubs and boxes with mashed potatoes, coleslaw, and biscuits onto a metal cart and leave. Frank pushes the cart over to the team. A cheer goes up and out, and Dyani Dehiya is sure her Little Sister hears it.

∞

For the next few days, Ryanne is smug. "He's not just a loooooooser, he's a poooor loooooooser." She wears her "I voted" sticker until the stickum on the back no longer sticks and reminds the team that their votes mattered. Dyani lets it be known with a smile that the mood of the house has dramatically changed since election day.

On Monday, November 9, the drug manufacturer Pfizer announces that in trials, its vaccine is 90 percent effective. The CDC says that over 250,000 Americans have died so far of the virus, and Frank shudders. As a pediatrician, he wonders how many children have lost their parents. Orphans now.

SJV makes it official. No fans will be allowed to attend the games. Contests will be played with essential personnel only. Not only will the excitement crowds generate evaporate, so will the money. Molly expected this turn. She thinks about last week's meeting with Dr. Calhoun and has second thoughts. She texts him suggesting they meet again early in the week. Mose texts Molly saying he's willing to work without pay. Molly knows his part-time salary will not cover any significant deficits, but she appreciates the gesture. She texts back declining his offer. She also knows that he donates his entire salary to various clubs in Oxnard.

Six of Molly's ladies have family members who have contracted Covid. So far, none have died, but it hits home, nevertheless. Molly's mother starts to work as a housekeeper again back in Colorado despite her daughter's warnings. In her late 50s, she tells Molly that it is something she enjoys. Ryanne's mother behaves the same way. Intransigent!

Monday's practice is late. The arena's custodians, along with the team's managers, sanitize the gym area after the men's team finishes. The expenses for this extra cleaning and for Covid testing compromise the university's budget. Ken Davidson's blog considers this, and he wonders how long colleges can sustain athletics under these circumstances.

Practice begins as usual. Martina points a temperature gun at each player's forehead, asks how she's feeling, and notes the results on her computer. Martina has already tested the coaches and managers. Individual pre-practice routines begin, twelve masked girls jogging and stretching at social distances. In fifteen minutes, those distances will be eliminated as drills require the team to bump and screen and touch.

As Emerson jogs past the coaches, she says, "This is all so weird." On the next lap, she says, "Not that weird is a bad thing." Another lap around, "I so need a game!" On the next lap, as she passes Joyce, Emerson slaps her teammate on the butt and laughs. "Maybe it's just me who's weird." Joyce yells out that there's lots of truth in that.

Coach Rascon blows her whistle and brings the team together for opening remarks. "I know it's difficult but keep up with the protocols. Good work. Martina tells me that all of you passed your health checks."

Kaori yells out, "The new cafeteria food sucks!" Her teammates laugh in agreement.

Molly looks over to Ryanne. "Maybe I could get the university to grant us a waiver and you could all eat at least one meal at Coach Powell's." Ryanne shakes her head no, and Molly continues. "Today's emphasis is on defensive transition. I'll lean heavily on Coach Dyani since she so loved to play defense." That sarcastic remark brings all kinds of vocal responses, since they remember that Dyani was not known as the most disciplined defensive player during practices over the past two years.

"Do as I say, not as I did," she says sternly. "Remember who has the punishment whistle."

Practice goes well. Maddie, Claudia, and Addie struggle with the vocal aspects of defense and with the "help the helper" concept. It's Claudia who tells the coaches, "We just played zone at my high school, and I was allowed to take chances." Dyani shakes her head. "No excuses, C-Simp. You defend or you'll never get off Coach Rascon's bench. I had to learn the hard way."

Two hours of difficult drills with lots of collisions, each drill culminating in rebounding work. Joyce and Kenti relish defense which makes practice more enjoyable for them. Dyani hovers over Maddie, often taking a fistful of jersey to move her quickly into the proper defensive slot. "Travel with the pass! Don't watch it and then move; that's too late." Known for their offense which can overrun an opponent in just a few minutes, it's SJV's defense that is the silent assassin, especially in the Ring of Fire Conference which doesn't have the talent of the Pac-12 and, therefore, can't just tell a star player to take over. La Colonia this season will once again employ several defensive schemes, but all of them are based on hunger and aggression.

∾

Joyce texts Coach Rascon on Wednesday to tell her she will miss practice. The Fresno hospital has filled up again and two nurses have come down with Covid, so the ward is short-staffed. Molly lets Martina take Joyce's place in several drills. So far, the team has avoided any serious injuries, no sprains or broken bones, just bruises and blood around the mouth and nose. Experience counts, and the top eight look sharp. The coaches' main concern is the backup point guard. Claudia Simpson is coming, but she's a rookie who was a shoot-first guard in high school. Dyani constantly harps on her to "Pass ahead! Eyes up! You've got two studs running the wings. Give it up!"

Ryanne, whose mood is always upbeat these days now that Biden won the presidency, laughs to Molly. "I wonder where Dyani heard those phrases before?" Dyani was not a pass-first point guard when she arrived from Tucson, because she had been the best scorer on every team she had ever played on. "When did you learn to pass?" asks Ryanne to Molly.

"Never did," says Molly tongue-in-cheek. "Sort of like you, I suppose."

❧

"Before we talk contract, Coach, I need to give you bad news," says Dr. Calhoun on his end of the phone on Thursday morning. "Santa Barbara canceled your game just before you called. Their coaching staff has a Covid case, so the whole team will go into quarantine for fourteen days. I know that will disappoint your girls. They'll cancel at least two others, so I've got calls in to see if either one of those would want to pick up a game with us."

Molly is not surprised; she's been following the outbreak closely. "Maybe starting play this month is a bad idea. I just heard this morning that the Ivy League is cancelling its entire season, all sports."

"I know. It's been rumored for over a month now. They're in a different boat than we are. No athletic scholarships and huge endowments, so their programs can weather this pandemic." Dr. Calhoun pauses, and Molly doesn't rush in. "Coach, I think our conference is still going to play, albeit with no fans and limited exposure. You and your ladies have been amazing in your protocols."

"They've done all we've asked, but you know it just takes one unlucky contact, and it all goes to hell. With the added expenses for safety, I know how tenuous our finances are."

Dr. Calhoun harrumphs into his cellphone. "Nice lead-in to our contract talks."

"Yeah, I thought some things over since we last talked about it. Frank and I had a long discussion. I think Covid, for all its evils, puts some other things into perspective. One of my main concerns about Tulare is the air quality and its effect on my son. Frank says he can manage that though, and that living in any urban area would be just as bad. Can't run away from it, so, I took that issue off my list. Actually, I made out a new list. SJV can't come close to my original salary request so if other parts of my list can be agreed upon, I'll continue at my current contractual salary for the next two years. At that point, regardless of my team's wins and losses, you bump it up ten percent, and then every year after that I get a cola increase or four percent, whichever is higher."

"That's generous," says Dr. Calhoun whose face registers mild surprise.

"Hold on. I want an immediate twenty-percent pay raise for Coach Powell. She's a gem and underpaid. That would cost the university about twelve thou. Next, I want my other assistants to get a ten percent raise. Coach Robinson's is negotiable since he gives it all away anyway."

"You only have two assistants, not counting Mose."

"I know, but down the road, you know, when I have a staff that resembles other Division 1 universities."

"You said you didn't want one that large."

"I'm kidding about a staff that large, but I am operating this year with one less coach than I need. That's my next demand, that when the pandemic is over, I want one more coach, one like Coach Aikins was, an analytics geek who also knows basketball."

Dr. Calhoun's noise resembles an "Okay, that's probably doable. Go on."

"Alright, here's the *what's in it for me* part. I want a guaranteed contract. Ten years. You know what my work ethic is, and that I will represent the university honorably. You know the ladies I recruit, that I don't waste my time on multi-star athletes who won't be committed to SJV, those who could bolt under the new transfer rules. You and I can sit down later and build in some modest bonuses for the team's on-court successes, for graduation rates, and so on, but those shouldn't be a hang-up." Molly pauses. "And, again, when this pandemic subsides and I get that extra coach, I'd like to teach a summer class related to opportunities for women athletes, a serious class about leadership. And, I'd also like to be included somehow in the Environmental Science Department, not as a lecturer or professor, of course, but as maybe someone who students in that department can call upon for extra help. Kind of like a special projects consultant. I can work into that, but when my time as a basketball coach ends, maybe I can continue working here in an academic field."

Dr. Calhoun puts down his pen after noting Coach Rascon's

requests. "Coach," he pauses. "Molly. These are fair points. Give me a few days to write something up that I can present to my superiors. Before I do that, I'll get with you about them, to make sure we're on the same page. If we are, then, I'll see what I can do."

The call ends with assurances that Molly's team will be playing the first week that the NCAA allows for competition, the last week in November. Dr. Calhoun reviews his note, tapping his pen on one item. Ten-year guaranteed contract. *Tenure for a coach, just like a valued professor,* he thinks.

Molly clicks off, holding her phone. Immediately, Freddie Mercury alerts her to another call.

"Coach, my mother's in Los Angeles and wants to see me. What do I do?"

∾

The Dreamer, Esther Santiago, meets her coach in the basketball office. Molly asks Esther the obvious question, "How long has it been?"

"Almost two years ago at Christmas. At my tia's house. That's when she left for Mexico City to find my brother. She hasn't been able to get back in and see me. Remember when you talked with her?"

"Forgive me for asking this question, but do you want to see her? I know you've been angry with her."

"Yes, oh God, yes."

"Well, then, I think you should."

"But what about Covid? I'm sure she hasn't been as careful as she should have been. Then, I'd expose the whole team."

Molly thinks for a moment. "Do you know how long she'll be staying?"

"Not really. My cousin drove her up from the border. That's where she called from."

"All of your classes are online, aren't they?" asks Molly.

"Yeah."

"How about if we get you to LA, to either a restaurant or your aunt's house where you can spend some time with her. Whether that's an hour or a day or longer, we can play that by ear. You'll have to go into quarantine after that, but we'll keep you apart from your teammates. I can get you tested when you get back."

"That means I'll miss the first set of games."

"Yes, it does, but there will be more. Besides, we may get all the early ones canceled anyway. You need to go see your mother." Molly smiles to get Esther's assent. "Call her. Now."

❧

Coach Rascon explains to her ladies why Esther and Coach Powell aren't at practice.

"Won't Coach have to go into quarantine too then?" asks Kaori, a question that others on the team also have.

"No. Coach will not come in close contact with Esther's mother. She'll be dropping Esther off at a restaurant where she's meeting up with her mom. Coach will stay well away. Esther will be staying overnight, but Coach will come back this evening."

"How will Esther get back?"

"Probably her cousin will drive her back tomorrow or the next. She'll quarantine in a motel here, at least until her Covid tests come back, and then she goes into one of the quarantine rooms on campus. I think we have it covered, but she won't be available to play until the second week in December."

Like every practice La Colonia has had this fall, Thursday's is spirited and productive. Maria slides into Esther's slot as a Big and seems to be comfortable there. "It's temporary, I know, and I'll be back at a pretty position when Esther gets back." Maria fluffs her hair to emphasize the humor of her comment, but during the toughness drills with Coach Robinson, she gives better than she gets, something that her sister notes and compliments her on. On one repetition, Sylvia hits the deck, to which Coach Robinson asks which girl is the younger sister. Sylvia pops up and says, "Oh, it's on now!"

At the other end of the court, the seven perimeter players work on ball movement that leads to three-point shots. Dyani corrects the three rookies about poor passes, and after each comment Keilani says, "Every drill's a passing drill. It's Coach's mantra." Dyani tells Claudia to deliver the ball into the shooting pocket, so all Emerson or Kaori have to do is execute the proper fundamentals. "Then, we score!"

Kenti has a particularly good practice, harassing Keilani as usual but also on offense as the third point guard. Now in her second season, the soccer star's hands begin catching up with her feet. Molly sends Keilani, Claudia, Maddie, and Kenti to a side basket with Coach Dehiya to work on "all things point-guardish," meaning ball-handling skills and decision making, while she drills Kaori, Emerson, and Addie on finishing at the basket. In this area, Emerson's skills as an impromptu dancer help her take on the contact without losing her balance. If games are played, Emerson will lead the team in scoring, will demonstrate on a nightly basis why she was an all-Southern California high school selection, will make UCSB regret letting her get away.

Molly's phone beeps. A text from Dr. Calhoun. "I've replaced UCSB with USC. Their AD said they want pay-back for last year. At their place. Same date. You're welcome." A second text adds an addendum. "I need to speak with you about your contract."

Practice comes to a close. Molly tells her team about the replacement game, and they whoop in excitement. USC will be a difficult game. "No fans in the stands, and we'll need to wear our masks. Bus down, no planes for any California games, and it looks like that's all we'll have. Keep Esther in your prayers, . . . along with the hundreds of others you care about. Proud of you all. Excellent practice. Get back to your rooms and shower. You stink!"

At social distance the ladies extend their hands and yell "La Colonia!"

Ken Davidson calls to find out about Esther. He'd like to write a blog about her, but Molly dissuades him. "Her mother is illegally in the country. Esther doesn't need another thing to worry about just now. All my ladies are traumatized. Their young lives have been turned upside down, as you're well aware. She'll be missing some games, and when she comes back, she'll be even more isolated than the team already is. They all have their own rooms, but at least they can mingle some at practice and meals. Esther won't have that for a couple of weeks. If you need a topic, you might think about mixing together

Joyce and Kenti. One works evenings in the Fresno hospital, and the other spends her days studying soils on the farm. Neither complains, but they both are tired at practice, and both need to take double precautions because of their associations."

Ken thanks Molly for her time and tells her that he will run anything he writes by her to protect her girls. "Ladies," she corrects.

Molly has texts from both Ryanne and Esther. Ryanne's is brief. "Back home. Watched them hug in the parking lot. Stayed until she gave me a thumbs up. Good decision, Mol." Esther's text is longer with emojis. "Thank you so much, Coach. We had a late lunch and now we're with a friend of my tia. Yeah, I'll need to quarantine, but I can do that. I think I'll stay here through the weekend. Home Sunday. I'll let you know. Sorry I'm missing practice."

Molly is tired, exhausted actually. She lays her head back against the couch and closes her eyes, not responding to either text immediately. Her two men are washing dishes and cleaning the kitchen, both laughing at silly things. She wants only to hear those sounds; she does not want to hear another news report about Covid just now. She thinks about her own mother and wants to hug her, to simply melt into Mama's chubby arms and smell the combination of her perfume and cigarettes. Molly hated that her mother smoked, that she still sneaks a cigarette frequently, but sometimes when she walks past a smoker, she's reminded of her mother. Molly falls asleep until Frankie beeps her nose telling her it's time for dessert.

Friday and another day without school for Frankie. He is a resourceful child, but even he struggles without his friends and teachers. He is surrounded by La Colonia, but they are masked and social-distanced. He has a backyard, is skilled with his computer, and reads, but how many weeks and months can an elementary school boy be sheltered before it affects his mental and emotional growth. On a Zoom call with the parents of a recruit, Frankie leaned in to say hi, to give the family touch to the recruitment. When asked what grade he was in, Frankie said, "I'm a no-grade boy; we don't have school anymore." This scenario repeats itself with the 6,000 Tulare County students, mostly poor and brown, mostly without full-time access to a computer. They are falling behind.

Friday the 13th. Frankie's paternal grampa tells him over the phone not to walk under any ladders or behind any black cats. "Why would I do that?" asks Frankie. Grampa Martinez likes to tell jokes, but the family hasn't been together since the lockdown was ordered last March. Dr. Frank's parents have followed the medical guidelines strictly and avoided "The Covid." Both were laid off from their jobs and mostly now sit at home watching television. Money is not too much of an issue since Frank is well-paid and their home is paid off. They have lived in it for 40 years, but now, Frank and Molly want them to move to Tulare, either in with them or into a nearby house. There are plenty for sale for a modest price. Frankie hands the phone back to his mama.

"Did you talk with the real estate agent that Frank called?" asks Molly.

"We did. Nice lady, young, I think, but with that damn mask, I can't tell. We're meeting with her again next week."

"Well?"

"You're a persistent cuss, you know. Frank gives me the pros and cons, but you demand action right away." Frank's dad laughs on his end. "If we sold this house and moved out, we'd have to move in with you right away while we looked for a place in Tulare. Mama and me don't want to be an imposition."

"Stop that. You aren't." It's Molly's time to joke. "Anyway, I'd get free childcare."

Molly remembers her time as a player at State Tech. She practiced every day, no days off. Now, the NCAA mandates one day off each week. It's a good thing, at least it would be without Covid. Coach Rascon knows that basketball practice, regardless of the intensity and demands, is a respite for her ladies. Life is stressful, but for two to three hours each day, her ladies can just be themselves. The Team. The Sequoias. La Colonia. Sisters. All the players would gladly come in on Sundays to forget Covid again, suspend the pandemic for that three-hour block. Because of their day off, she expects today's practice to be energetic. Esther returned last night, but she will be quarantined for two weeks. The three recruits aren't ready for USC yet. Joyce is a zombie, but a trooper zombie. Having just seven or eight quality players for a game against a Tier 1 university is courting danger, but if that's what Molly has, then that's what Molly will go with—and no excuses will be permitted.

As the team stretches around the center circle, the four coaches make the rounds, checking on their schoolwork, their bumps and bruises, their boyfriends via Zoom, and their emotions. "Are you sleeping? You know you can get fruit from The Pantry, don't you?" The rookies were unsure of that option. Coach Powell tells them what they already know that there are just eight practices before their first game. Coach Robinson asks them if USC recruited any of them. He knows the answer. "It's always nice to stick it to those people who doubted you, who doubted your spirit." Coach Dehiya wears a Chinle High School Wildcats sweatshirt rather than a San Joaquin Valley Sequoias coaching shirt. Claudia Simpson knows only snippets of her coaches' backgrounds that mostly relate to their college careers, or in Coach Robinson's case, his NBA career. She asks Coach Dehiya about her shirt.

Dyani looks down at her shirt. "It's where real basketball is played. On the rez, basketball is a player's game, not a coach's game. No set plays, just me and my basketball against the world. Run. Run some more. Keep running. It's what I'm still trying to instill in Coach Rascon. She's almost got it; maybe this season." Dyani looks over to Molly as if to check on her attention. "Coach gets it more than most, but I'm still working on her."

Molly uses Dyani's words as her cue. "Here's where we are, ladies. Missing those two weeks hurt our preparation, set us back, so this week we will be all over you for hustle and conditioning. We can't waste time having you run sprints; we need to sharpen our game skills. As Coach just said in so many words, we run."

Keilani raises her hand, and Molly knows her question won't be serious. "So let me get this straight. You don't want me to walk it up and call out a number?"

Molly looks over to Kenti Solorzano. "Kenti, be ready to start next Thursday." The team laughs. Kenti looks at Keilani, points, and grins. Keilani can grate on her teammates' nerves at times as she learns how to lead the team, but Kenti hasn't ruffled any feathers for her attitude in two seasons, only frustrated guards by her persistent defense.

Molly speaks again. "No, I don't need to tell you that, but you three rooks need to understand. SJV runs every possession, make or miss, regardless of the score. Old news, but this week you're all going to be pushed to new heights. We will demand energy and execution, and if we don't get it from every one of you, we won't be satisfied. Southern Cal is bigger, taller, and more experienced. We have speed, and as the saying goes, *Speed kills*!"

Molly looks back at Keilani. "Everything I say to you, every piece of information that Dyani gives to you, pass it on to Claudia and Maddie. Crash course in point guard play. Emerson and Kaori, you do the same with Addie. Bigs! You need to be the anchor until the pretty ladies get synched." She looks over her team and nods approvingly.

Ryanne blows her whistle. "Okay, let's go. Get up off your asses and let's go 3 on 2, 2 on 1." It's a favorite drill of the team. Every player gets to play every position and aggression counts for everything. Bodies collide, and no one takes pity on a teammate who hits the floor hard. "Get up and get back! Get up and catch up! You've got to block out, Claudia! That back side is vulnerable! "

For ten minutes La Colonia warms up, because this first drill is designed only to set the tone. Next up, rebound block outs. Not box outs, but BLOCK outs. And so it goes. Two hours later, Coach Powell blows her whistle, and the team again gathers around the center circle, sits, and listens while they stretch. Ryanne holds up seven fingers.

Coach Rascon is sweating profusely, as are the other coaches, including Coach Robinson. She has little to say, just nodding as if to acknowledge her team's great effort. "Yep, that'll work." As the ladies begin to rise, four coaches fist bump them and smile.

Moses Robinson whispers to Molly Rascon, "Championship effort tonight. Good job."

"Yeah. We got a little better."

༄

At dinner, after Molly and Frankie have talked about their day, Frank says softly, "Moderna announced its vaccine is testing out at 94 percent, a little better that Pfizer. We should have a vaccine soon. The government will rush through approval." He breathes out heavily. "We can get this virus in the rearview mirror."

༄

On Tuesday, Molly returns Dr. Calhoun's call. "Please don't tell me USC has canceled our game," says Molly.

"No, we're still on. Did you get Esther's test results yet?"

"Good news there. She'll get another test tomorrow, so we're keeping our fingers crossed, but regardless, she won't practice with us for a while, and we won't have her for the first game."

"How much will that hurt you?

"She's a force and a big part of our inside game. Really a smart player too, so it could be significant. USC is big inside and tough, so we'll be stretched a little thin there."

"Well, I think you made the correct call anyway. You won't be sneaking up on the Trojans though, after last year," says Dr. Calhoun. "My guess is they've watched last year's game several times. Back in the day when we were playing, Coach, I know I hated being subjected to film after a loss. My coach was obsessive about it. Have you shown your kids last year's game much?"

"Not at all. We've used our allotted time on the court. I knew going in that we would be a different team without Dyani, but I didn't realize how much different. Keilani has come a long way, but she's not Dyani. Different skill set. We need court time, plus after our top tier, we're young, so scrimmages tend to be lopsided at times." Molly laughs. "However, when I insert Dyani onto that second team for scrimmages, it evens out the score."

"I'm pretty sure your kids will give a good accounting of themselves. They always compete well." It's the pause leading into the purpose of the conversation. "I spoke with Dr. Harper about your contract demands."

Molly interrupts. "Suggestions. Hardly demands."

Dr. Calhoun smirks. "Semantics aside, Dr. Harper had some questions. You are not technically a faculty member, but staff. She compared you to our chief financial officer in that you are vital but not a professor."

"Semantics?" teases Molly.

"Yes, but important semantics. Anyway, Dr. Harper wants to consider the ten-year guaranteed contract more, wants to get some input from our legal department and some other universities. She was concerned about honoring a contract that long if your team isn't performing well." Molly starts to respond, but Dr. Calhoun cuts her off. "I know, I know, but she doesn't know you like I do. She didn't say no, she just said that she wants to consider it a little longer. I think she'll accept all your salary requests, both for you and your staff. Because of the stresses on our budget right now, I may have to battle a bit on the 20-percent raise for Ryanne, but because you all took voluntary pay reductions this past year, that works in your favor. Which leads me to your last request. Do you know how many D1 coaches teach?" Dr. Calhoun pauses for emphasis. "None that I could discover. Back in the olden days, they did, but no longer. It's a unique request."

"I'm serious about it, and I'm not looking to pad my salary with a Basketball 101 course designed for my players. I could teach a leadership course and never mention basketball. If this Covid pandemic has taught us nothing else, it's shown us that the old men making the decisions about our future are bereft of new ideas, and they've been willfully ignorant of the significance of demographic changes for our democracy. It's like they forgot about what democracy is built upon. And my request for an environmental class is kind of based on the same thing. Our current students fear climate change because they know it will impact their lives. Hell, it already is. Our little part of the earth here in the San Joaquin Valley is being bombarded by climate change. Our students get it."

"Slow down," says Dr. Calhoun. "I'm on your side here. We just need to present your request in a way that Dr. Trevino understands why you should teach these courses instead of a faculty member with a science degree."

Unseen by Dr. Calhoun, Molly cocks her head with a new thought.

"Can I ask you a question?" He consents, and she asks. "Are you thinking about leaving?"

There is an uncomfortable pause before Dr. Calhoun answers. "I've been approached." He corrects himself. "That's not accurate. I've put out some feelers. I'm looking. My wife has problems with the air pollution here; she's paying the price for being a smoker. I like it here, but . . .:"

"I get that part," says Molly softly. "You would be missed."

"Thank you. We'll see what comes up. You'll need to put up with me for at least the rest of this year. Getting back to your contract, I have another meeting scheduled for Thursday with Harper and Trevino. I'll keep at it. I'm pretty sure the salary parts are a go, both for you and your assistants."

"I appreciate it. Thanks." Molly taps off. Her thoughts return to Frankie's asthma.

Chapter 16

"The men's game has been postponed," texts Molly to Ryanne. "Dr. C is trying to find another. Doubtful so late."

"Five days until USC. Girls feel like they're living in a convent," replies Ryanne.

"What a great idea!!!!" texts back Molly.

"Mom and Pop have accepted the bid," texts Frank. "Two days on the market, five bids. They want a place of their own up here."

"I know. Your mom texted me too. Virtual house hunting now. They'll be able to afford something nice here," texts Molly.

"I need a game!" texts Keilani.

"We all do. Lol," texts Coach Rascon.

"This is just crazy!!"

"Who should back you up at SC? Claudia or Kenti?"

"I'm not coming out until we're up 20, so it doesn't matter."

"Dr. T on board with guaranteed contract. Still not sure of science class. Leadership course a go for next summer. Start on lesson plans, Teach," texts Dr. Calhoun.

"Thank you. Do you want to team teach it with me?"

"Lol. No!!! You're too driven. I couldn't keep up."
"Bullshit!!!"

∾

"I got a NICE raise from the hospital! Remind me. Is practice at 1?" texts Joyce.
"Yes. 1. Congrats. You've put your heart and soul into helping. So proud of you!"

∾

"Coach, my parents want to have dinner catered for us after practice today. Not pizza!! Real food. What can I tell them?" texts Kaori.
"Ask your teammates. Get a consensus. Have the delivery over here. Dr. F and F will set up the chairs in the backyard. 5:00. Weather should be good. Tell your parents thanks. They are special people."
"Team wants Asian food. Lol! Just because I'm Asian. We eat other things."

∾

"I heard the men's game got canceled. Is ours still on?" texts Emerson.
"Yes. Covid was detected in their opponent. Our men are fine still. Are you excited?"
"God, YES! My whole family got tickets."
"Fans aren't allowed. Remember?"
"Teasing. Got ya. See you at practice."
"Extra running for that."

∾

Molly sets her phone on the counter, turns on the TV, and slides her legal pad in front of her. The news is bad again. Covid deaths are rising nationwide with nearly 2,000 deaths per day. *Should we even be playing?* she thinks. *How is this flattening the curve? Maybe we should use cutout players and coaches too.* Trump continues to rant about the rigged election, the phony ballots in Pennsylvania, the voting machines owned by Dominion. Molly tells him to shut up and accept the outcome. She turns off the TV. Frankie comes into the kitchen still wearing his pajamas.

"Well, good morning, Sleepyhead."

He gives his mama a hug. "Where's dad?"

"He had to go to the clinic for a few hours to see a couple of special cases. You know, worried moms."

"But it's Saturday."

"He'll be home by 11:00. Let me get you some breakfast. Have a seat." As she stands, her phone buzzes. It's Dyani.

"The rez is on lockdown again. Everything closed. Not good."

"I know. Saw a bit on TV. So tragic."

"See ya at practice. Gotta go pray."

Molly knows Dyani does pray.

Only Esther is missing, otherwise, there is a full complement at practice, including the student managers. Mose shoots baby hooks while the team jogs. Several of the ladies bump him as they pass or try to block a shot. Even at 73 with gimpy knees he protects the ball. As the initial warmup ends, the ladies put the balls in the cage and assemble around the center circle to stretch. Now, the coaches mingle and ask about any topic. Except for the masks and Esther's absence, it's a normal practice.

"Today, Monday, and Tuesday," says Coach Rascon. Three practices left before they play. "Make every minute count."

Dyani's phone buzzes, an incoming text, and she steps away to read it.

"Today's emphasis, for those of you who didn't read the schedule before practice, is transition." Coach looks at Maddie, number 11 on the depth chart. "What's the rule for defensive transition?"

She knows. "Read the defensive end as we sprint back. Turn at half-court. Talk and pick up with pressure. Basket then ball."

"Very good, young lady." Molly points at Maddie as she's complimenting her. "USC will have us scouted. They want your asses after last year, so we need to be better than last year. Our defensive transition has to be instantaneous. Whether we score or not on the offensive end, we apply pressure. Bigs, that will require lots of end-to-end sprinting. All four of you will get lots of minutes. Maria. Joyce." Coach Rascon smiles at them as if she has just promised these two reserves fifteen minutes of game time. Molly looks to Ryanne.

"USC will want the game in the low 60s. We want it in the high 70s. Ergo," Ryanne pauses and smiles. "Therefore, either we run or lose."

"Everybody up. Zig-zag! Go!"

Mose walks to Dyani and asks her if everything is okay. A middle-aged Navajo woman from Chinle, a friend of the family, has died from Covid. Mose puts an arm around Dyani's shoulder.

"Nothing I can do. Can't go back because of the lockdown. Can't do anything." Dyani breathes out heavily, bumps her head into Mose's chest, and thanks him. "We carry on, huh."

Mose nods. "Yeah. You okay taking your three girls today?"

"Yeah, we got work to do."

Every time Molly has had her team assemble at her house, in her backyard, she has gotten approval from the university's health officials. This Saturday is no exception, and they approve with the same requirements. Dr. Frank greets the Sushi Lin delivery girls in the driveway and guides them around the side to the tables in the back. They've delivered to this house several times during the pandemic. He tips them. The temperature hovers just under 70, above the normal for this time of year. No wind, so the picnic should be pleasant. Four bottles of non-alcoholic Martinelli champagne are on ice. One has been opened and Papa Frank and Frankie sip and giggle, celebrating a made-up occasion, in this case, Frankie's victory in chess over his grandma. Online game. Good enough.

Kaori arrives first with Emerson. She wants to be the host. Ryanne and Dyani are next. Frank turns the gala over to Kaori. Kaori prepares one meal for delivery and hands it to Dr. Frank.

"Come on, Champ. We have a delivery," says Frank to Frankie. They drive over to the dorm to leave dinner outside Esther's door. Frankie texts Esther and giggles. "Dinner awaits." She opens her door, looks down the hall to where the delivery boys stand, waves, and yells "Thank you."

Coach Rascon instructs the managers to go through the line first. Martina insists her assistants go ahead of her. When every lady and Tom Cooley have filled their plates, Molly and Ryanne walk around and fill the team's plastic cups with faux champagne. They fill one for themselves and then lift them above their heads. Molly warns, "Take small sips after each toast; we have a few. We don't want any drunk people here. First, to all of you for your wonderful adherence to the protocols. I know it's been a pain in the butt, but you've been troopers. Next, to Esther. She'll be back with us next weekend. To Kaori and her family for the meal. Please thank your parents for this, Kaori. Finally, to Dyani." Molly looks to her new assistant coach and nods. "Dig in!"

Frank and Frankie return, the little one carrying a McDonald's sack. His mama squints at her husband. He sits next to her and asks about the team's play at practice, asks if they're ready for USC.

"Honestly, I don't know. No scrimmages. No exhibitions. I have a good group, but going against only ourselves isn't the optimum situation. Guess we'll find out Wednesday."

"Game is still a go?"

"As of 3:30 this afternoon. Reminds me of last March when teams around the country kept cancelling, and I was on my phone with Dr. Calhoun constantly seeing what our conference was going to do."

"That was so disappointing," reaffirms Frank. He taps his wife on her thigh. "Think positive thoughts."

The dinner has a time limit, as per health directives, so at 6:15, the team puts their paper cups and plastic utensils in the proper containers and drifts off into the dusk, social distance walking.

Ryanne has real alcohol after the dinner/picnic. Dyani has coffee. Ryanne asks her about her first coaching assignment.

"Harder than I thought," replies Dyani.

"What part?"

"It just seems like there's a task to complete at every moment, but to be fair, I think Covid has a lot to do with that."

Ryanne nods. "It's been a trying year for sure. Not as much fun. I hope you give this gig a fair chance. You're good at this."

Dyani smiles. "I didn't say it wasn't fun. Yelling at Keilani is a kick." Dyani shakes her head as if to signal to Ryanne that her words were a joke. "That girl is going to do just fine next week. It wouldn't surprise me if she has a double-double."

"Have you noticed how much Coach has aged these last six months? Like you said, something every minute. Not just basketball either."

"She's allowed me to be the point guard coach. I know she monitors them too, but it's like she swallowed hard and turned that position over to me. Three years ago, I thought I knew it all. I was a JC all-American. She took all the swagger out of my game at first, let me know I wasn't bigger that her team. *Her team!* When she sent me home after the summer practices, I wasn't sure I wanted to come back. I didn't like her. Just my obstinacy made me not quit. She refined a few of my skills, mostly taught me to make fewer great passes that were risky. Made me respect . . . maybe myself more." Dyani reflects on her comment and takes a sip of coffee. "She said I was more than just a basketball player."

Ryanne picks up the thread. "Coach told me with certainty that you would be an All-American D1 player. You would have been too if we'd have been allowed to play in the tournament. The nation would have seen you."

"I know. Coach was, I think, more disappointed than me. That's the coach that I want to be. She has such high expectations of the team, but more, I don't know, for herself. And it seems like she doesn't confuse goals with purpose. Does that make sense?"

Ryanne nods and smiles warmly. "She had her time as a player. She, her team, State Tech, came close to winning it all a couple of times. It was all about that chance. She wanted that for you last year. It hurt her that you didn't get that chance. She built a team to surround you, to give you that opportunity. She believes she'll never see one like you again."

"Well, then I guess you and I will just have to get Keilani to that stage."

ༀ

Molly feels a little guilty not attending church, but she knows she isn't going to put her family and team in jeopardy by praying in person. Frank told her months ago that God knew where to find her and would understand. She stayed up late after dinner watching film of USC, trying to find that one last tendency to gain an edge. This Sunday morning, she pours over her notes from film study, her notes as well as Ryanne's and Dyani's. Mose refuses to watch film from previous years. Because of Covid, how teams qualify for The Tournament this season might be different. Last season's victory over SC was huge for seeding purposes, at least it would have been if the tournament had been held. This year, who knows. A Quad 1 win probably will count for an improved seed, but again, that's in a world that hasn't been turned upside down. Frank comes into the kitchen wearing an old t-shirt, pours himself a cup of coffee and refills Molly's. He kisses the top of her head, lays his hand on her shoulder, and squeezes gently. She reaches up and squeezes his hand. "It's doable," she says.

"What did you find last night?" asks Frank.

"That Sylvia and Greta will have their hands full."

"Oh, if that's all, then you'll be fine." He removes his hand from her shoulder, unplugs his iPad, and opens it to read the news.

A buzz alerts her to an incoming text. It's Ken Davidson. "FYI. Their leading scorer from last season is going to play." Molly smiles. Ken has a multitude of sources from the LA area. There had been some question about the SC forward from last season who led the Trojans in several categories. Sprained ankle. *I guess this means they're taking us seriously.* Molly makes a check mark by one of her bullet points. This afternoon, she will meet with Ryanne and Dyani and Mose in the War Room and transfer her notes to the whiteboards. There will be an immediacy to their activity, as if the world outside that room isn't important, but this year, that outside world hovers over that coaches' room and every coaches' room around the country.

Molly will listen to her assistants as they discuss who backs up Keilani for this first game, but Molly has already made her decision. Claudia. She's not ready for D1 competition yet, but she was recruited for this role. Kenti has her role, and it has never been as the reserve point guard; her offensive abilities are limited. Kenti's role is really a destiny away from the court. Learn everything she can about soils and take that knowledge back to Guatemala and pass it on to the small farmers in the hills. Kenti's game minutes will be directed at SC's point guard, defending her for brief minutes to allow Keilani a respite to concentrate on her offensive responsibilities.

Her cell buzzes. It's Izzy Soto, a high school teammate. Izzy's season is still on hold. Colorado high schools have had their season pushed back. "Hey sweetheart. Ready?" Molly laughs. The Cheetahs all begin any text now with "sweetheart" out of love for Queenie Roberts, their fairy godmother from Oro Hills who passed away from Covid in the spring. "So ready, Iz. How are your kiddos?' The two high school teammates text for a few minutes. Frankie walks into the kitchen. Molly takes a picture of him and sends it to Izzy. "He needs to comb his hair."

Sunday morning. This long year has only been eight months. The first Covid wave passed, but the second wave swells on the horizon promising to crest in the next weeks. Molly's task is to protect her ladies. Dr. Frank's role is to protect his extended community, Tulare and Visalia. Neither works alone.

Kaori, Emerson, and Keilani eat breakfast in Kaori's car in their pajamas. Emerson's idea. She didn't want another morning in the sterile cafeteria eating off a plastic tray, so they are eating mini-sandwiches, muffins, and coffee off the paper sacks that were handed to them out the service window. Giggling. They now will be starters and are expected to provide the bulk of the scoring this season, and who resemble triplets when they are wearing their masks. Except that Kaori is Asian, Keilani is Black, and Emerson is a dancer. Emerson's joke. An unopened sack sits on the backseat, a present for Esther so that she doesn't have to eat the pre-packaged dorm meal that students get when they are in quarantine.

The giggling begins when Kaori says she hasn't kissed a boy in over eight months. Actually, the giggling started when Keilani said she hadn't had sex in over eight months, and then Emerson said that sex was still sex even when wearing a mask. "Protest sex" is what she calls it, and that she indulged herself after one of the summer BLM protests in Los Angeles. "Protected on both ends," laughs Emerson, "but it doesn't leave this car."

They agree that not having a boyfriend is the one thing that truly sucks about social distancing. Emerson admits that it's not so bad not having a steady boyfriend, but not being allowed to pick up is interfering with her education. Keilani, who sits in the backseat of Kaori's car, slaps Emerson's shoulder at her remark. They leave McDonald's parking lot to deliver Esther's breakfast.

Kenti calls home to Nebaj, Guatemala, the one day each week when she can talk with her family. They always want to know about basketball practice, about the farm, and whether she has a boyfriend. Kenti's answers are much the same each week: "Fun. Rewarding. No." Her parents worry that if she stays in America, she will never find a husband, that she will get too old. Kenti assures them that she will be coming home as soon as possible after she receives her Ph.D. Sundays for Kenti do not involve outside work or basketball; they are set aside for reading, research, and writing her dissertation. Today, she tells her family about the upcoming game with the University of Southern California, that it is still scheduled to be played despite the surge in Covid cases, that yes, all the team will be wearing masks during the game. Her father wants to know if her team will win. "Papa, we always win."

Joyce Hensley works an eight-hour day shift at the Fresno hospital, The emergency rooms are near capacity again.

Maria is the team's loner, at least among the team. Maria is the party girl on the team, and a constant worry for Coach Rascon and Coach Powell. Both coaches have talked with Maria about her social behavior. "The talk." Maria is the only player on the squad who is not completely gaga over basketball. She likes it, but if it were to go away, Maria would find other things.

Molly's three freshmen recruits eat breakfast in the cafeteria, walk back to their dorm rooms, and then lay on their beds texting each other. Only Claudia expects to play significant minutes in Wednesday's game. Addie might get a few minutes if Kaori or Emerson gets in foul trouble. Maddie probably wouldn't take off her warmups. All are excited that their college basketball careers are about to begin.

"How's your lip?" texts Addie to Claudia referring to the blow delivered by Greta when Claudia drove the lane in Saturday's scrimmage. Greta helped her up, but the blood forced Claudia to the sideline and to the trainer's room. No stitches, just a very fat lip.

"Feels like a tennis ball. Icing it now. Looks like I got a double shot of Botox."

"Greta felt bad, I think," texts Maddie.

"She's so nice, but all of the Bigs are," texts Claudia.

"I can't guard anyone on the team," texts Maddie, "and I hate when Kenti guards me. What is she? 26?"

"Keilani says she was a star soccer player back in Guatemala," texts Claudia.

"A game. Can you believe it!!!!!" texts Addie.

Greta sits on the floor outside Esther's door, talking. "Coach Robinson told me he expects USC to be really tough inside, to be ready for a really physical game. I told him I hope so. He's been so good for me. Have you ever talked to his wife?"

"Just a little last year at that one party. She looks so much younger than Coach," says Esther. "They're a great couple. They're always holding hands."

"This summer when I was working with Coach, Sally . . . she made me stop calling her Mrs. Robinson; she said it reminded her of that actress in some movie. I can't remember which one, an old-time one, I think, but Sally would make me meals and sit with us when Coach and me would take breaks. Coach said she keeps him in line, but that was just his way of bragging on her. They met in college and have lived in Oxnard since they got married. She knows all about basketball. I guess living with an old NBA star will do that."

"I'm going to miss not going with the team this week," says Esther, "but I needed to see my mother. She's struggling, but she's going to move back in with my tia in San Diego. That will help."

These two were roommates until the pandemic forced them into separate rooms, and along with Maria became best friends in much the same way that college students bond during their freshmen years of dorm living. Neither thought much about college when they were in high school, but Coach Rascon found them both when she was scouting other girls. Coach Robinson knew of Greta because they both live in Oxnard, and he saw her play. She considers him her godfather.

"You'll be cleared to play later this week," consoles Greta.

"You guys better not mess up without me. I want to go undefeated this season," says Esther.

After breakfast in the cafeteria, Sylvia hits the books. Except for Kenti, Sylvia is the oldest player on the team. She and Joyce are seniors now. Both are hearing rumors that seniors will be given another year of eligibility because of the cancellation of last year's tournament, both have indicated this will be it for basketball. Joyce has made that decision for sure. Her work at the hospital is more important than being a backup Big, even if it is on a championship team. Joyce loves playing, loves her coaches, and loves her teammates, but her accelerated path because of the demands for nurses has led her into adulthood quickly. She almost gave up basketball over the summer, but Sylvia convinced her that she was needed for another run to a championship, and that she would miss her if she wasn't on the team. The only seniors, Joyce has been Sylvia's backup for their entire careers, but they have been paired in so many practice drills and shared rooms on trips that they know instinctively what the other is thinking. Only Joyce knows about Sylvia's two-year long crush on Coach's husband, a secret that they giggle about but is real.

On Sunday evening, Coach Rascon sends out a group text to her twelve ladies. "Read the scouting reports in the war room before you come to practice tomorrow. Two practices before USC. Let's make them special."

∽

Molly calls a former teammate from State Tech who now is an assistant coach at an Ivy League school. Coach Rascon seeks insight into the emotional state of players whose seasons have been canceled, not just the year-end tournaments, but of an entire year of competition.

"I can't speak for universities elsewhere or even for our men's team," says Nancy, "but our girls are devastated. Since it was announced eleven days ago, our staff has been meeting and talking with them daily. They cry, they yell, they tell us how unfair it is, they withdraw, and they cry some more. They're hurt and confused. I have to tell you, we've broken protocol more than once to hold our girls. Many of them have expressed a desire to transfer, especially the ones who get the most game minutes. The Ivy League doesn't give athletic scholarships, as you know, but we help with finances in other ways. These girls can play, and now they won't be given a chance."

Molly stays silent to allow Nancy a moment to control her own emotions. Molly remembers those hugs, those tears, and the anger.

Nancy begins again. "Molly, I don't know if we'll lose any via transfer. Afterall, they're getting an Ivy League education, and that's pretty hard to give up, but we could." Nancy makes a sarcastic noise. "Do you need some players?"

"No," answers Molly softly and sympathetically. "I'm sure some of them could help us, but they're not coming here. I have my team." The two old teammates share common experiences before ending the call. "I'm sure you'll hold your ladies close. They couldn't have a better person guiding them through all this. Take care of yourself, Nancy."

Molly clicks off and breathes out heavily. "This is a complete mess," she whispers. For whatever reason, Molly thinks of Kaori, the one lady on her team who could have been accepted into an Ivy League university after high school. It was what her family desired, but Kaori wanted to be known as an athlete first, at least for a few more years. *If the Ring of Fire Conference surrenders to the virus and cancels the season, Kaori and a handful of her teammates could transfer and play at other D1 schools. But it wouldn't be the same. This team is destined to be together, to go through the war together, with me and Ryanne and Dyani,* thinks Molly. *War, huh? Odd choice of words, but maybe this is what this has been. Is. Trench warfare.*" Molly doesn't think of herself as an officer at this moment, but as one of the foot soldiers marching in step with her ladies into battle, a battle of a different kind than ever before.

∾

Ken Davidson sits fifteen rows up in the stands watching the Sequoias practice. He has always liked SJV's nickname. *Strong, sturdy, lasting. It fits this team.* Ken sketches Sylvia, the sturdiest of the trees.

Every championship team needs an anchor, and Sylvia is this team's. He sees her differently this season; he sees all of them differently. Coach has always conducted a no-nonsense practice, but this season, there is an air of . . . *what's the word I need*, thinks Ken. He laughs at his drawing. He notes that Sylvia is working almost as Coach Robinson's assistant, coaxing Greta and Joyce to be just a little more precise with their footwork. Esther remains in quarantine for the rest of the week.

Mose adjusts his mask, not because it's uncomfortable for him, but because Greta bumped him while he defended her drop step from the left block. "That was excellent!" he says softly. "Just like this summer. Remember? Let's do it again. Joyce, try to push her three feet farther out."

Fellowship! Maybe that's the word I was searching for, thinks Ken. *Still the same demands, still the same sense of urgency to this practice, but more intimate.* He writes the word on his pad and circles it. He turns his attention to Coach Dyani who is demonstrating a pull-back dribble to Keilani. Coach hands the ball back to Keilani, moves behind Kenti, who is guarding Keilani, and talks this year's point guard through the drill. Kenti instinctively knows not to steal the ball in this drill, just to stay in front of Keilani and force her left. After two repetitions, Claudia replaces Keilani, and Maddie replaces Kenti. The drill continues. Coach Dyani puts one hand on Kenti's shoulder while she whispers a "Way to go!" to Keilani. Coach quickly returns her attention to Maddie. "What are you trying to get Claudia to do, Maddie?"

The first hour focuses on fundamentals, but Coach Rascon knows her team needs scrimmage time. The five starters go against the six reserves. When the reserves struggle to get into the flow on offense, Dyani replaces Claudia who shadows the assistant coach and listens to Dyani's running commentary. "You have to move the defense. Never be more than one pass away, Claudia. Create space in the halfcourt; clog space on defense."

Coach Rascon is pleased. Her team has one more practice before boarding the bus for Los Angeles. They are not mid-season smooth yet, but they are opening game ready.

Family, thinks the journalist. *Yeah, family is the word I'm looking for.*

❧

After dinner Molly receives a text from Stephanie Borges. "FYI. Endowment will be slightly more than originally promised. My sidekick Janet has Covid but isn't doing too bad. We are both in quarantine. Good luck Wednesday. Won't be able to attend because of f-ing Covid." A second text buzzes, also from Stephanie. "I know we couldn't have attended anyway because of the no fans order, but still, f-ing Covid."

"Honey," yells out Molly to her husband. "My endowment angels are in quarantine. One of them has Covid."

Frank walks into the dining room where Molly is working on her last practice preparation. "Serious?" He hands her a small bag of M&Ms.

"Just got a text. I guess not too bad, but they're both in quarantine. Thanks." She opens the bag and allows several pieces to spread onto the table. "I wouldn't be so chubby if you didn't buy me these."

Frank sits next to her and takes a couple. "You are the same weight as when I met you. Fighting weight still." He kisses her cheek. "They're both in their early 60s, aren't they? Should be fine. Esther's last test came back negative, didn't it?"

"Yeah. I don't know the answer, but the virus sure hasn't affected the young and healthy like it has the older generation. I wonder about all the school closings, what harm that will have as students move through the system. I suspect Frankie and kids like him will get through this fine, because we have computers in the home and we take the time to work with him on his studies, but so many of his classmates." Her sentence is incomplete, but Frank understands.

"Lots of his classmates will fall further behind, that's what." He takes a few more M&Ms, and Molly gives him a stare like he's stealing something of value. "Just trying to keep the fat off you." He gets up and returns to the living room.

She texts Esther. "Missing you. It will be good to have you back on Friday. You're only going to miss this one game."

Esther texts back with a heart emoji.

❧

Tuesday before Thanksgiving. SJV's last practice before their first game. Tulare County's coronavirus cases continues to spike, and the county is averaging over a death per day. It shows on Dr. Martinez's face. The county's fall harvests fill the air with both strong aromas and fine dirt particulates. "Essential workers" cover their faces with bandanas rather than N-95 masks. President Trump's team of lawyers files more lawsuits contesting the outcome of the election, all of which are rejected by courts in several states. Moses Robinson is reading *Moby Dick* and tells Molly that her gym is like the Pequod. Both have hardwood floors, "or decks," and each has a finite crew of diverse personalities and demographics. Both ships sail in isolated waters. Both the Pequod and the Sequoia gym serve as refuges from the ravages of the current conditions. Mose doesn't think Molly resembles Ahab, however, that that role is taken by Trump. Ryanne threatens daily to resign, move to Georgia, and work to elect Democrat senators in the runoff election there. Dr. Trevino continues to hesitate on Molly's contract, and the University of Washington's women's basketball coach receives no support from her AD.

Around noon, three hours before practice, Molly sits with Dyani on the filming platform eating lunch and watching Frankie play soccer with Kenti who has arrived early to speak with her academic adviser at one about her dissertation. At one end of the gym floor, Frankie has arranged two soft bench chairs to act as goal posts.

"What would you be if you couldn't be a coach, Coach?" asks Dyani.

"Don't know if I have any talents for anything else."

"Seriously. If organized sports went away, what would you do?"

"Hmm. Maybe something that ended at a set time, something that I didn't bring home with me to stew over each night, something that allowed me to just be a mother and wife."

"And" presses Dyani.

"I'd work for someone."

"You work for someone now."

"Sorta, but it never feels like it. What happens in here is my own doing. That was always good, until Covid. I didn't need to know everything about you guys, but now, I do need to know. Not knowing led to . . ." Molly stops herself from saying a name.

Dyani says it. "Char. What else could you have known that would have prevented it?"

"I don't know, but something, and I really don't like how I answered your question. I love this job. What about you?"

"You mean what other job?" Dyani smiles. "Yours."

Kenti allows Frankie to score occasionally, and each time he does, he throws his arms up in the air and yells, "Goooaaalllll!" Dyani stands after one long kick and claps, yelling, "Ole!"

Molly smiles under her mask knowing how lucky Frankie has been during this pandemic to have had space, both a backyard and the Kappa Sig court. She thinks of the children growing up in high-rise apartments or the Chicago projects. She thinks of her players, of how fortunate they've been to have had the team. Yes, they lost an opportunity to play in a tournament last season, but they were in a relatively safe environment. They're back together for another go at that tournament. Opportunity delayed.

Dyani sits back down. "That girl made me better," she says referring to Kenti. "Completely unselfish. As I think back on practices last year, I don't remember her ever being on my scrimmage team. You always put her against me." Dyani pauses. "You were hard on me, harder than on any of the others."

"Yep." Coach smiles. "You are the best I ever coached . . . or played against," she pauses and smiles again, "and so stubborn. Suggestions didn't penetrate. Only my anger seemed to get through. I saw so much more in you, and I think you were satisfied at first just being as good as you came. You blew off mistakes thinking your talents could overcome those on the next possession. I thought I could find you one more point, one more assist, one more steal, but more importantly, a ton more leadership."

"Was any of it staged?"

"My frustration was real, but sometimes the delivery was scripted."

"But it was all honest?"

"Every word, every comment." Molly looks out over the court, taking her eyes from Dyani. "Do you ever get tired of these old stories I tell you?" Dyani shakes her head no. "Anyway, I had a teammate who was quick as a cat but with no offensive skills. I think I played her a thousand times on the driveway and always won, not because I was so good, but because she couldn't score on her own. In games she was a great teammate, always covering the other team's point guard." Molly pauses to remember Stevie. "I got all the glory, and she did all the dirty work. Funny how that works out in life sometimes."

Dyani tilts her head, waiting for the moral of the story.

In a few moments, Molly delivers. "Surround yourself with good people, with decent people. I've got Ryanne and Mose and Martina, and you." She pauses, smiling under her mask. "This's the kind of job I'll always want."

On cue, Ryanne walks onto the floor and yells up to the media platform. "Come on down, girls. We have work to do."

In the War Room, Mose stands before one whiteboard, his back to the door as the rest of the coaching staff enters. Without turning around, he asks a one-word question? "Empty?"

His partners laugh. Ryanne answers. "We thought you needed to pull your weight more, so one of the four boards is for you. We filled up ours for the team, but you need to impart some of your vast storehouse of knowledge to the girls. The marker is on the ledge."

Mose nods, the only part of his body moving. Molly, Ryanne, and Dyani wait. In a minute, Mose reaches for the marker, pulls off the cap, and steps to the board. He writes in cursive, *Tomorrow isn't about Southern Cal.* He steps back, puts the cap back on the pen, turns, and flips the pen to Ryanne, allowing them a moment to read it. Then, he takes the eraser and wipes his words away. "Okay, what's the schedule?"

Practice is light. Lots of shooting, walk-throughs of in-bounds plays, a couple of shooting games. No block-out rebounding drills, no bump-the-cutter drills, no rez ball. After one hour, the ladies shoot free throws, jog their misses, and collect at the center circle for the coaches' comments. Dyani gently tells the team that Char will be watching. Ryanne reminds them to eat and hydrate and review the scouting report, emphasizing the rebounding comments. Molly, who always has the last word. speaks of intensity and the re-start, of opportunity as she always does, and how proud of them she is, not just for today, but for the past eight months. Then, she turns to Mose, and says, "Tell them what you told us before practice."

Mose uncrosses his arms and rubs his goatee, stepping slightly forward. "Games never are about who you're playing against, but who you're playing with and who you're playing for." He stares intently at the team, this collection of young ladies all of whom are a half century younger than him. He raises one arm with fingers outstretched and waits for the team to stand and raise their arms. "La Colonia," he says softly.

Chapter 17

November 25, 2020. Games are back. Some games are back. Across the nation universities are canceling games due to Covid outbreaks. No fans in the stands. Covid protocols. Masked officials, of course, since they're always the bad guys. Molly Rascon scans the internet to see if the NCAA will pull the plug just as they did on March 12. She's hopeful they won't, that it will be decisions made by individual members since football is being played, but that nagging fear hangs in her heart. Football is played outside, basketball indoors. SJV versus USC at 1:00 in the Galen Center, Los Angeles, California. Just one of a hundred scheduled, but it is the most important one.

At least, that's what Molly Rascon, aka Coach Rascon, believes.

It's 4:00 am, and Coach Rascon drives over to her arena to board a bus to another arena for a college basketball game between a Quad 1 team and a Quad 4 team. She knows that USC will not take SJV for granted this year, not after being beaten last season. Last year, Coach Rascon believed her team had a chance—if everything went well and SC did not sufficiently corral Dyani Dehiya. They played Dyani straight up for the first two quarters, tried to adjust at halftime, and ultimately could not believe how good this Quad 4 point guard could be. Coach Rascon hopes SC doesn't use last year's game experience as the playbook to defend Keilani. Keilani is improving, better than she should be after the restricted practice time she received because of Covid, but she isn't Dyani.

Molly's phone beeps; it's Martina. "Equipment is all packed. Double checked. Anything else?" Martina is an angel, Molly's angel.

She'll have coffee for her coach too.

Players are to be on the bus by 5:30 with their blankets, pillows, and favorite stuffed animal, if necessary. Three hours if traffic cooperates. Nice to have gps warnings. Bare bones travel squad because of Covid. Everything is "because of Covid." Twenty-six riders plus two bus drivers. Six males, 22 females. Esther remains in isolation Three hours, no stops. All meals prepared ahead of time. Breakfast will be eaten when the team arrives at USC, pre-game snacks, post-game dinner all prepared by the SJV cafeteria with menus from the new dietician. Molly thinks back to high school when her team always traveled by bus, the traditional yellow Blue Bird. *"Gotta go to the bathroom? Hold it 'til we get there."*

This morning's bus is an ultra-modern charter. BusBank. Spacious, comfortable, and safe. Not yellow. Wifi, deluxe toilets, a seat for every player. Social distancing even on the bus. Dr. Calhoun pulled some budget strings to rent a private charter instead of using a university bus. He told Molly this first game must be played with no distractions. There have already been enough of those. The team will travel in relaxed attire, their sweatsuits. The coaching staff will also travel in "less than formal wear," but still professional.

Despite the restrictions and concessions, there is still a game feeling in the air as the team boards the bus for the journey. Martina hands Coach Rascon the latest betting line. Vegas has SJV as a nine-point underdog, last year notwithstanding. The Sequoias lost their two best players, according to Vegas, to graduation. Yeah, nine points sounds about right. Molly whispers to Ryanne that their team has never been anything other than an underdog when playing a top-tier university, and usually Vegas was right, until last year. "Underdogs."

Dr. Martinez drives up at 5:40, Frankie in tow still in his pajamas. They exit the car and wave. Like everyone else in the parking lot, they are masked. Molly walks to them for a hug and receives a high five from her son. Frank hands his wife a card. They wait in the dark outside the car until the bus drives away.

"You're so lucky," says Ryanne when the bus doors close.

"Nobody knows that more than me, Ry." Molly stands as the bus begins to move and tells her ladies to settle in, to get some more sleep.

Seven-plus hours until game time. She and Ryanne sit next to one another, while Dyani sits across the aisle. Mose takes a seat behind Dyani and stretches out his six-six frame. He is all in with bus travel, especially charters when compared to plane travel. In the previous two seasons, Ken Davidson traveled with the team. Not this season. Covid protocols again, plus he's still weak. When the game ends, the team stats will be passed on to the several news outlets, of course, but Ken will receive insider views from Mose, who will be unflinchingly complimentary of both teams regardless of the final score. Nobody associated with the team has a better perspective on athletic competition than the grampa. No one is gentler either.

The bus leaves Tulare and pulls onto CA-99. It will pass through a dozen smaller towns, all based around agriculture, all struggling with Covid. Most of the team will not see any of this since they'll be sleeping. Maddie Martin watches as the bus passes through her hometown, Bakersfield, then she falls asleep. At various times one of the coaches will get up and walk the aisle to check on their girls. They know who's awake by the light from the cell phones. Dyani, Ryanne, and Molly all remember bus trips as kids, how much fun they were, the bonding that took place, but somehow, this trip is not like those. Maybe it will be on the way home after the game.

The route is altered at the north end of Los Angeles. An accident on the 5 forces the bus to divert to the 210. The journey is extended by a half hour, but the delay was built into the schedule. Arriving at the Galen Center, they are escorted to the visitors dressing room, a room much more elaborate and luxurious than their own in Tulare. USC is the consummate host wanting this first game of the new season, the restart, to go smoothly. The Sequoias eat breakfast. At 10:30 they hold a 30-minute shoot-around. Two hours before tipoff, they assemble in the locker room to go over game plans. "Sylvia, you have their big stud. She's a handful, likes to turn over her left shoulder, a bit slow in transition. Keilani, I know you're nervous about the offensive end, but you've got Templeton. She's experienced and the captain, so you need to focus on the defensive end. If you need extra help, look to Dyani. She abused her last year." Both Keilani and Dyani smile. The report goes on. Each girl is given a suggestion, her assignment, and a vote of confidence.

Each lady is taped. They dress out and head to the floor at 12:20, out onto a mostly deserted and quiet arena. The several dozen cardboard cutouts are silent. Both teams shoot and stretch before heading back to the locker room at 12:40 for hydration and a last word. Sylvia tells Keilani that USC's point guard played in Texas the same year as Sylvia did and that Keilani can handle her. "She's good, but you can do it. I've got your back."

Coach Rascon calls out, "Everyone up!" The team stacks high hands. Molly looks at each lady and then nods to Dyani.

Dyani nods back before saying, "Just for this first game, let's play for Char. I know she'll be watching." Dyani pauses. "La Colonia," she says in a quiet voice. The team responds, "La Colonia," with intensity and bring their hands down together.

As both teams go through their final shooting routines, an old Navajo man, unseen by anyone, sits high in the stands with the invisible girl. Like so many times in his life, how he arrives at a certain place is unexplainable. He looks calm.

∽

The Dreamer, Esther Santiago, waits in her dorm room for the first text from Martina Smith, who has promised to send updates on the game as often as possible. So far, Esther's Covid tests have been negative. Two more and she can rejoin her teammates on Friday and play in SJV's next game, Monday. Esther won't text back other than emoji thumbs up or down. She's hoping she can throw confetti at the game's conclusion.

Danelle Weston sits in class, 2000 miles from Los Angeles. Her complete attention is on an Army major explaining the military regulations regarding AWOLs. Later, after mess, she will sit at her computer reviewing the day's notes about military justice. She will receive a text from Sylvia about the game, but Danelle has moved on. She has had to.

Had the pandemic not occurred, Char Betany might be lining up along the center circle as the starting point guard against UC Santa Barbara, because that's the team SJV was originally scheduled to play, who SJV would have played without Covid. Likely, however, Char would be coming off the bench as Keilani's backup, except for Covid.

At 1:00 in the Galen Center, the starters for the two teams are introduced. Each player steps onto the court, masked, and looks back at the benches as her teammates are introduced. Of course, there are no benches, but plush chairs with *SC Trojans* imprinted on the backs. "Sylvia Castro. Greta Espinoza. Keilani Russell. Kaori Park. Emerson Loki. Emerson and Keilani grew up in LA suburbs, and their families certainly would be in attendance if fans were permitted. Greta's family would have listened on the radio whether the game was being played in Los Angeles or Santa Barbara and then returned to the fields or docks.

The teams huddle around their head coaches for last instructions before tipoff. Most of the Sequoias are still as Coach Rascon reminds her ladies of how they play. "We run!" Emerson Loki bounces with her right arm extended skyward toward the massive scoreboard that hangs over the floor. If the opening seconds go as planned, she will come off a down-screen from Greta on the right side of the court and fire up a three. Sylvia and Greta will begin to impose their will against USC's Bigs, and the three guards will "harass the shit out of USC's guards." Coach Powell's final pre-game instructions. Technical stuff.

Dr. Frank Martinez and his son begin preparations for tomorrow's Thanksgiving dinner. Both spent the morning at his clinic in Visalia, but he ended his shift early for the long holiday weekend. Unfortunately, Covid will not take a holiday break; if anything, the holiday will spread the virus further because of family gatherings. Dr. Frank knows he'll be called in to treat emergency cases, but in the hours his wife's team is playing down south, he picks up the turkey he reserved from the meat market, a fourteen pounder, and will shop for potatoes, yams, rolls, and the dozen other items on Molly's list. Frankie will not enter the stores with his papa, because of Covid protocols, protocols that Dr. Frank follows rigidly. He would be at the game if he could, and game thoughts dance around his head. Frankie's constant question during these two early afternoon hours, "Do you think we're winning?" As soon after the game ends and Mama has completed her post-game duties, she will call her boys, not text, and tell them the outcome. The call will be brief, but it will begin with the evaluation of her team that she always shares. "I'm so proud of my ladies; they played so hard." Win or lose.

Seemingly unconcerned with Covid, the Dow Jones closes over 30,000 for the first time ever. But Covid is out there, and on November 25, 2020, as the college basketball season begins, the death toll in America from Covid surpasses 250,000.

∽

The opening moments of the game go as planned. Greta tips the ball to Kaori who flips the ball back to Keilani as Emerson runs to the right block and waits for Greta's screen. She fakes across the lane and then comes out unguarded to the three-point line where her hands are greeted with a perfect pass from Keilani. Emerson rises gracefully from 22 feet, a shot every bit as elegant as one of her dances.

Martina texts Esther. "3-0 good gals." At the dorm Esther pumps her right arm.

High in the dark upper level of the arena, a masked Hector Dehiya smiles and leans forward.

Frankie asks his papa, "Do you think the game has started yet?

Coach Molly Rascon wore high heels just once and decided during that first game at Cal Coastal nearly a decade ago never to do it again regardless of the fashion of D1 coaches. This season, Under Armour Currys carry Molly along the sideline.

Moments of elegance disguise the physical nature of this contest. Southern Cal pushes, shoves, and grabs on every defensive possession and on every screen. La Colonia gives as good as it gets, and at the end of the first quarter, SC leads by four. Fortunately for both teams, the refs see only the elegance, so neither team is in foul trouble. Emerson plays all ten minutes. Kenti and Claudia spell Keilani and Kaori for 90 seconds, while Joyce plays two minutes and Maria plays about three minutes for Sylvia and Greta. The subs hold fast.

During the break, Coach Rascon demands her guards get up in ball coverage and fight over the screens. Coach Robinson demonstrates to Maria a trick to beat the SC Bigs to the block, and Ryanne encourages

Kaori to keep shooting despite going 0 for 3. "It's there; keep shooting, Kay-kay!"

Keilani's summer work schedule is rewarded in the second quarter. No turnovers against hard Trojan pressure, four assists and five points, and SJV surges to take the lead at halftime. Greta has solidly replaced Danelle as Sylvia's sidekick.

Martina texts Esther. "37-35. Emerson playing great. Greta and Sylvia making you proud underneath."

In the locker room, Maddie and Addie listen as Coach critiques the first half. Neither has played, but both hear the meaning of each phrase by all four coaches. Coach Rascon is precise in her instructions—and demanding. "Three steps higher on the block. Get your armbar out at a 90-degree angle. Make a fist, Maria." Coach Powell uses phrases like battering rams. "Knock that little turd, number 12, on her ass. You're allowing her free reign into the lane. I can't tolerate that!" Coach Dyani speaks to Keilani about seeing the backside corner when she drives the lane, not just the near corner. Coach Robinson circles up his four ladies, the Bigs, and compliments them on their battles inside. He especially praises his subs, Joyce and Maria. "Fantastic job, ladies. Now, take the next step. You'll get a few more minutes this half. Dominate your possessions!"

Southern Cal has the first possession of the third quarter, but it is met with a surprise trap when the ball is thrown to the corner. Keilani gets the steal and starts the break. She hits Kaori with a perfect bounce pass, and Kay-kay gets her first points of the game. Coach Rascon smiles at Coach Powell. "Maybe that will calm her down." It does, and Kaori scores six more in the quarter. Southern Cal doesn't wilt and surges when Coach Rascon subs Claudia in for Keilani for one minute. The quarter ends with the Trojans up one.

A basketball game played before no one, the first game back after an extended layoff, a game in a deadly pandemic with the players wearing masks, a game where turnovers should outnumber assists turns into an epic contest of will and determination. The teams execute like it's midway through the season instead of the opener. The lead changes hands six times before the last minute, and the crowd is on its feet at the end, at least the old man high in the stands is. As another old man once told his young point guard 25 years earlier, "You still have to put the ball in the basket." Emerson Loki and Kaori Park, the two players SJV most rely on to do just that, come through with a three to take the lead and a driving layup to secure the win, both off assists from Keilani.

Martina texts Esther. "72-69 us!!!!!!"

Frankie looks at his papa about 3:00 and says, "I have a good feeling about the game."

Hector Dehiya disappears just as quietly as he appeared, holding hands with a member of his tribe.

There is no end game congratulatory walk-through, just waves from in front of each bench. USC walks off the court to its dressing room, while SJV runs to its. There, after a few minutes of celebratory cheering, they take a knee and listen to Dyani say a Navajo prayer. Sylvia and Joyce, standing with their arms around one another, get the attention of the entire gathering, and Sylvia says, "No showers! We're going to wear the sweat of this game all the way home." And they do . . . in a luxury bus.

On the ride back to Tulare, Mose leans into Molly, smiles like a fox, and whispers, "Okay, maybe the game was just a little about Southern Cal."

∾

The following Monday, SJV's game with Cal State Riverside is canceled due to Covid concerns from Riverside. Stephanie Borges and Janet Caldwell, SJV's recent donors, are both isolated from Covid. Stephanie will end up in the hospital for three weeks. Dr. Calhoun tells Molly that all her contractual requests have been approved except for the teaching assignment in the environmental science department. "I'm still working on that one, Coach." Molly tells the University of Washington agent that he will need to find a new coach elsewhere, that she still has unfinished work to do in Tulare. Ken Davidson writes his blog about the SJV-USC contest without seeing the game and ties it closely to the farm workers who are mostly unseen to America but continue to harvest crops under dangerous conditions.

Joyce Hensley misses three days of practice working overtime at the

Fresno hospital because of the rise in hospitalizations due to the recent spike in Covid cases. By the end of November 2020, nearly 400 nurses nationwide have died of Covid. Doing their job.

EARLY DECEMBER 2020

Things are not and then they are.

Agriculture and Basketball. Blog, by Ken Davidson

Agriculture and basketball in The Valley have changed dramatically since I was a kid, but so has most everything else in America. I lived in town, in Tulare, and my parents were not employed in agriculture, so the intricacies of farming were never implanted in my DNA like sports were. My memories of cattle roaming freely in the fields, that pastoral image in my mind's eye, does not exist today. Dairy farms now are concentrated and include "harvesting manure." I shake my head at that image. I vaguely recall the friction between the field workers and the farm owners. Strikes led by the United Farm Workers occurred "out there in the fields." I also do not remember that the air pollution was as bad as it is today.

Likewise, the style of play for today's basketball is unimaginable to Boomers like me, most notably the pace of play, the skill level, and the physicality. That is especially true about the women's game. There were no girls' sports in school back in the Sixties. Title IX was not on the horizon in my youthful universe. The weekend games were always boys' contests. After graduation I moved on, leaving Tulare and The Valley in the pages of my yearbooks. I left with my blissful ignorance intact.

And then I returned. This blog was meant to be my retirement hobby, a way to ease my way into the last chapter of my life. My award-winning columns in the past, I would be able to appreciate my roots while I chronicled the local basketball teams. Farming and hoops in The Valley. Easy-peasy . . . satisfying. Still, something was missing.

Reenter Moses Robinson. My wife thinks it was predestined, a gift from God. This former NBA player, middle school math teacher, youth basketball coach, wry humorist whose daily chore was to contemplate life from an Oxnard beach with his wife met me for coffee in the SJV cafeteria. After catching up, he said without fanfare, "Ken, you might consider following the women's team here at SJV and getting to know its coach."

Enter Coach Molly Rascon. My blogs could return my life to a sense of regularity as I wrote about what I knew, albeit a women's team, but still about a coach, her team, and the pursuit of championships. I could write human interest stories about players much like the story I wrote about Moses Robinson 40 years earlier. Aah, direction and purpose again.

Tulare, California, is not the nation's basketball hotbed; it is not the spot recruits imagine when they consider their futures. Tulare isn't even a typical college town. SJV caters to low-income minorities from California, especially from the more rural areas of the state. No 5-star recruits. No 4-star recruits. Only a handful of 3-star recruits in any sports. Certainly not for basketball, for either men or women. The coaches know that and accept the hand they have been dealt. Except Coach Molly Rascon, who thinks that if you're going to play the game, you might as well challenge the highest hill. A word of warning to Dawn, Geno, Kim, and Tara: Molly is coming for you.

Because of the agricultural nature of the San Joaquin Valley, we are told from an early age that we are what we eat. Well, Molly has always eaten her Wheaties. I observed early on that championships to Coach Rascon did not stop at conference championships. That highest hill was the highest stage. Not just Mt. Whitney, but Everest. "To dream the impossible dream." Not just an NCAA bid, not just the Round of 16, not even the Final Four, but the Gold Ball as she called it. Mose told me at the start of this past season not to pooh-pooh that goal, not with Coach Rascon. In all my years of covering coaches, she is unique, but still, SJV in that rarefied air? Come on!

The 2019-2020 season! As the team prepared for their conference tournament, I wrote of their achievements and the conference championship and believed they had a shot at the Sweet Sixteen, the second weekend of the NCAA tournament! Molly and her dynamite core: Dyani, of course, the best player in the country that no one knew about. (They were about to find out.) And Emerson and Kaori and Sylvia and The Tribe. Yeah, they had a chance.

And then came Covid.

Like most everyone else associated with sports, I felt cheated. It wasn't fair. My last, great scoop. Canceled! But as I blogged about this team over the past eight months, the longest year of my career, I learned that Coach Rascon is not one of those who felt cheated; she saw the "Gold Ball," and it was not a trophy. It was life, and this was just one more obstacle to living that life with purpose. "Don't feel sorry for yourself, the entire world is in the same gym."

This past summer, before I came down with Covid and almost died, Coach and I sat in the stands of her gym, separated by six seats, and talked. I was frustrated about wearing a mask, frustrated that games were suspended, that the town was mostly shuttered, that friends were sick and dying. She said something that I wrote in my notebook but didn't get back to at the time. She said, "I don't lead the nation, I only coach this team." She paused and then said as a continuation, "And I will not allow anger to infect my team. I will use love and positivity to get through this."

Now, as the season has restarted, as the world races towards environmental catastrophe, as our country is being torn apart by political anger and greed, as Americans die by the tens of thousands monthly, I am encouraged, heartened even, by this little bit of a dynamo named Molly Rascon. She makes me believe America can get through this pandemic, not just the Covid pandemic, but the political, economic, and environmental pandemics. I hope she doesn't burn out because of The Pause; she has invested every part of her soul into getting her ladies through this pandemic. Please let there be something left in the tank to carry her beyond this crisis.

This afternoon, I will drive over to the gym to watch the Sequoias practice, share a few thoughts with Mose, and marvel at the resilience of those girls. Those women. I will search for another story shaped by the leadership of a woman raised in poverty, taught by other basketball coaches who saw the future, who seized her opportunity when it presented itself, who sees what we mere mortals do not. Obviously, she is destined to become one of the Basketball Gods. But not today. Today, she has a basketball team to coach, a team in my beloved San Joaquin Valley, to doggedly move it closer to the Gold Ball that isn't a trophy. Today, she still has hands-on gardening work to do . . .

to till the soil for her seeds to sprout,

to provide water and sunshine for her seedlings to grow and mature,

to teach her flowering plants perseverance and independence,

to cultivate in them the strength to weather the storms,

and become the produce of America's bountiful harvest.

To be visible!

The End